"TELL ME HO[W] YOU WANT ME, KATY."

Judson's voice was rough with desire. "Tell me," he commanded.

Somehow the words she needed to say wouldn't form. Kathryn could barely think, much less talk. Turning her head toward him, she sought the mouth that had fired her senses.

But Judson stepped back, letting his eyes roam over her face instead. His own features reflected what she was suppressing—the wanting, the needing and the hunger that neither time nor past hurts had been able to kill.

"Why do you want me?" he purred, running his hand slowly over one breast, then the other, still searching her face.

Kathryn's blood rushed hotly through her veins. Moving closer, she arched against him, anticipating his touch in other, more secret places. "I want you. The reason doesn't make any difference . . . even if it should."

RETURN OF THE DRIFTER

Melodie Adams

A SuperRomance from
HARLEQUIN
London · Toronto · New York · Sydney

First published in Great Britain in 1985 by
Harlequin, 15–16 Brook's Mews, London W1A 1DR

© Melodie Adams 1984

ISBN 0 373 70137 3

11–0485

Printed and bound in Great Britain by
Cox & Wyman Ltd, Reading

CHAPTER ONE

"I DO APPRECIATE your thinking of me, but—"
Kathryn Ryan continued to smile apologetically as
she spoke, although the curve of her mouth became a bit strained when she was abruptly cut off
in midsentence.

"I had hoped you'd agree to chair the committee this time, Kathryn. I was counting on you."
Diamonds flashed and gold glistened as Adelle
Henry waved a pudgy hand in a haughty gesture
of protest. "Won't you reconsider?"

"I'm sorry, but it just isn't possible." The edge
in her voice indicated her thinning patience. Hearing it, Kathryn attempted to soften her refusal
without retreating from her position. "The boutique keeps me very busy, Adelle. There simply
isn't time for me to take on more responsibility."
She shrugged lightly and hoped the subject would
be dropped.

"I see." But it was obvious that Adelle didn't
consider Kathryn's explanation an acceptable excuse. She seemed about to argue the point when a
middle-aged couple paused beside her, distracting
her attention. Immediately Adelle turned on a
practiced smile of delight and swiveled slightly to

greet the party's newest arrivals. Kathryn also murmured a few words of greeting, then fell silent, allowing Adelle to monopolize the couple.

An impatience stirred Kathryn as she listened to the polite voices and the meaningless conversation. But she was careful not to let her reaction show. Her features were smooth as she raised her wineglass and sipped the delicate white wine. Her glance strayed to make a sweep of the ranch-house living room, nearly filled to capacity with guests.

People were standing, sitting, milling about. The men were dressed in expensive suits and the women had apparently tried to outdo one another with their gowns and jewelry. The air was heavy with chatter and throaty laughter, and cigarette smoke.

Despite the air conditioner, the room was warm and stuffy. Kathryn's gaze wandered to a large window, darkness showing beyond the glass. It was fresh and relatively cool out there...and quiet, Kathryn thought, save for the natural country sounds of a July night. Miles of flat, fertile Kansas ground separated the Culpepper wheat ranch from the nearest town.

The distance made the ranch seem an unlikely gathering place. Yet in recent years, parties here had become the norm. It had all started seven years ago, when Horace Culpepper had invited the entire town of Deepwater to a barbecue. The discovery of oil on his land was the reason for celebration.

In one way or another, that discovery had

touched the life of every citizen of Deepwater, Kansas. An hour south of Topeka, the town had been little more than a wide spot in the road, with half a block of businesses lining either side of the county highway. The tiny community had been made up of merchants, farmers and small-time ranchers—the hardworking people who had always managed to scratch out a decent living, but little else.

All that had changed when the men had come in droves to work the oil fields. On their heels were others—contractors, carpenters, and all manner of businessmen and laborers, anxious to supply the necessary products and services to accommodate the flood of newcomers. The circulation of all that new money had breathed life into the bust town of Deepwater, and it had boomed.

For most of the locals, it had meant a financial success they had never dared dream about. The townswomen were now able to wear silks and jewels with the same frequency that they had once worn durable cotton housedresses. Yet for a silent few, the discovery of oil that long-ago summer had meant personal ramifications that would last a lifetime.

An audible sigh came from Adelle Henry, making Kathryn aware that the other couple had moved on and she was again the sole recipient of the older woman's attention.

"Well, Kathryn, since soliciting your help is obviously out of the question, I won't bother you with our problems anymore."

Kathryn recognized the appeal to her sense of charity but refused to feel any guilt. "I'm sorry, Adelle.''

"There's no need to apologize, dear. My sympathies are with you. I think it's just awful that you have so little time to call your own...not even a few hours a week to contribute to the betterment of your community.'' Again she sighed. The light of battle gleamed in her blue eyes, a contrast to her sympathetic facial expression.

Running the tip of her tongue along her back teeth, Kathryn silently counted to ten. Regardless of the impression she'd given, the demands of the boutique were not what had dictated her answer. The business did require a great deal of attention, but pleading a lack of time had been nothing more than a polite way of displaying disinterest—a tiny white lie used purely for the sake of sparing Adelle's feelings. Now the woman was challenging that excuse, trying to shame Kathryn into agreement. The idea turned her mild impatience into simmering anger.

"Now Adelle,'' a smooth male voice interjected, and Kathryn felt an arm slip around her waist in light possession. "I'm sure Kathryn genuinely regrets having to refuse you. But I'm also sure you can understand her position.''

First protest, then resignation stole across Adelle's heavily made-up face. "Yes, I suppose I can. Being a working woman must be quite taxing.'' Her voice had a condescending ring. Adelle was the banker's wife, and the reigning matriarch of Deepwater society, since a society had developed.

The line of her mouth kept its faithfully smiling curve, but Kathryn was forced to lower her lashes to conceal the irritation in her green eyes. Adelle, like most of the residents of Deepwater, was aware of Kathryn's status as proprietor of a boutique, but this woman could never seem to make the distinction between being a businesswoman and plodding away at a dead-end job. To Adelle, it all amounted to the same thing—something a woman did out of sheer necessity until she found a man to take her away from it all. Kathryn didn't want to be taken away. Not anymore.

Now, at twenty-four, she was perfectly content with her life in Deepwater, Kansas. If there were times when she felt that there should be more to her existence, they were rare. And Kathryn was always able to chase the vague emptiness away with a very valid argument. She had everything she wanted, so what was left? Nothing. She had it all—independence, financial security, Charles. . . .

Her gaze swung to the tall dark-haired man at her side. That perpetual smile of his was working its magic, easily smoothing any of Adelle's ruffled feathers back into place.

His features were well defined and classically handsome. The tailored black suit he wore made the medium gray of his eyes seem lighter and gave them an added intensity.

There was a sophistication about Charles, a certain panache that clearly stated that he was a newcomer to these parts, having lived in Deepwater a little less than five years. He'd been city bred, city raised and that fact somehow set him apart from the country-born people in the community. Not above, just apart.

Charles Court. He was the kind of man any girl would want. No, Kathryn corrected the thought. He was the kind of man any *woman* would want. And her own well-ordered life was also what any woman would want. That starry-eyed girl she'd been seven years ago would have seen things differently. But Kathryn had learned a lot since that summer. The important things in life were the things that lasted—the things you could count on.

"Isn't that right, Kathryn?" Charles prompted. Her blank look told him she hadn't heard a word he'd said. Charles didn't miss a beat. "Once we're married I would imagine that you'll be able to spend less time at your shop and more time on some of Adelle's worthy projects. Isn't that right?"

"Oh, do you think so?" Adelle brightened visibly. She looked to Kathryn for confirmation.

"Perhaps." Anything more definite would have been an outright lie. Kathryn's irritation was rapidly finding a new target, directed now at Charles for putting hope into the woman's head.

"Well, of course you will," Adelle decided with a little laugh. Now that the matter was settled, the battle won, she began to lose interest. She scanned the room. "Oh, there's Marion! I need to discuss next week's auxiliary luncheon with her. If you two will excuse me?"

"Of course," Charles said. Kathryn just kept smiling. Her cheeks were beginning to ache with the forced effort. Once the woman was out of earshot, Charles glanced at Kathryn. "That settles that." His mouth twitched with amusement. "She certainly is anxious to put you to work on one of her committees."

"Only because I keep telling her no," Kathryn stated. "Being selected by Adelle is supposed to be a privilege. She takes a negative response as a personal rejection."

"Then why don't you try saying yes?"

"Because I don't want to." Conscious of the clusters of people nearby, Kathryn kept her angry voice at a low volume. "And you had no—"

"Smile, Kathryn," Charles interrupted, and nodded politely at a passing couple.

"I don't feel like smiling, Charles." But she did so anyway, not wanting to draw attention to herself. "Why on earth did you tell her I would do it?"

"Why not? It made Adelle happy, didn't it? And she won't be bothering you for a while." There was a shrug of his shoulders as Charles gave her a puzzled look. "Why are you so upset? You both got what you wanted."

"But only temporarily," Kathryn retorted. "It would have been much better to give her a final no and leave it at that."

"The conversation wouldn't have ended so amicably," he pointed out.

Kathryn sighed impatiently. "Charles, haven't

you learned yet that it is impossible to give everybody what they want?''

"Yes, and there are two tricks to getting around that fact,'' he asserted with confidence. "Either make them think they want what you're giving. Or make them think you're giving what they want.''

"That sounds like manipulation,'' she accused.

"No.'' A frown briefly flickered across his face. Then Charles gave her an engaging grin. "It's good politics.''

Most of the heat of her anger had burned off, but Kathryn's position remained unchanged. "Whatever it is, you're not going to use that strategy on me. You can't possibly make me think that I want to get involved in Adelle's so-called civic work. Those meetings are nothing more than excuses for the more socially prominent women in town to get together for lunch, cocktails and gossip. I'm not interested, Charles.'' The declaration was made on a warning note.

His grin faded to seriousness. "Kathryn, once we're married. . . .''

"Charles!'' She stared at him. Although she wasn't a bit pleased with the way he'd handled Adelle, Kathryn understood his stalling tactics. But surely he wasn't expecting her to fulfill the half promise he'd made? "Our marriage isn't going to have any bearing on that decision—or how much time I spend at the shop.'' Had he meant what he'd said about the future, too? She frowned warily. "We've discussed this and you know how important my business is to me.'' The boutique was her security, her independence.

"It may not have any bearing on the shop," he murmured, gray eyes narrowed speculatively. "But I certainly hope it will have some bearing on the extent of your social involvement. After I'm elected mayor, you, as my wife, will be expected to take an active interest in community affairs. As I recall, we've discussed this, too."

Just for a second, Kathryn caught a g'impse of the attorney she'd met two years ago. Straightforward and stable, with a solid law practice, Charles had represented all the things she had desired in a man. They had been seeing each other regularly for a year when Charles had decided to pursue his true ambition—politics. And Kathryn had agreed to stand beside him, doing whatever she could to further his career.

"You're right." It was a reluctant admission, tinged with guilt that she hadn't been doing her part.

"Don't look so glum," he chided. A slow smile spread across his face. "You always have to run into a few thorns to get to the roses."

"I suppose."

"It will all be worth it, Kathryn. The sweetest rose of all is just a few thorns away. Mayor, governor—"

"Governor?"

"Why not? The sky's the limit. With the connections I've been making and—" he planted a warm kiss on her temple "—the most beautiful girl in the state by my side, how can I lose?"

"You couldn't possibly." Kathryn dryly mocked his certainty.

"That's the spirit," Charles said. "If we hang on to that attitude and play our cards right, we can make it all the way to the governor's mansion—and then some."

Nodding a response, Kathryn recognized the problem. Charles thrived on playing the cards right, and to her, it just seemed like playing a game of liar's poker. But a political career was his ambition, and he was perfect for it. Past experience had taught Kathryn that you couldn't change a person. Everyone was born a certain type, and that was the type he'd always be.

She would simply have to adjust to the political world. She was positive she could. There were too many things about Charles to admire, and she wouldn't lose him just because his choice of career wasn't hers. After all, he'd never asked her to give up her business. Besides, what were a few committee meetings?

"I mean what I said, you know." His arm curved again around her slim waist. "You are beautiful." In an almost absent fashion, his eyes studied her— the delicate bone structure that made her features as classic an example of female perfection as his were male, the ash-blond hair that made a pale frame for her face, and the emerald green of her eyes, fringed with thick dark lashes, that made such a striking contrast to the fairness of her skin. The black silk cocktail dress she wore was styled in the simplest of lines, an understated elegance in the design and fabric. The fit subtly showed off her slender yet mature curves.

She was on the verge of thanking Charles for the compliment when an elderly gentleman approached them, his short round body clad in a blue suit, the jacket unbuttoned. The protrusion of his stomach strained the buttons of the light-blue shirt he wore. Charles reached to clasp the man's hand and give it a hearty shake.

"Horace! Good to see you." Even though they'd been at the party nearly an hour, this was the first time they'd seen their host.

"Charles. Kathryn. Glad you could make it." The older man nodded his head, partly bald, partly gray, in Kathryn's direction. What hair was lacking on his head, Horace Culpepper made up for on his face. His gray muttonchop whiskers always reminded Kathryn of a walrus's.

To the people at the party, Horace was something of a celebrity. It was only natural that he would be credited with starting the boom of Deepwater, and the resulting affluence the people enjoyed.

Yet, in the beginning, Horace Culpepper had been looked upon as anything but a hero. While the townspeople had enjoyed the growing prosperity, many of them had objected to the sudden influx of people. The men who brought their families were accepted much more easily than the drifters. And there were plenty of them. They made up a good percentage of the oil-field workers.

Drifters were a tough lot. They had to be; the hours on the drilling sites were long and the work was hard. At the end of a shift, when they had scrubbed away the sweat, dust and grime, they went out in search of relaxation and entertainment. For most the search had ended at the tavern, where they drank and fought with the same drive they had at work. Some of the local residents hadn't taken kindly to that kind of disruption.

Especially Kathryn's mother. Mattie Ryan had been one of the strongest protesters, stating her opinions loudly, clearly and often. The only thing that could ever come of a drifter was no-good. According to Mattie, that breed of man meant nothing but trouble. Yet "that breed of man" had filled Mattie's boarding house to the rafters. The people she'd so zealously opposed had increased her income from meager to sizable. Later the savings her mother had accumulated, plus a small life-insurance policy, had enabled Kathryn to open the shop. Maybe something good could come of a drifter after all.

"We wouldn't have missed it, Horace," Charles responded heartily to their host's greeting, and glanced at Kathryn for confirmation.

"No, we wouldn't have." Her voice sounded like an echo.

"I'm glad to hear it," Horace declared, his twinkling look sliding briefly to Kathryn. "Because I've got a surprise for your young man." He clamped a hand on Charles's shoulder. As most people did, Horace liked Charles. He was backing him for mayor.

Amusement touched Kathryn's smile at Horace's choice of words. "Her young man" was forty-five. Which some people considered to be reason for concern, since his age was nearly twice hers. But Horace was well past seventy. Charles probably did seem young.

"Surprise?" Charles's curiosity was fully aroused. "What kind of surprise?"

"Now if that isn't a ridiculous question." He shook his head. "If I told you, it wouldn't be a surprise."

Both Charles and Kathryn chuckled and pretended Horace's was a new line.

"You'll just have to wait and see," the older man declared. Before Charles had a chance to respond, Horace Culpepper's alert gaze was on the foyer. "Stay right here, you two. I'll be back in two shakes." Then he was bustling off.

Kathryn blinked, surprised at the abrupt departure and the amount of energy Horace always had. A soft laugh bubbled from her throat. She watched him maneuver his way around the guests in his path and walk toward the foyer. Automatically her gaze skipped ahead to discover the older man's objective. A man was standing in the archway, having obviously just arrived. The sight of him struck a thousand responsive chords in Kathryn's memory. All of them jolted her system like an electric shock. The laughter died on her lips, choked off by a sharp, painful gasp. It couldn't be him. Not after all these years.

Yet there was so much about him that was achingly familiar. A couple of inches over six feet, he carried his height with a loose-limbed ease. He was broad at the shoulders and narrow at the hips, his lean muscled frame exuding strength. The sun had tanned his skin to the deep color of polished teak and bronzed the rugged planes of his face. In contrast, the sun's rays had picked out strands of his brown hair and gilded them, giving a light and dark, wood-grained effect.

As she stared, he ran a hand through the vital thickness of his hair. The action only enhanced its careless, windblown style and added to the virile, earthy appeal of the man. He was too roughly male to really be handsome, but there was something about his tough, rakehell good looks that held a devastating attraction.

Kathryn remembered him all too well; his looks, his mannerisms and the pain he had caused were all etched too deeply in her mind to ever be truly erased. She wanted to look away or close her eyes and open them again to find him gone. But he wouldn't be. He wasn't an illusion. Judson—the man she hadn't seen in seven years. The man she'd never wanted to see again. She pressed her lips together in a tight line to keep them from trembling.

There was a magnetic pull that kept her gaze riveted to him, but her side vision caught sight of Horace Culpepper, vaguely registering the information that he had been detained by another guest. Judson leaned a shoulder against the archway and let his hooded gaze make a slow sweep of the living room and its occupants. It paused to linger on Kathryn. Her heart stopped working, and a cold hand squeezed the breath from her lungs.

What was he doing here? Had he come back to claim the love he'd left behind? Outrage surged through her, raw and hot. Just as quickly, it was doused, frozen by the way his brown eyes touched her and moved on with no more than passing interest. Bitterness twisted her insides into painful knots. He didn't recognize her. Maybe he didn't even remember her.

Not that she cared. There was nothing left of what she'd once felt for Judson Taylor—not love, not hate—nothing. It was only the shock of seeing him again that made her stomach churn in such violent reaction.

Horace Culpepper managed to extract himself from the small group. With hurried strides, he went to meet Judson, who pushed away from the wall and extended a hand, all in a slow, lazy flow of movement. An equally slow and lazy smile pulled his lips apart to reveal a row of strong white teeth. The quick actions of the older man were a sharp contrast to the relaxed ease that characterized those of Judson Taylor.

"Who do you suppose that could be?" Charles murmured.

Swallowing past the tightness in her throat, Kathryn stalled for time. "What did you say?" She tipped her head back to look at him.

"I was just wondering—" His curious gaze left the two men to focus on her face. A frown of concern drew his brows together. "Kathryn, are you all right?"

She avoided a direct answer. "Why do you ask?"

"You don't look as if you feel very well."

"Actually, I don't." Charles had given her a way to escape, and Kathryn intended to take it. She fanned herself with her hand. "My stomach feels a little queasy. It's so stuffy in here. All the smoke. . . ."

"Maybe some fresh air would help," he suggested.

"I'm sure it would." It was a quick agreement, an unnatural streak of cowardice pushing to the surface.

At one end of the room, a set of French doors led onto a patio. The impulse to run and put as much distance as possible between herself and Judson was strong. Kathryn suppressed it with an effort. They hadn't taken two steps toward the patio when Horace was calling them back.

"Charles! Hold on a minute. There's someone I'd like you to meet."

"This won't take long," Charles assured her quietly, and turned to wait for the approaching men.

Kathryn was slow to follow his action, taking an extra few seconds to school her expression so it would conceal the tumultuous reaction within. All her defenses were up, and her back was ramrod straight as she mentally braced herself for this meeting.

A step behind Horace, Judson was chuckling at something the older man said. The soft, husky timbre of his laugh raked her nerves. For the span of a second, her eyes locked with his lazy brown eyes. There was no flicker of recognition in his look. Relief and bitterness warred for control, with neither the clear-cut victor. Kathryn divided her glances between Horace and Charles, but with adrenaline pumping through her veins, she was aware only of the third man.

"Charles, I'd like you to meet Judd Taylor, Monument Oil. And this is Charles Court, Deepwater's next mayor."

Out of the corner of her eye, Kathryn was aware of the upward lift of Judson's eyebrow. "I'm honored, Mr. Mayor." There was an undertone of dry amusement in his voice that subtly mocked.

Charles didn't appear to notice it, laughing appreciatively as he gripped Judson's hand. "The title is still a bit premature, but I do like the sound of it." False modesty did not come naturally to Charles, so it didn't occur to him to act hopeful or unsure of the future election results. "So you're with Monument Oil," he stated. "I've been hearing a lot of good things about that company. Of course it is new, but for an independent—"

"Excuse me, Charles." Horace looked uncomfortable. "I'm not sure that I made things clear when I introduced you two. Judd isn't *with* Monument Oil, he *is* Monument Oil." It was an obvious attempt to keep Charles from saying something to the owner of the company that he might regret.

The information took Kathryn by surprise, but she kept her reaction from showing. Charles wasn't so successful. There was a slight hesitation as he drew back in reappraisal of the situation and the man. Heightened interest and a new respect showed in his gray eyes.

"Of course," Charles said smoothly. "I knew that name rang some kind of bell. I hope you'll forgive me for not making the connection sooner."

"No problem." The dryness in Judson's voice was searing. It told Kathryn that she wasn't the only one who suspected Charles had never heard the name before in his life.

Irritation and a tinge of embarrassment for Charles brought a little of the color back to her cheeks. But waves of panic washed both feelings away as Charles took her by the hand and drew her forward.

"Mr. Taylor, I'd like you to meet my fiancée, Kathryn Ryan."

A chill raced down Kathryn's spine at the sound of her own name. Surely hearing her name again would be enough to prod Judson's memory back to that summer seven years ago. Yet his eyes revealed nothing, the deep-brown surfaces acting as barriers that wouldn't let her see in. She was glad, but there was a sharp stab of pain in the vicinity of her heart that she could be so easily forgotten.

"Hello, Katy. It's been a long time." The rich, low tone of Judson's voice vibrated through her and sent her heart skittering all over the place.

He hadn't forgotten. Never in her life had anyone called her Katy—except Judson. He had pinned the nickname on her the first time they'd met, saying simply that she looked like a Katy to him and that's what he wanted to call her.

And if Judson Taylor wanted to do something, that was all the justification he had ever needed.

CHAPTER TWO

"HELLO, MR. TAYLOR." There was a tightness in her throat that made her voice come out husky, but otherwise Kathryn managed to keep her poise. She coolly ignored the quirk of Judson's mouth that mocked her formality.

"You two are already acquainted?" Charles split his questioning look between them.

"You could say that," Judson agreed in a low drawling tone that suggested there was a great deal more to the story.

"Yes. Mr. Taylor roomed at my mother's boarding house for a while," Kathryn explained quickly—perhaps too quickly. Nervously she glanced at Charles. His look was thoughtful, yet he appeared oblivious to her tension and the subtle undercurrents in the air.

"That's right," Horace Culpepper recalled. "You did stay at Mattie's that summer, didn't you?"

"When was this?" Unaware of the connection between Judson and Horace, Charles was plainly confused.

"Judd worked some of the drilling sites on my land one summer," Horace explained, then frowned. "How long ago was that?"

Kathryn clamped her teeth down on the answer that sprang to mind—seven years, one month and three days since Judson had left. She hadn't consciously kept track of his absence for years, but old habits were so hard to break. When Judson hesitated, too, as if searching his memory, an ache started to hurt someplace in her chest.

"It must have been about seven years ago, wasn't it, Katy?" He tipped his head at an inquiring angle.

Her smile was brittle. "Something like that."

"I imagine you see a lot of changes in Kathryn, then." Horace ran an admiring eye over her. "Seven years ago this pretty little lady couldn't have been much more than a child."

Something flickered in Judson's expression, piercing the lazy aloofness of his gaze. Then his mouth slanted in a smile that was heavy with irony. "Yes," he agreed. "I guess she was."

A child. The words cut, and the truth of them was salt on the wound. Images flashed of those times when Judson had treated her as anything but a child. Yet she had been so naive, child enough to believe in him and the promises he'd never intended to keep.

"Well, Kathryn...." Horace Culpepper was getting fidgety again; that restless energy sent his eyes darting around the room. "You and Judd probably want to do some catching up. This looks like a good time to borrow Charles for a minute or two." Without waiting for a response from her, he turned to Charles. "The man over there in the blue is a former senator. If you haven't met him yet, you should. He might be valuable to you in the future.''

The subject was guaranteed to attract Charles's attention. "No, I haven't met him." His desire to do so was obvious. The glance he turned to Kathryn was preoccupied, lit with anticipation. "Do you mind?"

She did. Very much. But what could she say? "Go ahead." She faked a smile of encouragement.

"I won't be long," Charles promised a little absently.

A chuckle came from Horace as he clamped a meaty hand on Charles's shoulder and nudged him in the senator's direction. "Don't you believe this slippery-tongued public servant. I hear that same promise every time one of them gets up to make a speech." He winked at Kathryn, then lifted a hand in a farewell gesture. "Judd, enjoy the party and I'll see you a little later."

There was a faint nod of his head in response. "I'll do my best, Horace."

With a sinking feeling, Kathryn watched her moral support and her buffers disappear into the crowd. For all intents and purposes, she was alone with Judson Taylor. In her mind she had pictured an occasion such as this at least a thousand times. Half of those times she had confronted him with the past, ripped him to shreds with scathing remarks, then turned and walked away. The rest of the times she imagined herself rushing into his arms. She knew she wouldn't play out either scene.

"It isn't necessary for you to keep me company." Kathryn's voice was stiff, like her carriage.

"Are you asking me to leave?" he inquired with a lazy kind of dryness.

"Of course not." She managed to smile and look slightly taken aback that he should suggest such a thing. "It's just that there are so many other people here for you to either meet or get reacquainted with. And since you and I really don't have any catching up to do, I didn't want you to feel obligated by what Horace said." So cool. So composed. Kathryn was proud of herself.

"I don't feel obligated." It was a flat statement, issued too decisively to be only a casual reply.

After all this time it wasn't a message Kathryn needed to have reinforced. She swallowed the bitterness that choked her, determined to show him the past meant as little to her as it did to him. She lifted her chin a fraction of an inch and donned an expression of polite interest.

"It's obvious that you and Horace have kept in touch since you worked for him. I wasn't aware that you'd gotten to know one another so well back then."

"We hadn't. At the time I was just one of the workers. But a few things have changed since then. Horace and I have been doing business on occasion for the last couple of years." The corners of his mouth deepened in a wry smile. "Horace was a little surprised when he realized the president of Monument Oil had worked for him just a few years earlier.''

"I can imagine," Kathryn murmured tensely.

By most standards, including her mother's, Judson Taylor had been a no-account drifter, irresponsible and undependable. They were traits that went along with the breed, the same as wanderlust and that easygoing, reckless brand of charm. Drifters were notorious for the latter. Men who were rogues always seemed to hold a fatal fascination for women. At seventeen, the attraction had been too druggingly potent for Kathryn to fight off, despite her mother's warnings.

"Are you surprised?" There was something probing about his gaze.

"About what? Your success?" At his faint, affirmative nod, Kathryn shrugged and looked past him instead of at him, unable to deal with whatever was in his eyes. "A little." But she wasn't surprised, not really.

"Why?" The question was slightly challenging. "I told you I was going to make something of myself."

That was one thing she had never doubted, not in all this time. "You told me a lot of things, Judson." Feeling that she was betraying herself, Kathryn groped for another topic. "So," she said quickly, "what brings you back to Deepwater?"

"Business."

Apprehension shot through her system. "Does that mean you're going to be in town for a while?" She struggled for a light note.

There was a narrowing of his eyes as they surveyed her features. "Just for a day or two. Horace and I are signing some contracts tomorrow. I'm flying back as soon as we tie up all the loose ends."

"I see." There was relief in her reply and it brought a measure of cynical amusement to his smile, hardening the line of his mouth. "Where is it you're flying back to, Judson?" Nearly every time she opened her mouth, Kathryn wanted to take back what came out. The last thing she wanted was for Judson Taylor to think she was the least bit interested in anything about him.

"Dallas," he said, then answered the question she wasn't about to ask. "That's where Monument Oil is based. I'm not there much anymore, though. I do a lot of traveling."

"So you're still a drifter. You just traded in your Levi's for a three-piece suit and your pickup truck for an airplane." Bitter sarcasm crept through to sharpen the observation. "Success hasn't changed you at all." The words had the sound of an accusation.

His expression became complacently aloof. "I didn't know it was supposed to." He watched her with lazy interest. "What about you, Katy? You look different, but are you still the same?"

The same what? The same naive teenager who had fallen for him and swallowed every line he'd thrown? "No." It was a quietly forceful denial. "Some of us do change, Judson. Drifters don't."

"Is that right?" he wondered idly.

"Yes."

If she needed proof, it was standing right before her. The only changes the intervening years had made were minor—surface differences that ran no deeper than skin or clothes. Time had whipped the softness of youth from his features. Experience had carved lines in the lean bronze of his face, slashed grooves alongside his mouth, and etched a network of sun creases that fanned out from the corners of his eyes. There was a slight crook in the bridge of his nose that told Kathryn that it had been broken. She stifled the impulse to ask how it had happened and resented the fact that she cared. She also resented the changes in him, because they only added to the aura of tough virility he exuded. Against her will, she was conscious of it.

"If I didn't know better, I'd swear I was hearing Mattie's voice." There was a lift of one corner of his mouth, but it held little humor. "You sound just like your mother, Katy."

"And you sound as if you're surprised about that," she retorted in a burst of bitterness.

He studied her for several seconds. "I guess I shouldn't be, should I? Some of her was bound to rub off on you." He smiled wryly as he shook his head. "Whew. That woman did have a burning dislike for me. She never thought I'd amount to anything and didn't mind telling me about it." He glanced down at his suit, then met her gaze. His brown eyes glittered with reckless challenge. "I wonder if she'd think I was respectable enough now to rent me a room?"

The question chilled Kathryn, making it clear that while Judson had kept in touch with at least one resident of Deepwater, he obviously hadn't bothered to inquire about her. At least not in the last five years.

"Deepwater has gone through a lot of changes, Judson. There are several motels in town now."

"I know, but since I'm only staying one night, I thought I'd rent a room from Mattie—for old times' sake." The last part was drawled with exaggerated mockery.

"As far as I can remember, you two never had any old times worth resurrecting." Kathryn bristled. "I suppose what you'd really like is to show her how successful you've become and prove that she was wrong on that score?"

A muscle tightened in his jaw as his facial expression became hard. He took a pack of cigarettes from his pocket and shook one out, then replaced the pack. There was the clicking sound of a lighter. Only then did Judson release her gaze and lower his eyes while the flame touched the tip of the cigarette. When he looked up again, it was through a thin screen of smoke.

"If you're wondering whether I'm harboring a lot of old grudges and want a chance to retaliate—don't. I never fought Mattie before, even when I had damned good reason to." The hardness of steel ran beneath his tone.

"That's true. You didn't." It was a grudging admission. The restraint he'd exercised in the face of her mother's verbal attacks had been incredible. Kathryn hadn't had nearly so much control, a fact she now regretted.

Judson took a drag on the cigarette and released the smoke on a long breath. "On second thought, I think I will stay in a motel. Going back to the good old days even for one night sounds less appealing all the time."

Kathryn was in complete agreement. She wanted the memories to remain just as dead and buried as her love for him was. So why did it hurt when he echoed her sentiments?

"Here we are, Kathryn." Horace Culpepper came to stop beside her while Charles slipped around to the other side. "And you can thank me for returning your fiancé so promptly. If it hadn't been for me, those two long-winded politicians would have been swapping lies all night." Amusement danced in his eyes and Kathryn wondered why their host couldn't sense the tension in the air. She could feel the oppressive weight of it all around her.

"In that case, Horace, I will say thank-you." Her smile was stiff with the effort to make it appear normal. "If there's one thing a girl can't stand, it's being deserted." Kathryn realized her poor choice of words instantly and regretted it. Instinctively her glance darted to Judson's, but her statement had made no impression. She saw the bland indifference in his eyes and died a little.

Her reaction confused her. It also forced her to wonder whether using the word "deserted" had been less accidental than she wanted to believe.

Had it been an unconscious attempt to rake up the past? To confront him with what he had done and see his reaction? What had she expected? Guilt? Remorse? Regret? After seven years?

"Why, Judd! You haven't even got a drink yet," Horace realized with a guilty start. "What do you say we remedy that and then you can bring me up to date on a few things?"

"Sounds good, Horace. I could use a drink about now." His narrowed eyes took in Kathryn at his side, then he glanced at Charles. "Nice meeting you, Charles. I'm sure we'll run into each other again before the evening is over."

"I'll look forward to it," Charles assured him. There was a speculative gleam in his gray eyes as he watched the broad-shouldered figure disappear into another room. He turned to Kathryn. "Did you and Taylor have a nice visit?"

"I guess so," she replied with studied indifference.

Lifting a squat glass, Charles took a sip of his drink. "Tell me about him."

"What do you want to know?" She gave him a carefully blank look. Inside she was shaking.

"What *should* I know?" Charles countered.

"You're acting like a politician," she accused lightly, buying time. "If you're hoping to get any information out of me, you'll have to be more specific."

Charles smiled absently. "How well did you know him before?"

"He was only here for a few months." Averting

her eyes, Kathryn shrugged and hoped Charles would draw his own conclusions from her answer. She didn't want to lie, but neither did she want to explain.

"How long is he planning to stay this time?" Charles swirled the ice cubes in his glass.

"A day or two." She shot him a quick glance and wondered where the questions were leading.

"Is he married?"

The casually asked question stiffened her. Kathryn felt hot and cold all at the same time. "I don't know. I didn't ask." It was a slight shock to realize that the possibility had never occurred to her— not once in all this time. The muscles in her throat constricted, and she drained the last of her wine to ease the sudden tightness.

"Did Taylor mention anything about seeing you again while he's in town?"

"Why should he, Charles? We knew each other very briefly a *long* time ago." The rawness she felt came through in the sharpness of her reply. Then her eyes widened on another thought. "Are you jealous, Charles?"

"Do I have any reason to be?" A hint of suspicion darkened his eyes.

"Of course not," she said briskly. She was impatient with herself for presenting the idea when it obviously hadn't occurred to him. Mutual trust was too important to permit such careless remarks. She slipped an arm through the crook of his arm and gave him a reassuring smile. "Why so many questions anyway?"

"I was just curious about him. Monument Oil is a fast-growing company. Horace pointed out that it might not hurt to get to know the man behind it all."

Kathryn didn't bother to contradict that statement, but she knew Horace and Charles were wrong. If Charles got to know Judson Taylor, a lot of damage could be done—damage to her relationship with Charles. Before him, there had been only one man in Kathryn's life. Charles knew that, and so did the rest of the town. What they didn't know, was that the man was Judson Taylor. Everyone in Deepwater believed exactly as they had been led to believe. It still amazed Kathryn that her secret had been so successfully kept.

Maybe she had been wrong not to confide in Charles, but prior to tonight it hadn't seemed necessary. Judson had been nothing more than an unpleasant memory. The past was dead and all Kathryn had wanted was to forget. No matter how understanding Charles was, Kathryn couldn't visualize herself telling him about Judson. Not at this late date. The time for confessions was two years ago, when she and Charles had started seeing one another regularly.

"Can I get you another drink, Kathryn?" Charles noticed her empty glass.

"Please." She handed it to him, aware that her eagerness was to have him gone so she could get a firmer grip on her emotions. As she watched him move in the direction of the bar, she told herself there was nothing to worry about. The shock of seeing Judson again had merely made her over-react. In a day or two, he'd be out of the state. She wouldn't see him again after tonight. Her life would continue on the same smooth course she had set, well planned and ripple free.

Confidence and poise were traits Kathryn had worked hard to develop, especially since she'd met Charles. Both began to return to her now and the internal shaking was reduced to faint tremors. She began to realize that fate had provided her with an excellent opportunity.

She had come a long, long way in seven years. The simple little country girl who'd spent most of her time in cut-off jeans and old T-shirts had evolved into a woman, a lady with style, elegance and a hard-earned sophistication. She was finally comfortable with herself. The desire to show off just a little was too much to resist. Judson might be richer and his clothes more expensive than the day he left, but he was essentially composed of rough male edges, something fine clothes and success couldn't hide. He would never have Charles's polish—or hers, for that matter.

For the next two hours Kathryn ignored the pounding pain in her temples. She mixed, mingled and subtly campaigned at Charles's side. If Charles noticed that she was taking a more active part than usual, he didn't comment on it. Each time she found herself within close range of Judson, Kathryn made a show of ignoring him. Whoever she and Charles happened to be talking with received the benefit of every ounce of her social charm. She wanted her actions to make a definite statement. She was totally unaffected by Judson's second intrusion into her life—and totally unscarred by the first.

In the beginning, she derived a measure of satisfaction from her efforts. But as the evening wore on, Kathryn found herself swallowing the bitter taste of irony. She might be ignoring Judson, but he wasn't paying any attention to her, either. The covert glances she sent his way usually saw his back turned to her. Her pride was suffering. She wanted to do the ignoring, the brushing off, the rejecting. She was disgusted with her childishness. What did it matter whose idea avoiding each other was? Staying apart was the objective, and it was being achieved.

Her headache was getting worse, the pain drumming insistently. She drew Charles aside and gave him an apologetic look. "I'm really not feeling well at all, Charles. I've got a splitting headache. Could we please leave?"

"Of course, darling," he agreed without hesitation.

But it was another half hour before they were seeking out Horace to make their excuses. They found him stationed near the foyer, surrounded by a trio of men. The one leaning indolently against the wall was Judson. Kathryn gave him a wintry smile and tried to concentrate on what Horace was saying. Very little of the old man's lengthy anecdote sank in. Kathryn was so tense, she nearly jumped when the punch line came and the men burst into an appreciative round of laughter. Relief coursed through her when Charles began the goodbyes.

"You can't leave yet, Charles!" Horace declared in startled protest. "That surprise I mentioned earlier hasn't arrived yet." Impatient fingers tugged at a gold watch chain as Horace frowned at his pocket watch.

"I'm sorry, Horace, but we're going to have to—"

"Stick around a few more minutes," Horace insisted and stuffed the watch back into his pocket. "If you don't, I'll guarantee that you'll wish you had." His enigmatic grin promised some rare treat.

Charles was wavering. Kathryn could sense it. She quelled the vague rush of irritation. She could hardly blame Charles, considering the way Horace kept dropping hints to deliberately whet his curiosity.

"I'm afraid we can't do it, Horace." The insistence was firm, if a little reluctant. "Kathryn has a headache and she wants to go home."

"Oh." It was an abrupt sound as Horace lost his grounds for argument. "I'm sorry to hear that, Kathryn."

She accepted his sympathy with a faint smile, but Kathryn was conscious of the brown eyes that narrowed on her in a measuring study.

Without looking directly at Judson, Kathryn was fully aware of his skepticism about her early departure. Just this once, she wished Charles would have left her out of his explanation. Usually, even if it wasn't the whole truth, Kathryn provided the excuses for leaving a function. She didn't normally mind playing the role of wet blanket, and she understood the purpose of that duty. It was better for Charles's image if he always appeared reluctant to part with what was invariably "excellent company."

The door opened and closed, and a breath of warm night air swept in to freshen the stuffy atmosphere. For a split second there was silence in the immediate area. Then everyone was talking at once, the subdued murmur of voices transmitting an undercurrent of excitement that seemed to ripple through the room.

"The surprise has arrived," Horace said in an aside to Charles. Quickly excusing himself, he made his way to the door.

"It's the governor," Charles declared in an impressed whisper. "No wonder Horace wanted us to stay." With deliberate nonchalance, Charles let his attention linger on the hovering group that surrounded the tall, distinguished politician.

Aware of the anticipation Charles had to be feeling, Kathryn silently admired his outward show of mild yet respectful interest. At the same time, she realized how selfish it would be to expect Charles to sacrifice such a prime opportunity. She was just going to have to tough it out, regardless of her headache *and* the cause of it.

Her glance strayed to Judson. Unlike the others, he was paying little attention to the governor. The drink he was holding was neither wine or a cocktail; it was a beer. Taking a long swallow, he appeared restless, letting his eyes survey the room. He looked relaxed and slightly bored with the whole affair—and the company. Her lips tightened as she planted her teeth together and tried to emulate his air of indifference.

While people crowded around to welcome the newest arrival, Horace came to rejoin them. "Well, Charles? Are you positive you have to leave?" He grinned confidently.

There was the smallest hesitation before Kathryn inserted, "I think I'll survive a couple more hours." She avoided Judson's look and worked to keep the resignation out of her expression. The reward came in the grateful glance Charles flashed her way.

"Good, good." Horace nodded his approval and turned to Judson, raising heavy gray eyebrows in a questioning fashion. "How about it, Judd? After the governor makes the rounds, a few of us are going to slip away to the den and let him tickle our ears with something worth hearing. Care to join us?"

"No thanks." A half smile accompanied the refusal. "I'll leave the politicking to those of you who have the patience and stamina for it." Tipping his glass, he downed the rest of his beer and handed the empty glass to Horace. "I think I'll call it a night."

"You're leaving?" The old man blinked.

"Yeah. I've got a lot of work ahead of me tomorrow. I'll see you in the morning."

"Nine o'clock?" Horace asked to verify the time of their appointment.

"Right." His chest expanded on an indrawn breath, his eyes resting on Kathryn. He held her gaze for a pulse beat, a thread of tension tying them together. Sensations that had lain dormant for so many years surfaced in a rush. Kathryn could feel fires long banked suddenly kindling. She averted her eyes, breathing with difficulty as she blocked out the memories assaulting her. Then Judson was nodding, preparing to take his leave.

"Say, Judd." Horace stroked his whiskered chin with a thumb and forefinger. "You're staying in town, aren't you?"

The question checked the initial step he'd taken to leave. "That's right."

"Since Kathryn isn't feeling well, maybe you could give her a ride home?" The rising inflection of his voice put a question mark at the end of the sentence. Kathryn went white.

"I could," Judson replied evenly, and didn't sound too thrilled at the prospect.

"That won't be necessary," she inserted quickly, and added a lie. "I'm feeling much better now."

Judson slid her an amused look, silently taunting and mocking. He shrugged in acceptance and started to turn away. This time it was Charles's voice that stopped him from leaving.

"Maybe that would be a good idea," he decided.

"It isn't." That was too forceful. "I mean, it

isn't necessary to put Judson to the trouble,'' Kathryn amended.

There was the shortest of pauses before Judson yielded to the pressure of propriety. "It's no trouble." The assertion was smooth, but not very convincing.

"Thank you for the offer." The cloak of false politeness was difficult to maintain, so Kathryn shifted her gaze to Charles and willed him to read the message in her green eyes. "But I'll stay until you're finished, Charles."

"That could be hours," he warned.

"I don't mind, really." She laced her arm through his in an attempt to hold on.

Charles made a quick study of her face, missing what she wanted him to see. "I appreciate your being so supportive, darling, but I can see that you aren't feeling well. Judd's generous offer will solve the problem for both of us. You can get home and get a good night's sleep, and I'll feel better knowing that's where you are." He grinned persuasively. "I won't have to wonder whether you're about to pass out on me, either."

"But I'm fine—"

"Really, Kathryn. I insist." Disentangling her hand from the crook of his arm, Charles wrapped an arm around her shoulders and urged her toward Judson. "Go home, take an aspirin and get some rest. I'll talk to you tomorrow."

Her mouth opened to protest, but common sense made her reconsider. If she made too much fuss, Charles would begin to wonder why. He knew she wanted to leave the party, so the next natural assumption would be that she wanted to avoid being alone with Judson. Which was true. Since it wasn't a reaction she wanted to explain, she held her silence.

There was a stilted exchange of farewells. Then Charles was turning to accompany Horace to the den, and Kathryn was left with little choice but to follow Judson. He was already halfway to the door and gave no sign that he intended to wait for her.

She was unwillingly made aware of the comparison between his exit tonight and the one he'd made seven years ago, the last time she'd seen him. In both instances, he had walked out without looking back. And just like the last time, Kathryn felt the sharp sting of tears in her eyes. She blinked them away, because this time she didn't care.

CHAPTER THREE

THE SKY WAS DARK as black velvet, with shadowy clusters of clouds forming occasional gray patches. Fistfuls of stars glittered like diamond dust and a white half moon tossed a little light over the flat, empty Kansas plains. A collection of outbuildings edged the large ranch yard. Near them, a fluorescent security light blazed from a tall pole. The powerful glow cast a gray-blue sheen over the white ranch house and the surrounding area, turning the darkness into artificial twilight.

Pausing on the wide wooden porch, Kathryn let her eyes adjust to the difference in light. Frowning, she looked around for Judson. A footstep sounded behind her, loud on the board floor. She turned in time to see Judson push away from the wall and flick a half-smoked cigarette over the porch railing.

"Ready?" he asked.

"Yes." The response was a grim sound as she followed him down the steps.

The parking area in front of the large garage was filled with cars. Vehicles lined either side of the long driveway and cluttered the graveled ranch yard. With long, easy-flowing strides, Judson veered left and started down the driveway. The delicate high-heeled sandals she wore forced Kathryn to slow her pace or risk twisting an ankle on the slightly rutted, gravelly ground.

Glancing over his shoulder, Judson stopped to wait for her. His hands were on his hips, pushing his suit jacket back and emphasizing how the leanness of his chest tapered to a flatly muscled stomach. Drawing even with him, Kathryn brushed past Judson as quickly as her high heels would allow.

Even though she concentrated on the careful steps she had to take, Kathryn nearly stumbled when a large hand curved itself under her elbow. The contact jolted through her like an electric current. Even more of a jolt was the discovery that Judson's slightest touch could still have the same disturbing effect. The realization made her stiffen and her pulse quickened, sounding loud and primitive to her own ears in the peaceful quiet of the night.

It was a relief when they stopped near a tan car and Judson released his hold. He opened the passenger door, but didn't wait to help her inside. He was already walking around to his side when she slid in and pulled the door shut. A second later, Judson climbed in behind the wheel and turned the car toward the highway. Moon-silvered wheat fields flanked the two lanes, the asphalt emptiness broken by the grasshopper-headed pumps of a smattering of oil wells.

"I've made this drive a lot of times," he mused idly. "And the trip back to town always seemed twice as long as the trip out to the ranch."

Kathryn made some meaningless comment and stared straight ahead. She wasn't in the mood for small talk, and she had the feeling that the hour-long drive would be infinitely longer tonight than on any previous occasion. She twisted her fingers together in her lap, dreading every second of it.

The car was standard size, but its interior felt very small. Long and lean, Judson's frame seemed to fill every inch of it. He filled Kathryn's side vision, too, until she could hardly see anything except the shadowy cut of his profile. With each rotation of the car's wheels, her awareness of him increased. The silence between them became stifling. She needed a distraction from the direction her thoughts kept trying to take.

"By the way," she said. "My home isn't a boarding house anymore." Just in case Judson had changed his mind about where to stay, Kathryn wanted to let him know the choice had been taken from him.

"It isn't?"

"I turned it into a boutique almost five years ago."

Judson let his eyes leave the road long enough to search her features in the darkness, then returned his attention to the narrow highway. "Are you serious?"

The disbelief in his voice rankled. "Don't you think I'm capable of running a business?"

"I wouldn't know about that." There was an irritating indifference to his reply. "I just can't imagine Mattie giving up her boarding house. As much as she complained about it, I still think she loved every minute of it.''

"Considering the short time you were there, that is a very astute observation.'' Kathryn sighed heavily, wondering why she had started the conversation. Then she remembered and decided to continue. "Yes,'' she admitted on a more civil note. "She did love it. Besides me, the boarding house was her life. It was all she had. Business dwindled away to nothing when the motels started going up in town. Buck was the only boarder left at...at the last. He still has a room upstairs.''

"At the last?'' He questioned the reason for her hesitation.

Turning her head, Kathryn stared out the side window. She probably should have said something earlier, but she hadn't wanted to discuss personal topics. "Mother died five years ago.''

"Mattie?'' Surprise mixed with concern as he blurted the name. "How?''

"Cancer.'' Kathryn's voice was flat, lacking emotion. It wasn't because she hadn't loved her mother. She had, in a distant, sad sort of way. They had never been close like mothers and daughters should be, arguing more than they discussed, shouting more than they talked. Yet, Mattie had always been there when Kathryn needed someone. There were times when she truly missed her mother. But the passage of years allowed Kathryn to speak of her death without grief.

"That must have been rough on you.'' It was a subdued comment.

"Yes, well...I made it," she said, reflecting how she had made it through other losses, but all of them had taken their toll.

"How did Buck take it?" Judson asked quietly.

Turning away from the window, Kathryn met his concerned look, then turned away. For nearly twenty years Buck Weston had boarded with Mattie, and Kathryn couldn't remember or imagine a time that Buck didn't have a place in her life. He had been many things to her—baby-sitter, play-mate, confidant, disciplinarian, comforter—the father she had never known.

His relationship with her mother was a little more difficult to describe. Kathryn could only guess how deep the couple's feelings had run. There had never been any outward signs of love between them. In fact, the opposite had been true. Rather than exchanging affectionate words and glances, Buck and her mother had traded insults and scowls. Yet beneath it all, Kathryn had sensed a mutual understanding. Others had always been put off by her mother's abrasive manner, but the rough cowboy had instinctively known how to deal with Mattie. He'd fought fire with fire, and Kathryn suspected they had carried on a romance in their own odd way for years.

"He took it hard," she remembered. "Of course he never talked about it very much." That wasn't Buck's way. Most of what she learned about what he was feeling was from observation and by reading between the lines. "I think he still misses her. He seems kind of lonely, and—"

"He always did seem lonely," Judson said tautly. "I never could understand why he didn't find a woman who would appreciate him instead of—" The sentence was abruptly cut off before anything derogatory was actually said about her mother, but his meaning was clear. He rubbed a hand over his mouth, the gesture hinting at regret.

"Obviously he didn't want another woman," Kathryn said coolly. A sense of family loyalty made her defensive and protective of Mattie, but in truth, she too had often wondered why Buck had tolerated her parent for so long. Mother or not, there was no pretending that Mattie Ryan had been a likable person. Kathryn wavered between being glad for Buck's steadfast loyalty to her mother, and feeling sick over the waste of a good man who deserved a lot more than Mattie had been capable of giving.

"I'm sorry about your mother, Katy." Judson's sympathy sounded sincere.

Still, all things considered, Kathryn couldn't help being skeptical. "Why?" she challenged softly. "You two never liked each other."

"Mattie never gave me a chance to like her," Judson pointed out. "She hated me on sight."

"You were a drifter." It was a simple explanation—and complete. Mattie hadn't needed any more reason to dislike Judson. She herself had married a drifter, a glib-tongued Irish charmer who had swept her off her feet and left her a year later—eighteen, pregnant and alone. It was little wonder that she had been bitter.

"Translated: the devil reincarnate," he said dryly.

"You're exaggerating," she snapped.

"Oh, no I'm not." His tone was wry, with a trace of sad amusement. "But there isn't much point in going into all that." This time it was his heavy sigh that seemed to linger in the air.

"No," Kathryn agreed, because there wasn't any point. Especially since most of Mattie's judgments and predictions about Judson had eventually come true. Her mother had recognized his type right from the start, and she had been wary. Unfortunately Kathryn's reaction to him had been the direct opposite—right from the start.

The first time she'd seen Judson, Kathryn had been fascinated, intrigued and mesmerized by some force beyond her control or understanding. Without half trying, she could remember every single detail, every sensation of a moment seven years ago.

It was July, and she had been in the big kitchen all afternoon, helping her mother fix supper for the boarders. There had never been enough extra money for luxuries such as air-conditioning, so the kitchen had held all the heat and humidity of a midwestern summer day, plus the additional heat from the stove and oven.

To combat the sweltering temperature, Kathryn had coiled her waist-length ash-blond hair into a loose knot atop her head and dressed in soft-pink cotton shorts and a matching T-shirt. Wisps of hair had escaped to curl damply around her neck.

She experienced the uncomfortable sensation of perspiration trickling into the valley between her breasts. The stickiness of the day had made the thin material of her tee shirt cling like a second skin, outlining her ripe young curves.

Since her mother had told her to set an extra place at the table and the instruction had been given with an uncommunicative grimness, Kathryn's curiosity had been naturally aroused. When the screen door squeaked on its hinges, she hurried to finish slicing the roast and arranging the meat and vegetables on a serving platter.

Water had splashed noisily into the deep laundry sink on the back porch, the sound mingling with the rumble of male voices as the men took turns lathering up with pine-scented soap. Her curiosity had led Kathryn to the opposite side of the kitchen where she could unobtrusively get a look at the new man. Standing to one side of the sink, he'd been rubbing his sun-browned face and arms with a thick towel. Then he'd replaced the towel and combed his fingers through the variegated tobacco brown of his hair in an attempt to tame it into some kind of order.

Kathryn had felt dangerously excited as she watched Judson, who seemed so strong and lean, young and rawly male. He was not the usual, run-of-the-mill boarder. He was younger than most, but it was more than that. The exact quality had eluded Kathryn, but something made him different, and special somehow. Maybe it was the sparkle in his eyes that seemed to suggest a big appetite for all life had to offer. Or maybe it was the determination in his stride, so self-confident it was almost a swagger. Kathryn would have been content to stand there unnoticed and study him all day, but the sharp edge of her mother's tongue had sent her scurrying to fill the glasses with ice cubes and iced tea. In the meantime the men had filed into the dining room.

Kathryn could remember so clearly the way she'd kept stealing glances at him as she'd carried the food from kitchen to table. Once she'd looked up and found herself gazing directly into his brown eyes. Nothing could have made her look away, not even the hot color that stained her cheeks. Then his mouth had curved slowly and lazily into a smile. It was the kind of smile Kathryn had read about but never seen. The kind that took a girl's breath away and left her feeling dizzy.

She experienced all sorts of new reactions. Some crazy, heady sensation had turned her legs to jelly, and afraid her knees were going to give out, Kathryn had made a hasty retreat to the kitchen. Smiling in wonder, she'd leaned against the counter and tried to catch her breath. The conversation that drifted in from the dining room had made that impossible.

"Quite a looker, huh, Taylor?" one of the boarders had asked, referring to her. And Kathryn had stood motionless, feeling that she was hanging on the edge of a precipice while she waited for the newcomer's response.

"She's beautiful," Judson had stated matter-of-factly.

Then the other boarder had taunted him, his words taking away a little of the glow Kathryn had felt, but none of the heat. "You'd better be careful, young buck. She may look like a woman, but she's still jailbait."

"Oh yeah?" A long silence had followed before Judson Taylor finally asked, "How old is she, anyway?" It was a reluctant question, as if he'd wanted to deny any interest in her but couldn't.

"Seventeen, just barely."

"Oh."

Kathryn had heard the flatness, the grim disappointment in the reply that said he was categorizing her as unavailable. But that handsome older man of twenty-six had called her beautiful and subsequently captured her heart. From that moment on, she'd done everything in her power to make him recognize her for the woman she thought she was instead of the child against whom the other men had warned him.

In the end it seemed she had convinced him only too well. Looking back, Kathryn could see that Judson's resistance had only been a token gesture, but at the time, his initial indifference had presented quite a challenge to the feminine charms she was just discovering and learning how to exercise. Eventually his surrender had been complete. As had been hers. Kathryn had fallen in love.

Leaning back she let her head rest against the car seat and stared at the flat emptiness of the fields speeding by. Seven years, and the impressions of her time with Judson had not yet begun to dim.

"Do you realize this is the first time you and I have been alone together in a car," Judson mused.

Kathryn looked at him for a blank instant. Considering their past relationship, his observation didn't seem possible. But it was true. Her mother had never allowed her to actually date Judson. Of course they had found ways of getting around that rule.

"That's true," she murmured.

"Hard to believe, isn't it?" There was a dry quirk of his mouth.

"Yes." Kathryn's throat tightened.

When he turned his head to look at her, the atmosphere thickened with shared memories. This was the man she had once rested all her hopes and dreams upon, and he was only an arm's length away. She recalled the joyful abandonment of that summer, the sheer sweetness of those long lazy days and languid starlit nights. It had been the happiest time of her life, yet she couldn't recall even the good times without feeling a choking surge of bitterness. The hurt was much more recent and long lasting than those fleeting weeks of pleasure and discovery.

"I'm sorry for the way you were railroaded into taking me home," Kathryn said crisply, regretting the recent unguarded moments, and wanting to rebuild a wall of aloofness.

He shrugged and looked back at the highway. "You can't help it if your boyfriend isn't the chivalrous type."

"Charles isn't my *boyfriend*," Kathryn bristled. "He's my fiancé."

"I guess boyfriend is the wrong word." Judson's voice was dry as he revised his opinion. "Charles is old enough to be your father."

She bridled at the implied criticism, yet it was hardly something she could deny. "We're both adults. Age doesn't make any difference."

"If you say so." He dismissed the subject with expressive indifference.

"I do," she stated unnecessarily, and remembered his earlier comment about Charles. She didn't want to talk to Judson about him, but she did feel obligated to defend Charles in his absence. "And just for the record, Charles is very much the chivalrous type. He's always a perfect gentleman." That was a large part of his charm.

"Mmm-hmm." It was a lazy, mocking sound. "That's why he was so quick to pawn you off, rather than take you home himself."

"He did not pawn me off!" she declared indignantly. "This was simply a convenient solution for both of us. Charles knew I wasn't feeling well. He was concerned about me and wanted me to go home."

"It seems to me, he was perfectly content to let you suffer, once the governor arrived. You offered to stay at the party, and I don't recall hearing Charles argue," Judson pointed out.

For a stunned second Kathryn was at a loss because she realized Judson spoke the truth. "Tonight was very important to Charles," she finally retorted. "And I understand."

"I understand, too," he replied calmly. "Probably better than you do."

"What are you talking about?" she demanded, the tone of her voice communicating a message of careless disdain for whatever his answer might be.

"I've known a lot of Charleses," he stated simply, untouched by the ice in her voice. "He's not the type of man who can make you happy."

It was said so calmly, so matter-of-factly, that Kathryn wasn't entirely sure she'd heard him correctly. Then she was outraged that Judson, of all people, would have the nerve to make such a judgment. She curled her nails into her palms.

"And I'm sure you are an authority on how to make a woman happy." She bit out the words, then tempered the sharpness of her voice with cloying sweetness. "Tell me, Judson, do you have a happy little wife waiting for you at home?"

"No, I don't have a wife." He threw her a quick, challenging look. "As a matter of fact, I don't have a home either."

The knowledge that he had neither taunted her, because Kathryn knew that one would come as easily to him as the other—if he wanted them. He obviously didn't. He never had. He had only claimed to want them, knowing that's what a seventeen-year-old had wanted to hear.

"No, of course not." She was trembling, awash again with all the old hurt and bitterness. "That was a stupid question on my part, wasn't it? How could I have forgotten that you're not the type of man to be tied down to one woman or one place.

Considering that, you're hardly in a position to pass judgment on Charles—or me!''

His gaze was fixed on the dark ribbon of highway. There was no change in the impassive set of his features. ''I wasn't passing judgment—just stating facts.''

His calm, all-knowing attitude was additional fuel for Kathryn's flaming temper. ''The *facts* are that Charles is a good, reliable man.'' She stressed each adjective, the cool inflection of her voice implying that Charles was the antithesis of Judson. ''He has a stable future, and I know for a fact that I can count on him. No matter what, Charles will always be by my side.''

''Like tonight?'' It was a soft challenge. ''Try it the other way around, Katy—you'll always be at his side. Not that I think Charles would actually leave you,'' he went on to clarify the point. ''But he's a taker. His loyalties will always lie with whoever can give him the most. Tonight it happened to be the governor. Tomorrow...?'' He slid her a long sideways glance. ''Can you be satisfied with that?''

Kathryn refused to even consider the question. ''I don't want to discuss it,'' she snapped. ''Especially not with you.'' She was irritated with herself for letting the conversation go as far as it had.

''Why?'' he wondered, then supplied his own reasoning. ''Because the truth hurts?''

''There are a variety of reasons, Judson, but that definitely isn't one of them.'' She would have left it at that, but she had the feeling Judson would merely draw more faulty conclusions. She'd sooner supply her own reasons. "Mostly, I don't want to discuss it with you because you don't know Charles, you don't know me and you couldn't even begin to know what would or wouldn't make me happy. Besides, it isn't really any of your business."

"I *do* know you," he countered, smoothly ignoring her attempt at disqualifying his opinions. "At least, I know how you used to be—sweet about half the time, sassy when you were crossed. Furious one minute and passionate the next." He stared out the windshield, his head tipped to one side. "And I also know what used to make you happy."

There was a heavy silence, one of those moments that seem to stretch on and on while Kathryn searched through the sudden turmoil of her thoughts for something suitably scathing to say. Judson turned to look at her and she felt the almost physical touch of his gaze. The breath in her lungs felt trapped.

Like his smile, Judson's eyes held a sensual magic all their own. They traveled with slow familiarity down her body, lingering on the agitated rise and fall of her breasts, which betrayed her altered breathing. Then his eyes wandered on in a lazily knowing inspection that left a tingling trail of fire as a small reminder that what he'd said was true. He had been able to make her happy in many ways—in all ways.

Any real feelings she'd had for him were dead and gone, yet the physical attraction between them still existed. The rapid pulse in her neck was further proof. Kathryn resented his potent male sexuality, which affected her simply because she was a female.

"I've changed," she said flatly. A hardened glint entered her green eyes as she swung her gaze to him. "It takes a lot more to make me happy now." Or a lot less, she considered.

"I don't believe that." His statement was just as flat, as he returned his eyes to the road.

"And I don't particularly care." She spoke curtly because she was quivering inside. Kathryn was afraid he might be right, and she wanted desperately for him to be wrong.

"So cool. So poised," he mused, drawling the words. "You're the picture of sophistication, Katy." It wasn't a compliment. "Too bad I don't believe that elegant shell is the real you. I'd lay odds that the hot-tempered, hot-blooded girl I once knew is still in there. Eventually, she'll find her way out, and she'll be bored to death and miserable when she finds herself stuck with someone like Charles."

Kathryn was seething, her stomach churning with a violent combination of emotions. She managed to hold her fury in check, not wanting to prove him right by letting him see that he could still arouse anything in her, even her temper.

"I'm sorry to disappoint you, Judson, but you're wrong. And I'm sure you won't take offense if I say that while I appreciate your concern for my happiness, I don't need your advice. I've been taking care of myself for a long time now, and I've gotten to be very good at it."

He gave her a long considering look, then lit a cigarette and blew out a stream of smoke. "You're right." His voice went flat with disinterest. "It's none of my business."

The lights of Deepwater were growing more distinct. Houses began to dot the landscape. Then whole subdivisions were crowding close to both sides of the highway. During the boom rows of new frame houses had been built almost faster than the town could put in streets. Mobile-home parks and mobile-home sales had become very lucrative as people had scrambled for housing.

Passing the last trailer park, the car bumped over the railroad tracks that had once marked the edge of town. Grain elevators stood nearby, looking incongruous now that they were practically in the center of Deepwater.

Kathryn breathed a sigh of relief. *Just five more minutes.* She couldn't remember when she'd ever been so anxious to get home. Often it made her feel lonely to walk into the dark emptiness of her apartment above the shop. Tonight it seemed like a haven, safe and secure.

The two-lane highway turned into Main Street. Judson slowed the car to comply with the posted speed limit. There was something reflective about his expression as he observed his surroundings. The town had changed, but there were some things that Kathryn guessed would always be the same.

On the whole, the streets were deserted and peaceful, except for the block that contained the Main Street Tavern. Cars and pickup trucks were parked at the curb in front of it. Cowboys in crisp Levi's and straw Stetsons lounged outside the doorway, drinks in hand as they indulged in a round of good-natured ribbing and jostling. With a few more beers, the jostling would lean toward the rowdy side and probably result in a fight. Kathryn suspected the men would be disappointed if it didn't. To them, confrontation was part of the fun—a good way to blow off steam.

Judson let his glance linger on the cowboys as the car passed the tavern. "I'll bet those boys are having a better time than anybody at that party we just left."

"Yes. I noticed you looked rather bored." She wished she could say that he'd also looked out of place in the distinguished gathering, but she couldn't.

"Weren't you?" His tone challenged her to tell the truth.

"Not in the least." She'd been much too nervous and on edge to get bored, but of course she didn't tell him that.

At the next intersection Judson turned left and drove another two blocks. The area was an odd combination of residential and commercial properties. Many of the big old houses had been turned into businesses. An equal number were still private homes. Without hesitation or asking for confirmation, Judson stopped the car at the curb in front of the shop. Kathryn glanced at him, surprised and a little irritated that he'd recognized it so easily when it had changed so much since the last time he'd seen it.

With its fresh coat of white paint and various other improvements, the large, two-story frame house retained just enough of a homey atmosphere to give a welcoming impression of hospitality. The front had been remodeled, equipped with display windows and a large sign bearing the name of the boutique in dusty-rose lettering. It was a far cry from the deteriorating boarding house, with its chipped gray paint and covered front porch.

Kathryn was proud of the changes and of the obvious success she'd made of her business. Everyone had predicted that a town like Deepwater couldn't—wouldn't—support a place that sold only exclusive, and expensive, lines of women's wear. Despite the fact that the townswomen had more money to spend on clothing than they'd ever had in their lives, everyone had insisted there wasn't a demand for such things as silks and satins and designer gowns. Kathryn had suspected it was only because such things had never been made available. Her healthy bank balance proved she'd been right.

Her hand was on the car door handle, yet she found herself hesitating. Kathryn didn't know why. Maybe because she was waiting for Judson to comment on what she'd done with the old place. Or maybe it was because something needed to be said after all this time. But what? It was much too late for words to change anything.

She glanced at Judson, who was staring out the side window at the shop. There was a stillness about him that was unnatural, as if something was holding his gaze and he couldn't look away. His jaw was tightly clenched, every muscle rigid with a sudden tension that Kathryn didn't understand.

It seemed to have something to do with him seeing the boutique, yet that didn't make any sense. She'd told him about it earlier, and he had reacted with indifference—the same way he'd acted about practically everything else she'd said. Yet, he clearly wasn't indifferent now.

She pulled the handle and released the latch. The sound seemed to break whatever spell Judson had been under. His head snapped around as the car door opened. Strong fingers seized her arm to prevent her from leaving.

"Katy, I. . . ." A controlled urgency was in his low voice, and there was something probing in his gaze.

Kathryn lowered her eyes to the hand that gripped her arm. Unwanted sensations quivered along her nerve ends. She hated the weakness that was spreading through her limbs, a weakness she had felt too many times before. Why did he still have this power over her?

She twisted away, trying to break free of his grip. There was an instant when his fingers tightened, digging into her flesh. Then Judson released her. As she started to climb out of the car, Kathryn heard the driver's door opening. The sound sent a clamor of alarm through her system.

"There's no need to see me to the door." She had already spent too much time in his company. Her crispness stopped his actions. The door slammed shut.

"That's right." Sarcasm curled his mouth. "You can take care of yourself now, can't you?"

Kathryn ignored the gibe and pushed the door all the way open. It was purely an afterthought that made her hesitate. "Thanks for the ride," she said with a brittle smile. "I hope you enjoy your stay in Deepwater."

Judson inclined his head in mocking acknowledgment. "Maybe I was wrong," he decided. "Maybe you are perfect for Charles. You already sound like a politician's wife."

Turning sharply, Kathryn stepped out of the car. The flat of her hand was pushing the door when Judson said, "Goodbye, Katy." It sounded so permanent. Some invisible force made her stop and turn around.

"Goodbye, Judson." But the tan car was already pulling away from the curb. She watched as the taillights grew smaller and the car eventually turned a corner, disappearing from view. A chill inched slowly along her spine until she felt frozen.

She drew a deep breath and tried to shake off a feeling of depression. Opening her evening bag, she took out a set of keys and jingled them absently as she walked to the shop entrance and let herself in.

It was dark, but Kathryn knew her way around all the display racks and mannequins without needing to turn on a light. Her eye caught the shimmer of rich fabrics as she threaded her way through the showroom. At the back of the shop, a set of dusty-rose curtains hung in the archway that divided the business area of the house from the living quarters. Kathryn stepped into the narrow back hall and hesitated. The light in the kitchen was on, which meant Buck was still up.

Her headache had intensified with the emotional strain of the ride home. She really didn't feel like talking, and she doubted she'd be very good company. What she needed was to get some sleep. The decision made, Kathryn turned toward the staircase. She hesitated again when her foot touched the bottom step. She suddenly couldn't face the idea of being alone. Not just yet. She went to the kitchen. A lanky, wiry man was slouched at the kitchen table, the run-down heel of his cowboy boot hooked over the arch of the other. His large knuckled hands were curled loosely around a coffee cup, while his faintly frowning gaze was focused on the steam rising from the hot liquid.

Observing him from the archway, Kathryn was struck anew by the air of loneliness that surrounded him. How many nights had she come home to find him like this, sitting alone in the silent kitchen? If questioned, Buck would claim he liked having the house to himself; it gave him time to think. But judging from his expression, his thoughts weren't pleasant.

Turning his head, he looked at her as she entered the kitchen. Although Buck was in his early sixties, his brown hair was just beginning to gray. His rough and weathered features were darkly sun browned, his skin the color of oiled leather. His blue eyes were faded to a washed-out color, but they were piercing and direct and they gleamed with intelligence.

"You're early tonight." Like his demeanor and appearance, Buck's voice was gruff, belying the true sensitivity of his nature.

"A little," she agreed. "I have a headache, so I wanted to come home." She walked to the cupboard and reached for the bottle of aspirin and a glass.

"How was the party—other than your headache?" Buck asked.

That wasn't an easy question to answer. Kathryn shook two white tablets into her palm and popped them into her mouth, then chased them down with a glass of water. She set the glass on the counter and turned to look at Buck.

"If you mean, did I have a good time—no. If you mean, was it profitable for Charles—yes. At least I think so. He was just getting going with Governor Ashworth when I left."

"When you left?" Buck frowned, his heavy brows knitting together. "Charles didn't bring you home?"

"No." Agitation swept through her.

"Who did?" he voiced with curiosity.

"You'd never guess in a hundred years." She still couldn't quite believe it herself. Shaking her head, she poured a cup of coffee and joined Buck at the table.

"A hundred years?" One eye squinted at her in speculation. "Since this old carcass doesn't have even half that many left, maybe you'd better just tell me."

Kathryn took a sip of coffee, then set the cup back on the table. "Judson Taylor," she said flatly.

The mention of the name brought a second of shocked silence. Then Buck blurted, "Judd Taylor! What's he doin' here?"

"Business. He's leaving right away," Kathryn replied evenly. "It seems he is very successful."

"Well that don't surprise me one bit." The line of Buck's mouth cracked into a grin. The news of Judson's unexpected appearance was still sinking in. For the moment Buck seemed to forget about Kathryn. "That boy had a lot on the ball," he remembered with satisfaction and barely veiled affection. "Your mother might have seen him as nothin' but a drifter, the aimless, wanderin' kind. Me, I saw him as a man who was headed somewhere—goin' places." He shook his head and the grin broadened. "I'm glad he made it."

Kathryn sat silently, staring into the mirror-black surface of her coffee. She sensed the change in atmosphere the minute Buck recovered from the initial surprise of the announcement. The silence lengthened. Buck had always liked Judson; theirs had been a special relationship.

But Buck was also aware of how shattered Kathryn had been seven years ago when Judson had left, voluntarily joining one of the company's exploratory crews when he had the choice of staying in Deepwater with Kathryn. Of course, he claimed he'd rather stay, but the money he'd been offered was too much to turn down.

It still pained Kathryn to remember the way

he'd steadfastly ignored her declarations of love and flatly refused her request to go with him. Judson had had a reason for that, one against which she could hardly argue. She was seventeen, a minor. So Judson left, promising to come back for her in six months, on her eighteenth birthday, with enough cash to make a sizable down payment on a house. They'd planned to be married.

His promise to return was something Kathryn had clung to like a lifeline. She had never doubted that he would keep his word. Her lips pressed tightly together at the memory. She had been so young, so trusting, so stupidly naive. She had been willing, even eager, to let Judson become her whole life. Everything had revolved around him. When it finally sank in that he wasn't coming back, her world had totally collapsed.

During those long anguished months of waiting, Buck had been there to console her and provide excuses to explain Judson's continued absence. But the lack of letters or phone calls had been a little more difficult to explain. Buck had tried, not wanting to believe the worst despite the damning evidence. Eventually Judson's name was eliminated from their conversation entirely.

"So...how was it for you tonight?" Buck shifted uncomfortably. Concern sobered his expression.

Kathryn's shoulders drooped tiredly. "To tell you the truth, I'd rather forget all about it."

"Did you ask him why he didn't come back?"

Her breathy laugh was bitter. "No." She

wouldn't deliberately invite that kind of humiliation. "I think it's always been rather obvious why he didn't come back. He never intended to."

"I don't know, Kathryn. It takes a lot to fool old Buck. I'd have swore Judd Taylor meant everything he said to you." Buck held with the theory he'd had years ago.

Kathryn gave him a pitying look. She'd believed that, too, for a while. "Maybe he meant them while he was here. But in his case, absence did not make the heart grow fonder."

"Why don't you talk to him before he leaves?" Buck suggested. "At least you'd finally have some answers."

Kathryn shook her head to firmly reject the suggestion. "If he had any explanations, or if he even felt he owed me any, he would have made them tonight. He had plenty of opportunities."

"I suppose you're right," he muttered, reluctant to agree even now. "You were just kids. It's probably all for the best if it's forgotten."

"It is," she agreed. "I don't want answers or anything else from Judson anymore. I just want him to drift on through Deepwater and out of my life like he did before—only this time for good."

She lifted the coffee cup to her lips and ended the conversation, but her mind wouldn't let her bury the past. If she closed her eyes, she knew she'd recall every glorious moment of loving Judson—and the agonizing experience of losing him.

Once she had placed the sole blame on him. Now she took partial responsibility—not for the dissolution of their affair, but for the traumatic effect the experience had had on her. That part was entirely her own fault.

Her biggest mistake had been in putting her happiness in the hands of someone else. Since Judson, she had learned to maintain control—of her life in general and her relationships with men in particular. Now she looked for different things in a man, things that promised emotional security. It was a practice she definitely intended to continue.

The coffee in her cup had grown cold. Kathryn drank it anyway. But it didn't wash away the bitter taste in her mouth. So far, nothing had.

CHAPTER FOUR

IN SLEEP, Kathryn twisted fitfully. Tears trickled from her closed eyes, clung to the tips of her lashes, then splashed onto the satin pillowcase as she moved her head restlessly from side to side, fighting off ghosts from the past.

The sob that choked her throat awakened her. Stiff with tension, Kathryn tried to get her bearings. She listened to the steady ticking of the clock on the bedside table. Gradually she began to relax. It had only been a dream.

Images from the nightmare continued to haunt her. In an attempt to banish them, Kathryn rolled onto her side and pulled the covers more securely around her. She was plagued by a deep familiar sense of loss. For the first time in years, she had dreamed of Judson....

"Judson." Kathryn pushed herself into a sitting position as last night's events came flooding back. Judson *had* been here. That part hadn't been a dream. She cradled her head in her hands, for she had sat up too quickly and now had a throbbing headache.

Kathryn felt as if she'd barely slept an hour. Glancing at the brass alarm clock, she saw it was only quarter past six. The alarm wouldn't go off for another hour, but Kathryn didn't want to go back to sleep, not when there was the possibility that the dream would continue.

Moving carefully, Kathryn pushed the covers aside and got out of bed. Decorator blinds covered the two large windows, blocking out most of the morning light. Drawn by a vague curiosity, Kathryn reached for the cord and opened the blinds.

The day was bright and clear, the Kansas sky a vivid blue, dotted with cotton-ball puffs of clouds. The old neighborhood was graced with a multitude of shade trees. Birds were perched among the spreading limbs, singing a cheerful wake-up song in the early-morning stillness.

Kathryn thoughtfully studied the scene. The day promised to be hot but beautiful, just like most other July days. In fact this morning could have been any midsummer morning; there was nothing special or out of the ordinary to distinguish it. Kathryn didn't know what she had expected to see outside, but she was somehow surprised that nothing had changed.

Yesterday her world had suffered a major jolt. Today it seemed only natural to expect some visual aftereffects. Kathryn shook her head to dismiss the thought and immediately regretted it, for the action produced more throbbing in her temples. Moving away from the window, she went into the private bath off her room and took a couple of extra-strength aspirin. The combination of the pain reliever and the tingling warmth of the shower spray had a revitalizing effect.

With a towel wrapped turban-style around her wet hair, Kathryn pulled on her blue satin robe, then glanced at the alarm clock on the bedside table. It was a few minutes after seven. Since she didn't open the shop until nine, there was plenty of time before she had to start getting ready for work. She knotted the sash of her robe and went downstairs.

The inviting aroma of brewed coffee greeted her as she neared the kitchen. Buck was standing next to the coffee maker, one hand resting on his hip and the other holding an empty coffee cup. He looked impatient with the gurgling machine.

The glass pot was nearly full. When the coffee stopped dripping, Buck grabbed the pot's handle and began to fill his cup. There was another gurgle from the machine as the last bit of water was sent to drip through the grounds and filter. Hearing the noise, Buck hurried to replace the pot, but some of the liquid dripped onto the burner where the heat made it sizzle and dance.

Buck flicked a disgusted glance at the dribble of coffee he'd managed to pour into his cup. He downed it in one swallow and glared at the coffee maker. "Don't hurry on my account," he grumbled to the machine. "Just take your ol' sweet time. I ain't got nothin' better to do today anyway."

Kathryn had to smile. "You're getting old, Buck. Now you're talking to machines. That's a bad sign."

"I ain't gettin' old," he denied with a snort. "I'm just gettin' smarter. I can say anything I like to a machine and it won't give me no back talk." At that moment, the coffee maker gurgled for the last time, making a long, low growling sound.

"It won't, huh?" Grinning, Kathryn went to get a cup for herself.

"I take it you're feelin' better this mornin'." Buck poured the coffee, filling her cup when she held it out. "You seem to be back to your old sassy self." His keen eyes swept over her as if to verify his statement.

"Good as new," she assured him, but it was an exaggeration and they both knew it. She couldn't deny that seeing Judson again had been a shock. It was only natural that it would take a little time to recover.

Buck eyed her closely for another second, then swung away from the counter to head for the table. Kathryn followed, pulling out the chair opposite where Buck usually sat. But he remained standing.

"I think I'll fix me some breakfast," he declared, and went to the refrigerator.

"Breakfast?" Kathryn frowned, watching him take out a carton of eggs. Then he was bending over to get a better look at the shelves. When he pulled out the meat drawer, Kathryn's response was automatic. "There isn't any bacon." It was something she rarely purchased since Buck hardly ever ate breakfast at home and Kathryn was usually satisfied with juice and toast. Today, she doubted her knotted stomach would tolerate even that.

"Guess I'll have to improvise then. A meatless breakfast ain't no breakfast at all." Straightening, he held up a package of bologna. "This'll do fine."

"Why aren't you going to Ruby's this morning?" Kathryn asked, because that was where he always ate breakfast, and usually lunch, too. For dinner, he was generally home, but Kathryn had often suspected that wouldn't be the case if Ruby's small café was open in the evenings. Like a lot of small-town restaurants, it catered to the business people, opening very early in the morning and closing at two in the afternoon.

Officially the restaurant's name was The Deepwater Café, but the place had been commonly referred to as Ruby's ever since Ruby Weatherby had bought it a few years back. Her husband, Jake, had been one of Buck's closest friends, but he had passed away the same year as Kathryn's mother died.

For a time Buck and Ruby had found comfort in each other, drawn together by a mutual understanding of grief and a need to share the burden. Their longtime friendship had been strengthened by the experience, but Kathryn had hoped the friendship would blossom into something even deeper. Apparently, that wasn't to be.

At the stove, Buck slapped four slices of bologna into a large iron skillet. "I feel like cookin' my own breakfast today." He answered Kathryn's question, then fired one at her. "Anything wrong with that?"

"No." She smiled at the gruff defensiveness in his voice. Buck was hiding something. "How is Ruby doing these days, anyway?" She tried to sound very casual. "I haven't seen her in a while."

"She's fine." Kathryn could glean nothing from either Buck's words or facial expression about the present status of their relationship.

"And the café?" She tried a less personal approach, hoping it would lead somewhere.

"What about it?" Using another skillet, Buck cracked four eggs and watched them sizzle in the hot grease.

"I assume it's doing well?" Kathryn prompted. As usual, she was getting nowhere with her questions about Buck's personal feelings. He kept them inside, as if revealing deep emotion was a display of weakness. Yet beneath that rough exterior was one of the most sensitive men Kathryn had ever met. If anyone deserved to find true happiness, Buck did. Kathryn doubted he had ever experienced it, and feared he never would.

"Yep." With a fork, Buck turned the bologna slices. He put bread in the toaster, then went back to check the eggs, expertly flipping them with a spatula.

"I'll bet Ruby gets tired of having to cook all the time," Kathryn said in a musing tone. "Why don't you invite her over for dinner one of these nights? She'd probably enjoy a meal she didn't have to cook herself." Years ago Ruby had often been their dinner guest. Kathryn wondered who was responsible for breaking the habit.

"I might." Buck was busy buttering the toast, and he mumbled his reply. When he'd finished, he dished the food onto two plates and set one in front of Kathryn.

"What's this?" Her smile was puzzled. Her stomach began to churn at the sight of the food.

"You wanted some, didn't ya?" Buck didn't look at her as he settled into his chair.

And Kathryn suddenly knew why he hadn't gone to Ruby's. It had nothing to do with the woman. Buck was worried about Kathryn, so he was going to take care of her. There was nothing he or anyone else could do to erase the effects of seeing Judson, but Buck wanted to do *something* to help.

Food was the first thing people usually thought to offer in a crisis. And it was the last thing the troubled person usually wanted. But Buck's gesture touched her deeply, and Kathryn picked up her fork.

"I'm starving," she lied.

CRYSTAL CHANDELIERS were suspended from the high ceiling of the boutique, their glittering light combining with the sunshine spilling through the large display window that looked out onto the street. Yards and yards of rose-colored fabric draped the window, the voluminous folds tied back with thick satin cord.

The same rich fabric framed the archway to the

four dressing rooms, which were as big as small bedrooms. In them, a woman could relax and take the time to study the fit of a garment from every angle. The mirrors were large and well placed, the atmosphere conducive to fantasizing. Furnished with settees of cream brocade, marble-topped tables and crystal lighting fixtures, the boutique provided the farm and ranch wives with that touch of glamour every woman occasionally craves.

Crossing the shop to unlock the street door, Kathryn felt the plush dusty-rose carpet give beneath her feet. A certain ease ran through her, soothing the tension that seeing Judson had created. Kathryn felt a combination of things, some of which she couldn't even identify. True, there was the expected pride and satisfaction. Yet there was more.

All sorts of emotions were tied up in this place. When Kathryn had decided to open a store, she had been a shattered and vulnerable girl of nineteen. A year before, she had been forced to accept that Judson had abandoned her. A month after that she had suffered another devastating loss. During that time, Kathryn had leaned heavily on her mother, relying on Mattie's strength. But then her mother had died, leaving her, too.

It was then that Kathryn began to see that if she loved, she lost. The two went together hand in glove. And each time she lost, some vital part of herself died in the process. In a bid for self-preservation, she had buried her emotions deep inside, where no one could ever shatter them again.

People were the cause of heartache, people who were allowed to get so deep into your feelings that they took part of your soul when they left. Having lost so much already, Kathryn knew she couldn't afford to let it happen again.

So it was this shop that had carried her through. Its solidity had taken the place of Mattie and Judson. The boutique had become the object of her attention, devotion and her affection. And it had blossomed under her loving touch. In return, it had made her the woman she was—confident, independent, strong. So when Kathryn looked around the place, as she was doing now, she didn't see a thriving business. She saw a symbol of her ability to survive, and as always, it gave her strength.

She walked to the tall marble-topped counter and let her fingers trail over the cool surface. Preoccupied, she took a seat on the stool behind the counter. Maybe she should think about expanding the shop. There were vacant rooms upstairs, and her thoughts drifted, focusing on plans and possibilities and furnishings. . . anything but Judson.

Late that afternoon the silver bell above the door tinkled musically as someone entered the shop. Kathryn glanced up with a smile, automatically closing the ledger and pushing it aside. When she saw Charles, Kathryn didn't have to look at her watch to know she had worked past closing time.

Charles always came at five-thirty. During the week, they had a standing dinner date. Sometimes they went out, and sometimes Kathryn fixed something for herself, Charles and Buck at home.

She liked the definite pattern of her life. It was busy and uncomplicated, and she always knew what to expect.

"Hi." Charles moved farther into the shop, glancing around to make sure there were no lingering customers. Kathryn was sitting behind the tall counter. Charles stopped a few feet away, his handsome face wearing a smile. "How come the shop's still open? Were you working with someone?" He was well aware that if a customer wanted to browse, Kathryn kept the boutique open as long as was necessary.

"No. I guess I just lost track of time." The day had practically flown by. Kathryn guessed it was because she'd made such a point of keeping busy.

"That can happen all too easily." His smile widened as he shook his head. "I did the same thing at Horace's party last night. It was three in the morning before I knew it."

The comment reminded Kathryn of the circumstances under which she had left the party. She felt vaguely irritated. Apparently the concern that had prompted Charles to insist she let Judson take her home had faded. He hadn't even asked how she felt.

"Three o'clock," she murmured. "That must mean you were having a good time." She slid off the stool and walked over to hang the gold-lettered Closed sign on the door.

"I had a wonderful time." Charles made the distinction. He caught her arm as she started to pass. "Absolutely wonderful," he repeated.

"Kathryn, I really believe I will eventually be governor of this state. Everything seems to be going my way."

In his sober expression she saw a burning ambition, something that was usually concealed by the charm of Charles's smile. Then his mouth was coming toward hers, and Kathryn automatically tilted her head back to accept his kiss of greeting. Its pressure was firm but brief, lasting mere seconds. Nothing about the kiss made her heart pound or turned her knees to jelly, and Kathryn was glad. Those were sensations she no longer trusted, no longer wanted. "All those hours I spent out at Horace's were a sound investment," he stated. "The contacts I was able to make last night are going to be invaluable later on. One in particular."

"I assume you mean Governor Ashworth?" She went back behind the counter to remove the money from the till, placing it in a bank-deposit pouch.

"That's exactly who I mean. We hit it off right from the beginning. Harold has invited me to the capitol tomorrow so I can meet some of the honchos up there."

"It's Harold already," Kathryn observed dryly, almost mockingly.

His gaze sharpened at the bite in her voice. "I told you we hit it off," he reminded her, and frowned. "What's wrong, Kathryn? I've just told you about an incident that will probably be a milestone in my career, and you're acting as if you couldn't care less."

"I . . . I'm sorry." Kathryn was irritated—with

herself. She suddenly became aware of the roots of her impatience with Charles. She was reacting to some of Judson's comments. Especially the one about her being pawned off and his implication that she wasn't really very important to Charles.

"Aren't you happy for me...for us?" Charles wanted to know.

Kathryn disliked the way her imagination picked up Charles's quick change from singular to plural, magnifying it until it seemed important. She was being unreasonable and overly sensitive, thanks to Judson's snide remarks. But she didn't intend to let that continue.

"Of course I'm happy," she insisted forcefully, her smile deliberately bright. "For *us*." Kathryn wasn't going to let anything spoil this victory for her and Charles—or their chances for happiness together. Silently she cursed Judson for planting seeds of doubt. He hadn't known what he was talking about. And Kathryn was disgusted with herself for even listening.

The next morning Kathryn had barely opened the shop for business when the bell above the door chimed to announce the first customer of the day. Perched on a stepladder in the storeroom, she hurried to finish stacking shoe boxes high on a shelf.

The ladder was an old, none-too-steady, wooden affair with rough edges that were known to give splinters to the unwary. Kathryn kept that in mind as she stepped down, careful to avoid snagging the emerald-green silk of her dress and the sheer nylon of her panty hose. She dusted off her hands before smoothing the dress over her hips and running testing fingers over her blond hair to make sure no stray wisps had escaped the sophisticated coil at the back of her head.

Leaving the no-frills storeroom, Kathryn entered the main showroom of the boutique.

"I'm sorry to keep you waiting...." Like her voice, her step faltered when she saw Judson standing near a mannequin. He appeared to be absorbed in the inspection of a gold lamé designer gown.

"No problem." He spared her a brief glance as he brushed aside her apology—as if she would have made the apology if she'd known the "customer" was him! Then he was looking at the dress again, a large hand reaching to touch the material. He looked totally relaxed, totally at ease.

Kathryn wasn't. A cold anger was building inside her. The night before last, they had met by accident. Today, Judson was definitely forcing a meeting. She'd never dreamed he'd have the nerve to come strolling into her place of business just as if nothing had ever happened between them. But then again, remembering some of the wild things he'd done in the past, Kathryn should have known he'd have the nerve to do anything.

She recovered from the initial moment of shock to inquire in an amazingly professional manner, "Is there something I can do for you?"

With a slight turn of his head, he looked at her. "I doubt it." His shoulders lifted in a shrug as his gaze released hers to sweep curiously over the shop. "But you never know. Do you mind if I look around?"

"Not at all." She met his challenging look with a cool glare. "You're welcome to stay as long as you like. This is a place of business, Judson, not my home." The last was offered to let him know that if the situation was reversed, her answer would have been different. "I'm afraid you'll have to excuse me, though. I have a lot of work to do." Pivoting on a spike heel, she walked over to stand behind the counter.

"Of course," he murmured dryly, and turned his back to her while he caught the long sleeve of the gown in front of him and inspected the price tag dangling from it. His low whistle sliced through the thick silence.

The sound prompted Kathryn into action. She stopped staring at the tapering width of his shoulders and the tobacco-brown hair that grew just long enough to curl over the back of his shirt collar. Bending down, she pulled a stack of catalogs from the shelf beneath the counter. When she straightened, Judson had moved on to look at another well-dressed mannequin.

Taking the top catalog from the pile, she started poring over the pages. Her gaze was fixed on the columns of facts and figures, but Kathryn was seeing none of it, too conscious of Judson's presence in the room. It was impossible to ignore him, no matter how badly she wanted to. What was he doing here?

On the surface, Judson seemed to be taking an

inordinate amount of interest in the merchandise. His hands were pushed into the front pockets of his tan slacks as he wandered around the racks, frequently checking a garment's price tag. Kathryn found it difficult to believe he was that interested in women's fashion.

The clothing in the boutique was quality—and expensive. In fact, everything in the shop was costly, including the furnishings. By design, it looked more like an elegant sitting room than a clothing store. There were garment racks and mannequins, but they had been positioned strategically, giving the large room a spacious and airy look. It was all carefully planned to make shopping seem like a treat instead of a chore.

"Nice place you've got here, Katy." Judson let his attention return to her as he approached the counter. "Classy and very elegant, yet it isn't gaudy or intimidating. You have very good taste."

"Thank you." Kathryn didn't want a compliment from him. Or anything else.

"You're welcome." The courteous response mocked her. Leaning an elbow on the counter, he gave her a bland look. "Did Charles set you up in business?"

Kathryn stiffened visibly at the remark, and his subtle implication that the attraction Charles held for her might be based on his ability to provide her with material luxuries.

"No, he did not." Kathryn could barely suppress her resentment. "I had already had the place three years when I met Charles."

His mouth thinned into a disgruntled line, giving him a brooding look. His dark gaze moved over her features—features that were becoming flushed and hot under his steady regard. Kathryn wished he wasn't standing so close. Against her will, her senses were stirring in direct reaction to his presence. She couldn't breathe without inhaling the spicy musk smell of him—that stimulating combination of an after-shave and his own male scent. Impatient with herself and irritated with him, she picked up a pencil and started flipping quickly through the catalog pages, as if looking for something in particular.

"So you're really planning to marry that guy," Judson stated in faint disgust.

Kathryn put a check mark beside an item she had no intention of ordering. "That's generally what one does with a fiancé, Judson." She tried to sound preoccupied.

"Really. Tell me, Katy. What else does one do with a fiancé?" The question was heavy with suggestion.

There was only a split second's pause before she turned another page. "Nothing that would even come close to being any of your business." The waver of her tautly controlled voice betrayed her strained composure.

There was a moment of stillness, then the flat of his hand came down on the countertop in a hard slap. "You're right again."

He discarded his lazy pose and swung away from the counter in a surge of restless energy. The distance he put between them brought immediate relief to Kathryn. She stole a resentful glance at him and hoped he was leaving.

Instead he paused about midway between Kathryn and the door. He turned back to face her. "So when's the big day?"

"Why?" She challenged the reason for his interest with false sweetness. "Would you like us to send you an invitation?" She'd send one to the devil first.

"Not especially," Judson refused smoothly. "I try to stay away from potentially depressing situations. When is it?"

"We haven't set one yet," she said crisply, and felt defensive about admitting it to him.

His eyes narrowed. "How long have you been engaged?" He tipped his head to one side, watching her closely.

Kathryn had to stop and think, since Charles had never actually proposed. Their relationship had just evolved to the point that they were seeing each other exclusively. Such an arrangement would naturally result in marriage. Shifting uncomfortably, she dropped her left hand below the counter to hide the bareness of her ring finger.

"We've been seeing each other for two years." But to answer his question, Kathryn had to estimate when the relationship had become serious. "And we've been engaged for a year."

"A year?" Stunned, Judson released an incredulous laugh. "What's he waiting for?"

"Nothing," she snapped. "We just don't want

to rush into anything.'' But lately Charles had been talking about marriage with increasing frequency. It occurred to Kathryn that she was the one who kept holding back. The insight surprised her, since Charles could give her everything she wanted in a marriage.

Judson chuckled. ''I don't think you have to worry about that.'' He shook his head in wryly amused disbelief. ''Good ole Charles has got a helluva lot more patience where you're concerned than I ever had.''

Her breath caught sharply in her throat at his offhand reference to the intimate side of their past relationship. It was as if the subject was so insignificant in his mind that it didn't even deserve a tactful evasion. The more she thought about it, the less surprised she was. It was typical of Judson to never make too big a deal of anything. Nothing was ever too important. As it turned out, not even herself. She already knew all that, but she bitterly resented the way he was flaunting it—and right in her own shop!

''That's true, Judson. Charles does have a lot more patience.'' Her temper flamed. ''So far, he's stuck by me for two long years. You only lasted two months.''

His expression hardened and his smile straightened. There was something mixed with anger in his dark eyes. Was it pain? Regret perhaps? It was veiled before Kathryn could read it, but its poignant quality tugged at her. She resisted its silent appeal.

His mouth slanted in a mocking line. ''Two

years and not a wedding in sight,'' he drawled. "What's the matter, darlin'? Is Charles afraid of settling down?''

"Hardly,'' she scoffed, stung by his sarcasm. "Charles doesn't have any hang-ups about commitment—unlike some people.''

"Some people,'' he repeated, then arched an eyebrow. "Meaning me, of course?''

"Who else?''

"Who knows?'' he countered. "I have a hard time keeping up with who the current man in your life is, Mrs.—'' He stopped, prompting her to fill in the blank.

The title threw her for an instant, especially since it had come from Judson. Actually it wasn't so surprising that he knew. He had kept in touch with Horace Culpepper the last couple of years. The whole town knew the story about the young airforce officer Kathryn had eloped with, but no one ever brought that up in her presence any more, believing the subject held painful memories. For the same reason, nobody ever called her by her married name. Just as no one had ever questioned her desire to forget.

"*Miss* Kathryn Ryan is my legal name—now.'' The qualifying word was tacked on as an afterthought. "I would appreciate it if you'd use it.''

There was a faint, negative movement of his head. "You'll always be Katy to me.''

"Don't call me that,'' she snapped, because the way he said the pet name had always disturbed her—and still did.

"Why not?" He wandered toward the counter, a knowing glint in his brown eyes that played havoc with her pulse.

"Because I dont't like it." Her chin lifted to a defiant angle.

"You don't?" A few slow steps brought him near the counter. He angled his course to come around behind and stand next to her. When he stopped, he was much too close for the thin thread of her poise to handle. Alarm was flooding her system and making a mockery of her normal breathing rhythm. She turned back to the catalog, conscious of his raw male vitality.

"No, I don't."

"That's funny." Her side vision caught his movement as he bent to reach for something on the shelf below the counter. There was a faint shuffling noise. Then Judson straightened, sliding an unassembled cardboard gift box on top of the opened catalog so Kathryn would be forced to look at it. She stared at the dusty-rose lettering of the boutique's logo and felt something inside start to crumble. The sting of tears was in her eyes.

"Katy's." Judson read the name on the box in a falsely puzzled tone. "With all the names in the world to choose from, I wonder why a person would give her shop a name she didn't like."

Further denial at this stage was pointless. Kathryn was trembling as she snatched up the box and shoved it back under the counter, loathing the sight of it and all it revealed. She hated Judson, too, for pushing the issue and taunting her with his knowledge of the feelings she'd never quite been able to forget.

Desperately seeking a diversion, she started flipping through the catalog again, then changed her mind. That was pointless, too. She slammed the book shut with a loud bang and marched around to the front of the counter, putting some needed space between herself and Judson.

"You wanted to see the shop—you've seen it! I would appreciate it if you would leave now." Her arms were folded tightly across her middle, her nails digging into the soft flesh of her upper arms.

Bending slightly at the waist, Judson placed both hands on the countertop and challenged her with his lazy glance. "You invited me to stay as long as I liked."

"I changed my mind." It had already been fairly well established that Kathryn wasn't exactly indifferent to him. So there was absolutely no reason to pretend she didn't mind him being there.

"Ah." Judson nodded in cynical understanding. "The proverbial woman's prerogative." He straightened and walked around to face her, stopping a few feet away. "Don't you think you've abused that privilege?"

"What are you talking about?" she demanded.

"I'm talking about the way you found yourself a husband before my trail was even cold." There was a grimness about his mouth. His gaze was hard and probing.

"You're exaggerating," she snapped, and found it impossible to hold his look. "You had been gone three months by then. That was plenty of time for your trail to cool." And plenty of time for Kathryn to realize that he might not come back.

Her mother had "told her so" right from the beginning, but Kathryn had steadfastly refused to listen, positive Judson was different. Yet the days and weeks kept dragging by and she never heard a word from him. It was the waiting and wondering, the not knowing, that had made the time so difficult to endure. As long as she hadn't heard from him, there was hope.

Then she had discovered she was pregnant. She had been seventeen and terrified. Between morning sickness and her emotional state, it had been impossible to hide her condition from her mother. Kathryn could still feel the burning shame and humiliation of the moment of confession. Considering all the warnings her mother had given, Kathryn had expected angry lectures and recriminations. Instead, her mother had given her what she needed most—support and understanding.

From that point on, her mother had taken control of the situation, doing her best to make things as smooth as possible for Kathryn. It was something that had surprised her, and something for which she would always be grateful.

Judson let a contemptuous breath slide through his clenched teeth. "For someone who claimed to be so much in love with one man, you certainly changed your mind in a hurry."

"Well, Judson, when you find a good man, you can't waste time and let him get away. There aren't that many of them out there." She struggled for an airy note, hoping to convince Judson that she'd gotten over him whether it was true or not. If nothing else, she could salvage a piece of her pride.

"So how come he got away?" he taunted. "Or did you just change your mind again?"

Kathryn's green eyes widened in surprise. If he'd heard about her marriage, why hadn't he heard the rest of the story? "He's dead, Judson." The flat statement brought a grim dismay that took the harshness from his handsome features. Kathryn felt uncomfortable with the lie and just a little cruel.

"I'm sorry, Katy." His voice was roughly subdued. Impatiently he raked a hand through his hair. "And I'm sorry about resurrecting the past. You've been through a lot, and I imagine you'd just as soon forget about it—all of it." A nerve twitched along the side of his jaw as he waited for her reply.

"Yes. I would." But she had to squeeze the assertion past the huge lump in her throat. After seeing him again, it wasn't going to be easy.

Swinging away to stand at right angles to her, he sighed heavily and stared out the display window. "I should have just done what I came here to do and left it at that," he muttered.

"What exactly did you come here to do?" She frowned warily.

"I wanted to see...Buck." The hesitation was so slight, Kathryn wondered if she imagined it. "Is he around?"

"No." An odd sense of deflation came with Judson's announcement. Kathryn preferred not to acknowledge the feeling because it was senseless. And she'd already had a painful lesson in the cost of listening to her feelings instead of her head. She walked around the counter and sat on the high stool. "Buck is working today."

"I thought he'd be retired by now." He frowned in surprise.

"Semiretired," she corrected, feeling safer with this line of conversation. "He hires out on some of the ranches every now and then, doing whatever they need. Today I think he's working the wheat fields."

"Tell him I'll stop by this evening and see him." Judson turned toward the door.

"He won't be home then, either." The information stopped him, and he looked back at her.

"Oh?" The one-word question sounded skeptical.

"His bowling team is in the finals of a tournament tonight," she explained.

"Oh." This time he sounded disappointed. "I'd hoped to see him before I left." He sighed in resignation. "Tell him I stopped by anyway." Without waiting for an agreement, he walked to the door.

"Buck should be home tomorrow night." She felt obliged to tell him, for Buck's sake. The older man would be delighted to see Judson again. Kathryn was glad that Buck wasn't nursing seeds of vengeance on her behalf and that his feelings about Judson had no bearing on his feelings for her. In Buck's opinion, mistakes were made, forgiven, and eventually forgotten. It was a healthy attitude that stopped the growth of debilitating bitterness. Kathryn wished she could develop such an outlook.

With a hand on the doorknob, Judson tossed back an answer. "That's no good. I'm leaving in the morning."

The silver bell jingled as he opened the door to let himself out. Kathryn hesitated for an instant, her mouth going dry. She forced herself to think about Buck and how disappointed he was likely to be if the two men missed each other. It wasn't her place to stand between them.

"Judson." Her voice was very matter-of-fact. "Buck will be here for dinner tonight." She faltered, unable to issue an actual invitation.

When he looked at her, a faint smile touched his mouth, mocking but in a warm way. "Thanks, Katy. What time?"

"Six o'clock. The same as always."

"I'll see you then." He flashed her a smile and Kathryn felt dizzy. Biting her lip, she watched him leave. She had the feeling she had just made the second biggest mistake in her life.

The feeling nagged at her throughout the day. Every time she thought about having dinner with Judson, Kathryn wished she'd kept her mouth shut. It didn't help a whole lot to remind herself that she'd only invited Judson over for Buck. As the supper hour approached, the desire grew stronger to renege on the offer. But of course, she couldn't.

OPENING THE OVEN DOOR, Kathryn grabbed a pot holder and used it to pull out the wire rack so she could check the bubbling casserole. She had prepared a Mexican dish that immediately filled the air with a tantalizing, spicy aroma. She slid the rack back inside and turned the oven thermostat to warm.

The back door opened and footsteps clomped on the floor of the enclosed porch, just off the kitchen. Water splashed noisily into the metal laundry sink. Aware that Buck was home, Kathryn prepared the rest of the meal. She took a head of iceberg lettuce from the refrigerator, rinsed it with cold water and started tearing the crisp leaves to make salad.

"Something smells good," Buck declared, sniffing the air as he entered the kitchen.

"It should," Kathryn told him. "It's your favorite."

"Mexican casserole?"

"Yep." She smiled over her shoulder and put the large bowl of salad in the refrigerator. She had no idea whether Judson liked Mexican food or not, but it was what she'd planned and there hadn't been time to run to the grocery store. She doubted that she would have anyway. This dinner wasn't for Judson's benefit.

As she went to the cupboard for plates, Kathryn paused, wondering again if she could survive the evening. Then she realized there was no reason to try. Why hadn't that thought occurred to her before? She didn't have to be there. She didn't feel the relief she'd expected to feel, but the nervous churnings of her stomach began to settle down. She took two plates from the cupboard and started setting the table.

"You're having company tonight," Kathryn told Buck as she put out the glasses and silverware.

The silence that followed the announcement made Kathryn glance over her shoulder. A glowering frown darkened Buck's features.

"What's wrong?" She frowned back in confusion. It was rare for Buck to be angry. Since he loved having company, she wondered what had brought the scowl to his face. "Aren't you going to ask me who's coming for dinner?"

"I already got a pretty good idea." It was a taut, grumbling comment. His eyes swept the table, then came back to glare at her in accusation. "You went and invited Ruby, didn't ya?"

For a second Kathryn was thrown by Buck's assumption. Then she remembered suggesting that Buck ask the widow to dinner some night. Obviously he thought she'd taken the matter into her own hands. She was puzzled by Buck's attitude. He liked the woman, so why the objection?

"You don't want Ruby to come over?" Kathryn deliberately failed to correct Buck's mistaken impression of who the company was going to be. First, she wanted to find out the reasons behind Buck's odd behavior. Knowing Buck, he wouldn't reveal anything once he realized the woman wouldn't be coming.

"If I wanted her to, I would've asked her myself." Buck fairly snapped out the response.

"But you've always liked Ruby." Kathryn was becoming more and more confused. Maybe something had happened to break up the friendship.

A sudden agitation came over Buck. He hooked his thumbs into the waistband of his worn Levi's and shifted his weight to the other foot while he looked everywhere but at her.

"We're friends," he stated gruffly, then looked at her. "And that's all. I don't want her to start thinkin' I got other ideas."

But Kathryn noticed the touching wistfulness that briefly entered the faded blue of his eyes. "And *do* you have other ideas?"

The question appeared to strike a nerve, bringing his chin up sharply. "Don't you go pushin' for no romance between me and that woman," he warned. "I told ya, we're friends. That's the way we like it." He shifted his weight back to the other foot. "Why, if Ruby comes here tonight and sees just them two plates, she'll think I was plannin' a date or somethin'. She'll be uncomfortable. Then I'll be uncomfortable—not to mention, I'd feel like an old fool. Pretty soon, we'd start avoidin' each other, and—" He stopped abruptly, then changed whatever he'd been going to say. "Put another plate on that table, Kathryn. You ain't leavin' me and Ruby here alone."

"Buck," she said gently. "Ruby isn't coming here tonight. It's someone else." Kathryn regretted leading him to believe otherwise. Buck was surprisingly upset.

The relief that flooded his face stole the tension from his expression. His long, wiry frame slouched against the counter, the tautness slowly easing from his muscles.

"Well, I don't mind tellin' ya I'm glad to hear that," he declared with a shake of his head. "If Ruby was to start thinkin' I had my eye on her—hell, we couldn't even be friends no more."

"Her friendship means a lot to you, doesn't it?" Kathryn tipped her head to the side, studying him. She couldn't tell for sure whether Buck wanted more from Ruby or not. It was obvious, though, that even if he did wish for a more intimate relationship, he wasn't going to let Ruby know, and possibly spoil the friendship they shared.

For Buck to feel that way—*if* he felt that way—Ruby must have indicated a lack of interest in a deeper involvement. Or maybe, Kathryn thought, she was reading too much into this whole conversation. It was more than possible that the pair was in complete agreement on the subject, and each was fully satisfied with the situation as it was.

"There ain't too many people my age who can go out and do things whenever they feel like it," Buck said. "Most 'em got husbands or wives tellin' 'em when to come and go. Jobs tyin' 'em down. Kids and grandkids needin' attention." Buck grimaced to show his distaste for the hassles of a home and a family. Then he shrugged a shoulder and smiled. "But me and Ruby, we're kinda in the same boat. We both got our freedom."

"That's true," Kathryn murmured.

"We don't have to get home by a certain time," he continued. "We don't have to go to work if we don't want to—me bein' as good as retired and Ruby bein' her own boss. We can do just what we please and there ain't nobody to tell us any different."

"I see." But it seemed to Kathryn that he was trying a bit hard to convince her—or himself—of the virtues of being alone. There were no obligations, no one to tell them what to do or when to do it, but there was also no one to care, no one with whom to share the joys of life or grumble about its frustrations. No matter how close, a friend couldn't take the place of having someone of your own.

It was a truth Kathryn herself had to deal with two years ago, when Charles had started showing so much interest in her. The experience with Judson had left her shaken and wary of men, so it took a while before she began to realize that all men were not alike. It was Judson's kind—the drifters, the rogues, the rebels, the rakes—that were dangerous. Rules had no meaning for them, except maybe one: love 'em and leave 'em. It was a phrase they all lived by, including her father.

But there were safe men out there, those who were dependable, responsible, willing to settle down and build a life with one woman. Keeping that in mind, Kathryn had opened her eyes and looked at the long lonely years ahead. Then she'd looked at Charles with a new clarity of vision.

Charles, who was attractive, charming, successful. Charles, who had moved away from the excitement of the big city to settle down in Deepwater. Charles, who was now running for mayor and someday hoped to be the governor of Kansas, which proved he had made this town his home. And finally, most importantly—Charles who would never love her and leave her.

"That Ruby, she knows how to have a good

time, too,'' Buck declared with obvious fondness. ''Since Jake passed on, I've taught her how to fish, bowl, shoot pool. More'n half the time she beats the guys at their own game. And you talk about a poker face! That woman can look just as blank as a piece of paper and all the time she's sittin' there holdin' a straight flush. I've lost more money than I care to count by tryin' to read her face.'' His look became thoughtful, and he sighed. ''Nope, sometimes you just can't tell what the ole gal's thinkin'.'' With a shake of his head, he appeared to clear his thoughts, his attention moving back to the table set for two. ''So who is comin' for dinner, anyway?''

''Judson.'' Just saying his name stirred up the butterflies in Kathryn's stomach all over again. What was it about men like him that could affect a woman even when she already knew the score? Nothing would ever come from an attraction to the drifting kind, except heartache. Yet women continued to fall prey to such men's charms, lured by the excitement danger usually arouses. Or maybe the real lure was the desire to try to tame such a man. The challenge of being woman enough to satisfy someone whose hunger for change was insatiable. Either way, it was a battle lost before it was even begun.

''Judson?'' Buck echoed in surprise.

''Yes. He wanted to see you before he left.'' Wiping her clammy hands on the front of her apron, Kathryn checked the casserole again.

''I thought he'd be gone already.'' But Buck was

obviously delighted that he hadn't. "Will it bother you to have him here?"

"Not in the least," she assured him with a weak smile.

She put salt and pepper on the table, then went to the refrigerator for Tabasco sauce.

Buck watched her for a moment. "Because you're not going to be here," he deduced.

"Bingo." She stood back to survey the table, deciding it was fine. But the satisfied gleam in her eye was a result of the alternative she'd found to spending time in Judson's company.

"So where are you gonna eat?" Buck demanded gruffly. "And don't tell me you're goin' out, because Charles is out of town and I know you don't like to go to restaurants alone."

"Don't worry. I'm not going to starve." Turning to face him, she chided him for his unnecessary concern. "I'll have some of the casserole later."

"Why don't ya just eat with us?" he asked quietly.

She clasped her hands together, her gaze dropping to study the pattern of her fingers. "I think you know the answer to that."

"You still care about him." It was a statement that made no pretense of being a question.

"No." She shook her head, but didn't meet the discerning blue of his eyes. The tip of her tongue darted out to moisten lips that suddenly felt dry. "Buck...how could I still care about somebody who treated me the way Judson did?" There was too much confusion in the question for it to be taken as a challenge. Which was the way she'd wanted it to sound. "It's impossible," she insisted.

"Maybe so," Buck conceded, and walked over to the coffee maker, pouring a cup from the glass pot.

"Isn't it?" she asked hesitantly, since Buck didn't seem totally convinced.

There was a shrug of his shoulders. "I s'pose that depends on whether it was true love to begin with."

"And if it was?"

He took a drink of coffee, studying her over the rim of the cup. "If it was, I'd say it's not only possible, it's likely that a person would still care."

"But how?" Stormy confusion darkened her eyes.

"Kathryn, when a heart gets broken, love don't just die out automatically, although I'm sure a lot of people wish it would." His mouth quirked ruefully. "Instead, it stays right where it started—in the heart. It's just broken up into so many little pieces that it's hard to see it for what it is. It's easier that way. It almost lets us forget."

Almost. That was the problem. No matter how hard she'd tried to blank him from her mind and memory, Kathryn hadn't been able to forget Judson. His image was always there, even if it had acquired a bit of a tarnish. But she had also come to believe that she could have a happy and rewarding life without him. It was imperative that she cling to that belief, for the sake of survival.

"Why don't you have supper with us, Kathryn?" he persisted.

"Why?" After what he'd just said, it didn't

make sense. "Spending time with Judson certainly isn't going to help me forget him."

"Maybe it's time you started rememberin'," he suggested softly.

"No, thank you." With a curt shake of her head, she dismissed that idea and walked to the sink, her fingers curling over the counter edge as she stared out the window. "I lived through it once, and I don't want to do it again. Not even if it's only in my mind."

"You're talkin' about the bad times," Buck pointed out. "What about the good ones?"

That was even more dangerous ground. Kathryn had no intention of traveling it. "What could possibly be the point?" she challenged.

"You two were happy together," Buck stated, as if it was relevant now. "You enjoyed each other's company. Sure, you were crazy about each other, but you just plain liked each other, too—as people."

Kathryn shot him a look of sheer disbelief. "I hope you're not suggesting that Judson and I could ever be *friends*?" It was a ludicrous thought.

"No. But I am sayin' that you two had a lot more goin' for you than physical attraction or romantic love. You were also buddies. That's a lot to have all in one package, and it's a lot to lose, too." Something in his look suggested that he might be talking from experience. "Maybe there's a chance of gettin' it back. If so, tryin' would be worth it."

His last sentence seemed to hover in the air. It was difficult to believe that Buck could even think such a thing, much less say it. Crazier yet, he looked completely serious.

"Oh, no." Her voice quavered on the firm denial. "Any chance of that went trailing along at Judson's heels when he walked out and forgot to come back."

"So maybe the guy made a mistake," Buck said calmly, not giving up the idea that there might be something of the relationship to salvage. "Maybe he's regretted it all these years. Why don't you find out his side of the story?"

"No." It was a clipped answer that didn't leave the subject open for more discussion.

Buck ignored the not too subtle hint. "What have you got to lose? If it turns out I'm wrong, you'll be in exactly the same position as you are now. If not...."

The uncompleted thought hinted at all sorts of possibilities, all of them bright and shining. They might have appealed to the young romantic with stars in her eyes, but Kathryn wasn't a love-struck teenager anymore. Her feet were planted firmly on the ground. She hadn't survived the last seven years without learning a few basic truths.

"Forget it, Buck, I'm not going to talk to him, and I'm not going to see him." Glancing at her watch, she went to the oven and removed the casserole, leaving it on the counter to cool. If she wanted to avoid Judson, she needed to hurry. It was ten minutes before six. "Everything is ready. I'll just set out the salad and rolls and you two can help yourselves."

"Okay." Buck wandered closer to the counter, sniffing the rising steam appreciatively. "I can hardly wait to sink my teeth into that," he declared, showing a sudden and apparently exclusive interest in the food.

It was the way he let the topic of a minute ago drop that made Kathryn wary. Plus, there was a trace of smugness in the older man's expression. Buck looked entirely too pleased with himself.

Running their conversation over in her mind, she recalled Buck's interest in hearing the reasons behind Judson's behavior. It didn't take much figuring to reach the conclusion that Buck intended to ask some questions if she wouldn't. The last thing she wanted was for Buck to start asking Judson for explanations. If they sounded at all reasonable, Buck would relate them to Kathryn. And Kathryn didn't feel safe enough to hear any excuses. She knew how willing she'd been to believe them in the past.

"I've changed my mind, Buck," she announced, and untied the apron protecting her emerald dress. "If you'll do me a favor and set another place, I'll run upstairs and freshen up."

CHAPTER FIVE

STANDING IN FRONT OF THE BUREAU MIRROR, Kathryn dipped a fingertip into a small pot of lip gloss and applied a light, shiny coat of color to her mouth. She capped the container and stood for a second, listening. Male voices drifted up from the lower level of the house. Judson had arrived.

If she wanted to keep the men from having more than a few minutes of privacy, there wasn't time to change out of the silk dress and heels she'd worn all day. She quickly freshened her eye shadow and blusher, then tucked a few strands of hair back into place. Pressing a hand against the tightening muscles in her stomach, Kathryn drew a steadying breath. Then she went downstairs and paused in the kitchen archway.

The two men didn't notice her immediately; they were engaged in the kind of back-slapping, hand-shaking greeting that often marks the reunion of good friends. One was aging and tending to gray, the other just coming into his prime. Yet nothing seemed to hinder the respect and camaraderie they'd always shared—not age, time, distance or circumstances. Watching them, Kathryn felt oddly left out.

She began to question the necessity and fairness of imposing on them. The tension that always coursed between Judson and herself would hardly add to the enjoyment of the evening. But when Judson turned his glance to her, so lazy and alive with interest, Kathryn felt anything but tense. His look warmed her all the way to her toes.

"Hello, Judson." Her voice had a breathy catch.

"Katy." He nodded and let his gaze slide to the table, which was now set for three. "I'm glad you're planning to join us. Somehow I had the feeling it would be just me and Buck."

"It almost was," Buck inserted, observing the exchange with keen interest. "Kathryn changed her mind at the last minute."

"Oh yeah?" Instead of mocking her, Judson was curious. His dark eyes probed for the reason behind that decision.

"I...." Aware that cowardice had been the motivating factor, Kathryn felt awkward. "Buck didn't think you'd mind." Which was hardly an explanation.

"I don't." It was a quick agreement, laced with something warm that seemed to suggest pleasure.

A little late Kathryn realized that both her answer and her presence were being interpreted all wrong. Naturally Judson would assume that she had a desire for his company. Judging by the difference in his attitude toward her, it seemed obvious that he liked the idea. There was a strong, unnerving flutter of her pulse.

"Well." Her smile was tight, her nervousness building under Judson's steady regard. "Shall we eat before the casserole cools off too much?"

While she went to the counter for the baking dish, chair legs scraped on the recently tiled floor. The two men sat opposite each other at the small round table. Along with setting an extra place, Buck had put the salad and other items on the table. The only thing left to do was fill the glasses.

A pitcher of iced tea was waiting in the refrigerator. As Kathryn carried the pitcher to the table, she felt the clock turn back to a time when serving these two men had been a nightly ritual. Of course, there had been other boarders, but these were the only ones to whom she had become attached.

The almost comfortable sense of familiarity was increased by the way Judson was dressed. The expensive suits were gone tonight. Instead, he wore a pair of crisp Levi's that molded to the length of his thighs and hugged the leanness of his hips. His shirt was white, unbuttoned at the throat, the sleeves rolled up to expose sinewy forearms.

Kathryn could almost believe she was back in the past, if the sophisticated picture she made wasn't so out of place. Suddenly, despite the way her feet were aching from the artificial arch of her high heels, Kathryn was very glad she hadn't had time to change into something more casual. She needed a reminder that this wasn't the way things were anymore.

All through dinner, the old patterns reemerged,

with Buck and Judson ribbing and laughing as if they'd seen each other just yesterday. More than once Kathryn caught herself being swept into the conversation. When she realized what was happening, and how easily it was happening, it frightened her. Then she would lapse into silence, struggling to hold herself aloof. It wasn't as easy as it should have been.

Buck was the first to finish eating. He pushed his plate aside. "So you're a big success now, eh, Judd?"

"I do all right." It didn't seem to be modesty that downplayed his success. Rather, it was as if Judson didn't see his accomplishments as important.

"I'll just bet you do," Buck said. "Always knew you would. So how'd you get started?"

Pushing his plate away, Judson grinned. "I just did a little research, did a lot of talking, got some investors and got lucky."

"And that's all there was to it." Buck was skeptical.

"That's it." Lights danced in Judson's eyes.

He made it sound easy, but Kathryn was certain there had been plenty of rough times. The evidence of them was grooved into his face, in the harsh lines. But she didn't doubt that it had been easy for him to convince people to back him. He had been able to make her believe anything.

Sliding her chair back, she rose and collected the plates. "Coffee?" she suggested.

"Please," Judson replied, and Buck simply

held out the half-full cup he'd brought with him to the table.

Kathryn took it, dumping the cold coffee down the drain. She returned with three steaming cups.

"I see you got your nose broke, boy." And Buck had no compunction about calling attention to it.

"And I see you're still as sharp as ever." Judson's was a friendly gibe.

"You'd better believe it!" Buck snorted. "What happened?"

"Nothing too exciting," Judson said ironically, lifting his cup to take a drink of coffee. "I was passing through some little town down around Houston, and I ended up in a poker game. You know how it is. All the local boys are anxious to let you in the game so they can sucker you out of your money. The only problem was, I ended up winning most of the pots."

Buck was nodding slowly, visualizing the scene. "Not smart," he concluded. "Anybody with a lick of sense knows better than to try to take too much money out of a strange town. Especially if it's a small one and especially if you're alone."

"I don't play to lose," he stated flatly. Then he grinned. "But I got a souvenir, so it wasn't a total loss." He rubbed a finger over the bridge of his nose.

Irritation bristled along Kathryn's nerve ends at the way Judson still took everything in stride. What did it take to faze him? She certainly hadn't, or he wouldn't be sitting here talking and reminiscing as easily as if they were all old friends. However, she had to admit that she, too, was considerably more relaxed tonight than the last two times they'd seen each other. That in itself was dangerous.

"You were pretty wild as a young'un," Buck recalled, his gaze narrowing on Judson in speculation. "Are you still?"

Setting his coffee cup on the table, Judson leaned back in his chair and lit a cigarette. Kathryn sensed that there was a method to Buck's questions, as if he was trying to determine whether maturity had altered Judson's reckless attitude and life-style enough for there to be a chance for him and Kathryn again. Wise to such futile hopes, she flashed Buck a warning look as she got up to get an ashtray for Judson.

"I've settled down some," Judson assured him, and Kathryn closed her ears. It wasn't safe to listen to such information. The ashtray was set in front of him with a little more force than was necessary.

"Some," Buck repeated, testing the word. "But not completely."

"No," he admitted. "I doubt if I ever will settle down completely. Life would be too boring."

There was a tightness about her mouth as Kathryn brought the coffeepot to refill their cups, then sat down. Her hands were folded in her lap as the coffee cooled and the first silence of the evening settled over the table.

Taking a drag on the cigarette, Judson inhaled

deeply and eyed the other man with knowing humor. "Why are you scowling at me, Buck? You were about fifty-five when I saw you last, and you had a wild streak that still came through every once in a while."

Buck narrowed his eyes warily. "What do you mean?" he asked hesitantly.

Judson shrugged with a little too much vagueness. "Oh, I was just thinking about one night when a few of us were down at the tavern." He slid a twinkling glance at Kathryn. "The place was relatively peaceful until Buck decided to get rowdy."

Such behavior from Buck was news to Kathryn. "What happened?" she prompted.

"Nothing much," Judson replied casually, but silent laughter was crinkling the corners of his eyes. "At least, nothing much was happening until Buck started the fight."

"Fight?" Her eyes widened in surprise.

"I didn't start it." Grimness pulled the corners of his mouth as Buck stared into his coffee cup.

"You threw the first punch," Judson countered.

Kathryn pressed her lips together in faint disgust. "You should have been old enough to know better."

"I was," he muttered, not one bit pleased with the turn of conversation. "There's just certain things a man's gotta fight for."

"Such as?" Her tone indicated her doubts that physical violence was ever the only solution.

"Things." The grumbled response made it clear that Buck did not care to discuss it.

Amusement twitched around Judson's mouth without materializing into a smile. "It seems to me, Mattie had come with you that night."

"I don't remember." And Buck threw a quelling look across the table.

Judson didn't take the broad hint, enjoying the fact that the turnabout was fair play. Buck had put him on the spot more than once tonight. "Yeah, she was there," he remembered. "And some lonely cowboy kept dropping quarters in the jukebox and asking her to dance. Wouldn't take no for an answer as I recall."

"You're recallin' too much for your own good, boy," Buck growled the warning.

In spite of herself, Kathryn was intrigued. The long-standing relationship between her mother and Buck was something rarely discussed.

"What happened?" She tilted her head to the side. Buck showed no signs of answering, so she shifted her curious gaze to Judson.

He obliged with a grin. "Since the cowboy wasn't receiving Mattie's message, Buck decided to spell it out for him. 'N—' and his right fist connected with the guy's jaw. 'O—' and his left got the message across."

It was difficult to hide a smile. "Why, Buck." Kathryn blinked innocently. "I never knew you were so gallant."

"Gallant, hell!" His face wore a disgruntled look, slightly embarrassed but not really angry at this recounting of one of his more chivalrous moments. "That didn't have anything to do with it. You just have to fight for what's right. Ain't that the way it is, Judd?" Tired of being the object of discussion, he shifted the topic from himself.

Judson seemed strangely thoughtful as he toyed with the handle of his coffee cup. Lifting his eyes, he let them meet Kathryn's. There was an unsettling concentration in his steady look. "It's true," he agreed. "But I do most of my fighting with my head these days." He finally released her eyes to flash a wry grin Buck's way. "It's a lot easier on the knuckles."

"No kiddin'." Buck laughed. "My hand was sore for a week after I hit that guy."

It was almost an hour later that Buck thought to glance at his watch. The action prompted Kathryn to look at hers, too. She could hardly believe the time had passed so quickly.

"This has been great, Judd." Buck pushed back his chair and got to his feet. "If there was any way to get out of it, I'd cancel my plans for tonight and stay here. But I'm bowlin' in a tournament. Can't let the team down. Are you sure you can't stick around for a few days?"

Judson stood up, too. "I wish I could, but I'm due back in Dallas tomorrow morning."

"If you've a mind to, you could come up to the bowlin' alley and—" His eyes made a quick sweep of the room, briefly lingering on Kathryn before returning to Judson. "You gotta be back tomorrow mornin' you say?"

"That's right." He frowned slightly.

"Well, then, you probably got an early plane to catch. You'll have to be gettin' home at a decent hour tonight for some shut-eye."

Judson hesitated. "That probably would be a good idea," he agreed slowly.

"Well...." Buck shifted awkwardly, then gripped Judson's hand in a strong handshake. "You take care of yourself, boy." His voice was more gruff than usual, a little choked up.

"You, too," Judson said meaningfully.

The two men stood there, not wanting to appear sentimental. But it was an emotional moment for everyone, only hinting at the ties that nothing had managed to sever. Without words, it was understood that considering Buck's age and any number of unfortunate possibilities, this could conceivably be the last time they'd see each other.

Not wanting her presence to make them feel awkward, Kathryn slipped over to the sink. There might have been a mistiness in Buck's eyes when she passed. She couldn't be sure. But her back was to the men and water was splashing in the sink, granting them a degree of privacy as they said their goodbyes.

A few minutes later, the back door was closing behind Buck. Footsteps sounded on the tile floor, drawing Kathryn's sideways glance to Judson. He approached her leisurely, his expression thoughtful.

"I'm going to miss him." His eyes darted to the door as he leaned against the counter and crossed one scuffed cowboy boot over the other. "When I was a kid, I lived in a lot of foster homes. And I've met a lot of people since then. But the old man that just walked out that door is the closest thing to a father I've ever had." His breath came out in a silent chuckle. "That sounds silly, doesn't it? Considering I only knew him a couple of months."

"No." Kathryn remembered how quickly the men had taken to each other. Judson's parents had been killed in a car crash when he was small. There had been no brothers, sister or relatives. Buck had no family, either. The friendship between them had been instant, helping to fill a shared void. "I know what you mean. Buck has always seemed like a father to me, too."

"Most people like you or dislike you, accept or reject you on the basis of your behavior," he went on in a musing tone. "But Buck, he was different. I always knew I had a friend whether I was right or wrong." He slid her a dryly amused glance. "Which is not the same as saying he didn't let me know flat out when I was wrong."

"Same here." She rolled her eyes expressively. "He isn't one to mince words."

"No, but when he gets done cussin' you out, there aren't any hard feelings. Remember the night I came home drunk and parked my truck outside your bedroom window?"

"Yes." A smile edged her mouth. It was something that happened involuntarily every time she thought about that particular night. "It would be hard to forget, Judson." She arched an eyebrow and gave him a dry look. "You do know you made a fool of yourself."

"I suppose you're referring to the way I was sitting on the roof of the pickup, just so I could get a little closer to your window—and you." The last two words were added softly.

"You fell off," she reminded him, conscious of the sudden rush of blood through her veins. She quickly made herself busy, rinsing the dishes under the tap in preparation for the dishwasher.

"I know." It was a rueful acknowledgment, filled with amusement at himself. "Buck wasn't thrilled with me that night. Yet he was the one who helped you half drag, half carry me to my room so Mattie wouldn't find out and throw me out on my ear."

"You would have deserved it if she had," Kathryn stated, but couldn't quite manage to sound disapproving. She couldn't quite manage to breathe evenly, either.

"Thanks a lot," Judson murmured dryly.

"Well, you would have." She turned to look at him with the utmost of patience in her expression. "Anybody who would perch on the roof of a pickup truck, singing at the top of his lungs at two o'clock in the morning...." She shook her head, letting the ridiculous scenario speak for itself.

"Point taken." Amusement ran warmly through the drawled agreement. "But you were mad at me. You wouldn't even talk to me. It was the only way I could think of to make you listen."

"Me and the rest of the neighborhood," she murmured.

"I only wanted to make up." His tone was so sensually low, it seemed to take some of her breath away.

"What a crazy way to do it." Her voice was husky, a direct result of the knot in her throat.

The past was tugging at her—the past and the man standing so close to her now. Her resistance to both was crumbling by the second. The most Kathryn could do was move a couple of steps away and start loading the dishwasher.

The results of the evasive tactic weren't very satisfactory. Automatically Judson followed suit, picking up dirty glasses and putting them in the top rack of the dishwasher as if it was the most natural thing in the world for him to do. It was insane, but the action had a seductive effect on Kathryn's senses, because it had been his habit that summer. Except then Judson had dried the dishes while she washed them, helping so she could finish her chores and have more of the evening to spend with him.

"It might have been crazy," he admitted. "But it worked."

"Only because you tricked me," she insisted.

"What? Do you mean you didn't fall for my irresistible singing?" He drew back, thumping a hand on his chest in mock dismay. "Could that be possible?" He frowned with dramatic incredulity. "I mean with a song like, 'K-K-K-Katy, beautiful Katy.'" He sang the words and captured her gaze.

His gilded brown hair had fallen carelessly across his forehead. It gave him an arrogantly rakish look that matched the gold-shot sparkle in his brown eyes. "Could anyone resist?" he wondered.

And Kathryn found herself wondering the same thing. When he chose to exercise it, Judson was a master at the fine art of persuasion. His charm was so lethal and flowed so freely. It was almost laughable that she'd thought seven years would have granted her immunity.

She laughed, struggling to make it a natural sound. "Believe me, it's possible." She nodded to add emphasis to the statement. "To tell the truth, I was laughing behind the curtains the whole time."

"During my romantic song?" He looked aghast, then his expression became brooding. "I'm crushed." But humor glowed in the darkness of his eyes. "How could you?"

Her shoulders lifted in a helpless shrug and she giggled, venting some of the sexual tension sizzling through her nerves. She forced her mind away from the present and back to that night. It really had been a sight—and sound!

"I'll bet you laughed the hardest when I lost my balance and fell," he accused.

"From where I was standing, it did look awfully funny. It must have only been a few seconds, but it seemed like you teetered up there for a long time." The laughter tumbled helplessly from her as she pictured him, arms and legs flailing in the air.

"For your information," Judson said dryly, "the bed of that truck was hard."

"I didn't think it was funny when you actually fell," she assured him, sobering slightly. "If I had, I wouldn't have gone running out there in my nightgown. Actually I was scared half to death."

Her amusement faded to a faint smile. Absently she dropped a handful of silverware in the dishwasher basket. "There you were, lying so still on the bed of that truck, not making a sound. I thought you were dead. Or at least unconscious." Even now she barely suppressed a shudder.

"And you came creeping into the back of the pickup, peering at my face. I guess you were trying to see if I was alive." Chuckling, he bent to put some plates in the bottom rack.

"And you grabbed hold of my wrist!" she recalled with exasperation. "If I had been a little less terrified, I would have been able to scream. The whole town would have come out if I had."

"It was all worth it, wasn't it?" His voice was different, soft and low now, a disturbing sensuality in it.

When she turned her head to look at him, he was right beside her, bending over the open dishwasher. Thousands of tiny electrical impulses seemed to spark the air and charge it with an elemental tension, which had always existed between them. His mouth was only inches away, so close that the warmth of his breath was caressing her lips—almost a kiss in itself.

"What was worth it?" Kathryn couldn't remember what they were talking about. Worse, she couldn't seem to turn away from the strong, firm line of his mouth near her face.

"All of it," he murmured. "We made up."

If her breathing hadn't already been affected by his nearness, it was permanently disrupted when she met the velvet intensity of his gaze. They both knew what had come after he had grabbed her wrist. Kathryn could almost feel the thrilling pressure of his kiss as he'd taken possession of her mouth. The taste of alcohol and tobacco hadn't offended her. It had only increased the excitement of the forbidden.

A similar excitement was running through her veins at this very moment, a hungry desire to taste the sweetness of forbidden fruit. Kathryn fought desperately to ignore the craving.

"Th—there must have been an easier way." Her attempt at a smile was stopped when Judson's eyes drifted to the parted curve of her lips. Her face felt hot and flushed, but Kathryn didn't think it was a result of the way she was bending over the dishwasher. She started to straighten, but the large hand that curved itself to the side of her neck checked the movement.

"There probably was an easier way." His fingers applied a light pressure to the back of her neck while his thumb traced the softness of her cheek. "But it wouldn't have been nearly as interesting." His warm breath whispered over her face, tripping her pulse as his mouth moved closer. "Or as exciting."

"No." It was an agreement, not a protest, spoken with a husky throb of desire.

The hand on her neck tightened to pull her that last inch. Only it wasn't necessary, because Kathryn was closing the distance of her own accord, swayed by the dizzying sense of déjà vu that engulfed her. She was the girl of seventeen again, longing to know the kiss of the drifter, the sense of adventure, the thrill of the untamed.

She wasn't disappointed as his mouth covered her lips with confident possession. There was no curiosity in the kiss, no testing, no experimentation. But there was heat. There was fire. And there was too much space between them after being so long and far apart. Her hand moved to the back of his head, her fingers curling into the thickness of his hair as they both straightened, maintaining the hotly fused contact of their lips.

His encircling arms pulled her to him so their bodies were reunited as well. Kathryn melted against him. The kiss grew deeper, hungrier, ravenous in its desire for satisfaction. The explosion of her senses was even more awesomely wonderful than she remembered, the chemistry between them stronger than ever, its potency only increasing with time. The sweet agony of being in his arms brought a sob to her throat. The sound was muffled by his mouth.

The roaming pressure of his hands as they moved along her spine was restless and evocative. They investigated the curves of her hips and arched her more fully to the masculine contours of his body.

Kathryn could hear a loud, strong heartbeat and wasn't sure whether it was his or her own. Her caution was obliterated by his touch, and she gave herself up to sensation. Her fingers gripped the muscled ridge of his shoulder, holding on to him, and she felt as if they were in a world of their own.

Judson dragged his mouth from hers, the warm moistness of his lips moving to graze a path across her cheek and down the satiny column of her throat. Her head fell backward to give him free access to the highly sensitized area of her neck, where her pulse was throbbing so wildly.

"Katy." There was a rough edge to his voice as he spoke against her skin. Her body quivered with excitement. There was satisfaction in knowing he was as excited as she was. "It's been too long, Katy." His teeth nipped at the side of her neck, then he nuzzled the curving line with teasing roughness.

Time was irrelevant—nonexistent, allowing her to forget the ultimate cost of knowing him. She *was* Katy again—Judson's Katy. Her mind didn't even try to separate the past from the present as his intimate caresses set her afire with a yearning for fulfillment.

His hand cupped a breast and it swelled to his touch, straining against the thin material of her dress. It could well have been the thin cotton of a summer nightgown. It didn't matter. This man was stroking and arousing the rosy point to hardness. That's all that mattered. Kathryn arched against him, wanting to absorb, and in turn, be absorbed.

"Where's the bedroom?" he muttered thickly.

Dazed, Kathryn lifted her lashes to look at him. She was totally fascinated by the passionate light in his eyes. His eyelids were heavy with desire, his breathing ragged.

"The bedroom, Katy." His huskily demanding voice finally penetrated the swirling mist she was drowning in.

The golden clouds of emotion and sensation were split by the dark shadows of a threatening storm. She had lost the distinction between the past and the present. And in one way they were the same. Judson wanted her tonight, and he was leaving in the morning. He had made a fool of her once. Kathryn had nearly let him do it again. Splaying her hands across his chest, she pushed, but his arms tightened to keep her within the circle of his embrace.

"No." It was difficult to string two words together, so she settled for the single word that would get her message across.

"Yes." His gaze burned over her face, seductive and smoldering. "We need each other."

When she opened her mouth to deny it, his fingers pressed against her lips. "Don't try to tell me it isn't true. I can feel you trembling. And—" his hand moved to cover the throbbing pulse point in her neck "—your heart is racing, the same as mine. Seven years hasn't changed it for either of us. The only thing that's different is we're not kids anymore."

"No, we're not kids anymore, and that makes

everything different." With more force she pushed against his chest, needing to get away from him and clear her senses. This time he didn't try to hold her. She twisted out of his arms and took a couple of quaking steps backward. "I'm all grown up now, Judson." Her hands were shaking as she nervously smoothed her dress. "And I do have a woman's needs, but not for you to take care of."

"Maybe I'm the only one who can take care of them," he suggested while his dark gaze traveled from her eyes to her mouth and back again. "Maybe you're the only one who can take care of mine."

Wary and trembling, she shook her head in mute denial. She didn't want him to make it sound as if she was special. She knew better. It was simply that she was here and available.

"That kind of response doesn't just happen with anybody, Katy. But I'm guessing you've found that out in the last seven years."

"It's chemistry, nothing more," she insisted.

"What's between us is more than physical attraction," he stated. "It always has been. Admit it. We belong together."

"It seems like I've heard that line somewhere before," Kathryn mocked bitterly. "Where could that have been?" She scratched her head in a thoughtful fashion, but the gesture was heavy with sarcasm. "Maybe it was just before you walked out on me."

His eyes narrowed. "I didn't exactly walk out on you." There was a hardness behind his frown. "We *agreed* I would leave."

"Yes, after you *told* me that was the way it was going to be. I didn't have a whole lot of choice in the matter." She pivoted and walked to the table, gripping the back of a chair for support.

"You're still bitter about that, aren't you?" The question was almost accusing.

"Whatever gave you that idea?" Kathryn practically choked on her own question. She could still remember her feelings of helplessness, her sense of desperation. "I couldn't care less about the past. In fact, when you left, it was the biggest favor anyone ever did for me. Now I finally have the chance to thank you." But it hurt to speak, the lump in her throat making her voice a raspy sound.

"I know you were hurt when I didn't take you with me," he began with growing impatience. "But you were seventeen! A minor! Your mother would have had me arrested!" The statement accepted none of the blame, and it ignited Kathryn's fiery temper. She whirled to glare at him.

"That's good," she flared. "Blame it all on my mother!"

"You know it's true," Judson snapped. "We wouldn't have made it to the state line if I'd taken you with me. Mattie couldn't stand the sight of me."

Kathryn didn't deny it. "I often wondered why you put up with the way she treated you. Why you bothered with me when you could have taken your pick of the women in this town and avoided all the hassle of being involved with someone who was underage." Her head was tipped at a challenging angle, daring him to respond while letting him know she wouldn't accept his answer.

His mouth was a hard, grim line. "I did it because I loved you." The declaration was pushed through clenched teeth.

"That's what you said." She didn't try to hide her skepticism, only her pain. "But after you left, the real reason became very clear."

"Did it?" he taunted, reacting to the hostility that was emanating from her.

"You knew you'd be moving on soon, and you also knew my mother would never allow me to go with you. Mattie was your insurance policy. A guarantee that you wouldn't be saddled with me when you left."

A silent rage trembled through him before Judson finally erupted. "I told you I was coming back!" he snapped.

"Yes." It was a bitter agreement. "The insane part is that I believed you would."

"Did you really?" Judson demanded in contemptuous anger. "How long did you believe it? A day? A week? A month?" There was a short pause while he studied her with accusing dark eyes. "I know it would make you feel better to say that everything is my fault because I left, but you can forget it. It isn't as if you were moping around, waiting for me to come back. You stand there making all the pitiful noises of the wronged virgin, and you were off somewhere married within three months! If you'd loved me the way you claimed to, you would have waited!"

An incredulous light entered her eyes. "How long did you expect me to wait, Judson? Seven years?"

"I expected you to wait until you turned eighteen," he said harshly. "That was when we agreed that I would come back. That was when I was supposed to be able to take you out of this house without your mother's interference." There was a sudden mocking slant to his mouth. "But it wasn't your mother's interference I encountered. It was your husband's."

"My husband's?" Kathryn frowned, thrown by the turn of conversation, because what he was suggesting was impossible.

"Indirectly," Judson said in clarification. "Mattie was the one who told me about him. And she took great pleasure in breaking the news." His eyes broke away from hers, and he stared at the screen door. "It was the last thing I expected to hear when I walked up to that door—even though I probably should have guessed."

It took a second for the implications of his words to sink in. When they did, Kathryn felt faint. Reaching behind her, she gripped the back of the chair. Her head moved numbly from side to side.

"No," she murmured. "You haven't talked to my mother since you left. You haven't been back here since—"

"Since your eighteenth birthday."

For a moment his statement seemed to reverberate in the absolute stillness of the room, while

Kathryn stared at him. He looked completely serious, and she felt the color drain from her face.

"That's impossible."

"You knew I came back." His voice was accusing, but he also sounded doubtful. "You have to know. Mattie would have told you—" His jaw snapped shut with a surge of anger. "No, she wouldn't have," he muttered the realization. "Just in case there was a slim chance that you still cared about me."

"No." It was a small weak sound, but it gained force as Kathryn repeated it. "No!" She shook her head violently in denial. "It isn't true, and you're not going to convince me that it is. I never heard from you once, Judson! Not one word after you left. And now you expect me to believe you came back?"

"I did come back, dammit!" Grim and restless, he began to pace the large kitchen, angry frustration written in the taut lines of his body. "All those letters I sent—" he stopped abruptly to give her a piercing look "—you never got them?"

Her laugh was harsh with disbelief. "Don't try to tell me you wrote."

"Oh, yes, I wrote." His voice was dry, his mouth grim. "When you didn't write back, I told myself that you were still hurt and angry because I'd left. I figured you just needed some time to cool off. I never dreamed that your mother was intercepting your mail—but I sure as hell should have." He shook his head. "I should have known Mattie would do something to keep us apart."

Kathryn stared at him, frozen and calm on the outside while a tangle of emotions churned within. The part of her that had loved him wanted to believe the past seven years had all been a mistake. But the part of her that had believed him before and had suffered for it won out.

Bracing his hands on the counter behind him, Judson observed her closed expression. "Can't you see what happened? The pieces are all falling into place."

There were too many holes in his explanation, which placed all the blame on her mother—the one person who had always been there for Kathryn. Anger cut through her like the slash of a double-edged sword.

"Since my mother isn't here to defend herself, it makes it all very convenient. A nice, tidy, pat explanation," she said bitterly.

"It's the only explanation," Judson asserted. "Unless you're lying about how much you knew back then." Pushing away from the counter, Judson slowly made his way toward her. "I don't think you're lying. I think you really believe I deserted you."

At his approach Kathryn's head snapped up like an animal's, an animal scenting danger. Seeing the way she stiffened, Judson stopped.

"It isn't surprising that it didn't work out for us," he murmured. "We had everything against us—your mother, your age, my life-style. But time has taken all the old obstacles away. The past is all that stands against us now. Let's put it behind us, Katy. Let's start afresh."

"No." It had been a mistake the first time. Only a fool would fall into the same trap twice. "It's over, Judson."

"I thought so, too." His eyes roamed lazily over her features, lingering on her lips. "But you have to admit that there's smoke coming from the old fire and the ashes are still hot."

"I don't have to admit any such thing." Not to him anyway, she thought. "I got caught up in the memories, that's all. Everyone is susceptible to them on occasion. Especially after they've spent several hours talking about the past." Careful to avoid his eyes, she walked to the door and opened it. "I think I've done enough reminiscing for one evening. So if you don't mind, I'll say goodnight."

"Why?" he challenged. "Because you're afraid of what might happen? Because you still care?"

"Care?" Her head jerked around to face him, an incredulous expression on her face. "Is that what you think? That I could possibly have any feelings left for you?" In a surge of agitation, she slammed the door. The glass rattled. "You haven't been listening, Judson!"

"I've been listening," he assured her. "But not to your words. I've been listening to the messages your eyes, your mouth and your body have been sending out. I don't need to hear any more, Katy. You told me all I need to know with one kiss. You still want me. In fact—" his gaze roamed over her, measuring her for a silent second "—I think you're still in love with me."

"In love with you!" The angry way she repeated the words made them a shocked denial. "Don't make me laugh!" Her head was held high and proud as she glared at him, hating his calmness and the arrogant certainty in his manner.

"But you're not laughing," he pointed out quietly. "You're crying."

It was true. Hot tears of pain, anger and frustration were streaming down her cheeks, and she hadn't even noticed. Her shoulders drooped and an overwhelming tiredness overcame her.

"Leave me alone." She made a halfhearted attempt to wipe away the tears as she walked past him, intending to leave him standing in the kitchen while she retreated to her room.

"I can't." It was a decisive reply, followed by the sound of footsteps. A pair of arms stole around her waist from behind, stopping Kathryn in her tracks. "I can't leave you alone," he murmured near her ear. "Not now."

Kathryn shut her eyes tightly and swallowed hard. "Sure you can, Judson. It's easy. Remember?"

"It was never easy," he said huskily. "But the bad times can be over if we let them. Let's concentrate on today—here and now." Bending his head, he rubbed his mouth over the side of her neck, confident of the power he held over her.

Despite the traitorous responsiveness of her body and his effect on her emotions, Kathryn retained control. She pried apart the arms crossed in front of her and stepped coolly away. Then she turned.

"You walked out on me seven years ago, and I begged you to stay." Her low voice matched his calmness. "I'm not begging anymore, Judson. I'm *telling* you to leave. Get out of my house. Get out of my life."

He studied her through narrowed eyes, lazy and calculating. "I'll leave," he said slowly. "But I won't get out of your life."

The assertion took her by surprise, but Kathryn recovered quickly. "I'm sorry to disappoint you, but you don't have any choice. There isn't room for you in my life."

"Then I guess you'll just have to make room," he drawled with calm determination.

"No."

"Then I guess I'll have to do it." Shrugging, he walked to the door. He pulled it open and paused to look back. He grinned recklessly, a possessive light in his eyes. "Night, darlin'. Sweet dreams."

The door closed behind him. Kathryn stared after him for a second, then moved to sink numbly into a chair. With her elbows propped on the table, she pressed her fingers against her mouth. What had Judson meant? What was he going to do? From experience she knew it was impossible to second-guess him. He had his own way of thinking, an odd kind of logic that she had never really understood. The frightening part was, he usually got what he wanted. And he wanted her— again.

Night sounds drifted into the kitchen through the open window above the sink. Crickets chirruped and june bugs beat their wings against the screen, drawn by the light inside. There was another sound, too. A happy, tuneless whistle. Kathryn listened to it and felt threatened by its message of confidence. It faded and disappeared. A car door slammed in the narrow alley behind the house. An engine started and Judson drove away.

Kathryn prayed he was leaving for good, but she suspected it was only wishful thinking.

CHAPTER SIX

THE COFFEE MAKER WORKED with its usual slowness, the volume of its grumbling, gurgling sounds
exaggerated by the early-morning silence of the
kitchen. Beyond the window above the sink, there
was darkness. The only light burning in the kitch-
en was the small one above the stove.

Lost in thought, Kathryn leaned against the
counter, her arms crossed and her sightless gaze
directed at the floor. Her head was reeling with
large doubts and small suspicions, all of them
centered around Judson's claim that he had come
back for her seven years ago.

What if it was true? What if her mother really
had sent him away? Kathryn tried to shake away
the thought. Yet it nagged at her.

"Do you know what time it is, girl?" Buck
ambled into the kitchen, startling Kathryn. Light
flooded the room when he flipped on the switch.
He blinked at the sudden brightness, his craggy
face becoming drawn with a scowl. "What are you
doing up at five o'clock?"

"I couldn't sleep." Rubbing her elbows, Kathryn walked to the table and sat down. "I'm sorry
if I woke you up."

Buck yawned before he could reply. He rubbed a hand over his face to wipe away the sleepiness and headed for the coffeepot.

"Had to get up sometime or other anyway," he muttered. "I s'pose now's just as good a time as any." When he joined her at the table, Kathryn barely glanced at him. "Somethin' wrong?"

There was and he knew it. But Kathryn shrugged aside the chance to confide in Buck, not certain whether she wanted to voice the doubts that were plaguing her. Judson's story seemed incredible, and it angered Kathryn that she couldn't put it out of her mind.

Dwelling on his tale was disloyal to her mother. Whatever else Mattie may have been, she had been truly loving to Kathryn. That had become surprisingly evident when she had been so sympathetic and understanding upon being faced with Kathryn's pregnancy. And now, in return for her mother's support, Kathryn found herself entertaining these absurd suspicions. She felt like a traitor. What on earth would it take to teach her not to listen to Judson's lies?

"I've just got a lot of things on my mind," she told Buck.

"One of these 'things' wouldn't happen to be Judd Taylor, would it?" A twinkle brightened his blue eyes. Buck made no attempt to conceal his hope that Kathryn and Judson could work out their differences.

"Not the way you think." Kathryn was quick to set him straight. A frown marred the smoothness of her features as she debated telling him her doubts. She suddenly wanted to, needing to see Buck's reaction and hear him say it was all ridiculous. "Something he said has been bothering me," she admitted, then hesitated.

"Yeah?" he prompted.

Kathryn leaned back in her chair and gave him a level look. She took a deep breath. "He says he came back to Deepwater on my eighteenth birthday." She saw the flicker of surprise in his eyes and paused to let the information sink in. "And he also says mother sent him away."

The surprise changed to a mixture of shock and outrage. "He said that?" Buck demanded, instantly defensive of Mattie.

"Yes." Kathryn understood his anger and skepticism because it was exactly what she'd felt when she'd first heard the accusations against her mother.

"Are you sure he was serious?" His frown deepened as Kathryn nodded. "But that don't make sense!" he declared, rejecting the information while trying to find a reason for it. "Under the circumstances, Mattie wouldn't have run him off—not when you were pregnant. She knew you were over there in Wichita, just waitin' for the day Judd came back. If he had, it'd be more like Mattie to get out the shotgun and force him to marry you, since a baby was on the way." His face was pinched in a scowl. "Besides, why would Judd have listened to Mattie? He never did before. Why would he give up so easy without seein' you first?"

"He says she told him I was married."

Buck drew back, eyeing her warily. "Naw." He shook his head. "Even Mattie wouldn't have gone that far."

There was a degree of comfort in seeing Buck's skepticism. It was the support her own opinions needed.

"That's what he said." She lifted a shoulder in a shrug.

She'd been right about Judson all along. While she couldn't take any satisfaction in the knowledge, she was glad the wondering was over. If Judson's claims were at all plausible, Buck would have been the first person to give him the benefit of the doubt.

"You know, Buck, I think I would have felt better about the whole thing if Judson had simply admitted that once he left Deepwater, he realized he wasn't the type to be tied down. I know that, and I've accepted that some men can't handle a long-term commitment. But apparently Judson felt he had to give me some excuse for the way he acted."

"What's the matter with that boy?" Buck snapped in frustration. "I'd have never suspected Judson would stoop so low as to try to turn you against your own mother. I always figured he had enough guts to own up to his mistakes like a man."

"I suppose he thought I would be glad to hear that everything was my mother's fault," Kathryn murmured, remembering an instant when she had wanted to believe him. She shuddered when she realized what could have happened if her loyalty had been misplaced. She had nearly let Judson get to her again.

Buck pushed back from the table and got to his feet, his tall, rangy frame towering over her. "It's time somebody straightened that boy out," he declared. "And right now I'm just about mad enough to do it. Did he say what time he was leavin'?"

"I . . . I'm not sure that he is leaving," she admitted. "At least not this morning."

"Why not?" Buck demanded. "That's what he said last night."

"He wants me back." Kathryn shot him a worried glance. "Or so he said." She was still uncertain about what Judson intended to do. Was he really planning to try to win her back? Or had he only said those things in the hope of getting her into his bed?

Buck's mouth tightened as the pieces fell into place. "And that's why he told you all that stuff," he realized. "So you'd forgive him."

"I guess so."

"He must want you back awful bad," he mused, some of the anger draining out of him as he mulled over the reason for Judson's behavior.

"He isn't going to get me," Kathryn declared sharply. Judson's attempts at weakening her resolve had only served to strengthen it. A bitter smile tugged at her mouth as she glanced up at Buck. "You should have heard him, Buck. He had it all worked out. He even suggested that mother had intercepted my mail."

"What?" He frowned, his eyes narrowing at the introduction of this new point.

"Oh yes. He said he wrote me lots of letters, but mother just got hold of them before I did." Her laugh was dry and humorless. "Can you believe he expected me to swallow that?"

Buck's gaze made a sudden shift away from her probing eyes. "That, uh. . . ." He licked his lips. "That'd be quite a story if it was true."

A tragedy, Kathryn thought. "Wouldn't it, though," she said with an edge of sarcasm that masked a quick stab of pain. In the back of her mind there had always been a vague hope that there was a reasonable explanation for Judson's desertion. Maybe he had been kidnapped. Maybe he'd developed amnesia. She had come up with a thousand excuses that would exonerate him, anything that would keep her from feeling the agony that accompanied the knowledge that he simply hadn't cared. Now there was no more hope. The excuses he had finally provided her with proved what she'd known all along.

"Well. . . ." Buck seemed suddenly antsy. For the first time in several minutes, his eyes met hers. Then he turned away. "I'll see ya later, Kathryn. Got some things to take care of this mornin'."

"Are you going to see Judson?" She asked, because that's what he'd said before. But something in Buck's attitude had changed since then. Kathryn wasn't surprised when he shrugged and shook his head.

"Don't know." His head continued its side-to-side negative movement as Buck turned and walked to the door. ''Haven't decided yet.''

The door banged shut behind him. Kathryn stared at it for a long time. But it was Buck's eyes she kept seeing, and the expression that had been in them that last time he'd looked at her. It was the expression of a man who was deeply troubled and fighting the bitter pain of disillusionment. Kathryn knew the feeling.

Finally she left the table and went to get ready for work. She was ready to embrace the comfort of the boutique with open arms.

CHAPTER SEVEN

LOOKING OVER THE INVOICE for the latest shipment of dresses, Kathryn wondered how many more times she would have to read it before she knew what it said. Her concentration was nil, and her nerves were very close to being shot. With Judson's parting words still ringing in her ears, she kept expecting him to pop in, welcome or not. The last thing she wanted was for him to catch her off guard again. Last night her decision to stay for dinner had been made at the last minute. There hadn't been time to emotionally brace herself for their meeting. Considering what that laxity had cost her, it wasn't a mistake she intended to repeat.

Every time the shop door had opened this morning, Kathryn had jumped. When the silver bell jingled again, her reaction was the same. Her wary, expectant glance darted to the entrance. But Charles didn't look anything like Judson.

"Charles!" She smiled in surprised relief. "I wasn't expecting you to come by this morning." She glanced at her watch and saw it was almost noon. She supposed he had come to have lunch with her.

"Did you miss me?" It was a question, but Charles wasn't unduly concerned about her answer, confident and secure in his position.

Kathryn frowned at him, finding his question strange. Then she remembered he'd been out of town the previous day.

"Of course I missed you." But she realized he hadn't once entered her thoughts. While the fact didn't exactly please her, she wasn't overly troubled by it. She'd had a lot on her mind.

Walking around the counter, she accepted the invitation of his outstretched arms and lifted her mouth for his kiss. Charles was not without experience or expertise in the way of technique. His kiss was firm and affectionate, a pleasant experience that usually left her with a warm comfortable glow.

This time was no exception. When he ended the kiss and wrapped her in his arms, Kathryn felt safe and secure, wanted and protected. There was nothing about his embrace that shook her senses and left her feeling vulnerable. It was a comfortable relationship for both of them. It satisfied certain needs; there were no demands made that couldn't be met. With Judson, Kathryn had had the fire and she'd been burned. With Charles, she had the benefit of a slow steady warmth without taking the chance of being left out in the cold.

Drawing back, Charles reached to bring her hands down from around his neck. "I'm going to have to go away more often," he teased, and set her away in a silent reminder of where they were.

"Don't you dare." The warning matched his light tone, but Kathryn meant it seriously. If Charles had been home last night, the scene with Judson would never have happened. And she wouldn't be feeling these sudden pangs of guilt. She wondered why she hadn't felt guilty before, but Kathryn wasn't prepared to deal with that issue at the moment. "Can I get you a cup of coffee?"

"I'm afraid I don't have time." He glanced at his watch.

"Oh." She was disappointed. "It's so close to noon, I thought maybe you stopped by to have lunch with me."

"No. I already have a lunch date with a client. We're meeting at the café down the street in a few minutes. Since I was in the neighborhood, I decided to stop here and let you know I was back."

"How was your trip?"

"Interesting." He nodded with satisfaction. "The time I spent with the governor wasn't as productive as I'd hoped, but I did meet someone who could prove to be a valuable source of information."

"Who's that?" Kathryn prompted.

"Louise Mariner." Charles frowned thoughtfully. "She's the daughter—the divorced daughter—of a congressman. She seems to know everything about everyone and doesn't mind telling it—to the right person." He qualified the observation.

"Such as you," Kathryn inserted.

"Such as me," he affirmed.

"And what makes you the right person to receive these interesting little tidbits?" Kathryn knew she was minimizing the importance of the information he could glean. The right knowledge in the right hands could be priceless if used correctly. But she also knew that anything important was rarely free. "What do you have to do in return?"

"Call her from time to time. Wine and dine her when I'm in the city. In short, give her a little of the male attention she craves. With sufficient flattery and a few martinis, I think Louise will spill all the secrets between here and Washington."

"I see." Turning, Kathryn wandered back toward the counter and tried to appear casual, but the mention of the woman made her uneasy. There was a nagging suspicion that Charles had done more than wine and dine the congressman's daughter. It wasn't the first time Kathryn had suspected something like this, and she doubted it would be the last.

The situation didn't please her, yet Kathryn chose not to confront Charles on this issue. She honestly didn't feel that she had the right. After two years of courtship Kathryn had still not taken that step into intimacy with Charles. It was an intimacy Kathryn had never felt ready to handle. And Charles had never tried to pressure her into anything, telling her patiently that when the time was right, she'd know it.

But she also knew that he was a healthy adult male with normal biological urges. If she wasn't capable of satisfying his physical needs, it didn't seem fair for her to object to him seeking some other outlet. Of course, once they were married, things would change. Eventually she would be able to take that final step—a huge step, in Kathryn's opinion.

She hopped onto the stool and leaned forward, bracing her elbows on the counter and feeling the heaviness of guilt settle onto her. Charles had always been so patient and understanding in the face of her inability to respond to his advances. Yet her aloofness wasn't his fault. He was a very attractive man. It was just that sexual desire had been absent from her life ever since her disastrous affair with Judson. Now, after last night, it was back. In a few short hours, Judson had accomplished what Charles hadn't been able to do in two long years. And Kathryn wasn't pleased with the knowledge.

She avoided Charles's gaze, afraid her eyes would reveal her thoughts. "So," she said brightly. "Tell me more about Ms Mariner. She sounds very colorful. How did you meet her?"

"There was a small dinner party. As the only single guests, we were more or less thrown together," he explained with a rueful grin. "It worked out, but it would be nice to have you by my side in the future. We need to get down to the serious business of deciding on a wedding date. Soon." With the change of topic, his expression grew serious. His gray eyes roamed over her face in open admiration.

"Yes," Kathryn agreed. "We'll talk about it." But not now, she thought. The time wasn't right.

She looked at him, so maturely handsome and refined, and she wondered why she kept holding back. She knew what she wanted in a marriage— something safe and solid, secure and comfortable. In a lifetime mate, Kathryn wanted someone she could care about but not someone who aroused those intense emotions she had known with Judson. She wanted someone she could be happy living with, but not someone she couldn't survive without if it ever became necessary.

Charles was offering her everything she sought. Yet this discussion about marriage was making her uncomfortable. Or maybe it was just her conscience. She tipped her head to the side and gave Charles a teasing smile, trying to lighten the mood.

"You know, Charles, I have the unkind suspicion that you really want a wife as a shield—to keep the Louises of this world from getting any serious ideas about you."

"Merely a side benefit, Kathryn," Charles responded in the same light vein. "One of many."

"Are you saying you want to marry me because I'll be a career asset?" She was only half teasing.

"Of course," he agreed without hesitation, only half teasing, too. "Do you think I'd deliberately set out to find someone who would be a liability?"

"I guess not." Put that way, it made her feel silly for asking the questions with any degree of seriousness. "Will you be coming for dinner tonight?"

"It's Friday," he reminded her. "I'm taking

you out. After we eat, you can decide what we'll do for the rest of the evening. Anything you want.''

"Anything I want? Why the special treatment?'' She was curious, since Charles generally had things planned in advance.

"Because you're a special lady,'' he explained smoothly, charming her with his smile. "And because I want to make up for your having to spend last evening alone.''

"I. . . .'' Kathryn hesitated, debating the necessity of telling Charles. Buck was bound to mention it at some point, so the wise thing would be to get last night out in the open. Trying to hide it would only make it seem important. "I wasn't exactly alone. Buck was here. . . and Judson Taylor.''

"Taylor?'' His surprised eyes narrowed on her. "What was he doing here?''

Something in his attitude made Kathryn suspect jealousy. There had been a hint of it the other night. Now it was stronger.

"He came to see Buck.'' She hurried to assure him that there were no grounds for the suspicion she read in his eyes—at least not on her part.

"He and Buck are old friends. Last night was their only chance to get together before Judson left.''

"Has he left already?'' Charles questioned sharply.

"He said he planned to leave early this morning.'' Kathryn hedged on a definite answer because Judd had said some other things, too. After last night she wasn't at all certain that his original plans were still valid.

"He's probably back in Dallas by now." Charles didn't seem disappointed by the possibility.

"Probably." Even though she wasn't sure, Kathryn added her agreement. She wondered about Charles's change of attitude toward Judson, remembering the interest he had expressed upon meeting him. Maybe, like her, Charles sensed that Judson posed some kind of threat. Also, there was the fact that Judson hadn't returned the interest Charles had shown. Kathryn preferred to think it was the first reason that had prompted the change.

Charles glanced at his watch again. "I have to go. I'll see you tonight."

"Okay."

With his departure, Kathryn felt suddenly calm. Just knowing that Charles was close by and that, true to pattern, he was coming to take her to dinner, made it seem as though things were back to normal. He usually had that kind of effect on her, steadying and calming. It was the complete antithesis of the effect Judson had on her—now or in the past.

Her ability to concentrate returned and Kathryn gave all of her attention to the invoice. There had been a mix-up in a shipment of dresses. She had received twice as many as she ordered, and the dresses were in two sizes instead of four. She could probably sell them all, but having too many women running around in the same dress could be disastrous, especially in such a small town. Her reputation had been hard earned, and this was just the type of thing that could spoil it. Kathryn decided to send half the shipment back. She was in the storeroom repacking the dresses when she heard someone come into the shop.

Entering the showroom, Kathryn recognized the Harper sisters, two delightful elderly women who frequently drove in from one of the tiny neighboring towns to shop. Every time Kathryn saw them, she marveled that two women who looked so different could be sisters. One was short and considerably more than pleasantly plump; the other was tall and rail thin.

"Can I help you find something in particular?" Kathryn knew the answer before she asked.

"Oh, no, no." The plump one shook her head and smiled. "We're just browsing."

"Take your time. If you need any help I'll be right through that doorway." Half turning, Kathryn pointed a finger toward the curtained exit. "Just call me."

Amusement pulled at her mouth as she went back to the storeroom. The sisters were always "just browsing," and they invariably left with no less than two garments each. They were giggling and exclaiming over the merchandise with girlish excitement when the bell above the street door tinkled again.

With a sigh, Kathryn returned to the showroom. Her smile of welcome faded at the sight of Judson standing in the middle of the large room. Her silent steps faltered and her natural grace disappeared. Again he had caught her with her guard down. She stiffened at the realization.

The thick carpet had muffled any sounds of her approach, so Judson hadn't noticed her yet. Taking advantage of that, Kathryn stopped and drew a few quick breaths to steady her shaky composure. He was wearing a dark suit and tie, which only set off his deep bronze tan and the muscular width of his shoulders.

From the back of the store came the faint buzz of whispering voices. His lazy glance drifted in that direction. The whispered conversation was instantly halted, indicating that Judson had been the object of the Harper sisters' conversation. The white-haired women looked like children caught with their hands in the cookie jar.

Then Judson flashed them a white grin and both of the women actually blushed. Suppressed feminine giggles came from the back of the shop, proving that even seventy-year-old females weren't immune to the potency of one of his smiles. It rankled. Moving behind the counter, Kathryn deliberately made enough noise to attract Judson's attention.

He let his gaze linger on the sisters for another second or two, then turned, leveling the force of his smile on Kathryn. "Hello, beautiful Katy."

Her stomach felt like a quivering ball of nerves as he approached. Kathryn waited until he reached the counter. "I thought you were leaving today." Her voice was very cool and very low.

"I thought I was, too." His glance made a

sweeping inspection of her, taking note of the way her beige summer-weight dress hugged her curves. Chunky jade jewelry gave the outfit color. Instead of the usual French twist, her pale hair hung in soft, shiny waves about her shoulders. "But it seems I have some unfinished business here," Judson said.

"Do you?" Kathryn pretended to take his remark at face value, ignoring his insinuation. Unfortunately her pulse couldn't ignore it. "Buck isn't here," she informed him stiffly. "If you'd like to leave a message, I'll—"

"I didn't come to see Buck. I came to see you." Casually he leaned an elbow on the countertop and let his hand slide over to touch hers.

At his touch, Kathryn recoiled, as if she'd been burned. She jerked her hand away and down toward her side. In her haste she cracked a knuckle on the edge of the counter. There was an involuntary gasp of pain before she gritted her teeth.

Judson wasn't very successful at looking sympathetic. Amusement glittered in his eyes, mocking her. "Careful there." The grooves alongside his mouth deepened. "You might hurt yourself."

But not nearly as much as he could hurt her if she gave him the chance. She kept her hands behind the counter, out of his sight while she rubbed the injured knuckle. Tension threaded through her veins.

"I thought I made it plain that I wasn't interested in seeing you." Kathryn ignored his words of caution and dealt with the issue.

He shook his head slightly. "You didn't make it plain at all."

"I told you last night that I don't want you here," she insisted quietly, conscious of two sets of curious blue eyes watching from the back of the shop.

"And I told you that I was receiving other messages," he murmured.

His gaze moved to the curve of her lips, as if searching for traces of his kisses. Kathryn imagined she could feel the pressure of his mouth, experience again the sensual warmth of his kiss and the taste of him, heady and male. There was a very real quality to the fantasy, and Kathryn was disturbed by last night's sensations all over again.

"You're wrong," she stated firmly, but her voice quavered. She hated this weakness, this vulnerability that took nothing into account except the potency of his attraction.

"No, I'm not." A knowing smile crooked his mouth. "After last night, you aren't going to convince me otherwise. Too much truth came out during our...conversation." He hesitated in his search for the word to describe all that had taken place the previous evening. "I know you were upset when you learned the truth about your mother. I was too, when I realized what her meddling had cost us. But I want you to know that I don't have any ill feelings toward Mattie. She—"

"Don't start on my mother again," Kathryn warned in a low angry voice. "I'm not interested in hearing any more of your lies."

A hard glint entered his eyes. "You still don't believe me," he accused.

"No."

His faintly narrowed eyes measured her for a long second, then a slow smile spread across his face. "The news came as a shock. You need more time to adjust to the idea. Why don't we discuss it over lunch?"

Kathryn stared at him. "Didn't you hear me? I don't want anything to do with you. I'm certainly not going to have lunch with you!"

"Then how about dinner?" he persisted, ignoring her coolness and looking amused by it.

"No."

But Judson rarely listened to what he didn't want to hear. "Dinner would be better anyway," he said thoughtfully. "It will give us more time to talk. I'll come by for you at closing time." Taking her acceptance for granted, he straightened from his relaxed stance against the counter.

Before he could move away, Kathryn spoke up. "I already have a dinner date tonight. Which is really irrelevant, since I wouldn't have dinner with you anyway, for any reason."

He paused, studying her with a bemused smile as he digested what she'd said. "In case you change your mind—"

"I won't," she insisted, angered by so many things—his presence, his arrogant confidence, and the way her remarks seemed to bounce off him, impotent and unheeded.

"But if you do," he continued, a heavy run of

amusement in his voice, "I'm at the Sands, room forty-two. I'll wait to hear from you."

"Don't hold your breath," Kathryn retorted.

His grin widened. "You know where I am if you want me."

"I don't want you!" she hissed in angry frustration.

"Liar," he said softly, and leaned over the counter until barely a foot separated them. "You do want me, and before I'm through, you're going to admit it to both of us."

"Never." It took all of her control, but Kathryn stood her ground, determined not to move away and reveal how much his nearness unnerved her. He was so close, she could make out every detail of his face, from the tiny sun creases fanning out from the corners of his eyes, to the pores of his tanned skin. She could see each individual spiky black eyelash.

"You wouldn't care to place a little bet on that, would you?" Judson challenged. He was far too sure of himself . . . and her.

"Why don't you just leave me alone?" Kathryn demanded in taut bewilderment. "Just run along back to Dallas and forget you ever heard of Deepwater, Kansas. You did that for seven years, so it shouldn't be too difficult to do it again."

The smile faded, his expression growing serious and thoughtful. "Last night I asked myself the same question over and over. But I guess the answer had something to do with a point Buck made. He reminded me that there are certain things a man's just got to fight for. That's something I never should have forgotten. Last time I took Mattie's word for the way things were. This time I'm trusting my own judgment. I think what's left between us is worth fighting for.''

"Don't bother," Kathryn advised. "You'll lose." She was going to make certain he did. If he didn't wind up the loser, she would.

"Uh-uh." Shaking his head, he rubbed a finger over the ridge of the otherwise straight bridge of his nose. "Remember? I don't play to lose. And the way I see it, the odds are all in my favor. Why don't you just give up now and we won't have to waste time doing battle?" His lazily seductive look suggested other, more pleasurable ways to spend the time.

And all of them were a fast road to heartache if she was fool enough to give in to temptation. The pressure of the moment got to her. "Get out of here, Judson! I mean it!" she stormed, forgetting they were in the boutique as she pointed a finger toward the door.

Whispers and suppressed titters pulled her attention to the back of the shop. Her cheeks reddened as Kathryn guessed what the Harper sisters must be thinking of her. As a businesswoman, her behavior was hardly commendable.

"Temper, temper." Judson clicked his tongue in reproval.

"If you don't leave my shop right this minute, I will call the police." Her clipped words were barely audible. Kathryn definitely didn't want their rapt audience to hear the threat.

"The police?" Judson echoed loudly, and the two sisters started buzzing again. "Don't go to all that trouble," he said with lazy amusement. "I was just leaving anyway."

He winked at her and walked leisurely to the door, then turned back to run his bold gaze over her one more time. "As always, Katy, it's been a pleasure." With a little tilt of his head, he gave a smiling salute to the Harper sisters, who were peering curiously through the racks of clothing, their blue eyes glittering. "Afternoon, ladies."

They were flushed and giggling as he left the shop, thoroughly charmed by his rakish manner. In contrast, Kathryn was simmering. She felt raw and unsettled.

What kind of woman was she anyway? A man could seduce her, desert her and lie to her, and she couldn't even hate him for it? Granted, she had learned her lesson. She would never again trust her heart to someone like him. In fact, she would never totally trust her heart to anyone. Her happiness was too precious and fragile a thing to place in hands that might one day turn callous and uncaring.

Her own hands were shaking badly. Kathryn glanced at them and knew she had to pull herself together. So many things weighed heavily on her mind. She needed a few minutes alone to try to sort them out.

The minute the Harper sisters left the shop, Kathryn locked the door behind them and decided to fix some lunch. She wasn't hungry, but common sense insisted that she eat something. When she entered the kitchen, she stopped at the sight of Buck seated in his usual chair at the table.

"What are you doing home?" she exclaimed. Buck was rarely around the house at noon, so Kathryn was surprised to see him. But she was so preoccupied with her own problems that she didn't notice when he failed to answer and walked past him to open the refrigerator. "Would you like me to fix you something to eat?" Kathryn bent over to view the contents of the refrigerator with disinterest. This time she noticed Buck's silence. "Buck, are you hungry?" She repeated the question and glanced over her shoulder.

Instead of his usual relaxed slouch, Buck was leaning forward, forearms resting on the tabletop, wide shoulders slightly hunched. There was a tight, pained look to his expression that brought a frown to Kathryn's face.

"No, I'm not hungry," Buck finally replied, a hoarseness in his already gruff voice. "I just came from Ruby's."

But Kathryn was no longer interested in the answer to her questions about lunch. She closed the refrigerator door and walked quickly to the table, alarmed at Buck's pallor.

"What's wrong, Buck?" She tried to be calm for his sake. He looked ill—or badly shaken. Maybe there had been an accident. "What happened?"

He finally lifted his eyes to her face. Kathryn was shocked by the look on his face. Instantly her mind traveled back to earlier that morning, and the bitter pain she had read in the faded-blue depths of his eyes. This was that same emotion— only now it was stronger. And there was a haunted quality now as well.

"Sit down, Kathryn." It was a sober order. "I have to tell you somethin'."

Her knees suddenly went weak. Kathryn sank into a chair. Whatever Buck had to say, she wasn't going to like it. It was obvious, too, that Buck dreaded relaying the news. He opened his mouth several times, but no words came to him.

"Aw, hell," he muttered in frustration. "There ain't no easy way to say it. I'm just gonna tell ya straight out." Still he hesitated. Finally he blurted, "It's true, Kathryn. It's all true. Everything Judd told ya last night is true."

"What?" It was a wary, one-word question. "Surely you don't believe him?" She felt betrayed.

"I didn't want to," he admitted. "Because I didn't want to believe it of Mattie. But somethin' clicked in my head when you started talkin' about those letters."

"What?" Kathryn didn't want to ask. A cold feeling of dread started in the pit of her stomach.

"Do you remember how I always used to go to the post office and get the mail?"

She nodded slowly. "Yes."

"I started doin' it right after I moved in here. Did it every day for years." Grimness carved the lines more deeply into his face. "One day Mattie told me she was goin' to start pickin' it up again. Said she needed the fresh air and exercise." Reluctantly he met her gaze. "That was right about the time Judd left."

"So?" Kathryn challenged out of fear. "That doesn't prove anything."

"No, not by itself," Buck agreed. "But it started me thinkin'. I figured out a way that might work to prove him right or wrong. I figured we oughta know the truth one way or the other."

"And?" It was a croaking sound. Kathryn's mouth felt so dry she could hardly speak.

"And, I went and talked to Ruby."

"Ruby?" She frowned. "You didn't tell her all this, did you?"

"No. But she was the one who convinced me it was true. Her and Jake used to own the grocery store, remember?"

"Yes, but—" Nothing was making any sense.

"And up until a few years ago, the post office was stuck in a corner of the grocery store. Ruby and Jake ran both of 'em until the town got so big and the new post office was built."

"That's right," Kathryn recalled. She clasped her hands in her lap, twisting her fingers so tightly together that the action produced a physical pain.

"Today at Ruby's, I just casually mentioned that Judd Taylor was back in town. She remembered him right off. Said he always used to flirt with her and give Jake a hard time whenever Judd came in to collect his mail. Then Ruby started talkin' about how you two always made such a cute couple. Said she never could understand what happened to make you run off and marry someone else." He paused, his expression grim. "She also remembered all those letters Judd kept sendin', because every time she saw one of 'em, she'd shake her head and think it was a cryin' shame things didn't work out different for you two."

"No." Kathryn shook her head. "I don't believe it." She didn't want to believe it. If it was true, it meant it had all been needless—all the pain and heartache she had suffered, and the lie she'd been living all this time.

"Kathryn—"

She met Buck's eyes and knew he shared her pain. She also knew what he'd said was true. Judson had come back and her mother had sent him away. And Kathryn felt the cold hand of betrayal squeezing at her heart. "When I think how much I trusted her...." The words trailed off bitterly. "After I told her I was pregnant, she was so understanding, so sympathetic. I told her how much I wanted to marry Judson, how he was coming back for me and...." A sob rose in her throat, choking off her voice as Kathryn remembered her mother's reactions to those statements.

Mattie's pale-blue eyes had regarded her daughter with a knowing kind of pity. He won't come back, those eyes had said, but Mattie had left the words unspoken. Instead she had taken Kathryn in her arms and told her that everything would be all right. They'd deal with this together. Then

Mattie made arrangements for Kathryn to stay with an aunt in Wichita until the baby was born.

Kathryn went along with the plan, but she made certain her mother intended to abide by her wishes. "When he comes back, you'll tell him where to find me?"

In her mind's eye, Kathryn could still see the incredible softening of her mother's usually hard features. "I love you, Kathryn Elizabeth Ryan. And I will do what will make you happy. Don't ever doubt that."

And Kathryn hadn't doubted her. Which made what was happening now an even more bitter pill to swallow. Kathryn's hands curled into tight fists.

"Why, Buck?" It was a hoarse, choked sound. "Why did she do it?"

"I can only guess at the answer to that," Buck admitted. "Your mother loved you very much—"

"Don't talk to me about love!" Kathryn snapped. After what she'd just heard, it was too much. She got to her feet, angry, hurting tears stinging the backs of her eyes. "She never loved me. She couldn't have."

"She did," Buck insisted. "More than anything else in the world."

"She deliberately ruined my life!" Kathryn hurled the words at him, sharp with the knife-edge of pain, and Buck winced. "Was she so miserable she couldn't stand the thought of anybody being happy? Even her own daughter?" She bit down hard on her lower lip. "That isn't love Buck."

"I know it don't seem like it, but it is," he insisted. "It's a scared kind of love. A kind that tries to hold on so tight and protect so much, that it crushes the very thing it wanted to keep safe. I think that's what happened with you. Your ma saw you fallin' for a drifter, and she wanted to protect you."

"She had no right, Buck!" An anger born of pain made her lash out against the injustice of it all.

"She was your mother, Kathryn," he reminded her quietly. "She had the right and responsibility to do what she thought was best for you. If she was wrong, just try to understand that she thought she'd be protectin' you. Judd was a drifter, and Mattie thought she knew all about that kind of man. After all she was married to one. I imagine Mattie was only tryin' to spare you the hell she went through with your father."

"That's no excuse," Kathryn said bitterly. "The situations weren't the same."

"Maybe not," Buck conceded. "But it is a reason. Don't make it right, though." He shook his head slowly from side to side. "Nope. It sure don't make it right. Your ma had her problems, and I think I knew her well enough to understand why she did what she did. But you two kids paid an awful big price for somethin' that really had nothin' to do with you."

A silence settled over the kitchen like a thick, heavy blanket. Suddenly drained, Kathryn sank into a chair. She tried to adjust to what she'd learned, but none of it seemed real yet. It was like a dream—a nightmare. For seven long years she'd been blaming the wrong person. It was going to be difficult to change a complete pattern of thinking that had become so firmly cemented with time and suffering.

"Course, you realize this all means Judd got a pretty raw deal, too." Buck leaned forward to wrap his hands around a cup of coffee that had long since gone cold. "You ain't the only one who got hurt in this tangled-up mess."

Kathryn lifted her gaze, the statement splintering through her. Judson had been hurt, too. He was also a victim of her mother's deceit.

"No, I guess not," she agreed, but the image of Judson as a victim wouldn't jell in her mind. All she could see was the man who'd walked out on her, a picture she'd held on to for so long. Now it was no longer valid—but it existed. Old scars and wounds couldn't be wiped away by a simple correction of facts. The hurt was real, even if the circumstances were fabricated. And the heartache was something Kathryn would never be able to forget.

Salty tears slipped off her lashes and made wet tracks down her cheeks. "Everything could have been so different," she murmured, thinking out loud.

"It's not too late," Buck said softly.

She looked at him, considering his words. A part of her wanted to believe him, a part of her wanted to try to recapture those golden days. But deep down, Kathryn knew it was a time forever lost to them. She felt a thousand years old, so far removed from the innocent trusting girl she had been.

She had loved with every fiber of her being, and she had felt the loss to the core of her soul. She had no desire to love that way again, with such completeness, such abandon. Ever. With any man.

And it would be so easy to fall in love with Judson all over again. The chemistry between them was still strong, pulling and drawing her toward him as the flame draws the moth. Before it had been relatively simple to protect herself from becoming involved with him. The past had been her armor, something for which she could blame him. Now she didn't even have that to cling to, and Judson posed even more of a threat.

For that reason she'd have to keep her guard up all the more. Just to be certain she stayed safe. The only insurance against pain was independence, that emotional independence that becomes impossible to attain when a woman loves too deeply.

"It's too late, Buck." With a sigh, she leaned forward and propped her chin on her hand. "It's all over between Judson and me. It has been for a long time."

Now she had Charles. It was on him that she needed to concentrate. Together they could build a life with which she could be satisfied. She had been content before Judson's return, and she was determined to regain that contentment once he left. But while he was there, it wouldn't be easy.

"You do know that ya have to tell him," Buck said, eyeing her closely.

"Tell him what?" Kathryn frowned, then wondered which "him" Buck was referring to. There were things she was keeping from both men—Judson and Charles.

"You gotta tell Judson you weren't ever married. He has a right to know."

"Why?" She sat up straight, alarm shooting through her. One barrier from the past had already been broken down. Kathryn didn't want to take another obstacle away. Knowing that there hadn't been anybody else, and knowing that she'd carried his child would only increase Judson's determination to revive the old fires. The last thing Kathryn wanted to do was encourage him. She only had so much strength with which to fight.

"You've got the advantage of knowin' the truth—that he didn't desert you. Judd deserves to know why you weren't here when he got back. It musta been hell thinkin' you were married to some other guy."

Buck obviously wasn't pleased with having to spell out Judson's side of the story. His scowling look held disapproval. It made Kathryn feel selfish, but she couldn't bring herself to agree to impart information that would give Judson an advantage she was afraid to let him have.

"I'm not ready to take that step, Buck. And it's my decision to make." She saw his mouth tighten and knew Buck was disappointed in her. It hurt to let him down. Yet she had to protect herself in any way possible. "I want you to swear you won't tell Judson about the baby—or the marriage. Leave it to me."

There was an instant when Kathryn was positive he was going to refuse. Then Buck reluctantly agreed.

"I won't tell him," he grumbled. "But I still think you should."

THE INCIDENTS OF THE MORNING left Kathryn tense and troubled. She considered taking the afternoon off, but almost immediately decided against it. Work had always proved to be the best therapy for her. Besides, she needed to get back on track, settle back into the well-carved groove of the life she had made for herself—the one she had built from the absolute nothingness she had had after losing Judson.

During the afternoon only a handful of customers visited the shop. Kathryn was glad there weren't more, because as the day wore on, she found it more and more difficult to deal with the women in a pleasant and patient manner. Their problems seemed so trivial when compared to her own. Kathryn couldn't generate any of her usual sympathy for a woman whose major concern was what on earth she was going to wear to the charity dinner on Saturday night. *Who cares,* Kathryn wanted to scream, but instead she bit her tongue.

All in all, it was a trying day. It seemed to take forever for time to drag itself around to five o'clock. When it finally did, Kathryn was more than ready to close up shop. She put the sign in the window, then began posting the day's receipts and preparing the bank deposit. The door swung open, startling her.

"You're a little jumpy, aren't you?" Charles observed as he walked in, ignoring the closed sign.

"Yes, I guess I am," Kathryn confessed with a loud sigh. "It's been one of those days." She didn't elaborate.

"If you're ready, we'll get out of here and go someplace where you can wind down," he offered sympathetically.

"That sounds like exactly what I need," she agreed, and stashed the receipts and paperwork in a drawer, leaving it until the next day. "Just give me two minutes. I'll get my purse."

It took even less than the requested two minutes for Kathryn to hurry upstairs, run a comb through her hair, apply a fresh coat of gloss to her lips and spritz some cologne on her wrists and throat. She was anxious to leave the shop and the nerve-racking day behind her.

When she locked the shop door for the night, Kathryn felt as if a weight had been lifted from her shoulders. She sighed and smiled up at Charles, amazed at how much better she felt now that he was around. She had a definite sense of being safe. Which seemed silly, since she wasn't in any physical danger. But Kathryn knew that the security Charles provided her with was emotional. With him, her heart was safe. With Judson, it wasn't.

"Shall we ride or walk?" Charles asked.

"Let's walk," she decided. She would have time to relax and soak up some of the lingering sunshine after being cooped up all day.

Although the July sun had begun its slow descent in the western sky, the lateness of the afternoon hour hadn't alleviated the heat and humidity of a lazy summer day. A light shimmer of perspiration gave Kathryn's skin a faint glow as her body adjusted from the air-conditioned coolness of the shop to the moist heat outside.

As they started in the direction of the restaurant, a car pulled up to the curb and stopped in front of the boutique. Even though she had no intention of reopening the shop, Kathryn cast a mildly curious glance backward to see if the customer was anyone she knew. Something about the tan sedan was vaguely familiar.

The passenger door opened and Buck stepped out. Kathryn's memory of the car instantly sharpened. It didn't take any guesswork to know who was driving.

"Hello, Buck." Charles walked over to shake the older man's hand. Kathryn had little choice but to follow. "Who's that you're with?" Charles didn't wait for Buck to answer and satisfy his curiosity. He bent down to peer in the window. "Why it's Judson Taylor." There was confusion and suspicion in his look, but it was quickly masked by a smooth smile. Moving closer to the car, he stuck his arm through the opened window and shook Judson's hand. "Nice to see you again."

Judson's reply was lost to Kathryn as Buck mumbled something about changing clothes. With a promise to be right back, he walked to the rear entrance of the house.

"I thought Kathryn told me you'd left for Dallas." It was a question, put in the form of a statement. Charles sounded only mildly curious, but Kathryn knew better.

"I'd planned to, but there have been some changes." Thankfully Judson didn't go into detail.

"No problems, I hope." Under the guise of politeness, Charles subtly dug for more information. Kathryn was half-afraid Judson would give it to him if Charles didn't stop fishing. Judson was hardly the shy type.

"Nothing I can't handle," Judson assured him, amusement liberally lacing his tone. But the message in his remark was meant for Kathryn.

"Good. Good." A frown was tracing lines in his forehead as Charles straightened from the window. His sharply questioning glance darted to Kathryn, as if he sensed he was the butt of some private joke. He was not pleased.

"Are you ready?" Her voice and expression were bright as she tried to prompt him into leaving.

"Yes," he agreed readily. "Judson, take care."

"Will do, Mr. Mayor." Again, there was a trace of mocking amusement that Charles noted, but didn't fully understand.

His professional smile was a bit tight as he gripped

Kathryn's elbow in a decidedly possessive manner, reasserting his claim even though he didn't seem at all sure whether or not it was necessary. No direct reference had been made to either Kathryn or her relationship with Charles. Judson hadn't said a word to her. He had arrived with Buck and obviously intended to spend the evening reminiscing with the old man—not Kathryn. Yet there was tension in the air, a thread of unexplained animosity running between Charles and Judson. Kathryn sensed Charles's frustrated confusion.

"Oh, by the way," Judson drawled, casually calling them back.

"Was there something you wanted?" Charles's expression was pleasant enough, yet there was a stiff reserve about him. He was polite and nothing more.

Judson had slid over to the car's passenger side. An arm was hooked over the window frame, a cigarette dangling loosely between his fingers. He studied the ribbon of smoke curling from the burning tip.

"There's something you might be able to help me with, Charles." He looked completely serious now.

"What's that?" It was a wary question.

"I need some legal work done on this end." Taking a drag on the cigarette, he glanced up. His brown eyes were narrowed against the smoke. "Would you be interested in handling some business for Monument Oil?"

Interest flashed in Charles's eyes, then his eyes

dropped to conceal it. Kathryn was too stunned to even attempt to hide her reaction. She stared at Judson, who didn't even look at her.

"I might be very interested," Charles admitted slowly, as if silently weighing the value of the opportunity against his instinctive dislike and suspicion of the man.

"I hope you are," Judson declared. "I've asked around, and the local consensus seems to be that you're the best counsel in town."

Charles's guarded expression began to dissolve, some of the old confidence returning to gleam in his eyes. Faint disgust went through Kathryn as flattery turned him into putty right before her eyes. What was the matter with Charles? How could such an intelligent man not know when he was being manipulated?

"I'm grateful to whoever passed the recommendation along," Charles replied to the compliment. "It's always nice to hear that someone thinks you're doing a good job."

"Everyone thinks so." There was a small smile lurking around Judson's mouth. "I was going to give you a call in the morning, but since you're here—" When he glanced at Charles, his expression was convincingly devoid of humor. "Maybe you can give me your answer now. I need someone right away."

"I would certainly be interested in looking over what you've got," Charles was quick to assure him. "And I do appreciate the offer."

"Good."

Kathryn watched the self-satisfaction settle into Judson's expression. Irritation forced her teeth together. It was easy to see the purpose of his plan. With Charles on his payroll, Judson could control much of his time, hence much of her time. Apparently she had underestimated the extent of Judson's determination. She wasn't flattered by the lengths he was willing to go. She felt threatened and angry. Charles was her shield and he was defecting to the enemy.

Buck sauntered around the side of the house, all slicked up for a night on the town. He was dressed in stiff Levi's and a white shirt, his leathery cheeks freshly shaved. When he rejoined the group, his glance made a swift arc to assess the situation.

"You're looking ornery tonight, Buck." Charles commented on the keen sparkle in the older man's eyes, failing to discern the cause of it. "Are you two going out honky-tonking?" he guessed, the last words sounding funny and inappropriate coming from him.

"Nope. Me and Judd were just goin' out to have some supper." He grinned and ran a dryly amused eye over Charles's suit and the chic design of Kathryn's dress. "Are you two goin' out honky-tonkin'?"

"Not tonight." Charles laughed, because it wasn't something they'd do any night. The local taverns weren't Charles's style. "We were just headed for Tiny's. You and Judd are more than welcome to join us." He glanced at Judson and explained, "Tiny's Restaurant has a fantastic smorgasbord on Fridays. Why don't you come along?''

Kathryn panicked. She wanted to nudge Charles or kick him or come right out and tell him to shut up. But of course, she couldn't. Charles had no idea what he was doing.

He couldn't even begin to guess how difficult it would be for Kathryn to spend time in Judson's company—or how dangerous. Being exposed to a man she had once loved beyond reason was tempting fate. It wasn't the way to cement her commitment to Charles, and that's what she desperately needed to do.

''That's where we'd planned to go anyway, wasn't it Buck?'' Indirectly Judson gave his approval of the plan.

Buck only hesitated a fraction of a second. ''Yeah.'' He watched Kathryn closely.

''Then it's all settled,'' Charles declared. ''Kathryn wants to walk down. You can either join us or we'll meet you there.''

The car door opened and Judson stepped out. ''We may as well walk, too.''

''Might as well,'' Buck agreed, and the four of them set off down the sidewalk.

CHAPTER EIGHT

THE SIDEWALK WAS JUST WIDE ENOUGH to walk two abreast. Buck and Judson had taken the lead, with Charles and Kathryn a step behind, bringing up the rear. Before they'd walked half a block, the arrangement was changed. Kathryn found herself strolling beside Buck, while Charles moved forward to talk business with Judson. Actually Charles did most of the talking, subtly injecting his credentials and some of his more impressive past experiences into the nearly one-sided conversation. Judson nodded and responded in all the right places, but Kathryn sensed his disinterest and impatience.

All the way to the restaurant she watched the two men. With the two of them walking side by side, it was impossible not to make some comparisons. Aside from the obvious physical differences and the difference in age, there was an air about each of the men that set them even further apart. Charles was so smooth and worldly; Judson was ruggedly virile and earthy. Both were men of distinction, yet Charles seemed to fade into the shadow of the younger man.

It wasn't something that happened often.

Charles normally stood out in a crowd. The more people there were, the brighter the light of his charismatic charm would shine. At the moment that light didn't even seem to be flickering. Kathryn wasn't sure whether that impression was caused by her imagination or by the way Charles was practically humbling himself as he worked continuously to sell Judson on his capabilities.

The conversation was interrupted when they entered the restaurant, a drab one-room establishment that got its good reputation strictly from the quantity and quality of the food it served. Black vinyl-upholstered booths lined one wall, and a long sideboard heaped with food ran the length of the opposite wall. A half-dozen tables took up the remaining floor space.

It was still early, so Tiny's was just beginning to fill up. A handful of people formed a short line at the sideboard. Charles insisted the other two men go first, then led Kathryn to join the line.

"Buck?" A slim woman of about fifty-five approached them from the opposite side of the dining room. Her hair was black, sprinkled with gray, and cut short in a no-nonsense style that seemed in keeping with the almost piercing directness of her pale-green eyes.

Buck turned at the questioning use of his name. His hard-bitten features were instantly softened by a wide grin. It seemed to light up his whole face.

"Ruby!" He greeted the woman with the pleasure of someone meeting a long-lost friend.

Since he'd been with the woman only that

morning, Kathryn's eyes narrowed on the pair in quiet speculation.

"What are you doin' here?" Buck asked. "Checkin' out the competition?"

"Actually, I—" That clear, penetrating gaze shifted away from Buck's face. It lighted on Judson. "Judd Taylor," the widow identified him instantly. "I heard you were back in town."

Judson looked at the woman, one eye narrowed slightly. Then a slow, dazzling grin appeared as he recognized her. "Ruby Weatherby. If you ain't a sight for sore eyes. I think you're looking even prettier than the last time I saw you."

The words, the tone of his voice and that smile all combined to make his comments an outrageous form of flattery. Most women would have blushed, become embarrassed, or would have tried to turn his compliments aside. Ruby Weatherby didn't even bat an eye.

"Darn right," she said, and held his sparkling look with that level green gaze of hers. Only a hint of a smile tugged upward at the corners of her mouth.

She had a poker face, Buck had said. And Kathryn was inclined to agree. It was impossible to tell what the woman was thinking. To go along with her deadpan expression, Ruby had a delightfully dry sense of humor, but most people had to get to know her before they could tell for sure when she was joking. Even then, it could, at times, be difficult. She was a hard person to get to know, but Kathryn had always liked her and felt the effort had been worth it.

Those pale-green eyes looked straight at Kathryn, then Charles, then Judson, revealing a razor-sharp intelligence, but little else. "What brings you back to Deepwater, Judd?"

"Business. But the trip's turning out to be a pleasure—in several ways." Although he never looked at Kathryn, she knew the remark included her.

"Will you be around here long?" Ruby asked Judson. Kathryn unconsciously held her breath, waiting for his answer.

"That's something I don't know for sure." Judson shrugged. "The answer's riding on a lot of things. I've never been a patient man, but this is one time I'm going to have to bide my time. The deal I'm trying to put together here will be worth it if it all pans out."

Again Ruby let her glance drift to Kathryn. "I hope you succeed."

Ruby knew, Kathryn thought. Somehow Ruby knew the "deal" Judson was talking about meant that he wanted to start afresh with Kathryn. And the widow was sincere in her hopes for Judson's success!

Why didn't Ruby think that Charles was the best choice of the two men? With a younger woman, Kathryn wouldn't have been surprised at an endorsement of Judson. But Ruby Weatherby had been around a long time. She'd seen men like Judson come and go, leaving a trail of broken hearts in their wake.

Yet, according to Buck, Ruby had always

thought Kathryn should have been with Judson—right from the beginning. Before his success, before he'd had a chance to prove that his intentions were honorable, before he'd had a chance to prove anything.

Like Kathryn, the widow must have sensed something different about Judd, something special that separated him from the other drifters. True, he had that reckless, restless streak universal to the breed, but he had loved Kathryn. She had known it. Even Ruby, a relative stranger, had been able to recognize it. Only Mattie had doubted him. And Kathryn had paid a brutal price for her mother's bitterly suspicious outlook.

The line moved forward. Judson, Buck and Ruby had turned to face Kathryn and Charles and include them in the conversation. Now Judson glanced over his shoulder.

"Shall we all grab a plate and find a place to sit down?" Judson suggested. "You will join us, won't you, Ruby? And Jake. Where is the old rascal?" His eyes made a quick sweep of the dining room as Judson remembered Ruby's husband.

Kathryn glanced at Ruby, wondering if such questions bothered her. It had been five years since Jake's death, but some people were never able to talk comfortably about a lost mate. Typically, Ruby appeared unfazed.

"I guess you didn't know," she said matter-of-factly. "I'm alone now." Nothing about her attitude asked for pity.

Still, Judson's face became etched with grim

sympathy. "No. I didn't know. I'm sorry Ruby. Jake was a good man."

"Yes, he was," she agreed. "And I'm glad to have had the time together that we did. It was good."

By her phrasing Ruby made it clear that it had been good, but it was over. She had obviously loved her husband, but she had also been able to let him go. It was something Kathryn had wondered about—whether Ruby was still clinging to Jake's memory and that was the reason she and Buck had maintained a friendly distance. Apparently that wasn't the problem. Buck must have just been stating facts when he'd told her they were only friends and that's the way they both wanted it.

"After Jake died I sold the store," Ruby said. "Now I'm doing what I always wanted to do. I own a restaurant on the square—run it myself. You'll have to stop by some morning. You never know—if you can catch me in a generous mood I might give you breakfast on the house."

Judson smiled, put at ease by Ruby's remarks, which assured him she wasn't upset by the mention of her late husband. "You'd do that for me?" He tipped his head to the side, flirting with the widow.

"I might." There was an impression of a shrug, but Ruby never moved a muscle. "You'll have to take your chances." She watched him for a second, straight-faced, then let a half smile curve her mouth. "Be sure to stop by." She turned to Buck. "See you in the morning, as usual?"

"You bet." He frowned slightly, realizing she

was going to leave. "Aren't you going to sit down with us?"

"No, we were just on our way out."

With a final goodbye that included everyone in the group, Ruby moved off toward the door. Buck's slightly frowning glance followed her, as did Kathryn's.

The cash register was situated to the left of the door. Ruby stopped beside it, although she didn't join the line of patrons waiting to pay. A balding, squatly built man gave the widow a quick smile as he handed the cashier a bill.

A blue plaid western shirt was stretched over the man's large belly, the worn-soft material gaping a bit between the pearl snaps. A toothpick dangled from the corner of his mouth. It bobbed with the motion of his lips when he said something to the cashier. Taking his change, he shoved it into the front pocket of his stiff Levi's and escorted Ruby to the door. As they left, the man clamped a straw cowboy hat atop his head.

"Well, I'll be—"

The softly muttered words drew Kathryn's glance to Buck. His expression was closed, as it often was. It didn't give Kathryn the slightest hint about what Buck thought of Ruby's date. She sighed inwardly, thinking that Buck and Ruby were cut from the same cloth. Trying to figure either one of them out was useless.

"Coming, darling?" Charles prompted her to follow him to the sideboard, heaped with enormous amounts of food.

Fried chicken, pot roast, ham and spareribs

were displayed alongside a variety of vegetables, salads and side dishes. For bread, there was a choice of whole wheat, white, corn bread, or blueberry muffins, all of which were freshly baked.

With so many things to sample, it didn't take long to fill their plates. Charles led the way to a round table for four. After Kathryn was seated, he pulled out the chair on her right for himself. Judson took the chair on her left and Buck settled into the remaining chair.

It was a small table, which made for close quarters. Especially when there were three long-legged men vying for a place to put their feet. Every time Kathryn moved, she found herself bumping knees with either Charles or Judson. In one case, she felt reassured by the contact. In the other, her senses were excited by tingly little danger signals. It seemed significant, a small-scale demonstration of what each man represented to her. It also seemed significant that she was sandwiched between them.

"You aren't eating, Katy," Judson observed, and it was the first time that evening that Kathryn noticed him directing a remark specifically to her.

"I've eaten a lot," she lied. "It just doesn't look like it because I put too much on my plate."

The truth was, she'd barely touched her food, spending more time playing with it than she did eating it. Her stomach wasn't behaving well at all, flip-flopping every time she felt the light brush of his leg against hers or became aware of his eyes running warmly over her. The latter happened less frequently than the former, because Charles resumed their earlier conversation and politeness demanded that Judson give his attention to him.

Kathryn had never known Charles to ramble on so much. He monopolized the table talk all through dinner and right up through the second cup of coffee. When they finally left the table and moved toward the cashier, Charles insisted on paying the tab. While he was taking care of the check, someone at a nearby table called to Buck. He walked over, leaving Judson and Kathryn alone.

"It seems we were destined to have dinner together after all," Judson murmured, looking very pleased with himself.

"Somehow I think you gave destiny a little help," she said tightly.

"Me?" He shook his head to deny the accusation. "I'm innocent. If you're going to blame someone, blame Charles. He did the inviting."

"You've been controlling the evening right from the start," she accused. The resentful green glint in her eyes dared him to deny her charge.

He didn't, shrugging and grinning instead. "It wasn't hard to do," he said dryly. "All I had to do was pull Charles's string."

"That isn't funny, Judson."

"No, it isn't," he agreed. "In fact, it's kind of stomach turning—but only because it's true."

Kathryn didn't like their conversation. It put her on the defensive and that wasn't the way to win. Ignoring his insinuations about Charles's character, she attacked instead.

"I was very surprised when you showed up to-night," she informed him with honeyed sweetness. "I thought you were going to wait to hear from me."

"I did wait," he insisted with a mocking lilt of his voice. "I guess, though, I'm like you, Katy. I don't like to wait too long."

It was on the tip of her tongue to challenge the remark and offer their lengthy separation as proof that he didn't mind waiting. It was still so difficult to believe that he actually had come back. She knew his comment had been a reference to the way she'd supposedly married someone else. While his remark made her uneasy, she wasn't about to deny it. But neither did she wish to discuss it.

"I thought you wanted to forget the past," she challenged him with his own words.

Surprise flickered across his face. "Do you?"

"Yes. I want to forget it—all of it."

"I came back," he declared grimly.

"Yes," Kathryn agreed, just as grimly.

He had come back, and his attempts to see her had been thwarted. But if everything had worked out the way they'd planned, who was to say how long it would have lasted? Judson hadn't changed. She remembered too well his comments at dinner that first night when Buck had asked him about settling down. "Life would be too boring," he'd said, and meant it. He would always need a change of pace and scenery. There would be no guarantees that he wouldn't eventually become bored with her, too. It wasn't a chance she was willing to take.

"It's over, Judson. I have a new life and I'm very happy with it. I have the shop. I have Charles. I don't need or want anything else."

"It isn't over." Judson's jaw was hard and unyielding. "Not by a long shot."

Kathryn was about to restate her position when Buck chose that moment to join them. A second later, Charles returned and they all filed out of the restaurant.

There was a languid warmth to the evening air, a lowering sun laying a golden glow over the peaceful neighborhood just off the town square. It was somnolent and still, with not enough breeze to rustle the leaves of the thick canopy of shade trees overhead. The clean smell of freshly mowed grass was all around them, some of the cut blades scattered on the sidewalk.

Everything was lush and green, a natural result of the richness of Kansas soil. Most of the houses in Deepwater were two-story, much like the structure of the boutique. White was the predominant choice for paint. The crisp coolness of the houses stood out against the vibrant green. Locusts were buzzing and other insects were warming up for their nightly symphony.

It was a peaceful setting, but being outdoors didn't help to ease Kathryn's tension. She watched the way Judson drew Charles forward to engage him in conversation, then skillfully involve Buck. Ultimately Judson dropped back beside Kathryn.

"Buck asked Charles a question." The mocking lift of an eyebrow indicated that Judson considered that to be a mistake on Buck's part. "It looks like he's going to be a while answering it."

"Buck asked how his trip was," Kathryn reminded him, fully aware that Judson had led him right into asking the question. "That's a pretty general question, so Charles will give a general answer, one that covers all the highlights."

"It's general all right—generally long," Judson murmured with mocking amusement.

The space between them and the two men in the lead had widened. Still, Kathryn kept her voice very low, although she doubted Charles could hear her anyway. He was talking louder than necessary as he gave a detailed account of his visit with the governor. Kathryn had the unkind suspicion that the speech was being given for Judson's benefit, not Buck's. The worst of it was, Charles was trying so hard to impress Judson, and Judson couldn't care less what he had to say. She felt sorry for Charles, and angry with Judson for making him look like a fool.

"That's your future," Judson murmured, inclining his head slightly toward Charles. He took a cigarette out of his pocket and lit it. "Are you sure you want to forget about the past?"

"If you find Charles so boring, why did you accept his invitation to join us?" Kathryn bristled, ignoring his question.

"Because I wanted to have dinner with you," he stated simply, and made no apologies for his underhanded tactics.

"And that's why you asked Charles to work for

you, too.'' She tossed her head in a show of angry disgust, unsure what upset her most—Judson's offer, or Charles's eagerness to accept.

''Now you flatter yourself too much.'' Judson's mouth quirked in a dry, humorless line as his glance flicked to her, then ahead. ''I asked Charles to work for me because he's a good attorney.''

''I suppose it's merely a coincidence that he happens to be my fiancé,'' she challenged.

''That would be stretching it just a bit.'' His laughing brown eyes sparkled. ''No, I wouldn't call it a coincidence—just a convenience. And I really do need some legal work done.'' He could tell how skeptical she was about the legitimacy of his claim.

''Well I don't like it.'' It was a vast understatement.

''Oh? Why not?'' The mildness of his inquiry was at odds with the complacent glitter in his eyes.

''I don't want you involved in our lives.'' The declaration was spoken through gritted teeth. ''Tell Charles you changed your mind and leave us alone.''

''Why should I do that?'' he wondered.

Kathryn bit her lip. ''So Charles and I can have a chance to be happy. It'll never happen as long as you're here.'' Kathryn was only beginning to realize and accept the bitter truth of that fact. With Judson around, it was too easy to find fault with Charles. It cost her a lot to admit it, but nothing else had worked. She felt desperate. ''I need that, Judson—a chance to be happy.''

His lips tightened, the line of his jaw growing hard. "I want you to be happy, Katy."

"Then you'll tell Charles you changed your mind?" It was less a question, more a challenge to the sincerity of his statement.

"No." There was no hesitation. "I told you before that you'll never be happy with Charles—or anyone like him."

And as before, Kathryn struggled against the conviction that he might be right.

"I believe that's something I should decide." But her decision would be a great deal easier if he wasn't so close to her. Kathryn was conscious of being slightly short of breath and knew it wasn't caused by their leisurely pace.

"I agree." He nodded. "But since you don't seem to be capable of making an intelligent decision right now, I'll have to help you."

"I don't need or want any help from you. I just want you to leave."

"If you and Charles have anything worthwhile between you, my being around won't make any difference," he said in a perfectly reasonable tone.

It shouldn't, but it did. "Let him go, Judson." Kathryn half pleaded, half commanded.

"It's his decision," he reminded her.

"You know as well as I do he'll take that job. You knew it before you asked," she accused.

"I know he'll do anything to get next to what he sees as power," he said quietly. "I guess he thinks some of it will rub off. In the long run, he's probably right. Connections and money will take him wherever he wants to go. He knows that.''

"I hate you for what you're doing." A sudden rush of tears burned her eyes.

"If you don't want him to work for me, tell him about us," he challenged. "That *should* stop him." But the way he emphasized the word revealed his doubts that it would.

"Why should it?" she countered, striving for airy sarcasm. "I don't think Charles would be either surprised, devastated or shocked to learn that I had a boyfriend when I was seventeen.''

"Would he be surprised, devastated or shocked to learn that what was between us isn't dead?" Judson mocked her for making their relationship sound so trivial—like nothing more than a teenage flirtation.

"It is dead." But her words sounded weak even to her own ears.

"Does he know we were together last night?" Dropping his cigarette, he crushed it beneath his heel and shoved his hands into the front pockets of his gray slacks.

"I told him." Her chin lifted to a haughty, defensive angle.

"Everything?" It was a low taunt, his glance sliding to her with amused skepticism.

"Of course not *everything*," she snapped as her mind returned to the heat of their embrace with much too vivid recall.

"Why didn't you?"

"Because!" she flared, then pulled her emotions together with iron control. When she looked at him, her features were a calm, cool mask. "Because I didn't want Charles upset over nothing."

"He probably wouldn't get upset over nothing," Judson pointed out. "Therein is where the problem lies, isn't it, my darlin'? If you won't admit it to me, at least admit it to yourself. There is a very definite something between us. Always has been, always will be."

Quickening her pace, Kathryn decided to put an end to the conversation with Judd. She quietly joined Buck and Charles and during the rest of the walk she kept her mouth firmly closed, her gaze fixed stubbornly ahead. On the surface, she was ignoring Judson. But only on the surface.

"Here we are already." Charles seemed surprised when they stopped in front of the boutique.

"Yes, here we are," Kathryn murmured dryly. The walk had seemed exceedingly long to her, grating on her nerves every step of the way.

No one seemed to have anything to say. The silence became awkward. This was the moment that invitations to come inside were usually issued. Under normal circumstances, Kathryn would have made the offer automatically. But these were not normal circumstances, and she had no intention of allowing propriety to pressure her into prolonging this situation.

"Come on in." When it became clear that Kathryn wasn't going to play hostess, Buck took it upon himself to extend the general invitation. But it seemed to be more a polite gesture than a gen-

uine desire for company. For Buck, that was unusual. "I'll put on a pot of coffee," he offered,
somewhat grudgingly.

Both men were going to accept. Kathryn could
see it in their expressions. She could have screamed.

"Count me out," she said bluntly. "I have a lot
of things to do yet before I go to bed." And her
agenda didn't include getting stuck between Judson and Charles for the rest of the evening. She remembered Charles's earlier promise that she could
choose what they'd do after dinner. A promise
he'd obviously forgotten. Suddenly she didn't
want to spend the remainder of the evening with
Charles, not even if they were alone.

"I've got some things to take care of, too,"
Judson said, even though Kathryn knew he'd been
on the verge of accepting.

Disappointment clouded Charles's expression
when Judson refused. There was little left for him
to do but follow suit. "I have some work I need to
catch up on myself." He didn't want to be the
only one with nothing to do. "I'll see you tomorrow, Kathryn."

It was more habit than anything that brought
Charles over to kiss her goodbye. He barely
brushed her lips with his mouth, then the kiss was
over. Yet this casual suggestion of intimacy in front
of Judson made Kathryn intensely self-conscious.

Involuntarily her glance traveled to him, darting
away when she saw how closely he was watching
the exchange. An uncomfortable feeling of dis-
loyalty went through her. The problem was, she

felt disloyal to Judson. Kathryn was shaken by the realization. Without a word to anyone, she pivoted and walked to the house.

Buck came in only a minute or two behind her. Kathryn had barely sat down at the kitchen table when he clomped up the back steps and walked in the door. She glanced at him briefly as her fingers drummed the tabletop in unconcealed agitation. She was seething and simmering, annoyed with herself, but also angry with Charles. He was to blame for the entire evening. If he hadn't been so anxious to do business with Judson. . . .

Kathryn pushed out of the chair, too restless to remain seated. "I don't know what's the matter with Charles," she said angrily, facing Buck. He was leaning against the counter, wearing a preoccupied expression. He didn't look much happier than Kathryn was, but of course it was hard to tell. "The man's a politician, for heaven's sake!" Kathryn declared, waving a hand through the air. "He's always using the same tactics Judson used on him tonight! Why can't Charles see through all that phony flattery?"

"Some people are just plain stupid," Buck muttered with a deepening frown. "But I'll tell ya one thing. I sure never thought Ruby was one of them people."

"Ruby?" The change of subject completely threw her. "What's she got to do with this?"

Buck's mouth went tight. "What I'd like to know, is what's she got to do with Hank Wright." The volume of his voice was low, but Kathryn realized he was angry. His large hands gripped the edge of the counter so tightly the knuckles were white. "What does she see in that potbellied rancher?" It was a question rife with impatience and frustration.

Kathryn's eyes widened. Buck was actually jealous! His present mood explained why he hadn't appeared very enthusiastic about inviting Charles and Judson in. Like her, he had spent the entire evening pretending to have a good time. And now, like her, he needed to blow off steam.

"You don't like the man?" Since Buck wouldn't normally let his feelings about Ruby come out in the open, Kathryn gave him a ready-made excuse for his statements about the rancher. It wasn't fair to question him now about information he would probably never confide when he wasn't upset.

"Aw, he's all right, I guess," Buck admitted grudgingly. "Can't say I know him well enough to say anything bad...course, I can't say anything good about him either." He kicked at the floor with the toe of a scuffed cowboy boot. "Never talked to him more'n a couple times in my life. That was enough, too," he snorted. "Pert near bored me to tears. Who would've ever thought a sharp gal like Ruby would end up fallin' for a stick-in-the-mud like him?"

"Just because they had dinner together, it doesn't necessarily mean Ruby has fallen for him." Kathryn argued the point logically, but she was reluctant to try too hard to convince Buck that the widow's feelings toward the rancher weren't serious.

Granted, such an assertion would improve Buck's spirits, but Kathryn had no way of knowing the truth about Ruby. She remembered thinking that Ruby must have indicated a lack of interest in Buck as a suitor. Perhaps the widow had rejected Buck's attempts at advancing the relationship beyond the stage of friendship. If that was true, there was no point in encouraging Buck. In the long run, it would only make acceptance more difficult.

"It means somethin'," Buck insisted. "Ruby ain't been out on a date with nobody since Jake died." He lowered his gaze to the floor, absently watching the scuffing motion of his booted foot. He looked defeated. It pained Kathryn to see it.

"Five years is a long time," she murmured, feeling the need to say something, yet aware that her words were inadequate.

"Don't I know it." One side of his mouth was pulled up in a humorless smile. "I been waitin' all that time, thinkin' maybe the day would come when Ruby would give me the signal—somethin' that would let me know she was ready to start thinkin' about another man besides Jake." His breath came out on a silent laugh. "I guess I got the signal tonight, loud and clear."

"What do you mean, you've been *waiting*, all this time?" It was obvious that Buck wanted to talk, so Kathryn was more than willing to oblige. Something about this conversation puzzled her, although she couldn't put her finger on exactly what it was.

"I just told ya," he muttered impatiently, not overly anxious to repeat himself. "I been waitin' for her to let me know she's ready to let another man in her life."

Kathryn frowned. She thought she was beginning to see the problem. "Have you ever let her know you were interested in...." She hesitated, choosing her words with care. "In being more than a friend to Ruby?"

An exasperated snort came from Buck. He lifted his head and looked at her as if she was dense. "How could I have helped raise somebody who ain't got no more smarts than to ask a question like that?" he wondered. "Don't you know what would've happened if I had started talkin' serious to her?"

"What?"

"Why, I'd have scared her off!" he explained. "It was up to her to let me know when she was over Jake and ready to get on with her life. I guess she just wants to get on with it with somebody else."

"Buck!" Kathryn stared at him. "If you've never indicated that you're interested, you have no way of knowing that she isn't."

"She's out with Hank Wright tonight," he offered as proof. "Not me."

"He probably asked her," Kathryn pointed out. "Did you?"

Buck walked to the table and sat down, his expression once again closed, as if the matter had been settled in his mind long before the conversation had ever been started.

"Kathryn, I been playin' poker all my life. Any good gambler knows that the secret to winnin'— or at least breakin' even—is knowin' when to keep bettin' a hand and when to throw it in. Only the fools play out a losin' hand. I ain't no fool. Five years of bettin' the same cards is long enough."

The chair legs scraped the floor as Kathryn pulled out a chair and joined him at the table. "I understand what you're saying, Buck, but I think you're giving up too easily. You're accepting defeat when Ruby isn't even aware that you were even in the battle! What happened to the man who believes in fighting for what's right?" She challenged him with his own words, words he had used in defending the barroom fight he'd started over Mattie. "You were willing to fight for my mother," she reminded him. "You fought *for* her, and you fought *with* her for twenty years. Why?" It was a question she'd wanted to ask for a long time. Now seemed like a golden opportunity. She studied him for a second. "Why did you put up with my mother all those years?"

Buck considered the question, then gave her a long, level look. "You're probably not going to understand this, but in her own way, Mattie needed me. She was too scared to admit to needin' or wantin' or carin' about anybody, but she needed me and I was always there for her."

"Even though she never gave you anything in

return," Kathryn said, unable to keep the bitterness out of her voice. Her mother had not only taken from Kathryn, she had also taken from Buck, robbing him of twenty years of his life.

"I didn't say that." Buck denied her assessment. "Mattie didn't have to tell me how she felt about me. I knew. We had our problems, but what was between us was somethin' special, so don't you try to make it sound like it wasn't. She needed me and I needed to be needed. I'm not sorry about the years I spent with her. The only thing I do regret is that your pa hurt her so bad she never could get over it. That's why she couldn't really open up with me. . . ."

The explanation brought an impatient sigh from Kathryn. Her parents' separation provided the excuse for everything her mother had done wrong, including Mattie's interference with Judson. In Kathryn's opinion, it was far from sufficient.

"I know it was hard for her when he left her, but—"

"Yeah, that was tough for her, but his leavin' was only part of it," Buck said. "When she first met him, she fell head over heels in love. Ran right off to Nevada to get married. After that, it was all downhill. They traveled around the country, never stayin' in one place for more'n a month or two at a time. He never held down a job long enough to make a decent living, so they spent a lot of nights sleepin' in the back of his pickup, parked along the highway. Whenever they did manage to scrape together a few extra dollars, Mattie never saw it.

Your pa either gambled it away, or spent it on liquor—or sometimes other women.''

Kathryn leaned back against the chair, letting the information sink in. She had never heard the details of how her mother had been forced to live. It came as a shock.

"Why did she stay with him?" she asked.

"What choice did she have?" Buck countered. "She had nowhere to go. She left home against her parents' wishes and wasn't welcome to come back. She had a baby on the way, and she was hardly more'n a child herself."

"I see," Kathryn murmured, and felt a rush of sympathy for the young frightened girl her mother had been.

"She went through hell with that man, Kathryn. So when you remember your ma, try to understand some of the things she did. It don't make 'em any more right, but she never in her life set out to hurt a soul. This trouble between you and Judd for instance. Mattie was only tryin' to make sure you never had to suffer what she suffered. Try to put yourself in her place. You might have done the same thing."

An instant denial formed on her lips.

"I told you to put yourself in her place," Buck stated. "Like the old sayin' goes, 'Don't judge a man until you've walked a mile in his moccasins—or somethin' like that.''

Kathryn bit at her lip, trying to imagine herself living her mother's life. No matter how hard she tried, she couldn't. Although the circumstances were somewhat similar to her own experience, there was one major difference that had made it all halfway bearable for Kathryn. She had had love to cling to—first Judson's, then her mother's. After that she had had the shop. Mattie had had nothing and no one at all. Kathryn had only a vague idea of what it would feel like to be in that position—except she knew it would be hell, as Buck had said.

Given the same circumstances, would she do what Mattie had done to protect her child? In all honesty, Kathryn knew she couldn't be positive about her answer. She hadn't lived it, so she really didn't know how the experience would have affected her judgment. But she had to admit, the impulse to protect—at any cost—would have been there. She simply couldn't say with any real certainty whether or not she would have obeyed it.

"I'm not sure what I would have done," she admitted.

A glimmer of approval appeared in Buck's eyes. "None of us is, Kathryn. That's what we have to remember."

She smiled and suddenly felt just a little bit teary-eyed. "I'm really glad my mother had you, Buck. For once in her life, she was a very lucky woman."

He shrugged the comment aside, but it pleased him. "We were both lucky. I knew the first time I saw her that we had something to give each other. I read it in her face." A quick grin came, then disappeared. "That's the gambler showin' up in me again. I've always had a knack for knowin' what the cards were by readin' people's faces. No matter what their mouth said, their eyes told me whether they were a friend or an enemy or whatever else I needed to know. 'Cept Ruby. She was a different story. I met my match in that woman. Never could tell if I had a winnin' or losin' hand, and I didn't want to throw it in until I was sure. Now, after five years, the cards are all on the table.''

With an air of acceptance, he stood up, stretching his arms over his head and letting them fall loosely back to his sides. ''It's been a long day. Think I'll have an early night.''

''But Buck, if you talk to Ruby—''

''The dealin's done, Kathryn. Leave it at that. I'm going to.''

CHAPTER NINE

SATURDAY WAS ALWAYS KATHRYN'S BIGGEST DAY at the shop. Traditionally it was shopping day for the local farmers, ranchers and their wives.

By noon she was swamped with customers as the day ran true to form. She skipped lunch and wished she'd remembered to take time for breakfast. From experience she knew there wouldn't be a lull all day. She was thankful for the business, but even more thankful for being busy. It kept her from thinking about Judson.

At two o'clock the small boutique was still brimming with women. Taking care of them all was no easy task, but Kathryn managed. She was kept constantly on the move, dashing from the cash register to the fitting rooms and to the numerous display racks to offer suggestions and assistance. Occasionally she expanded the route to include the storeroom where the fur coats and the easily damaged garments were kept, along with extra sizes or different colors of the merchandise shown in the store. Once in a while she helped a woman who was trying on a pair of shoes.

Her arms were laden with dresses as she waited patiently for a customer to decide there was enough of a selection to begin trying them on. The woman added another dress to the accumulating pile and turned back to the rack. Kathryn's restless gaze traveled around the shop, lighting on the Harper sisters. It was little wonder she hadn't seen them come in. Eileen nudged her sister and waddled over to greet Kathryn.

"I didn't expect to see you again so soon," Kathryn said, but let them know she was delighted to have them there.

"It's shopping day," Nadine declared. They were keeping to the tradition, despite the fact that they had the freedom to shop any day of the week, since neither of them worked.

"It certainly is." Smiling, Kathryn rolled her eyes in agreement.

"You should hire someone to help you out, Kathryn." Eileen was mildly scolding. "You're running yourself ragged. I don't see how you manage to keep up such a pace."

"It's usually only like this on Saturday." Actually, Kathryn had considered hiring part-time help, but the offer of so few hours a week—and on weekends—didn't appeal to many.

Kathryn was just as glad. Even though hiring someone would have lessened her work load, she always experienced a vague reluctance about giving someone else any rights to the operation of the boutique. She wanted to retain sole responsibility for the business. Its success or failure depended on her and her alone, and she liked the feeling of self-command that came with the knowledge that she was totally independent, relying on the contributions of no other person to succeed. Except, of course her clientele. But whether or not people chose her shop depended on Kathryn, too.

She smiled at Eileen Harper. "One chaotic day a week I can handle. Then I have all day Sunday to rest up from it."

"Still—" The woman would have added more, but she was interrupted by a series of hard, attention-getting raps on the large window facing the street.

The feminine chatter in the shop instantly died down. Everyone, including Kathryn, was staring at the man standing outside. Her eyes widened when she recognized Judson. His forehead was pressed against the window glass, his hands cupped next to his face to eliminate the sun's glare and enable him to see inside. For several seconds, he just stood there. Total silence descended on the shop.

Certain now that he had her attention, Judson grinned. Then he waved his fingertips and winked broadly. The other women began to chuckle at his antics, obviously finding them charming.

"Oh, look, Nadine!" Eileen exclaimed. "That's the man who was here the other day! He's out to catch Kathryn."

In the quiet of the shop, the remark seemed very loud. A blush stained Kathryn's cheeks with high color. She took a step toward the door, intending to meet Judson on his way in, then prevent him from causing another scene by sending him right

back out. An attractive brunet that Kathryn had
gone to school with caught her arm.

"If that man is out to catch you, don't run too
fast," she advised. "If I were you, I'd stand still!"

"I'll keep that in mind." Kathryn smiled stiffly
and walked to the door.

As she braced herself for another confrontation
Kathryn caught sight of more movement outside
the window. Judson was walking down the street—
in the opposite direction. Stunned, Kathryn stared
after him. Why hadn't he come in? What had he
wanted?

She was suddenly attacked by an overwhelming
curiosity. Maybe he had come to say goodbye, to
tell her he was leaving—for good this time. The
thought filled her with an aching emptiness, an
emotion Kathryn refused to name. There was no
place in her future for a man like Judson. The
sooner he left town, the better, she told herself.

But if he was leaving, she wanted to know.

On impulse, she hurriedly continued on her
path to the door. The heat of the afternoon
blasted her as she stepped out onto the sidewalk.
She felt slightly faint, but the giddiness had nothing to do with the fact that she might be about to
say goodbye to him.

"Judson!" There was something very urgent in
the way her voice came out to call him back. As he
turned to look at her, Kathryn forced a smile to
her lips in an attempt to appear casual. "Did
you...want something?" This time her voice
sounded cool and calm.

"Just to see your gorgeous face," he explained, and flashed her a devastating white smile.

"Oh." She controlled her expression with remarkable aplomb. "I thought maybe you had stopped by to tell me something. . . like goodbye." Her throat seemed to curl around the words. Kathryn felt a stab of fear. Already just the thought of him leaving produced symptoms of near-panic. It was only a small sample of how she would feel if she allowed herself to really care. It was a warning signal she couldn't afford to ignore.

Judson Taylor had the ability to break down every barrier she'd erected to protect herself— against love. . . and eventual loss. For her, this man spelled danger. It was something she had to remember, at all costs.

"Goodbye?" Judson frowned, as if the idea of leaving had never occurred to him. "No, that isn't why I came." He approached her with a long slow stride. "I just wanted to see you, but I saw how busy you were, so I decided not to bother you. Considerate of me, wasn't it?"

But he always bothered her and he knew it. Kathryn deeply regretted the impulse that had made her approach him. It both angered and frightened her that she hadn't been able to control it. Of the choices available to her, anger seemed the best weapon with which to defend herself against the fatal attraction of a man like Judson.

"So you just knocked on the window and made a spectacle of yourself," she accused. "If you didn't want to bother me, why didn't you just walk on by—or better yet, not come at all?''

"Neither of those ideas would have worked," he stated with a decisive shake of his head. "I had to let you know I was around." His half smile was loaded with lethal charm, flirtatious and persuasive. "Can't have you forgetting about me, now can I?''

If only that was possible. Kathryn started to back away. "I . . . I have to get back to work."

He nodded slightly to acknowledge the validity of her excuse. "See you later, darlin'. Count on it." With that, he winked and turned to continue down the street.

Kathryn glanced at the shop, seeing the milling customers through the window. Because of Judson, she had completely forgotten about them, leaving the boutique unattended to come running outside. All over again, her world was beginning to revolve around Judson, and when he was present, everything else ceased to exist. Just by being around, he was working his way back into her feelings, her life . . . her heart. Somehow she had to put a stop to it. Before it was too late.

With a worried frown, she entered the boutique. Someone came in right behind her, jangling the bell. Startled, Kathryn whirled around. Her hand slipped up to cover her rapidly beating heart. She laughed in relief as Ruby Weatherby, dressed in black slacks and a black-and-white print top, paused just inside the doorway.

"Ruby, you startled me." Kathryn explained

her nervous reaction and laughed again, a little self-consciously. She wondered if the woman had seen her talking to Judson. If so, Kathryn's rattled state probably came as no surprise.

"Sorry." But Ruby looked preoccupied. Her pale-green eyes made a searching arc over the shop.

"What can I do for you?" As far as Kathryn could recall, Ruby had never bought anything at the boutique. Most of the clothes weren't really her style. She hated wearing dresses and usually preferred casual slacks and blouses.

Her clothing suited her personality—basic with a total lack of pretentiousness.

In Kathryn's opinion it was a quality that only made the woman more attractive. She was completely natural, never trying to impress anyone. Either you liked her or you didn't, and Ruby never seemed to worry about it one way or the other.

"Is Buck around?" Ruby came to the point, making no excuses or apologies for not being interested in looking over the boutique's elegant stock.

"No, I'm afraid I haven't seen him at all today," Kathryn said. She was dying to ask what Ruby wanted with Buck—whether there was an interest beyond friendship or not. But she had no idea how to broach the subject. "Is something wrong?"

"Not with me," Ruby stated. "But I wasn't sure about Buck. He said he'd be in for breakfast and he didn't show up. He missed lunch, too. I was on my way home and thought I'd stop and find out what happened."

"I don't know," Kathryn lied, aware that Buck probably needed to avoid the woman for a while and give himself time to recover from the blow of seeing her with another man.

"He seemed perfectly fine last night," Ruby recalled. Then a small smile played at the corners of her mouth. "I would like to have stayed and talked to you all, but I don't think Hank would have been very happy if I'd suggested it."

"That's too bad. We would have enjoyed your company," Kathryn assured her, creating an opening to work the topic around to where she wanted it. "Charles and I haven't seen you in ages. Of course, neither has Judson. And Buck always enjoys talking with you. It amazes me sometimes when I think of how long the two of you have been friends. You make quite a team."

"Yes, we do," she agreed with a slow thoughtful nod of her head. "That's why Hank was so anxious to leave Tiny's when he saw Buck come in. He admitted to being jealous of Buck." The small smile gradually disappeared, leaving her face unreadable. "I told Hank there was nothing to worry about. Buck has no designs on me whatsoever."

Kathryn raised her eyebrows slightly, noticing Ruby's choice of words. There was the same ring about the widow's explanations as Kathryn had detected in Buck's. While he had claimed Ruby wasn't interested, she seemed to be saying the same thing about him.

In the light of what she learned last night about Buck having never approached Ruby, Kathryn wasn't surprised. It was becoming more and more apparent that the absence of any honest communication between the two might be the only thing separating them.

"Doesn't Hank believe that?" Kathryn asked, but what she really wanted to know was whether Ruby believed it.

"No." She sighed. "The way Buck comes in to the café every day had Hank convinced." Her clear green eyes suddenly looked tired and very wise. "But what Hank believes isn't really very important—as long as *I* am aware of what the situation is. Which I am." She blinked and cast another glance around the showroom. "I can see you must be very busy. And I have a few more stops to make on my way home. I should be going."

"Goodbye."

Watching Ruby leave, Kathryn couldn't help but smile. Nothing had been said to indicate in any way that an advance from Buck would be rejected. And Kathryn had gotten the definite impression that Hank wasn't exactly the love of Ruby's life. She obviously wasn't concerned enough about the rancher's opinion of Buck to want him to stop visiting the café. If anything, Ruby had seemed a trifle bored with Hank's insecurities and petty jealousies.

It was a good sign, and Kathryn intended to relay her suspicions to Buck the very first chance she got.

THE ROUTINE WAS BROKEN when Charles failed to appear half an hour after closing time. Kathryn was curious, but she wasn't particularly concerned about it. Occasionally, he got detained. He'd be there as soon as he could. That certainly was one of the many things that made her relationship with Charles so appealing. She never had to wonder whether or not he would come. He might be late, but he wouldn't be seven years late.

Turning the key in the lock, Kathryn decided to take advantage of the extra time she'd been allotted before Charles came to take her to dinner. The day had been hectic and tiring. Her legs and feet ached from the hours of standing and walking in high heels without a break. She was slightly light-headed from hunger, but she couldn't resist the lure of a hot bath before she did anything else.

Slipping her shoes off, she let them hang from two hooked fingers as she went straight into the bathroom and turned on the faucets, adding scented oil to the water. The rising steam lifted the fragrance of the oil into the air as Kathryn undressed and piled her hair on top of her head so it wouldn't get wet. By the time she'd collected a towel and washcloth, the tub was nearly full. She stepped over the edge and sighed as one aching foot felt the soothing heat of the water. The telephone rang.

In a burst of exasperation, she jerked her foot from the tub and sent water sloshing over the edge. Her short terry-cloth robe was hanging on the doorknob. She slipped it on and entered the bedroom, snatching the receiver from its cradle. She tried to sound pleasant when she spoke. "Hello?"

"Kathryn? Charles. Sorry I'm late."

"It's okay," she assured him, and wasn't curious enough to ask what had kept him. "I was just about to take a bath. Do I have time?"

"Plenty. I've made reservations for eight o'clock. It isn't even six yet."

"Reservations?" That did arouse her curiosity. There were very few places in town that required reservations. "Where are we going?"

He named a very elegant French restaurant—or at least it had all the trappings of one, even if it wasn't exactly the genuine article. It was another recent addition to Deepwater, the kind of place the townspeople had demanded once their financial situations had improved and they'd felt themselves being elevated to new positions of social importance.

The chef at the restaurant had once been the best fry cook in town, but he'd transferred his skills to French cuisine, learning from cookbooks and trial and error. The waiters wore tuxedos and spoke with French accents, which added to the atmosphere as long as Kathryn ignored the fact that they were local boys, most of them straight off the ranch. When she couldn't ignore the pretentiousness, the whole experience took on a slightly ludicrous aspect, and she usually ended up laughing. Either way, though, she always enjoyed her evening there, and an invitation to the restaurant usually denoted a special occasion.

"How does that strike you?" Charles already knew the answer.

"What's the occasion?" Kathryn wondered if this was an attempt to make up for last night and the way he'd forgotten about letting her choose the evening's entertainment. If so, she accepted the gesture.

"I thought we'd celebrate the deal I made with Monument Oil this afternoon."

"Oh," she said in bitter understanding. "I see."

"I've asked Judd to join us," he informed her, then thought to inquire, "I hope you don't mind?"

Mind? It wasn't exactly the word Kathryn would have chosen to describe the sinking sensation in the pit of her stomach. Her thoughts raced to come up with an acceptable excuse for refusing the invitation. But how could she suddenly change her mind when she'd expressed such delight less than a minute before?

It would certainly arouse Charles's suspicions. An explanation would be required. Kathryn wasn't ready to tell him why she wanted to avoid Judson. She was aware that the old reasons were rapidly becoming overshadowed by new ones. They were no less disturbing and they would be a lot more difficult to explain. Especially to Charles—her fiancé.

"Kathryn? Are you there?" He questioned the long silence that had fallen.

"Oh...yes. I'm here." She faltered guiltily.

"I...I was just thinking. It seems like there was something else I was supposed to be doing this evening. I have a feeling something has slipped my mind. I was trying to remember...." It sounded feeble, even to her.

"If you've forgotten about it, it couldn't be that important anyway," Charles reasoned. "Besides, you don't want to miss dinner at your favorite restaurant."

There wasn't an adequate excuse, so she stopped searching for one. "No...of course not."

"Good, I'll pick you up at seven-thirty sharp."

"I'll be ready," she replied with a lack of her usual enthusiasm and hung up the phone.

Chewing the inside of her lip, Kathryn sat down on the edge of the bed. This continual contact with Judson had to stop. She wasn't sure how much longer her nerves could stand the strain—not to mention her relationship with Charles, which she desperately needed to protect.

With the way Judson's mind was running, a little reverse psychology seemed to be in order. It stood to reason that if her resistance only served to convince him that she cared, perhaps a bit of polite and smiling acceptance would prove that the power he held over her wasn't so great after all.

By seven-thirty, Kathryn had bathed, dressed and was waiting just inside the shop door. In keeping with the elegance of their destination, she wore an off-white chiffon dress, soft and flowing as whipped cream. Her hair fell to her shoulders in shining waves, pulled back on one side with a gold comb.

When Charles stopped the car in front of the shop, Judson was with him. Slipping outside, Kathryn locked the door. She finished just as Charles reached the sidewalk.

"Right on time," he noticed with an approving smile. He was a stickler for punctuality—in others at least.

Cupping a hand to her elbow, he steered her around to the driver's side of the waiting car. Kathryn felt nervous as she slid past the steering wheel to the center of the seat. She didn't have to look at him to be conscious of Judson sitting beside her. Her senses were instantly alert, picking up the provocative scent of his after-shave and the heat radiating from his body. It was impossible to keep her breathing from becoming shallow as she turned her head and found herself eye level with his mouth, only inches away.

Charles climbed behind the wheel and Kathryn inched closer to him, not caring that he needed a bit more room in order to drive comfortably and safely. A different kind of comfort and safety was uppermost in her mind. The thought prodded her memory back to her earlier resolution.

"How nice to see you again, Judson." To her amazement, it sounded convincing.

The greeting obviously caught Judson off guard. A skeptical amusement twitched at his mouth. "I'm glad you think so. But I assure you, the pleasure's all mine."

Kathryn couldn't have agreed with him more, but it was not in her best interest to let it show.

"Charles tells me that the two of you will definitely be working together."

"Yes. And because of that, I imagine we'll all be seeing a lot of each other from now on." His gaze was half-lidded as he watched her for a reaction.

"I'll look forward to it." Kathryn purposely threw him a curve. There was satisfaction in seeing a flash of surprise. It didn't last long, replaced by a slow, spreading grin.

"I'm really glad to hear you say that." His tone was earnest, but there was something about it she didn't trust. "A lot of women would object to a fifth wheel tagging along."

"Don't give that another thought." Charles was anxious to dismiss any doubts about Judson's welcome. "Kathryn loves having people around, lots of them. Don't you, darling?" He patted the hand she had lying in her lap.

"Of course." In reality, she cherished her quiet time, preferring the company of one or two people to the crowded parties she was obliged to attend. But she was used to Charles saying whatever he felt was necessary to win someone over. It went along with the job.

"That comes as quite a relief to me," Judson admitted smoothly. "Since I know so few people in town, maybe I could just latch on to the two of you while I'm here." His lazy glance held a wicked glitter. It began to dawn on Kathryn how she was being trapped.

"I certainly hope you do," Charles stated,

snapping up the bait. "The more time we spend together, the better understanding we'll have of one another's goals. I think that's important. Once you know where you're headed, it takes a shorter route to get there."

"I tell you, Charles, it's amazing that you and I think so much alike." It was a drawled remark, rich with barely veiled amusement. "Those are my sentiments exactly. I think we'll make a good team." His mocking gaze moved to include Kathryn. "Maybe we should call ourselves the three musketeers," he murmured dryly.

While Charles puffed up a little at Judson's approval of his philosophy, Kathryn turned her gaze ahead. Grim resignation showed in her expression, an acceptance of defeat for the way Judson had outmaneuvered her, using her tactics for his gain. Now there was no such thing as his uninvited presence. Charles had offered him free rein to interfere in their lives. Apprehension weighed on her shoulders, slumping them slightly as she leaned back against the seat.

"Oh, Kathryn, before I forget—" Charles gave her a quick glance "—would you mind looking in the glove compartment for a refill for my gold pen? You know where they are; somewhere in the back."

Automatically she leaned forward to comply with the request. She pressed the button to release the latch and the small door opened, revealing an overstuffed glove compartment. A book of matches and some golf tees tumbled to the floor.

Charles laughed. "You see why I didn't ask you to try and find it, Judd? Kathryn has some idea of the order of that mess. I can never find anything in there myself."

As Kathryn reached to retrieve the fallen articles, Judson did, too, and as they bent over the length of his thigh pressed against hers. The heat of his solidly muscled flesh burned through the thin fabric of her dress to electrify her nerve ends. Her shoulder brushed against his arm as her fingers, becoming all thumbs, scrambled for the golf tees.

Charles was explaining that he always ran out of ink at an inopportune moment. The topic conveniently led to a detailed account of how he had acquired the fourteen-karat gold pen from an English nobleman. It was an impressive story. Kathryn began to suspect the story was the real purpose of having her find a refill at that particular moment.

She wondered if Charles would have used the same ploy if he knew about the sensual havoc the forced contact with Judson was creating. Their fingers tangled as they groped on the floorboards. Then her hand was captured in his. Her heart beat loudly against her ribs. His breath was warm on her cheek, and Kathryn felt an involuntary tightening low in her stomach.

Snatching her hand from his grasp, Kathryn straightened. She didn't dawdle over finding the ink cartridge. As soon as she had it, she snapped the little door shut and made a hasty retreat back to Charles's side of the seat. Her face was flushed and her breathing had an uneven pattern. She was disturbed. Judson's lazy glance noted the changes in Kathryn with satisfaction.

CHAPTER TEN

THE EVENING WENT FROM BAD TO WORSE. Although Charles tried to appear casual about being connected with Monument Oil, he was plainly thrilled at the prospect. Understandably the subject dominated his thoughts. He barely paid attention to Kathryn, directing the majority of his comments to Judson. Judson's replies were generally brief. By the time the food was served, Kathryn's ravenous appetite had diminished to the point that she hardly ate anything.

"Two could easily live as cheaply as one if one of them happened to be Katy," Judson remarked, subtly letting her know he was aware of her loss of appetite, which betrayed her inner turmoil. "She eats like a bird."

It wasn't normally true. Charles noticed her full plate, a look of concern on his handsome face. "Are you feeling all right?"

"No, not really," she admitted. "I'm beginning to get a headache." Between going all day without nourishment and the pressure of her present situation, it was only natural.

"Another headache?" Judson sounded concerned as well, but the light in his eyes mocked her.

"You have had several lately, Kathryn," Charles realized with a frown. "Maybe you should see a doctor to find out what's causing them."

"It isn't necessary," she dismissed the idea. "I already know the cause. It's nothing serious."

"Are you positive it's nothing serious?" Judson wanted to know. A smile lurked in his dark eyes, showing that he suspected he was the cause, and challenging her evaluation of the problem.

"Yes." Her answer was too quick and too sharp. She saw Charles frown in surprised disapproval. "I've been under a lot of stress lately, that's all," she explained.

"You really should do something about that," Judson advised. "Prolonged periods of stress could be damaging to your health."

Charles was nodding a steady agreement as he chewed a bite of food.

"I intend to do something about it," Kathryn insisted, and fired a glance at Judson. "Eliminate the problem." To allay any suspicions, she explained to Charles, "I've been having some trouble with a couple of suppliers. I'm thinking about dropping them." She threw a sweetly barbed look in Judson's direction.

"Getting rid of your...suppliers—" his mouth quirked with contained amusement as he hesitated over the last word to let her know he was referring to himself "—may not be enough to relieve the tension you're feeling."

"Why ever not?" Her voice was honeyed.

"Because it's very likely that the pressure doesn't really stem from annoying circumstances at all." His eyes were alive with lazy interest. He was obviously enjoying the challenge of discussing their personal relationship while Charles looked on, nodding and taking everything at face value.

"Oh?" Not wanting this to go on, she concentrated on her food.

"I've heard it said that the origin of stress is strictly internal, having no substantial correlation with external factors," Judson went on anyway. "The manifestation of stress is merely triggered by outside problems. In actuality, you are probably reacting to an underlying emotional conflict—according to what I've heard." The last was added quickly, to remind them that he was quoting a reliable source. When she met his dry glance, Kathryn knew better. He was fabricating this profound bit of wisdom as he went along. "If doctors delve deeply enough, they usually find an emotional problem that the patient has never really faced. Maybe that has something to do with your headaches."

"I don't think it's anything quite so dramatic." Kathryn pushed a crepe around with her fork. Judson's remarks were becoming bolder, less disguised. It was difficult to hide her irritation. "I must admit that I've never heard that particular theory before. It's very interesting, but it also seems very catchall." She challenged him with her glance. "If it is true, then it would be safe to say that solving the single emotional problem would insure that a person would never again be upset or tense." After pointing out the holes in his theory, she smiled with mock demureness. "Are you certain you didn't misinterpret what you heard?"

Grudging admiration registered in Judson's expression at the way she was outmaneuvering him. Her argument was sound, so the credibility of his statement was virtually destroyed. His mouth crooked in a wry acknowledgment that he had been bested. He started to add words to the silent admission, but Charles spoke first.

"No, Kathryn, I think Judd is right." An earnest frown knitted his brows as he tried to recall. "I believe I've heard that particular philosophy somewhere before."

Stunned, they both looked at Charles. He was nodding thoughtfully as he appeared to search his memory for verification of his claim. Knowing it didn't exist, Kathryn looked away. A vague sense of disgust tightened her mouth.

"It's hard to say what great mind it came out of." Judson consoled him with mockery, well hidden by a musing tone. "Little tidbits of insight like that just seem to float around, there when you need one."

As he had been all evening, Charles was quick to agree. "That's true."

Kathryn quit pretending an interest in her food. When she put her fork down, she accidentally met Judson's eyes. She read the challenge there—a silent dare to acknowledge what the evening had revealed about Charles.

A hovering blond waiter came to remove their plates, inquiring with an affected accent whether they wanted dessert. He bowed to acknowledge their negative response. Shortly after, the check was delivered to the table. Judson reached for it, but Charles was quicker.

"Let me get it tonight, Charles," Judson offered, and reached inside his suit coat for his wallet.

"I won't hear of it," he insisted. "I invited you to dinner." Keeping the check in his hand, Charles opened his wallet and took out a credit card. He used his gold pen to figure the amount of the tip and added it to the bill. The waiter collected the check and credit card and took them off to some hidden cash register. Judson ran his gaze over Kathryn.

"You're looking a little pale," he commented. "Don't you think so, Charles?"

"Yes, she is." He frowned with concern. "I hope you're not coming down with something."

"I'm not."

"Maybe some fresh air would help that headache," Judson suggested, and surprised Kathryn by adding, "Why don't you go ahead and take Katy outside? I'll wait until the waiter comes back with your credit card. As busy as this place is tonight, it could be a while before he returns."

"I could use some air." She was willing to grab at a few moments reprieve from the strain of keeping her guard up.

"I have to wait and sign the charge slip,"

Charles said. "Why don't you two go on out to the car." Fishing in his pocket, he pulled out a set of keys and handed them to Judson. "I'll see you in a few minutes."

Shrugging his acceptance, Judson stood up and helped Kathryn out of her chair. She saw the satisfied curve to his mouth that said Judson had known it would turn out this way. He wanted a few minutes alone with her and he had correctly anticipated the way Charles would react. Tight-lipped, Kathryn followed Judson to the door. She had been wanting to snap at him all evening. Now was her opportunity.

Outside he placed a guiding hand on the back of her waist. Kathryn moved away, stopping to glare at him.

"Don't touch me," she warned him angrily. "I don't know what you had in mind when you cooked up your little scheme to see me alone, but you wasted your time and your talents."

"I hope not." The declaration was made with an amused kind of candor. "So, you don't appreciate my efforts, hmm?"

"I do not," she said stiffly. "And I also don't appreciate the way you keep trying to make Charles look like a fool." If she intended to marry him—which she did—it was imperative that she was able to respect him.

"He doesn't need my help for that," Judson drawled. "Charles does a fine job of it all by himself."

"Only around you," Kathryn said, defending

her fiancé's behavior, placing the blame on Judson.

"Only around someone he's trying to butter up," Judson corrected smoothly. "Is that what you want, Katy? A yes man? Somebody who'll dance to anybody's tune if there's enough profit in it?"

"Charles isn't like that," she insisted, and started to brush past him toward the parked car. A hand snared her wrist. There was a definite shimmer of defiance in her eyes when she tilted her head back to look at him.

"Open your eyes, Katy," Judson said impatiently. "All night I've been trying to make you take a good, long look at the man you think you're going to marry. He—"

"I don't *think* any such thing," she flared. "I *am* going to marry him. And I don't care how many times I have to sit and listen to him butter somebody up." To herself, she admitted that was what Charles had been doing, despite her earlier denial. "I'm going to be right there by his side."

Anger flashed, then was banked as he made her the object of his penetrating study. "Not if I can help it. Whether Charles is aware of it or not, he's got a fight on his hands."

Kathryn was further irritated by the suggestion that she had no say in the matter, that the fight was strictly between the two men, when in reality the struggle was hers—her own common sense against everything else she was made of, including her heart, which wasn't nearly as discriminating in its interest.

His grip on her wrist loosened to allow his hand to make a slow slide up her arm, eventually stopping on her shoulder while his thumb absently stroked the curve of her neck. Kathryn remained rigidly still, refusing to let him see how much his touch was disturbing her.

"It doesn't really matter whether Charles is aware of it, because there's no contest as far as I'm concerned." It was impossible to hold his steady look, but when her gaze dropped to his hard, masculine mouth, it was just as impossible to look away. She was watching when his mouth slanted into a reckless smile.

"Then I guess all I can say is, may the best man win." Judson didn't seem troubled about the outcome.

His arrogance certainly roused a rush of anger, its heat overriding the hot disturbance of her senses. "Surely you can't think *you* are the best man?" Kathryn scoffed. "I admit that Charles has a few faults, but I have a list of yours that runs a mile long!" Once it had been true, but, unfortunately, that list had been shortened.

"I didn't say I was the best man all the way around," he murmured lazily. "I'm simply the best man for you."

An aching tightness welled in her throat. Kathryn didn't trust herself to speak until it passed. But she shook her head firmly to veto the idea. The best man for her was someone she could count on. Someone who could make her feel safe and secure, not threatened by emotions she couldn't control.

Judson wasn't fazed by her denial. One shoulder lifted nonchalantly. "Well, that's what I have to try to prove, isn't it? I hope Charles won't object to a little friendly competition?"

"I'm sure Charles could care less." Kathryn found her voice. "He knows he doesn't have anything to worry about."

Before she could guess his intentions, the hand on her shoulder tightened. His other arm circled around her waist to draw her against the hard length of his body and hold her there. When he lowered his mouth onto hers, her lips were parted in surprise. There was immediate ignition of sparks at the contact, a spontaneous combustion between two volatile chemistries.

Her hands had come up to ward off this intimate invasion, but now they lost their purpose. Although every logical, practical, sensible bone in her body decreed she shouldn't, Kathryn was kissing him back.

Her fingers were curling into the material of his suit jacket, then releasing it to slide under his coat and feel the heat of his body through his shirt. Beneath her splayed fingers, his heart was beating strong and hard, the vital pulse of life heightened by the elemental throbbing of desire. When she was weak and dizzy, Judson ended the kiss.

The coolness of the night air swept over her lips as he pulled away. Then her heated flesh was being cooled by the evening breeze and her mind began to clear, returning some of her balance. His hands framed her face and raised it for his inspection. Lazy satisfaction was in the crooked line of his smile.

"If I were Charles, I'd start getting worried." It was a low drawling statement to which Kathryn had no rebuttal.

His hands fell away, setting her free. It was a second before she realized it and took a step backward, her wariness returning too late to offer protection from Judson's attraction. She saw Charles as he walked out of the restaurant, also too late to remind her of the importance of their relationship. And some damage had been done this evening, Kathryn was positive. The question was, how much?

She received a hint of an answer when Charles stopped the car in front of the shop. Once they were standing outside, he turned to take her into his arms. It was dark and there was no one in sight. Even Judson couldn't see them from inside the car. Yet Kathryn found herself pulling away, unable to invite the kiss that had always seemed so pleasant and warming. She mumbled a nervous good-night, forced a smile, and walked quickly to the shop entrance.

THE SUNDAY PAPER RUSTLED as Buck lowered it to glance over the top at Kathryn. Her white summer heels clicked across the kitchen floor, the lightweight cotton fabric of her sky-blue dress swirling gently around her knees as she walked. A white cinch belt was at her waist, emphasizing its slimness.

"Where are you headed today?" Buck asked. The newspaper crackled as he turned to another section.

"Church." Kathryn took a pitcher of orange juice from the refrigerator. "I'm going to pray for a miracle. Care to come along?"

"Maybe next time," Buck replied, folding the paper back and laying it beside his coffee cup.

Kathryn put two slices of bread in the toaster. "Sure, Buck. Next time. You've been telling me that for years."

"I always mean it." Buck shrugged. "It's just one of those things I never seem to get around to doin'."

The remark prodded Kathryn's memory. She hadn't seen Buck all day Saturday. A lot had happened since the last time they'd talked. Gathering up her toast, juice and cup of black coffee, she carried her breakfast to the table.

"Speaking of things you never get around to doing," she began, "I think you should ask Ruby Weatherby out."

Buck scowled angrily.

"Wait!" Kathryn held up a hand in a placating gesture. "Hear me out. I have good reason for suggesting it, and I'm almost positive you'll get the response you want out of Ruby."

Reluctant interest flashed in Buck's eyes. "What makes you think so?"

"Ruby came in the boutique yesterday—looking for you." Kathryn sipped at her orange juice.

"Why?" Buck was startled. "Was somethin' wrong?"

"That's what she was wondering," Kathryn said. "She wanted to know why you hadn't come into the restaurant all day."

Kathryn related the entire conversation she'd had with Ruby to Buck, practically verbatim. He listened to every word with frowning but intent interest. When she'd finished, she sat back and watched him with a complacent smile.

"Well?" Buck prompted. "Is that it? That's all she said?" Plainly he didn't see the significance of Ruby's visit.

"What do you mean, 'that's *all* she said?' What more do you need?" Kathryn asked in exasperation.

"All you've told me is that Hank is jealous, but Ruby let him know there ain't nothin' to worry about." Buck was letting Kathryn know the information was nothing to get excited about.

"But Ruby obviously doesn't care if Hank's jealous," Kathryn pointed out. "She came here looking for you. If she was crazy about Hank, she would have been worried that coming here would cause problems." She paused to let the logic behind her statement sink in. "Don't you see? You thought Ruby had chosen Hank Wright over you. After talking to her I'm almost positive she just took whatever was available to her. If you had done the asking, she would have been at Tiny's with you that night."

"I don't know," Buck grumbled. "She's never given me no hints...."

"And you've never given her any," Kathryn interrupted. "You two are too much alike. You both play poker too well. But one of you is going to have to let his guard down and let the other know what he is thinking.'' She picked up a slice of cold toast and hesitated before it reached her mouth. "You did notice that I said 'he,' didn't you?''

"I noticed.'' Frowning, Buck stared at the newspaper. Kathryn knew he wasn't seeing a single word.

"It's worth a shot, isn't it?'' she urged.

"What if this woman's intuition you seem to be basin' everything on is wrong?'' he challenged, reluctant to put too much stock in her observations. "What if you're readin' somethin' that ain't there?''

Kathryn didn't think she was, but she couldn't be absolutely positive. "Then you will have at least tried. Which is more than you've done up until now.'' She bit into the toast and chewed it. "What is it they always say—nothing risked, nothing gained?''

There was a long considering look from his washed-out blue eyes. Determination began to settle over his craggy features like a mask, hardening them with new purpose.

"You just might be right,'' he said, nodding slowly as the idea grew firmer in his mind. "You just might.''

Kathryn certainly hoped she was.

When she'd finished her breakfast, she brushed a few stray crumbs from her lap and carried her dishes to the sink. She found her purse and rummaged for the car keys, then hesitated, returning the keys and slipping the thin leather strap of her purse over her shoulder.

"I think I'll walk to church today." It was only three blocks away and the day promised to be beautiful—hot, but beautiful.

Her announcement roused Buck from his own private musings. He tipped his head back to study her.

"You said you were going to pray for a miracle," he recalled. "Anything in particular?"

A quick smile came to her lips, along with a glib retort. But instead of saying it, Kathryn found herself answering honestly.

"Yes, actually. I'm going to pray that there's something left of me and Charles when Judson finally gets around to leaving. At the rate things are going, it will take a miracle."

Last night she hadn't even been able to kiss Charles, not when the memory of Judson's mouth on her own was so strong. And so devastating. Kathryn wished she could forget the way she had participated in the kiss. She hadn't exactly fought Judson off. That was the scary part.

So easily he could make her lose sight of the possible consequences of surrendering to those powerful emotions. How could she forget, even for a moment, what it was like to have her defenses suddenly ripped away? Heaven. Hell. With Judson, it would always be one extreme or the other. There would be no comfortable middle ground on which she could safely walk.

"So you're not going to try to patch things up with Judd," Buck said.

"No." The shake of her head was very definite. "There's too much risk involved."

He drew back to frown at her. "This, comin' from the know-it-all little gal who just gave me a lecture about risk? Nothing risked, nothing gained," he mimicked her earlier words. "Don't you believe your own advice?"

She gave him a tight smile. "I forgot to tell you. There's a flip side to that old adage that applies to people like me. Nothing risked, nothing lost." She especially couldn't take a chance on a man like Judson. None of the odds were in her favor. He was changeable as the wind, following any impulse that struck him. If he wanted to do something, he did it. He was a true free spirit, unbound by rules set down by others. It was desire that led him in a particular direction. When the desire fizzled out, he simply changed course.

He wanted her now the same as he wanted her seven years ago. But it was entirely possible that the desire was still there only because he'd never had her long enough to quench his thirst for her. She couldn't depend on him to be there for her day after day, year after year. She knew that. Yet she also knew instinctively how easily she could become dependent on him if she wasn't careful. And careful was one thing she'd learned to be.

"I'd better get going," she said, glancing at the clock. Actually she had plenty of time, but she didn't want to have to rush.

"Say a prayer for me, will ya?" The newspaper rustled as Buck picked it up again.

"I always do, Buck," Kathryn assured him, then left the house, smiling simply because it was Sunday.

The day was hers and hers alone. Right from the beginning, she and Charles had agreed that Sunday would be their "freedom" day. They wouldn't see each other unless one of them chose to issue a special invitation and the other chose to accept. That didn't happen often. They both believed in having space, giving each other a certain amount of room to breathe and think. Today the concept was especially appealing.

Kathryn felt at peace as she walked the tree-lined residential streets. The fresh air and sunshine were working their magic. Her pace was a leisurely stroll while she thought about how she would spend the afternoon. Sometimes she went for long walks, which usually took her to Old Bill's place just on the outskirts of town. It was a small farm she'd been visiting all her life—just as Old Bill had seemed old all her life. He owned horses and gave Kathryn unlimited riding privileges.

Then there were days when she curled up with a book, baked cookies or just lounged in the sun. Her Sunday schedule was rarely exciting, but it always included her favorite activities. She lifted her gaze to the cloudless blue sky and felt the increasing heat of the sun. Today she rather favored the idea of a swim in the river.

People were gathered in small groups on the lawn in front of the old white-steepled church. As briefly as possible, Kathryn greeted the people she knew and went inside.

"Good morning." A woman was stationed at the door, passing out bulletins, smiling as the members of the congregation entered. Kathryn walked to her usual place and took an aisle seat near the center of the sanctuary.

The church bells rang and everyone wandered inside. The congregation had grown along with the town, so most of the pews filled up quickly. By the time Kathryn had skimmed through her bulletin, the organist was striking a chord and the red-robed choir was filing in, with the minister trailing behind. This was Kathryn's favorite part of the service—the music. Although it was stimulating and enriching to hear the pastor expound on the scriptures, her spirits were always lifted by the old hymns.

She smiled faintly as the choir burst out in a lively song. There was movement on her left. Kathryn automatically turned her legs to let a string of people move to the inside of the pew. The last person sat down next to her. She turned her gaze in a kind of absent acknowledgment. The shock of disbelief rolled through her when she looked into a pair of lazy brown eyes.

For an instant she was too stunned to speak. Judson saw the shocked recognition register in her look. A half smile crooked his mouth. Kathryn felt the sudden acceleration of her pulse.

"What are you doing here?" she demanded in a low hiss, rife with impatience. Church was the last place she'd expected him to turn up.

"It's Sunday," he said, as if that explained everything.

"Since when did that make any difference?" she whispered tightly.

"I used to come here with you all the time." His expression was slightly affronted, although there was an amused gleam in his eyes.

"When I dragged you," Kathryn reminded him curtly, reacting to the tension that was destroying her peace. As usual, his appearance had thrown her off balance.

"Actually," he began, a slow easy smile deepening the grooves alongside his mouth. He leaned closer to whisper in her ear. "I woke up with this uncontrollable desire to see you."

"You shouldn't have bothered," she said coldly.

"I wouldn't have had to if you'd been lying on the pillow next to me where you belong."

Kathryn breathed in sharply, aware of her reddening cheeks. Of all the things to say, and of all the places to say it! "Ssh!"

At Kathryn's sharply reprimanding noise, the woman wearing the hat in the pew directly in front of them turned around. Her thin mouth was made thinner with stern disapproval. Kathryn felt certain her cheeks were on fire. Unabashed, Judson nodded and smiled at the woman until she was finally embarrassed into turning around.

Throughout the service Judson managed to maintain physical contact with Kathryn in one way or another. He reached for a hymnal at the same time she did and ended up grabbing her hand. Then he stretched his arm along the back of the pew so it brushed across her shoulders. Once in a while he would adjust his position and Kathryn would feel his muscled thigh rubbing against hers. Her glaring looks were ignored, returned with smiles that were much too blank. Judson knew his greatest weapon was this physical attraction that coursed between them. He was exploiting that knowledge to the fullest.

When the benediction was finally over, Kathryn's nerves were frayed to a state of rawness. Without a backward glance, she jumped to her feet and headed for the door, expecting Judson to get stalled by the people pouring into the aisle. Reverend Martin was at the exit, shaking hands with his parishioners as they left. Impatiently, Kathryn fell into the slow moving line. Finally it was her turn. She clasped Reverend Martin's hand and stiffly smiled a greeting.

"How are you this morning, Kathryn?" the minister inquired.

"Fine thank you, pastor. It was a wonderful service." Kathryn was certain it had been. She only hoped he didn't ask her what she thought of the sermon. She started to move on, but he retained his hold on her hand.

"Who's this you've brought with you this morning?" He was looking curiously past her.

She turned to follow his gaze. Dismay entered her expression when she realized Judson was right behind her. A self-satisfied grin was splitting his face.

"Allow me to introduce myself, reverend." He took the initiative when Kathryn showed no signs of satisfying the preacher's curiosity. "I'm Judson Taylor, Katy's fiancé."

Kathryn's eyes widened with shock. "That's not true!" she breathed. The minister looked a bit puzzled by the announcement, but he didn't ask any questions, sensing a storm brewing in the air.

Judson chuckled and leaned toward the minister to murmur, "She doesn't have the ring yet," as if that explained her denial. Then he grabbed her shoulders and propelled her forward. "Nice meeting you, reverend."

"Yes . . . you, too. And congratulations!"

Casting a glance over her shoulder, Kathryn saw the minister's smile. "But . . . ." It was too late to correct the false impression he'd been given. More people had stopped to greet him. Forced to abandon her attempts, she continued through the crowd, out the door and down the steps.

She was stiff under his guiding hands, but she didn't offer any resistance. There were too many people sending them curious looks already. She didn't want to call any more attention to herself, or to them as a couple. Once they were out of earshot, it became a different story. She moved rigidly away from him, boiling with anger.

"You've got some nerve, Judson Taylor!" Her voice trembled with the effort to keep it low, so it wouldn't carry back to the church lawn.

"Is something wrong?" Judson asked in false innocence.

"You stood right there and lied!" she accused. "And to the minister!"

Judson frowned and drew back a little, looking

insulted. "Do I look like the kind of guy who would lie to a minister?"

Her gaze raked over him, taking in the lines of his custom-made suit. He looked very respectable. "Appearances can be deceiving," she retorted.

"I didn't lie to him." Judson shook his head in denial.

"Well, you certainly did!" She wasn't in any mood for games. "What did you hope to gain by telling him that I'm going to marry you—"

"You are," he stated matter-of-factly.

Her lips parted on an angry breath, but she didn't waste her denial on Judson. It would only bounce off, like everything else.

"You are an insufferable, egotistical maniac!" The name-calling was for her benefit, since she had to have some outlet for her anger. It didn't have any effect on Judson.

"I've been called worse," he drawled, then gave her a deliberately engaging smile. "Let's go have some Sunday dinner."

"Judson." Frustration and impotent anger clenched her teeth. "Read my lips. I do not want anything to do with you." Each word was clipped and spaced.

To emphasize her meaning, she swung away and began to walk along the sidewalk in the direction of the shop.

"Now look who's lying," Judson taunted, falling in step beside her. "The truth is, you're *afraid* to have anything to do with me."

"Oh." Kathryn stopped abruptly, smiling with

false sweetness. "You think I'm afraid of you?" Her hands came up to rest on her hips in a belligerent attitude. "Is it so impossible for you to believe that I simply am not interested in you?"

"I think you're afraid of being a woman," he stated.

"Why?" she demanded. "Because you haven't succeeded in seducing me again? It may come as a bit of a shock to you, Judson, but there are women who don't find you irresistible! I happen to be one of them now. I want more than you can offer. A lot more! I'm not willing to gamble my whole life away on the chance that we can have something lasting. You can't guarantee me anything that makes me want to give up what I've already got."

A frown had been gathering on Judson's face during her tirade, narrowing his eyes to dark slits. Her fists were clenched at her sides as Kathryn glared at him, fighting back stinging tears.

"I'm not asking you to give up anything," he said tersely. "I meant what I said to the preacher."

She didn't want to hear that. Listening would be too dangerous. She had to remember that it was impossible to permanently tame a wild thing. And the permanent was all she was interested in.

"You shouldn't have told him we were engaged," she said tightly. "It isn't true and it never will be." Her tears were very close to the surface. With her head held high Kathryn swept past him.

"Don't follow me." She didn't look back when

she said it, because she didn't want him to see the tears that were slipping off her lashes. The order wasn't necessary anyway. She could hear his footsteps striking out in the opposite direction.

Her own feet seemed to drag, making the three-block walk a long one. Entering the house through the back door, Kathryn realized Buck had gone out. The discovery came as a relief because she didn't want to explain what had caused the redness of her eyes.

She went directly upstairs and changed into her swimsuit, a black bikini with a large red flower design. Her movements were quick but somewhat distracted as she put on a red terry-cloth beach robe and slipped her bare feet into backless sandals. Gathering up a beach towel and a bottle of suntan oil, she stuffed them into a canvas tote bag and went back to the kitchen.

There was a bowl of fresh fruit on the counter. As a substitute for Sunday dinner, Kathryn helped herself to a couple of big red apples. She bit into one and deposited the second into the canvas bag along with the other things.

In a matter of minutes she was pulling her shiny red convertible through the alley and onto the street that would take her to the country.

The top was down on the small car, allowing the breeze to comb its fingers through her pale shoulder-length hair. It lifted it from her neck and skimmed it back from her forehead. Kathryn could almost feel the tension receding from her muscles.

It wasn't far to Deepwater River, the town's namesake. Before she had driven five miles past the fringe of town, Kathryn was turning onto the old farm road. The wheels dipped into potholes, jarring Kathryn until she slowed the car to a crawling pace. Poking along, she decided she had glorified the narrow dusty lane by thinking of it as a road.

When she finally stopped the car, her gaze made a quick sweep of the riverbank. There wasn't a soul in sight. It had been several years since the town had built a public pool, but Kathryn still hadn't gotten used to seeing the old swimming hole deserted. She climbed out of the car, smiling faintly because she had this idyllic place all to herself.

Trees crowded close together, their spreading branches extending over the water. The grass underfoot was thick and tall. Kathryn waded through it and made her way down the rocky, sloping bank to the flatter, sandy surface edging the water. She spread her large towel on a patch of sunlit ground and sat down, tossing her apple core in the water.

Her arms were wrapped around her drawn-up knees as she let the solitude soothe her. Idly she let her gaze follow the floating apple core as it became a part of the slow lazy current, following the path of least resistance. Life would be so much simpler if she could do that. If she could flow with the current, follow her heart. With a sigh, Kathryn admitted that Judson was right. She was afraid of being a woman. The whole kind of woman a man like Judson would demand. That implied letting her guard down, being brave enough to let herself really feel. Which, in turn, meant being vulnerable, open to hurt. Kathryn had experienced both sides of loving, the joy and the agony.

She didn't think she'd ever be willing to take the chance again. It was so much safer to stick to something solid and reliable. With Charles there would be no mountain tops, but neither would there be those deep dark valleys she had walked through alone.

After shedding the beach robe and sandals, she spread a coat of suntan oil on her creamy light-gold skin. Then she stretched out on her back and closed her eyes.

A faint breeze rustled through the trees, its cooling breath fanning the sun's warmth to a comfortable temperature. The occasional lapping of the ever-changing river against the thirsty bank lulled her into limbo, half in and half out of sleep.

It seemed like a long time had passed when the vague sound of an approaching vehicle caused her to stir. Kathryn listened, then dismissed it as being unimportant. It was probably a fisherman. When he noticed her car, he would choose a spot farther down. A car door slammed nearby and Kathryn sighed in grim acceptance of the fact that someone intended to intrude on her solitude. A few people still preferred the swimming hole, the same as she did. Obviously one of them was here.

Behind her there was a clatter of rocks and dirt

sliding down the bank. Kathryn opened her eyes, suddenly conscious of how isolated the place was. She tried to appear casual as she tipped her head back to identify the person. Her eye caught a bright flash of yellow against tanned skin. A white towel was carelessly draped over one shoulder. A quiver ran through her when she saw it was Judson. She quickly lowered her lashes, still observing him as he came to a stop near her feet.

"Are you following me?" She kept her eyes nearly closed.

"Looks that way, doesn't it?" He sounded amused.

"I told you not to," she said curtly.

"In case you haven't noticed, I'm not in the habit of taking orders. Especially not from sassy blondes who say one thing and mean another."

"And I'm not in the habit of having men follow me around. Especially conceited dark-haired men who only hear what they want to," she retorted in kind.

Judson chuckled. "It may not please your ego, but I have to confess. I didn't follow you and I never dreamed you still spent your Sunday afternoons here. This meeting is purely by coincidence." His gaze took on a sparkling quality as it moved slowly over her. "Unless maybe fate had a hand in it."

"I don't believe in fate." She shut her eyes to block out his virile form—the sinewy length of his legs and the flatly muscled hardness of his chest and stomach. With his words from earlier that afternoon still ringing in her ears, she felt a little too vulnerable.

"I thought this place would be full on a nice day like today," Judson commented. He was moving around. A soft noise told Kathryn he had dropped onto the sand beside her.

"Nobody uses the swimming hole anymore. They use the city pool." She passed the information along with an outward show of disinterest. Inside, she was reacting to his presence. She could sense him lying next to her. The male scent of him was near, and her muscles tensed involuntarily. Kathryn could feel his gaze and the path it was taking over her length.

"You're a little red," he observed, but Kathryn knew the heat she felt had nothing to do with overexposure to the sun.

"I tan easily," she replied. "I'll turn brown by morning." But she did turn over to lie on her stomach. It seemed a safer position, exposing less to his interested gaze. Besides, Judson couldn't see her face when it was pillowed on her arms.

"Would you like me to put some oil on your back?" he inquired in a conversational tone.

Her eyes flew open to stare at the nubby texture of the towel. "No, thank you."

"You used to like it," he reminded her. "I'd pour some oil into my hands and wait a few seconds for it to warm up. Then I'd start on your shoulders, rubbing it on in slow circles. When I finished your back, I'd move down to your legs.

You had gorgeous legs,'' he remembered lazily. ''You still do.''

The stroking caress of his gaze made itself felt on the backs of her thighs. Gritting her teeth against the sensations, Kathryn remained silent.

''Then I'd massage your feet,'' Judson continued. ''You always liked that, too.''

''I used to like a lot of things I don't like now.'' Her muffled voice was husky.

''How do you know you don't like them now?'' There was a velvet sexiness in his tone. It curled around her and dragged a response through her limbs, a traitorous excitement building.

''I really wasn't looking for company.'' A change of subject was imperative. ''I came out here to be alone.''

''Sorry about that. I certainly didn't mean to bother you.'' Mocking amusement underlined the words, because his seductive reminiscing was bothering her and he knew it. ''I didn't come here to talk anyway. I came here to swim.'' He pushed himself into a standing position. A second later, Kathryn heard the sounds of his feet as they waded into the water. There was a loud splash and she knew he'd dived in. She was startled by his abrupt departure. Startled...and disappointed, she realized.

Turning her head to the side, she watched him through narrowed eyes, her alert gaze hidden by the veiled sweep of her lashes. He swam for what seemed like a long time, muscled arms cleaving the water with powerful strokes. Kathryn would have been less than honest if she didn't admit to enjoying this opportunity to observe him from a safe distance.

He surfaced close to the shoreline and glanced in her direction. She was glad her eyes appeared to be closed. Water streamed off him as Judson stood up. He shook his hair back, its wetness gleaming nearly black. Drops of water glistened all over his body, trapping the sun and giving his rippling flesh a polished look. The tanned length of him was blatantly virile.

When he finally began wading to shore, her pulse reacted to his approach, taking off and skipping beats. The moment seemed a part of a familiar pattern, that same old anticipation rushing through her veins. She made a determined effort to calm the thudding of her heart by reminding herself that things had changed. It was difficult to keep it in mind, though, when he was standing there, so long and lean, looking at her in that reckless way that was so exciting. A churning began low in her stomach and swirled outward.

At the edge of the river, Judson stopped. Then he was bending over to trail his hands behind him in the water, as if reluctant to leave its refreshing coolness. But Kathryn had only an instant's warning of his real purpose in stopping. He moved with lightning swiftness. She tensed, unable to avoid it in time as his cupped hands scooped up water and skimmed it toward her. The icy-cold drops rained on her sun-heated back and legs. She drew in a deep breath of shock. Then an immediate retaliatory anger took control.

CHAPTER ELEVEN

INSTANTLY SHE WAS ON HER FEET. Judson tipped his head back and laughed at the vengeful blaze in her eyes. Since he was already wet, similar tactics on her part would achieve less-satisfying results. Bending over, Kathryn snatched up the towel lying beside hers. Surprise flashed across his face, then Judson advanced a step, guessing her intention. Hurriedly, she wadded the towel into a ball and threw it. As it sailed over his head, an arm shot up, missing it by a few inches. He turned in time to see it land in the water.

"Aw, Katy," he muttered. "That's the only towel I—" The sentence wasn't finished as his yellow shirt made a little splash next to the towel. Judson spun around, his expression a mixture of disbelief and dismay.

"That was my shirt!" His hand waved impatiently toward the shirt, which was soaking up water like a sponge.

"Was it?" she purred, a smile lifting the corners of her mouth. "Sorry about that."

"I'll just bet you are." His irritated expression gave way to a glittering kind of amusement that promised consequences.

"You'd better get your shirt," Kathryn told him with a little smirk. "It's sinking." It was, along with the towel. Weighted with absorbed water and caught in the very fringe of the river's sluggish current, the items were slowly being pulled under as they drifted downstream.

Forced to abandon any ideas about revenge, Judson splashed into the water to rescue his things before the river carried them off. There was a wry twist to his mouth as he waded ashore, water streaming from the sodden articles. He held them both in one hand.

"Ooops." Her shoulders lifted in a shrug as Kathryn tried very, very hard not to smile.

Her amusement vanished when Judson swung the dripping things behind his back, then brought them around in a swift arc that sprayed icy droplets all over her. She took an instinctive step backward. The towel and shirt landed on the bank in a soggy heap, momentarily distracting her.

It didn't take long to realize her mistake. Her side vision caught his movement as he reached down to the water. She started to back away, but flying water splashed right in her face. Sputtering, she tried to blink the water out of her eyes. But she didn't have the chance, because more was quick in coming. Judson was using his hands as paddles, deluging her with one cold splash after another. Her hair was soaked and her eye makeup was running.

With upraised arms to ward off this liquid attack, Kathryn advanced on him. When she reached the river, she half turned and bent over to scoop some water. An arm circled her waist. Then a hand slipped behind her knees and Judson was swinging her up into his arms.

He paid no attention to her startled yelp of protest. Iron hands kept their grip on her, despite the way she pushed and kicked to struggle free. An awareness ran through her at the way he was holding her, with her body curved to his bare chest and his muscled arms curved so tightly around her back and under her legs. The discovery was sobering.

"Put me down!" she demanded.

Judson started to refuse, his gaze roaming over her face in a way that warmed her blood. Then a reckless smile stole any seriousness from the moment.

"That's the Katy I've been looking for." Lazy satisfaction was in his voice, along with a large measure of amusement.

The hand supporting her back shifted upward, and she held herself erect in his arms while his fingers brushed her cheekbone just below her eye. He rubbed his fingers together and Kathryn saw the darkness of running mascara on his hand. She could just imagine what she looked like. Injured pride lifted her chin. A chuckle came from his throat.

"Your sophistication is washing off, darlin'," Judson drawled. "Let's see if we can't get rid of all of it."

Like a mother rocking a baby, Judson began

swinging her back and forth. Kathryn realized he was trying to get enough momentum to toss her into deeper water. A second before he let go, she clamped her arm more tightly around the ridge of his shoulder and the other around the back of his neck. When his hands released her, she pulled him off balance, dragging him down with her. They both splashed into waist-deep water, going under and bobbing up with sputtering laughter.

"I ought to drown you," he growled. Beneath the water's surface, he grabbed her wrist.

"You asked for it," Kathryn retorted breathlessly. It was crazy how silly and carefree she was suddenly feeling. She hadn't felt this way in years. She had really begun to believe that wonderful, reckless sense of abandon only belonged to the very young. There was something enchanted and magical about having it back again.

Judson tugged on her wrist, trying to dunk her. Shrieking, Kathryn twisted away. The suntan oil remained on her skin, combining with the water to make her arms slick. Kathryn escaped his hold and struck out toward the bank. With a belly-flopping dive, Judson caught her around the waist.

"You slippery little devil." His laughing voice was near her ear. Lifting her out of the water, he heaved her away from his body. She landed, face first, her startled cry of protest going under with her. Kathryn was gasping when she surfaced. She pushed the wet mane of hair away from her eyes.

"Give up?" Judson asked, breathing hard from the exertion.

"Yes." Out of breath and laughing, she admitted defeat.

"Finally." His voice was husky.

Something in the dark gleam of his eyes changed the mood from playful to serious. As he glided through the water to let his hands rest on her bare shoulders, Kathryn had the feeling she had just surrendered a lot more than the water battle. She quivered under the possessiveness of his gaze as it lingered on the parted curve of her lips. She was tired of fighting her attraction for him. It was too strong and she was too weak. Her hands made a tentative reach for him, settling lightly on his chest. Curling gold hairs tickled her palms and made them itch to discover everything else male about him.

His mouth made a slow, thorough seduction of her lips, tracing their softness with his tongue until she trembled with the need to deepen the kiss. Her hands slid around his broad shoulders while his arms went around her waist to draw her closer. The buoyancy of the water made Kathryn feel as if she floated against him. It seemed natural and right to be in his arms.

It was crazy how just touching him could set off a chain of reactions that totally rocked her. It had always been like this. As his mouth settled onto hers and a response leaped and flared within her, everything else became unimportant. It was the feel of him—the warm, hard flesh of his chest beneath her hands, the taut muscles in his arms that contracted under her touch as she began to rediscover him—that mattered.

Her senses were heightened, driving out thoughts that no longer had meaning. Kathryn felt her heart pounding to the beat of some wild drum, a tempo she'd heard before, in the long-ago past, and never entirely forgotten. It was all she could hear, just as Judson was all she could see, feel and taste. The only awareness she had was of him—and it was enough. He was enough.

The message must have been transmitted to Judson, because the slow sensuality of his kiss flamed with a demanding passion as he tasted her eager lips. Her response to him was a rush of heat. Kathryn used her own desire to feed his hungry need, responding more fiercely to his kisses. The exchange continued for long moments while the blood pounded through her veins. Restless male hands roamed and caressed and excited her flesh. Below the surface of the water, one hand pressed against the base of her spine, pinning her to the thrust of his hips.

Kathryn arched willingly to mold herself to him, his hard male body imprinting itself on her feminine softness. Her breasts were pressed against his solid chest, her thighs rubbing the hair-roughened length of his legs. The taste of him filled her mouth, the intoxication of his possession remaining even when his mouth left hers to nibble her neck roughly. His hand tangled itself in her wet hair, gently tugging her head back to expose more sensitive skin to his arousing nuzzling. Kathryn barely stifled a soft moan of pleasure as his lips moved progressively along the ridge of her shoulder, taking little love bites on the way to her neck, where he licked at the rivulets of water resting in the hollow of her throat.

His tugging fingers pulled the strap to untie the bow at the back of her neck. It gave easily and her bikini bra slipped down to float atop the water. Bending at the knees, Judson let his mouth begin a downward path. Delighted quivers erupted as he explored the valley between her breasts and investigated the high, creamy swells.

A heady weakness seemed to melt her bones. She dug her fingers into the hard flesh of his shoulders as his arms curved around her hips. Then Judson was lifting her out of the water. She was held high in the air by strong arms that hugged her hips to his chest. His lips trailed fire over the white slope of her breast, then the warmth of his mouth took possession of the hard peak. Kathryn shuddered with uninhibited longing under the arousing manipulation of his tongue.

When he lowered her to let her stand, her legs barely supported her. The ultrasensitive tips of her breasts brushed the springy hair on his chest. A pressure throbbed within her, an ache in her loins to know the fulfillment of his total possession.

His arms were crushing her to him as he claimed her mouth again, his tongue probing with an urgency she matched, trying to get her fill of him. She was sharply aware of every place where skin touched skin. And there was a sharp, aching awareness that just being held by him wasn't enough.

Judson lifted his head, his breath coming ragged and hard. "I want you," he murmured roughly against her skin, burying his face in the curve of her neck.

"Yes." Kathryn's voice was husky with desire.

"I want to make love to you, Katy." Between the moist, fiery kisses he showered over her face, Judson went on to clarify exactly what he wanted from her. "I want you to be mine." It was a low possessive statement, spoken roughly against her ear. "I want you with me always."

His tongue traced her shell-like ear, and Kathryn shuddered in response.

"Judson...." Words wouldn't form. She could barely think, much less talk.

"Tell me, Katy," he urged in a voice rough with desire. "Tell me you want me."

"I want you," Kathryn admitted, because denying it was impossible. Turning her head, she sought the mouth that was firing her skin, wanting again to be captivated by the domination of his kiss.

But Judson withheld it, drawing back slightly to let his gaze roam over her face. His own features reflected what was expressed in hers—the wanting, the needing, the hunger that neither time nor past hurts had ever been able to kill.

"Why?" He wanted her to supply the reasons for these feelings. "Why do you want me, Katy? Tell me," he urged.

"I don't know." From the beginning, he had held a fatal attraction for her. Why it continued to exist in total conflict with her will was something Kathryn couldn't explain. "The reason doesn't make any difference."

Her fingers linked together behind his neck to pull him down to her once more. She closed her eyes in anticipation as his head began its descent, his mouth moving inexorably toward hers as he started to give in to the pressure of her hands and the invitation of her lips.

A second later, his fingers were gripping her wrists and pulling her arms from around his neck. "The hell it doesn't make any difference," he muttered thickly.

In dazed confusion, Kathryn opened her eyes and blinked at the harshness in his features.

"You love me," he stated. "And I want to hear you say it."

"No." Kathryn nearly gasped the word, shaking her head to reject the idea. That's what she'd needed to protect herself from. She couldn't have let it happen again...could she?

Judson saw the fear in her eyes—and the uncertainty. Then his expression was gentle, the harshness leaving it as he folded her again in his arms.

"Yes, Katy my darlin', it's true," he murmured. "You can't fight it. Neither one of us can. I think I've loved you since the first time I saw you. It's never changed. I still want you—as a lover, wife, friend, as the mother of my children someday." His dark eyes were intense. "Let me have you," he murmured, and claimed her mouth in an imploringly seductive fashion that had the blood instantly rushing hotly through her veins.

But neither that, nor the warmth of his hands could touch the chill that was seeping into her bones. With deadly certainty, Kathryn suddenly knew that what was happening now was not just the result of some powerful physical attraction.

In a way she wished it was, because then she would be able to enjoy the heaven to which he could take her, then walk away with no regrets. But that was impossible. If she followed where he was leading, she would regret it for a lifetime. Because she loved him. She had always loved him.

With the realization came a gripping tightness that choked her. It had all been so useless—her determination to keep anyone from possessing her heart; her fight to keep these feelings Judson aroused from taking root and growing into something deeper—all of it had been futile.

She was stiffened by an outraged kind of despair that sent her pivoting out of Judson's arms. There was no fairness in this world. Not when the only man she had the weakness to fall for belonged to the most dangerous breed in existence.

If she had to love anyone at all, why did it have to be Judson? Why couldn't it have been someone who could offer her at least a degree of safety? With any emotional commitment, there was always the risk of loss. But with Judson, that risk increased a hundredfold.

By nature he was a drifter, living on impulse and leaving on impulse. There was something inherent in his very makeup that needed and demanded more from life than the average person ever dreamed of getting, much less expected. It took so much more of everything to satisfy such a man. Kathryn wouldn't gamble on whether or not she would eventually bore him.

Strong fingers closed around her wrist. Kathryn let her gaze fall to his hand, deeply brown against the lightness of her tan. Its touch hinted at the potential power in his grip, although there was nothing forceful about the pressure at the moment. With a wariness that hadn't been there a few minutes before, Kathryn turned slightly to face him.

His comments about children and having a lifetime together kept ringing in her ears. It was impossible to forget that once she had carried his child, a child conceived in a love that had been complete in every way. Ironically, it was the totality of that love that had caused her to miscarry. She hadn't been able to cope with losing Judson. When he'd left, she had been devastated.

And she had vowed never to love that way again. At the moment she was only one step away from adding that completeness of physical expression to her love. If she followed through, she would be totally vulnerable. And if he left her again, it would destroy her.

Yet there had been a sincerity—a certainty of his own wants and needs—when he'd asked her to be his, always and in every way.

Meeting the intensity of his gaze, Kathryn believed him. Yes, Judson wanted those things now, in the heat of the moment. But what about tomorrow? What would happen when the moss began to grow beneath his feet and the call of the wind became too alluring. . .?

"What's wrong?" His eyes probed hers, warily asking for an explanation that he seemed reluctant to hear.

She couldn't meet that look. It hurt too much. How could she tell him that the reckless, adventurous spirit that kept drawing her to him was the very thing that kept them apart?

"Katy." It was a combination of a question and a demand. His expression had become grim. His hands moved to tighten on the rounded points of her shoulders, as if he was trying to hang on to what they almost had. He knew he was losing that moment of closeness. "Katy." Her name was said through clenched teeth, a kind of desperation mixed with anger because he couldn't stop the wall she was reconstructing between them.

"It's no good, Judson." Sadness clouded her green eyes, along with a mist of tears. "Damn, it's just no good." She shook her head, wishing it could be. "Please go away and leave me alone."

Without waiting for a response, she turned from his arms and headed for the riverbank. He didn't try to stop her.

"You don't want that!" he yelled after her. "You don't want me to leave you alone!"

Bending, she gathered up the towel and other

items, stuffing them into the beach bag. "I need that," she called over her shoulder.

"You need *me*!" Judson sounded totally frustrated and angry.

Instead of trying to deny it, Kathryn started up the sloping bank. She didn't dare look back. If she did, she'd probably run straight into his arms. Tears were brimming over as she marched steadfastly ahead. With this man there was no future for her love. She had to make a clean break while she still had a breath of a chance to get over him.

"I'll never leave you alone, Katy!" he shouted, his voice hoarse.

Glad to finally reach her car, Kathryn started the engine and turned onto the dusty lane.

TRUE TO HIS WORD, Judson was everywhere. At least once daily he passed by the shop window, only stopping long enough to wave. If she went out to lunch, he appeared at the restaurant. If she went for a walk, he was taking one, too. At each meeting they exchanged only a few civil comments. He never forced his company on her the way he had in the past, but seeing him so often kept her awareness of him at peak level. Although nothing personal was ever said, his brown eyes issued a constant challenge.

Charles continued to extend dinner invitations to Judson, which forced Kathryn to spend most evenings in the company of both men. However, the veiled jibes against Charles and the double-edged conversations stopped. Kathryn guessed that Judson no longer felt such tactics were necessary. The afternoon at the river had revealed a great deal. Instead of trying to prove anything more, Judson now seemed to be only biding his time until her resistance was worn down by his quiet persistence.

After nearly a week, she was surprised Judson hadn't grown tired of small-town life and his lack of progress with her. It had been weeks since his return, and Kathryn would have sworn he'd have moved on to greener pastures by now. Not that she claimed to be able to predict what he'd do at any given time. Predictable was the last word she would use to describe Judson. The one thing she was convinced of was that he would move on in time. That was the way of a drifter. Meanwhile Kathryn was living on the raw edge of her nerves. It couldn't last much longer.

On Friday Charles stopped by the shop at closing time to get her approval of the plans he'd made for the evening. For dinner, they would drive over to the next county, where there was a steak house that boasted a state-wide reputation for its choice meats. Of course, Judson would be coming.

"I thought we'd show Judson what a real steak tastes like," Charles said, laughing. "I bet him that even Dallas has nothing that can compare with Kansas beef."

Her smile was on the weak side. All day long Kathryn had been toying with the idea of staying home. She was tired and irritable and had had about as much of the triangle as she could stand.

"I think I'll pass tonight, Charles." She sat on the high stool behind the counter and kicked off her shoes. "I'm sure you and Judson can get along without me." More and more, she had the feeling that she was tagging along with the two men, rather than Judson intruding on her dates with Charles.

"Well, yes...I suppose we can." Charles frowned. He didn't like having his plans altered, especially on short notice. "About tomorrow night. I thought we'd—"

"We?" Kathryn interrupted with an edge of irritation. "I don't suppose I need to ask who this 'we' is?"

The frown deepened as Charles looked her up and down. "What's the matter with you, Kathryn?" he demanded.

"Nothing," she muttered. Letting a long breath escape through her teeth, she spread her hands on the countertop. "Yes, there is something."

"Well. What is it?" He showed an unusual lack of patience.

She studied him for a moment, tipping her head to one side. "Charles, do you realize how long it's been since we've spent an evening alone together, just the two of us?"

Clearly the question wasn't what Charles had expected. This desire for his company took the anger that had been forming away from his expression. "It's been a while, I know."

"Almost two weeks," she informed him.

"That long?" His lack of awareness annoyed Kathryn.

"That long," she mocked. "So what are we going to do about it? Or are we going to do anything about it?"

The challenge made him frown again. "What do you suggest?"

"That you stop including Judson Taylor in all of our plans. Or maybe I should suggest that you stop including me in the plans you two make."

"Jealous?" he guessed, smiling at the idea.

His amusement was not appreciated. "Is it unreasonable to want—to expect—to have some time alone with my fiancé? Is that asking too much, Charles?"

"Under normal circumstances, no," he said smoothly. "But I'm really surprised by your attitude. Taylor knows hardly a soul in town and you resent putting yourself out a little to make his stay more comfortable and enjoyable. Have you looked at the situation from that point of view?"

Kathryn bridled at the criticism. She had a malicious urge to blurt out everything that had happened between Judson and herself—in detail. She was becoming fed up with the way Charles had been ignoring her, and the way he always agreed with Judson, regardless of what she knew his true feelings were on an issue. And she was also fed up with the way Charles was constantly chiding her, like now, about her behavior.

"Judson knows Buck," Kathryn retorted. "And I know that Buck is probably very disappointed that he hasn't seen more of Judson in the evenings. If you're so all-fired concerned about keeping everyone happily entertained, why haven't you at least included Buck in your many generous invitations?''

A hardened glint entered Charles's gray eyes, revealing that Kathryn had hit her mark.

"It's business, Kathryn," he said flatly, and dropped the pretense of altruistic motives. "You know that."

"Yes," she admitted. "And I can understand the need for a certain amount of socializing. But surely it isn't necessary every night?"

"I think it is. It pays to know the right people— and to know them as well as possible."

"Does everything always have to pay? Does there always have to be some kind of profit involved? Some kind of angle?" Kathryn had never considered herself to be an idealist, but looking at Charles, she felt a twinge of disillusionment. She felt as though she was seeing him clearly for the first time, although she wasn't exactly sure what such clarity of vision meant.

"What am I supposed to say to that?" he questioned tightly.

"Nothing." She sighed, not sure why she'd brought the subject up or whether it even mattered. The one certainty in her mind was that she had to get Judson out of her life while she still had one left. Things were falling apart and Charles was the only one who could help her hold them together. "Do we have to see him so often, Charles?" She put the question to him again.

He ran an impatient hand through the hair silvering his temple. "If that's what he wants, yes." Period. Final. End of discussion. Her wants and needs didn't matter.

"Well, it isn't what I want!" she snapped, and hopped down from the stool, too agitated to remain still. Her arms were crossed in an attitude of defiance as she walked to the window and stared outside.

"Stop acting like a child, Kathryn," he reprimanded.

"A child!" She whirled to glare at him, furious at his calm while envying it. "Just because I express my feelings on a matter that involves me, I'm acting like a child?"

"You may express your feelings any time you like, but at the moment, you're acting like a spoiled brat who can't stand not being the center of attention. Dammit, Kathryn, this is my career we're talking about! If there are sacrifices to be made, I'll make them!"

"Are you willing to sacrifice us?" She asked the question quietly as she watched him closely.

"I assumed you were willing to stand with me," he challenged.

Again, the burden of responsibility was on her shoulders and Kathryn felt the weight. She was well aware that he hadn't answered her and wished she hadn't pushed.

"Kathryn." Sighing, Charles approached her, handsome and distinguished, arms outstretched. Her body was stiff as he gathered her close and rested his chin on top of her head. "I'm doing this for both of us, Kathryn, and I need you—by my side, not fighting me. It will all be worth it in the end. You'll see.''

What she saw was that she would always play second fiddle in his life. The strength of his ambition would always take precedence over his feelings for her, no matter how deep they might run. Instead of being hurt, Kathryn was ironically consoled by the knowledge. It made it a fair match, because Charles would never occupy first place in her heart, either.

"I've got to go," he murmured against her hair. "Are you sure you won't change your mind and join us?"

"No." Shaking her head, she backed away from the embrace. "I'm afraid I'm too tired to do a good meal justice."

"Maybe I could come by later," he suggested. "We could make up for some of the privacy you've been missing."

If he came to her tonight—after he'd seen to the *important* things, Kathryn knew she wouldn't be able to respond to him.

"No...I'm going to bed early. I'll talk to you tomorrow, okay?"

"Sure." He glanced at his watch. "Tomorrow."

After he'd gone, Kathryn locked the shop and went upstairs. She took a long luxurious bath, then didn't bother to get dressed, slipping into a powder-blue satin nightgown and matching robe instead. It was after eight o'clock when she finally surrendered to her growling stomach and went to the kitchen.

A solitary dinner was unusual, since she could almost always count on Buck or Charles for company. Friday was Buck's poker night. Sometimes the games were held in her kitchen. All the "boys" took turns hosting the weekly event, which usually lasted well into the early-morning hours. As she folded a slice of rye bread over a piece of ham, Kathryn thought about Buck—his bowling nights, his card playing, and the many friends he'd acquired over the years since coming to Deepwater. This was her hometown, where she'd spent all but one of her twenty-four years, and other than Buck, there wasn't a single person she could honestly call a friend.

Close friends were a luxury she hadn't afforded herself in a long time. There had been a few girlfriends in high school, but when she'd left town, she had let those relationships die. After she'd lost the baby and returned to Deepwater, supposedly a widow, she had avoided all but superficial relationships with both men and women. It was best not to get into a position where she could be tempted by a sympathetic ear. Her mother had carefully concealed the facts about Kathryn's affair with Judson, so nobody had suspected she'd left to have a baby. Kathryn had been very grateful to her mother for sparing her the humiliation. A good reputation in a small town was a valuable thing, one easily lost and hard to recover.

More than anything else, it was habit that had

kept Kathryn silent about her past when things began to look serious with Charles. Then, as time passed, it became more and more difficult to broach the subject, because she felt dishonest about not telling him sooner. It was that fear of destroying Charles's trust that had kept her silent since Judson had returned. But maybe it was time to tell him the truth. Surely Charles would understand. A man of forty-five was not easily disillusioned. Where her requests to avoid Judson had failed, an explanation might succeed in enlisting Charles's help in getting Judson out of her life.

Turning the idea over in her mind, she ate the half sandwich and drank a glass of milk. No definite decision had been reached by the time she'd finished eating. Confusion. Always confusion. She rinsed the glass and left it in the sink.

The books in the living room offered mental distraction. Kathryn picked at random from the shelf of paperbacks. But she did make a point of choosing one of Buck's Westerns, rather than one of her own favorite romances. With Judson in town, she didn't even want to think about romance.

To her surprise, Kathryn was able to concentrate on the story, losing herself in the Old West. Propped up in bed with pillows behind her back, the hours flew as she kept turning pages. She had started the last chapter when the telephone rang. She answered it absenty.

"Were you sleeping?"

The story was forgotten as she recognized Judson's voice. Its deep rich sound jolted her and she sat upright.

"No, I wasn't sleeping." She glanced at the clock, surprised that it was after one o'clock. "Why are you calling here this time of night?" she demanded. "Why are you calling here at all?"

"I missed you at dinner," he drawled, caressing her senses even through the phone wires.

"Did you?" She managed to sound cool.

"I just got back to the hotel." His voice was dry. "It's been a very long evening, just me and Charles."

"Why did you call?" Kathryn asked curtly.

"We need to talk," he stated. "But not on the phone."

"We have nothing to talk about." Her fingers curled tightly around the receiver. "It's all been said."

"I want to come over."

"No!" Kathryn was adamant.

"Why not?" But he wasn't really asking a question. He was challenging her to admit her feelings.

"You know why not," she snapped in frustration.

"Yes," he agreed. "I know you don't want to see me because you're afraid of what you feel. You know what will happen between us."

"Please." A weariness claimed her. "I don't want to talk about this." It was all very pointless and very painful.

"That's just too bad, because we're going to talk about it!" Judson sounded as if he'd lost all patience with her.

Instantly her temper matched his. "You may do

as you want, but I'm not going to discuss anything with you.'' She slammed the receiver down on its cradle.

Drawing her knees up to her chest, she stared at the telephone. As she expected, it started ringing almost immediately. Since Buck wasn't home yet and she didn't have to worry about it waking him up, Kathryn let it ring. After a while it stopped for a minute, then started again. Her fingers itched to pick up the receiver, but they didn't. Finally there was silence.

With a sigh, Kathryn leaned back against the pillows. She picked up the novel and searched for where she'd left off. After reading the page for the fifth time, she managed to grasp what it said. Eventually she relaxed enough to let herself be swept onto the Texas plains, far away from Kansas and its problems.

A faint sound filtered in from outside. Unconsciously, Kathryn frowned, her mind resisting the noise that was claiming her attention. Through persistence, it finally won out. She lifted her head, listening intently to identify it.

Then she wished she hadn't. Her mind clicked in recognition and her eyes widened in disbelief.

''Oh, no,'' Kathryn groaned and sank lower into the bed.

CHAPTER TWELVE

THE WINDOW WAS OPEN, a cool night breeze carrying the soft sound of a familiar melody clearly to her. Even if the words hadn't been recognizable, Kathryn would have known what they were.

"K-K-K-Katy, beautiful Katy. You're the only g-g-g-girl that I adore...." Judson held the last note, stretching it out with dramatic inflection.

Despite the shock, dismay and the mortification running through her, a tiny smile began to lift the edges of her mouth. There had always been a touch of the showman about Judson, an actor's flair for the dramatic that was rakishly charming and potent. This serenade scene had happened before....

Her lips tightened into a grim line as she registered what Judson was doing. She snapped the book shut and bounced out of bed, marching to the window. Judson was sitting on the roof of the rental car, his face tipped up toward her window as he sang. Irritated, she watched him for a moment, her foot tapping the carpeted floor. Thank heaven her bedroom faced the back of the building, Kathryn reflected. At least he wasn't standing in the middle of the street making a fool of himself—and her.

Judson finished the chorus and started over. Before he'd got out the first stuttering word, Kathryn was reaching for the window. She pulled it shut with a bang. She wasn't a starry-eyed kid anymore. And she resented that he thought such tactics would still work. She moved away from the window. He could go elsewhere and play his silly games.

But that obviously wasn't his intention. Instead of taking the hint, Judson increased the volume of his voice to overcome the obstacle of the closed window. Kathryn cringed as he started singing at the top of his lungs. Judson had never lived by other people's rules. He'd always made his own. He didn't care what others thought, but Kathryn did. Hurriedly she shoved the window open.

"Judson!" She hissed his name and he stopped to listen. "What is it you want?"

"I already told you," he stated. "I want to talk."

"About what?" she bit out impatiently, wondering what he could say that hadn't already been said.

"Come down here," he challenged. "Unless you want the neighbors to hear."

"Say what you came to say and leave." She called his bluff, knowing it would be impossible to conduct a personal discussion from their respective positions.

"Are you sure you want it this way?" He frowned skeptically.

"Positive." There was a smug satisfaction in

knowing she'd thwarted his plan to force her to invite him inside. After a moment's hesitation she heard his resigned sigh.

"Whatever you say," Judson gave in grudgingly. There was another pause.

"Well?" Kathryn prompted. She felt safe and smug. It came out in her voice. "It's very late, so I—"

In a flash, Judson was on his feet, standing on top of the car. Her eyes widened in sudden apprehension as she realized that in calling his bluff she had forced him into playing out his hand. Why hadn't she remembered that Judson never backed down from a challenge? He was always ripe for one. Now was no exception.

"Katy Ryan—" He spoke loudly, extending his arms as Romeo might have done to Juliet as she stood on the balcony. Ready to die of embarrassment, Kathryn started to retract the challenge. But she wasn't given the chance.

"I came to convince you that it's me you love, not Charles Court, who is twice your age and not your type—but me, Judson Taylor." He slapped a hand to his heart, pausing dramatically. "I was your first love. Your only love. Your—"

"Judson!"

"What?" He gave her an innocent look.

"Knock it off!" She hissed the demand.

"What's wrong? Was I too loud?" he inquired lazily. "I only wanted to make sure you could hear me."

"Everybody could hear you," she snapped. "I

wouldn't be surprised if one of the neighbors has called the police. This is a respectable neighborhood."

"I'm not doing anything illegal," he replied smoothly. "And I don't particularly care who hears how I feel about you. Of course, if you'd be more comfortable, I'll come in the house and—"

"You've already had your say," she cut in angrily. "Now just go."

"But I'm not finished." He cleared his throat and began again. "I know you love me, Katy, my darlin'. I could tell by the way you kissed me, with such passion, your flesh burning hot and—"

Kathryn gasped in horror. "Stop it!" she ordered. "Just stop it this minute!"

"Are you ready to talk to me privately?" he challenged.

"You're a raving lunatic!" she sputtered in disgust.

"No." He shook his head. "I'm just determined to see you—by fair means or foul."

He couldn't have made his intention more obvious. Kathryn ground her teeth in irritation.

"I'll come down," she muttered. She started to move away from the window, then stopped to point a warning finger at him. "Don't you dare say another word until I get there."

"Yes, ma'am," he replied with mocking acquiescence.

Not completely trusting him, Kathryn hurried from the room. She slipped her robe on as she descended the stairs and went to the kitchen. She took an extra second to tie the sash before she opened the door.

"Hi." Judson stood casually with his hand braced against the frame of the screen door. "I knew you'd want to see me tonight."

"Do I have any choice?" Kathryn watched him through the wire mesh that separated them.

"No, I guess not." He grinned lazily. "Can I come in?"

"It's very late."

"But not too late," he countered.

And Kathryn knew he wasn't referring to the time. "It is," she insisted.

"We have to talk," Judson said seriously.

"About what?" She was deliberately obtuse, postponing the inevitable discussion because it was going to be difficult.

"About us," he informed her patiently.

"There is no us." Her reply was clipped. "Why won't you accept that?"

"Why are you willing to accept it?" he challenged.

"Because I'm a realist, Judson. I gave up on dreams a long time ago." Her voice was low but steady.

"If that's true, I feel sorry for you." He gave her a long, searching look. "Without dreams, you might as well quit living. When there's nothing left to hope for, or work for, or pray for, the few small things you do manage to get from this life don't amount to much."

Kathryn didn't want to think in those terms.

There was definitely something to be said for settling for just a little less all along the way and ending up with more in the long run. Dreams were glorious while they lasted, but it was agony when the time came to wake up.

"Is that what you came here to tell me?" she asked coolly.

His chest expanded on an indrawn breath. "I didn't come here to tell you anything. We need to talk—both of us, and settle this once and for all."

"It's been settled for a long time." Her nails dug into the wooden door until she felt the paint start to dent beneath the pressure.

A yard light flashed on next door. Judson glanced impatiently toward it. "Are you going to let me in?"

"Will you leave if I don't?" She already knew the answer. The determination in his face was unyielding, his patience wearing thin. She sensed that he was feeling the same thing she was—that this waiting game couldn't go on indefinitely. Something had to happen, one way or another.

Woodenly she backed away from the door and gave him a level look as he entered. From the beginning everything had been building toward this moment, the time when the split would be final. Knowing it was almost over brought little relief.

She gave the door a push and it closed noisily. Judson took a couple of steps toward the table, then hesitated, throwing her a questioning glance. Kathryn neither moved nor invited him to sit down. She didn't say anything either, unable to initiate the discussion when she knew how it was going to end.

Judson looked around the kitchen. He seemed tense and uncomfortable. It was the first time Kathryn could remember seeing him uncertain.

"Is there any coffee?" he asked.

"I guess not." Her gaze moved to the empty coffeepot, fully aware that he was searching for a way to ease the tension.

"I'd make a pot, but I know you won't be staying that long."

He looked at her, his voice hard and accusing. "You're not going to make this easy for me, are you?"

Easy for him! Kathryn wanted to laugh, but it hurt too much. Didn't he have any idea what she had been going through ever since he'd come back?

"You're the one who wanted to talk," she reminded him. "Not me."

"So you're going to make it as difficult as possible," he concluded, a muscle jerking in his jaw. "All right. We'll do it your way."

Shoving his hands into the pockets of his navy slacks, Judson stared at her, as if trying to decide where to begin. His brooding gaze made her conscious of her attire. The thin satin robe molded itself to every dip and curve of her figure. A smoldering fire was kindled in his dark eyes as they wandered over her. Kathryn was shaken by the sensation that he was making love to her in his mind. A disturbing heat began to warm her blood. She had to stop this silent communication before his seduction of her ceased to be mental.

"If it's to be my way, we'll end it right now." Before it even started and before the pain of parting had a chance to grow more intense.

At her crisp response, he looked suddenly tired, the grooves alongside his mouth growing deeper with grimness. Kathryn had the feeling she had figuratively slapped him down one too many times.

"I don't believe that's what you really want. But since you keep insisting, I'll leave. There's no point in trying to talk to you in this mood." He studied her, his eyes shuttered and unreadable. "I'm beginning to wonder if there's any point in trying to talk to you at all." He crossed to the door.

Kathryn stared at him, shocked that he was actually leaving. This was what she wanted, what she'd begged and demanded that he do.

"No, there isn't any point," she agreed tautly, and wondered why she didn't just let him go. "There never was."

"I'm beginning to see that." It was a grim reply, dead with resignation and lack of feeling.

Its flatness sent strong emotions running through her, too many to sort out. She channeled the turmoil into anger.

"Good," she flashed. "I'm glad we finally understand each other!"

The screen door was partially open. It slammed shut when Judson released it and pivoted to face her.

"Whatever gave you that idea?" His voice and expression were hard with anger. "I don't understand you at all!" His hand sliced rigidly through the air. "When I came back, I didn't know what the hell had happened to us in the past, but after I saw you again, it didn't matter anymore. All that mattered was that we didn't have to lose any more years." He shook his head and laughed, but it was a sound loaded with self-derision. "When I saw what you'd named your shop, I gambled my pride on the chance that you'd want to try again, too."

"I told you—"

"Yeah. I know." He cut her off. "You told me. But I played a hunch instead of listening. I guess I was wrong." A brash grin slashed his mouth, a mask for his pain. "I lose, darlin'. You win. Too bad neither one of us is coming away from this with a prize. Just remember, Katy. This is the way you wanted it."

It was true, and that made her responsible for all the loneliness she'd feel when he left. But it wasn't the way she'd wanted it the first time.

"Since when has what I wanted made any difference to you, Judson Taylor? Everything always had to be your way! At first, you didn't want to get involved with me because I was too young, so you ignored me. Then you decided it didn't matter, so you gave me the treat of your attention. Then you felt like moving on, so you went running off to Texas. And now...."

She paused to draw a choked breath. "Now, after all this time, *you're* the one who wanted to come back, so you came, expecting me to forget about all those years in between visits and the life I've built in the meantime. You never did things according to what I wanted!'' She was trembling with fury, but unable to clearly identify the cause. Was she still so angry about the past? Or was it because he was giving up so quickly now?

"So what are you going to do about it, Kathryn?" His face was harder than she'd ever seen it. He never called her Kathryn, and the sound coming from him chilled her clear through. "Do you want to keep griping about the past? Or do you want to do something about the future?"

"I don't want to do anything," she snapped, unable to accept his challenge.

"No." There was an angry blaze in his eyes as he crossed the room to tower over her. His mouth twisted into a harsh attempt at a smile. "You'd rather spend the rest of your life wallowing in self-pity than summon up enough guts to try again."

"You have no right to talk to me this way," Kathryn protested.

"I have every right," he stated tersely. "I'm the one you're doing this to—me, and yourself. We've been given a second chance. Most people feel damned lucky if they even have a first! But not you." The derisive words were ground through his teeth as he roughly grabbed her by the shoulders and yanked her to him. His fingers bit into the soft flesh of her upper arms.

"I ought to shake some sense into that stupid, beautiful head of yours," he growled thickly.

"Let go of me." She lifted her chin haughtily, green fire sparking in her eyes. Her clenched fists moved up to his chest, pushing at him.

"When I'm finished," he muttered, and pulled her into his arms. She fought him wildly, pushing and struggling against the crushing hold that pinned her to his chest.

"Damn you, Judson Taylor," she cried in frustration.

"And damn you, Katy Ryan, for making me want you all over again."

The same frustration was in his voice, making it rough and raspy as his mouth came down to claim her lips in a final search for satisfaction. Kathryn strained to break free, but her hands were trapped. The steel band that circled her so tightly allowed no escape. The hardness of his mouth pressed her lips against her teeth.

The kiss brought a pain that was purely emotional as Kathryn realized she would never have to fight him again. It was over at last. The thought brought a sob to her throat. Her body went limp against him, the protest going out of her as she surrendered to the sensations of his kiss one last time. Her sudden lack of resistance produced a change in the pressure of his mouth. The force of the kiss began to ease, becoming less and less demanding and more and more persuasive.

His tongue traced a path over the love-swollen outline of her lips, his warm breath mingling with hers as she began to tremble under his sensual ministration.

There was tenderness in his seductive actions, mixed in with a raw kind of want that he held severely in check. He was no longer taking; he was asking, and for Kathryn, that was all it took.

Of their own accord, her fingers slowly uncurled from the tight fists she had made of them and spread across his chest to dig into the material of his shirt and the muscled flesh beneath it. His tongue probed past the white barrier of her teeth to mate with hers, and any remaining barrier of her resistance also collapsed. Again there was an intensity of feeling that was both physical and emotional. But this time the two were of one accord, both body and emotions responding to desire, not pain, and the hunger of her body was made ravenous by her love.

She strained against him, wanting to defy physical laws and fuse herself to the hard angles and planes of his body. His roaming hands expressed a similar need, pressing her to him with urgent, molding caresses that fevered her flesh and turned her blood into white-hot lava.

A groan sounded in his throat as he covered her face with searing kisses. "See how it is with us, Katy?" His husky voice was lower than a murmur, a faint tremor in it betraying how moved he was. "It'll always be this way." His mouth hungrily nuzzled the shell-like opening of her ear. She shuddered involuntarily. "Like a consuming fire...."

It was an accurate choice of words, and Kathryn had an instant mental image to go along with them. Harsh, cold reality came back to taunt her with the truth. When Judson moved to reclaim her lips, she turned her head, resting her cheek against his chest. She could hear his heart pounding, his breathing labored and heavy. The knuckles of one hand gently stroked her cheek and moved under her chin to lift her face up for his inspection. She closed her eyes tightly, resisting the light pressure.

"What's wrong?" There was confusion and concern in his husky request for an explanation.

"You're so right," she said on a painful sigh. "What we have is like a consuming fire."

"And that bothers you?" He frowned. "Why?"

The weighty silence didn't last long, but when Kathryn finally spoke, her voice was sad.

"Because that kind of heat will do just what it says—blaze furiously for a while, then burn itself out until eventually nothing is left." And then what? Where would she be? Kathryn already knew the answer because she'd been there before. Venturing over the same ground was a terrifying prospect.

For a long moment Judson was still. Kathryn could feel the conflict within him. She knew he wanted to argue the point, and she braced herself to withstand his brand of persuasion.

Instead of trying to kiss away her fears, Judson sighed heavily and set her away from him. She blinked, then watched with rounded eyes as he reached to cup the side of her face with his large hand. The other hand tenderly brushed a few strands of hair back from her face, then trailed in a feather caress over her cheek and jawbone.

"Katy." His voice was low and intense. "I love you." His stormy eyes probed deeply into hers in search of an echo to his declaration. She stared at the floor, so Judson couldn't see the answering depth of her love. "I've done all I know how to do to prove it to you. If it isn't enough, I'm sorry— for both of us. I really am sorry." There was a tightness in his words, a masculine attempt to restrain strong emotion that was nearly her undoing.

With his hands cupped to her face, thumbs under her chin, he lifted her lips to meet his descending mouth. It was a hard, brief kiss that never had a chance to flame out of control. It was a goodbye kiss, and the realization brought stinging tears to her eyes. They blurred Judson as he walked out the door.

KATHRYN SWIRLED THE WINE in the stemmed glass, staring absently at the play of candlelight on the pale-gold liquid. Across the small table, Charles was talking about something, but Kathryn couldn't keep her mind on the subject. She set the glass down, her gaze straying to the door as someone entered the French restaurant.

"He's not coming, Kathryn." The use of her name prodded her into an awareness of Charles.

"What?" A little guiltily, she pulled her eyes away from the door.

"You're looking for Judd, aren't you?" Rather than being a question, it was a smooth observation.

"I guess I was," she admitted, but an explanation was required. "I . . . I'm so used to having him impose on us, I guess I just keep expecting him to pop up."

At first that had been true, but she was beginning to realize it wasn't going to happen. It was Wednesday and she hadn't seen him at all since he'd walked out of her kitchen door the previous Friday night. She wished that she could feel happy about that, but all she really felt was empty. There was a hollow, gnawing ache inside that wouldn't go away.

"You're not missing him, are you?" Behind the teasing inquiry, there was a measuring quality.

"Missing him?" She tried to make it a scoffing sound, and avoided a direct answer. "I was the one who asked you to arrange it so we wouldn't have to see him so often. Remember?"

"Ah, yes." A trace of wryness edged his smile. "I remember that conversation well. You were feeling a bit neglected."

"Yes," she murmured.

"Then you should be very happy about the recent turn of events. Taylor's been so busy, I haven't seen him at all this week. The last time I talked to him was Monday, and that was just a quick phone call to check my progress on those leases I'm chasing down for him." His face bore a disgruntled expression, but it was quickly wiped away with a smile of chagrin. "I've just broken a promise."

She looked at him blankly. "A promise?"

"Yes, I promised myself that I wouldn't discuss business tonight."

"It's okay," she insisted with a wan smile. The subject didn't really matter to her since she barely heard half of what he said. She'd listened enough to know that Judson was still in town. That knowledge made it difficult to think about anything else.

"No, it isn't." He shook his head. "I want tonight to be ours, with no outside interference. You were right the other day. I have been neglecting you. It was unavoidable, but highly regrettable."

"I understand, Charles." She absently shrugged away the implied apology as her gaze wandered again to the restaurant entrance. It was another false alarm and her spirits dropped another notch.

Charles shifted his position and brought an arm up to rest on the table. The movement attracted her preoccupied glance. It was a full second before she recognized the small box in his hand for what it was. Charles instantly had all of her attention.

"What's that?" She darted him a wary, questioning glance.

Smiling indulgently, he opened the jeweler's box and set it in the middle of the table. An elaborate engagement ring sparkled brightly from a bed of blue velvet. A cluster of small diamonds surrounded a large center stone.

"I thought this might make you feel a little more pampered," he said, smiling broadly at her stunned expression. "Don't you like it?" It was a teasing question, carrying none of its implied concern.

"I...it's beautiful, Charles." Kathryn felt shaky inside, suddenly panicky because Charles was breaking all the rules. He wasn't following the comfortable pattern, the one where he casually mentioned marriage and then let the subject drop.

"I thought you'd like that style," he confided. "It suits you."

Actually it didn't suit her at all. The ring was gorgeous and had to have been terribly expensive, but Kathryn doubted that she would ever be comfortable wearing something so elaborate. A simpler style would have been more to her liking. But that had nothing to do with her reluctance. As Charles removed the ring from the box, her own hands slipped away from the table, out of reach.

The smile was replaced by a frown that questioned her action.

"What's wrong?"

"Nothing," she insisted with forced brightness. "This is just such a surprise."

"Surprise?" He continued to frown and there was a watchfulness about him. "Why should it come as a surprise? We've considered ourselves engaged for nearly a year. Actually, this ring is rather late in coming, wouldn't you say?"

"I suppose, but . . . ." The silence lengthened as she searched for reason to delay accepting the ring.

"But what, Kathryn?" It was a steel-hard challenge. "What's your excuse this time?"

"Excuse?" She was confused by both his words and the hardness of his tone. "What do you mean, my excuse?"

"Every time I talk about getting married, you pull back," he accused. "Yet you insist that it's what you want, too. Is it or not?"

"Of course it is," she replied automatically. "I just don't believe that marriage is something you should rush into."

"We've been together two years," he countered with dry impatience. "That isn't rushing, by anybody's standards."

"Well it is by mine," she retorted, resenting the way he was pressuring her.

"It wouldn't be if you were sure," he declared grimly. "Maybe you'd better give it some more thought."

He put the ring back in the box and snapped the lid shut. Kathryn flinched at the finality of the sound. It was on the tip of her tongue to reassure Charles. He'd advised her to give it more thought, but what was there to think about? Of course she wanted to marry him. Judson's reappearance hadn't changed that. She had never claimed to be wildly in love with Charles, so in that respect the situation remained the same.

Yet she continued to withhold the words that would prompt Charles into placing his ring on her finger—just as she had always avoided giving a definite answer to his suggestions that they set a wedding date. It wasn't a question of whether she intended to marry him. It was simply a question of when. Since Kathryn still wasn't ready to make that decision, she held her silence.

"Are you ready to order?" Charles stuffed the ring box into his pocket and picked up the menu.

"Yes." She sighed, turning her attention to the waiter.

CHAPTER THIRTEEN

THE EVENING WAS WARM and still, the stickiness of the day clinging to the night. A thick blanket of clouds hung low in the sky, refusing to relinquish the moisture they carried into rain. The air was heavy and almost wet.

There was an oppressive quality to the atmosphere as Kathryn and Charles walked slowly toward the house. She glanced at him and knew the heaviness between them wasn't caused by the weather. It had existed all through dinner and showed no signs of lifting. Even though the ring hadn't been mentioned again, it was uppermost in both their minds.

"I'm going to Topeka for a few days," Charles announced, breaking the silence that had followed the meal.

"You are?" She looked at him, mildly curious. His expression was thoughtful. "When?"

"I'm leaving tomorrow." It was a decisive statement.

"Tomorrow?" The information startled her. "Why didn't you tell me sooner?"

"I just now decided," he said flatly. "When I return, I want an answer."

"But..." Kathryn began. This wasn't like Charles. "I don't know if I can give you one by then."

"You'll give me one," he assured her. "If it's not yes, it'll be an automatic no. We've gone as far as we're going like this." It was not the words so much as his tone of voice that convinced Kathryn he meant what he said.

Her thoughts began to race, searching for a way to lessen his determination without forcing him into a position of breaking off their relationship entirely. Somehow she had to convince him the time wasn't quite right for marriage—yet. Waiting just a little longer would be better for both of them. They had been through this before and she had always managed to convince him. She would again.

"Let's not be too hasty, Charles." She linked her arm through his, smiling up at him. "You're upset. When you've had a chance to think it over, I'm sure you'll realize that a few more—"

"A few more what?" he interrupted impatiently. "A few more years? You're right, Kathryn. I am upset. But only because I have thought it over. It has finally dawned on me that you might be only stringing me along, keeping me around because you're a single woman in a small town and I'm a convenient escort."

"That isn't true," she denied, shocked by the accusation.

"Then set a wedding date," he challenged. "In the very near future."

"But Charles, I have to—"

"You have to decide," he insisted quietly. "It's just that simple." Automatically they had made the turns to take them to the house. A light was burning in the kitchen window as they walked to the back door. On the porch steps, Kathryn paused, facing him stiffly.

"Would you like to come in?" She sounded unnaturally formal. She was angered by the stand he had taken and frustrated by his refusal to listen to reason.

"No." There was no hesitation. "It's best if we leave things the way they are until I get back." Out of habit Charles began to lean toward her. In absent compliance, Kathryn tipped her head back to accept his kiss. Before there was any contact, Charles stopped his movement, abruptly pulling himself upright. "Goodnight, Kathryn." The words were clipped. Without waiting for a response, he turned and walked away. Her mouth dropped open in surprise, then a surge of irritation snapped it shut. No matter how impatient Charles became, she wouldn't be forced into taking a step she wasn't ready for. It was her decision, and she would make it in her own good time. She resented Charles for trying to rush her.

Pressing her lips tightly together, Kathryn opened the door and entered the kitchen. Anger and frustration drummed at her temples. Without conscious thought, she walked straight to the cupboard where the aspirin was kept. It was becoming a habit.

"Another headache?"

Startled, she looked over her shoulder. Buck was sitting at the table, a cup of coffee in front of him.

"Oh." Her small smile showed relief. "You're home."

"Yeah. I do stay home once in a while." Buck grinned.

"Not much." She filled a glass with water, then swallowed two pills. Leaving the glass in the sink, she glanced curiously at Buck. "What's been keeping you so busy lately? Ruby?" It was a hopeful question.

Buck had been out nearly every night, and Kathryn had had little opportunity to ask him about his activities. She assumed he was making some progress with the widow, but she also suspected the transition involved in changing their relationship would be a slow one. The line between friendship and courtship could be awkward to cross.

"I been seein' Ruby some." Buck lowered his gaze and sipped at his ever-present cup of hot, strong coffee.

Some. The admission seemed to confirm Kathryn's thoughts. Things were moving along smoothly but slowly. Ruby had obviously given him some encouragement, or Buck wouldn't have been seeing her at all.

"Course, I haven't been spendin' every minute with her," he stated, still concentrating on the white coffee cup and its contents. After a second or two, he lifted his eyes to look at her. "I been spendin' some of my evenin's with Judd."

Kathryn trailed her finger over the countertop, struggling to appear offhand. "Oh?" It was a prompting sound that asked for more information.

Buck considered her shrewdly. "Yeah," was the only response.

"How come you're not with him tonight?" she persisted brightly, pretending only an idle interest.

"He's busy." It was a noninformative reply and completely unsatisfactory.

"Buck . . . ." Kathryn hesitated.

"Yeah?" There was a knowing glitter in his eyes, a small smile denting his leathery cheeks.

She chewed on her lower lip. The determination that had kept her from asking about Judd was steadily being eroded by curiosity. She decided to give in to it. "What's he been doing with himself all week?"

"Workin' I guess. Haven't seen him since Monday, but me and him kept pretty busy over the weekend. 'Course, he wasn't in too good a mood. I suppose you know the reason for that more than anybody, though, don't ya?" Now Buck was the one probing for information.

A frown had gathered on Kathryn's face, her thoughts blocking out the last remark. Monday. A suspicion started to grow. Charles hadn't talked to Judson since Monday, either.

"What did he say the last time you talked to him?" she asked.

"Not a lot." The old man frowned, scratching his head through thinning hair. "He was real busy—and a little grouchy," he recalled with a laugh.

"And you haven't talked to him since," Kathryn reaffirmed, a tightness in her voice.

"Nope."

"Tell me, Buck. Don't you find that a little strange?" She suddenly felt raw and brittle. "I mean, the man has practically been a fixture around here for the last few weeks. If he wasn't with me and Charles, he was with you. Now, suddenly, no one has seen him since Monday."

"He said somethin' about bein' tied up for a few days. I don't see anything strange about that." He watched her with keenly assessing eyes.

"No, I don't suppose there is." Her breath-filled laugh was void of humor. "Strange is probably the wrong word for his behavior. Typical is more like it. Here today, gone tomorrow. That's very typical behavior—for a drifter."

Abruptly she turned and walked to the cupboard, conscious of Buck's gaze. She took down a mug, filled it with coffee, and sipped at it, nearly scalding her tongue.

"You're gettin' all worked up over nothin'," Buck chided. "Judd didn't say anything about leavin' town. Matter of fact, I got the feelin' he was gonna be around quite awhile. Last time I talked to him, he said he was fixing up his motel room for a temporary office." There was a thoughtful pause.

"I just can't get over what that boy's made of himself. I don't see how you can still call him a drifter."

"I called him a drifter, not a hobo," Kathryn differentiated between the two. "Money has nothing to do with it." The coffee lost its appeal. She set it on the counter, mindless of the way it sloshed over the rim. "It's his lack of commitment to people and places that I'm talking about. He breezes into town when he feels like it, then breezes out whenever the urge strikes him. He just leaves people dangling, wondering if...."

Her throat went tight, bringing an immediate halt to her words. It wasn't fair for him to do that, to let people go on indefinitely, always waiting, always wondering. Yet was that any different from what she was doing to Charles? Didn't he, too, deserve to know where he stood?

"There's one thing you don't have to wonder about," Buck insisted. "Judd's still in love with you."

There was a foolish leap of her heart, but Kathryn steadied it. "Any chance Judson and I might have had ended long ago. Nothing can change what happened."

With a deep breath and a faint lifting of her chin, Kathryn came to a decision. There was a calendar hanging on the wall near the door. She walked purposefully to it, lifting the page to study the dates of the following month.

"Charles formally proposed tonight. He wants to get married right away."

A loaded silence fell. Within seconds, it was shattered by Buck's explosive voice.

"You can't marry Charles!"

Kathryn flinched. Recovering quickly, she turned calmly to Buck. "You've always known that we planned to be married."

"Things are different now." His large-knuckled hands were flattened on the tabletop, restless energy evident in the tautness of his wiry frame.

"Why?" Her hands moved to her hips in challenge. "Because Judson came back, digging up all the old painful memories?"

"No." He met her look with a challenge of his own. "Because Judson came back, period."

Her eyes flashed, angry and incredulous. "Seven years, Buck! I didn't hear from him once in seven years! Don't you realize how long that is? I can't pretend that none of those things happened—that the past doesn't exist. I've spent all this time building a life that he can't fit into. You can't expect me to just be able to forget everything else and pick up where we left off."

"I expect you to have enough smarts to know you can't be happy with a man you don't love," Buck growled.

"I care for Charles a great deal," she insisted.

"You don't love him." The chair was shoved back as Buck pushed to his feet. "And you can't stand there and look me in the eye and tell me that you do."

Her gaze wavered, then held his. "No," she admitted. "I can't. But being in love has never done very good things for me.'' She tried to smile and joke aside the hurt in her expression. ''I think I'm better off being in like.''

Lately she hadn't even liked Charles very much, becoming irritated and impatient every time she turned around. But that was only because of Judson. She took consolation in the knowledge. She had been content with Charles before and she could be again. He had his flaws, but none that couldn't be overlooked.

''Don't you remember how happy you and Judd were?'' Buck challenged her with memories, all sunshine and golden.

''I try not to.'' Kathryn felt her composure splintering. ''Good night, Buck.'' She walked past him, too conscious of his gaze.

''You can have it, Kathryn.''

She paused in the archway, trying to keep her tears at bay. After a few seconds she looked back. ''For how long?''

''I can't answer that.'' The assurance she wanted so badly didn't materialize. It couldn't. ''But don't make the mistake of bein' so bitter about the past that you mess up your chances for the future,'' Buck warned.

The advice was too familiar. ''Has Judson been talking to you about me?'' she demanded, feeling betrayed.

''No.'' Buck frowned at the apparent change of subject. ''We usually talk about everything but you. Why?''

''He told me almost the same thing the other

night," she admitted reluctantly, and wished she hadn't asked. "I just thought...."

Buck was shaking his head, a sadly amused smile curving his mouth. "I don't have to talk to anybody to guess what you're doin'. It happens all the time. People get hurt real bad and it turns 'em bitter. That's what happened to your ma." His sigh held regret. "Too bad, too. If she'd ever been able to forget the way your daddy done her wrong, and forgive him for it, she might have been able to trust me a little more. But she was spoiled on lovin' and trustin' after that. Deep down she was afraid the same thing might happen again." He shook his head. "That's the really bad part about not forgivin'. It eats at your guts till there ain't hardly nothin' left inside except bitterness. You end up bein' just a tough, hollow shell. Ya don't feel much. Can't get hurt anymore. But ya don't really live anymore either. Don't seem worth it to me," he said. "Nope, it sure don't."

"But I've forgiven Judson," Kathryn said, to show Buck that she was not following in her mother's footsteps. "It wasn't his fault. I can accept that. But I can't forget what I went through when he left. I could never go through it again." She didn't want to have to try.

"Forgettin' is part of forgivin', Kathryn. Because if you can't forget what happened the first time, you can't trust nobody enough to let there be a second time. You still love Judd, but you can't forget, so you're runnin' like a scared rabbit. And you're gonna' mess up your chance for a future because of it, same as your ma did. I'd think on that, if I was you." He pulled out the chair and sat down, his piece said. "Night, Kathryn."

"Good night," she said absently.

As she climbed the stairs, Kathryn conceded that Buck was right. She was running scared... terrified, because there was so much potential for the scars from the past to open up into fresh wounds.

Over the years she had healed, but not completely. As Buck had pointed out, her recovery would never be final until the forgetting was accomplished. Without progressing beyond that last stage, there would always be fear.

Yet was that such a tragedy? It was fear that inspired caution in all things. It was what kept children from playing with fire or running into a busy street. It was a healthy emotion instilled for protection, necessary to survival. When someone gets burned, the memory of the pain lessens the chances of carelessness around fire and a recurrence of the accident is prevented. And Judson was Kathryn's fire.

The emotions that ran between them were too strong and too hot. They already rated at the top of the scale, so where could they go except down? There was no way of predicting how long it could last—or *if* it could last. Especially with Judson.

But Charles...he was a different story. With him she would be guaranteed a future. If it lacked the blinding sunshine of even a day spent with Judson, it would at least hold the promise of a lifetime during which there would be no dark lonely nights.

Lying in bed, Kathryn sorted through all the facts and knew there was only one way to go. The safe way. The one in which she was guaranteed a future of companionship with no risk of heartache.

More and more, she was coming to understand her mother—her pain, her motivation, her fears. It wasn't justification for some of her actions, but Kathryn could sympathize with Mattie and the painful events in her life that were responsible for the embittered woman she had become. Her hard shell had been her protection.

It was a natural result that Kathryn could understand. She too needed some kind of protection. In her case, fear of loss would serve as her armor, as opposed to the bitterness that had shielded her mother. Either way the result would be the same. Love wouldn't have any more place in her life than it had had in her mother's.

Kathryn closed her eyes, the decision for her future made. Sleep didn't come easily.

LIFTING THE TELEPHONE RECEIVER from the kitchen-wall base, Kathryn hesitated a few seconds before dialing. She bit her lip, staring at the push-button numbers and feeling the emptiness inside her that was never going to go away. Her only consolation was that it could be worse, so much worse, if she had listened to her heart instead of her common sense. With grim determination she jabbed her index finger at the buttons, dialing the number from memory.

The familiar, heavy tread of footsteps thumped on the porch, and Kathryn hesitated again. This was a call she wanted to make in private. The door swung open and slammed shut as she reached to replace the receiver. Kathryn jumped at the loud bang created by the forceful closing of the door.

"Buck!" With the receiver on its hook, she turned and gave him a startled glance.

There was a tight, closed look about his expression that told Kathryn the slamming of the door had been no accident.

"Who were you talkin' to?" His head jerked in the direction of the telephone, although he didn't really seem interested in the answer to his question. He continued into the kitchen, walking right past her.

"Nobody," she replied absently, watching Buck with a frown. "I was going to call Charles—"

"That figures," Buck snapped.

A chair was jerked out from the table with the same kind of angry force he'd used on the door. He dropped into the seat and leaned forward, resting his forearms on the table.

"What figures?" Kathryn asked, a little irritably. She was sensitive on the subject of Charles. The critical tone from Buck struck a nerve.

He flashed her a brooding look. "I don't know why I ever took advice from somebody who ain't even got enough sense to run her own affairs right," he growled.

"Advice?" She looked at him blankly, ignoring his criticism of her decision to marry Charles. "What advice?"

"About Ruby," he snapped. "She ain't interested in me." A flash of pain entered his eyes at the admission. Buck was hurting, and the pain was channeled into anger—a more manly emotion. "She told me today that Hank Wright has gone and proposed."

All Kathryn's defensiveness went right out the window. "I'm so sorry." Both for Buck and for having encouraged the romance. But she had been so certain that the widow's reception of Buck would be warm.

Impulsively she took a step toward him, then checked the motion. A physical display of her sympathy—like a hug—would embarrass Buck and make things that much worse.

"Aw, it ain't your fault," he muttered, slumping a little in the chair. "I knew it all along. Just wasn't meant to be, that's all. Some things ain't."

Kathryn already knew that, from experience. So she also knew how painful it was to accept harsh reality. She deeply regretted her matchmaking attempts.

"I guess you're right, Buck," she murmured, her voice full of the sympathy he wouldn't want her to verbalize. "I just thought...." It no longer mattered. She had obviously been wrong.

There was nothing more to say. Kathryn felt awkward. If Buck wanted to talk, he would do so. Obviously he didn't want to discuss Ruby. She sensed that her presence was unwelcome at this particular time; it was forcing Buck to contain his emotions.

"I should probably be getting to work," she said to excuse herself, and edged toward the hall that led to the shop.

The only response from Buck was a brief nod. Kathryn left him to lick his wounds in private.

The fact that she had contributed to his pain ate away at her. If she had only kept her mouth shut on the subject and minded her own business, Buck would be having an easier time of it now.

Guilt for her interference nagged at Kathryn. She had only been trying to help, acting on assumptions she believed to be true. Instead she had caused pain for someone she cared about very deeply.

It wasn't so much different from what her mother had done.

The thought plagued Kathryn for the rest of the day. And each time her mother's image appeared in her mind, there was more love in Mattie's expression than Kathryn had been able to see in weeks.

"THIS COLOR WILL BE BEAUTIFUL on you, Mrs. Morgan." Kathryn carefully folded the turquoise silk dress and placed it in the box.

"It's my husband's favorite," the young woman confided.

"Then I would say he has excellent taste." Kathryn smiled and handed her the box. "Thank you, and come back again."

She was looking through a dress catalog about an

hour later when she heard the boutique door slam. Startled, she looked up to see Judson, dressed in a red polo shirt and crisp Levi's. She hadn't seen or heard from him in over a week, not since that Friday night. She felt a hot rush of pleasure that couldn't be cooled, a crazy fluttering of her heart that couldn't be stopped. But she did try.

He was coming toward her, closing the distance between them with long urgent strides. It was a full second before Kathryn recognized his haste for what it was—the contained energy of anger. His brown eyes were darkened to black, his gaze demanding, accusing and condemning her all at the same time.

The air seemed to crackle around him as he came to a halt at the opposite side of the counter. Anger emanated from him in waves, paralyzing Kathryn, so she couldn't speak. Long charged seconds passed before he finally spoke.

"What kind of woman are you?" he demanded.

Kathryn was stunned by the force of all that male power and fury towering over her. "I...I don't know what you mean."

With savage energy he yanked a rolled newspaper from his back pocket and slammed it down on the counter in front of her. "This is what I mean." He clenched his teeth.

She pulled her gaze away from his face to stare at the paper. There was a picture of her, along with a wedding announcement. In the light of all the second thoughts she'd had since notifying the newspaper, it seemed impossible that she'd forgotten. Her fingers nervously twisted the diamond ring on her left hand.

"You knew we were planning this," Kathryn reminded him, and flinched at the censure in his eyes.

"I never thought you'd let it get this far," he snapped. "I thought you had more backbone than that!"

She stiffened at the assault. "Backbone has nothing to do with this, Judson."

"Is that right?" he taunted. "I suppose you're going to deny that you want to marry Charles because he makes you feel safe? Because he can shield you from all the unpleasant things, like thinking for yourself and making your own decisions—and living with the consequences of those decisions?" He snorted out a derisive laugh. "You're trying to take the easy way out and there isn't one. Believe me, Katy. I oughta know."

He swung away from the counter to stand at right angles to her, his gaze straying to the display window. A muscle twitched in his tanned cheek.

"For seven years I've been looking for an easy way—any way." There was a certain rawness in his taut declaration. "You might as well accept the fact that it doesn't exist. Sooner or later, those feelings inside you have to be acknowledged. You can ignore them all you want, but they won't go away. You can marry someone else, but they'll be there to haunt you." The ache of experience was in his voice, more convincing than any words could have been.

She slowly moved her head from side to side, but it wasn't a denial of his prediction. It was a gesture of sheer helplessness, a mute protest against the truth. Judson watched her shake her head.

"You've been lying to yourself for so long, you probably aren't capable of recognizing the truth anymore," he accused.

But she did and it was agony. She had two choices. She could live for the moment or plan for a lifetime. It was crazy, but she suddenly couldn't make up her mind. It should have been so simple. The scales were balanced unequally, but tipped to which side? Angry confusion prodded Kathryn to find out.

"I recognize a few things, Judson Taylor. Like the fact that Charles can give me a lot of things you can't." Or won't, she thought. She was holding her breath. Belatedly, she realized she was waiting for Judson to match what Charles had to offer—namely, a guarantee of a future.

"Is that a fact?" His sweeping look was deceptively lazy, missing nothing. "I never knew you were so calculating," he drawled. "I suppose you keep a running tally for all your beaux." Judson touched a forefinger briefly to his tongue, then lifted the finger to chalk up an imaginary mark in the air. "This one can give me this. This one can give me that." Abruptly he stopped mocking her and leveled a serious glance at her face. "Is that the way it works, Katy?"

"No," she protested, but in a sense, she had been guilty of that.

"I tried to warn you once that Charles is a taker, a user," Judson said tersely. "Maybe the reason you couldn't see it was because you're one, too. You're planning to use Charles—you've already used me. And fool that I am, I came back for more."

"I used you!" Kathryn was shocked by the accusation. "How did you manage to come to that conclusion?"

He studied her silently for a moment, his mouth quirking cynically at the trace of self-righteousness in her indignant expression. "What's the matter, Katy? Don't you believe men can be used? Or is it only poor defenseless females that can be hurt?" He wandered toward the counter. "You were seventeen. I was twenty-six. I was a drifter, a highway bum who broke all the rules. To you, I represented danger, the exciting kind a woman often feels with a first lover. But when it came to waiting, sacrificing, and all those other tedious things, you wanted off the merry-go-round. You—"

"What's going on here?"

The sharp demand from Charles startled both of them. Kathryn's gaze leaped guiltily to where Charles was standing just inside the door. The volume of Judson's voice had risen to a shout. Obviously it had overridden the sound of the bell. It was impossible to tell how much Charles had heard. His expression was grimly suspicious as he crossed the shop.

"Kathryn?" Again, he demanded an explanation.

"It's...nothing," she insisted with a poor attempt at a smile.

"Tell him." Judson's low voice broke over the room like distant thunder, rumbling and threatening. Charles looked expectantly at Kathryn. Her gaze ricocheted away before it even made contact with his.

"There's nothing to tell," she murmured tightly.

The room suddenly became very quiet, filled with a smothering tension. Kathryn kept her head down to avoid eye contact with either of the men. But Judson's gaze was boring into her. She could feel it. She heard the deep breath he took and the grim sound of its long, slow release.

"I guess she's right," he said flatly. "Maybe there is nothing to tell."

Her eyelids shut as relief washed over her. This was a confrontation she had desperately wanted to avoid. Beneath the counter, she twisted the diamond ring on her finger and tried to ignore its heaviness. It was an anchor, something steadying amid this churning sea of emotions.

But she didn't feel steady at all when Judson picked up where he'd left off.

"You see—" the steadiness of his voice was a challenge in itself and Kathryn cringed "—I was under the impression that Katy was in love with me." He paused, letting his statement sear the air. Then he was picking up the newspaper and showing it to Charles. "So when I saw this announcement, I decided I'd better find out if I was right or wrong."

"Obviously you were wrong," Charles stated. "The announcement is proof of that."

Involuntarily Kathryn glanced at Charles. It was amazing that such an intelligent man could be so blind about something so obvious. With a flash of insight, Kathryn realized that Charles hadn't seen what was happening only because he hadn't wanted to see it. An awareness required action. It would have forced him to choose between his fiancée and a major career opportunity. Her gaze went to Judson. He was watching her much too closely.

"Is that true, Katy?" Judson wasn't taking Charles's word for it. He demanded hers. "Was I wrong?"

At her hesitation, Charles spoke up. "Of course you were. We're getting married in two weeks—"

"Shut up, Charles," Judson muttered. "I want to hear it from her." His gaze never left her face, not for a second. "You were bitter and hurt because you didn't have any choice the last time," he told her roughly. "This time it's all up to you. I'll accept your answer as final. Now. Was I wrong?"

His fingers gripped her chin, forcing her to look at him. The black depths of his eyes nearly drowned her with their intensity, absorbing her and trapping her as securely as if he'd taken her into his arms. An ache of tormenting misery choked her. Kathryn couldn't deny her love for him and he knew it. Her silence was an admission, but Judson wouldn't settle for that. The pressure of his fingers increased, demanding a verbal acknowledgment.

Tears filled her eyes and blurred her vision. He was asking everything of her and offering nothing in return. Her surrender might bring a few stolen weeks or months. And then what? She closed her eyes, hating him for what he was doing. He had no right to take everything from her in the name of love. But that was his intention and she was helpless to stop him. No one would believe her protest when it was obvious her heart belonged to Judson. Not even Charles. A strangled sound came from her throat.

Pivoting sharply, Kathryn jerked away from his grasp and bolted from the room. Charles called after her, but she was beyond listening. She raced up the stairs to her bedroom and slammed and locked the door. Then she leaned weakly against it, a fist pressed to her mouth in an attempt to stop the sobs.

There was loud conversation in the room below. Kathryn couldn't make out the words, but she didn't like the sound of the heated tones. It occurred to her, too, that it was only a matter of time before one of the men—or both—climbed those stairs. She couldn't face either one of them yet. She wouldn't.

With jerky movements, she stripped out of her dress and pulled on a pair of jeans. She grabbed a white blouse and thrust her arms through the short sleeves. Her fingers were shaking as she fumbled with the buttons. The glare of the late-afternoon sun spilled through her window to flash on the diamonds of her engagement ring. The sparkling light seemed to mock her. She yanked the ring from her finger and slapped it down on the dresser. Charles wouldn't want her to wear it. Not anymore.

Her chest hurt, and Kathryn felt sick. There was no relief in knowing the engagement was off. Everything was all mixed up. For so long she had let logic rule and she had been reasonably happy. A part of her wanted things to go on that way. It was so much easier. Safer.

Without conscious thought, she rummaged hurriedly through her closet until she found her Western-style boots. She tugged them on and slipped quietly into the hall. On tiptoe she made her way to the kitchen and out the back door.

CHAPTER FOURTEEN

THE LOWERING SUN was warm on her back as Kathryn reined the bay mare through the gate. Behind her, chickens squawked and clucked, strutting freely around Old Bill's farmyard. Ahead of her, there was open pasture.

At the first urging from its slim rider, the horse bunched its muscles and stretched out into an easy, rolling canter. The bay seemed to need the feeling of space and freedom as much as Kathryn did. She began to relax in the saddle, some of the stiffness leaving her limbs.

A wide ribbon of green marked the course of the lazy river. Preoccupied with her thoughts, Kathryn had paid little attention to the direction she had taken. She reined in sharply when she realized where she was headed.

Directly in front of her, a huge old willow tree hovered close to the riverbank. When she was a child, it had been her favorite place, a secret place. Later, she had shared it with Judson. She hadn't been back since that last time when they'd come here together.

The urge was strong to turn and leave, but something pulled at her. Maybe it was a need to face things, to finally come to grips with reality. As Judson had told her, pretending a situation didn't exist wouldn't make it go away.

Dismounting, she let the reins trail the ground. The horse immediately started to graze. Kathryn patted the horse's neck and walked to the weeping willow. The massive tree was like an umbrella, covering and secluding the area beneath its branches. Pushing several of the long trailing limbs aside, Kathryn entered the shaded hideaway. It was cool and damp.

Memories assaulted her as her gaze dropped to the thick carpet of grass under her feet. This was where she and Judson had made love, a love so dazzlingly perfect that at seventeen, Kathryn had been sure it would last a lifetime.

Raking her fingers through the length of her blond hair, she walked over to the trunk of the tree and sat down, leaning against it. The breeze whispered through the supple branches. Water lapped rhythmically at the nearby riverbank.

The bay whickered softly and stomped a hoof. Her idle glance swung to the horse, visible through the screen of branches. Then she felt the slight vibration and heard the sound of drumming hooves. It had to be Judson. While Kathryn had no idea how he'd known she'd be here, she couldn't really say she was surprised.

The buckskin he rode came to a halt beside the bay. Kathryn brought her knees up and locked her arms around them. There was a rapid escalation of her pulse, an ambivalent mixture of pleasure and alarm. The saddle leather groaned as Judson dismounted. Seconds later, the willow screen parted and he ducked inside.

The instant he saw her, he stopped. His ruggedly handsome features were relaxed, but a disturbing heat burned in his eyes. Kathryn had to tip her head back to look up at him.

"I thought I might find you here." His voice was low, containing none of the anger of an hour ago.

"Why?" It was a soft challenge. She wondered if he thought she had come here with the hope that he would follow. Then she wondered if she had. She couldn't forget the way she'd ridden straight to the willow tree.

One corner of his mouth lifted to dismiss her suspicion. "Buck was out in his garden when you left the house. He said you hightailed it out of there in blue jeans and boots. With clues like that, I didn't have to be much of a detective."

"I guess not," she murmured.

"Are you all right?" His concern was genuine.

Like Judson, Kathryn felt no lingering anger. Actually she wasn't sure what she felt. A little sad maybe.

"Sure." Her mouth curved into a melancholy smile. She tightened the circle of her arms on her knees and lowered her gaze. "I'm just dandy."

He wandered over and dropped down beside her. "I wasn't trying to spoil things for you." His voice was softly grim.

"I know. You only said those things in front of Charles to help me."

"It's true," he insisted lazily. "To help keep you from making a mistake."

"Don't you think that's for me to decide?" It wasn't a very powerful retort, because Kathryn knew she hadn't been very successful in making a decision she could be happy with.

A short laugh came from his throat. "Think? I *know* it's for you to decide. Why do you think I've been working so hard to give you plenty of data to sift through?"

"What do you mean?" Kathryn frowned.

He shifted to face her more squarely, propping himself up on an arm. The position left one hand free. He reached with his fingertips to trace the curve of her cheekbone down to the delicate line of her jaw. It was suddenly very difficult to breathe.

"I mean, pretty lady," Judson drawled, "that every chance I have to be near you stacks the odds more in my favor."

"That is purely a matter of opinion."

"I know." His hand cupped the back of her head to draw her closer. With her hands clasped around her knees, Kathryn didn't have a great deal of balance. As he tugged her sideways, she put an arm down to brace herself. Judson took her other hand and lifted it to his mouth. "It's my opinion." He brushed a kiss across her palm, then guided her hand to rest on the ridge of his shoulder. "And it's your opinion, too."

"You don't know that," Kathryn protested, but the hand on his shoulder remained, holding onto him and glorying in the feel of the rippling flesh beneath her fingers.

"I do." Slipping an arm around her waist, Judson moved to brush his mouth over her forehead and temple, then let it linger tantalizingly close to her lips. "I also know that Charles is still there for you—" his breath was warm on her lips, feathering over them until she longed for his kiss "—if that's what you really want.... Is it?"

"I don't know," she admitted in a husky voice. At the moment it certainly wasn't what she wanted, but how long could the moment last? Soon it ceased to matter, because his mouth was on hers and there was nothing on earth that could equal this moment. There was a glorious rush of blood through her veins and a wild hammering of her heart. In his arms Kathryn felt completely alive and wholly female.

Judson dragged his mouth from hers, slowly, reluctantly. "I know what I want," he muttered against her throat.

"What?" she whispered.

"The same thing I've always wanted." His voice was thickly disturbed. "You, Katy."

Curving her hand to the back of his neck, Kathryn pulled him with her as she lowered herself to lie flat on the ground. With a muffled groan, Judson crushed his mouth onto hers in hard possession. Her lips parted to invite a deepening of the kiss to its fullest intimacy while her reaching hands went around his middle and flattened across his back, feeling his muscles straining to press closer.

His driving hunger was insatiable. There was a raw urgency in the restless, roaming caress of his hands. Her flesh was set afire, her insides knotted with sweet agony. She felt his fingers deftly slipping the buttons of her blouse free from their stitched holes, his hand pushing aside the material to expose a creamy shoulder, and her hunger matched his.

An appetite that had gone too long unsatisfied consumed her. While his mouth nipped sensually on the curve of her throat and the exposed ridges of her collarbone, her fingers tugged at his shirt.

Then Judson was aiding her, lifting his weight from her for seconds that seemed entirely too long as he pulled the shirt over his head and tossed it aside. The look in his dark eyes made her moan softly in anticipation.

Her own eyes were heavy with desire as he reached for her. With a slowness and sureness of purpose that had her trembling, Judson pulled her into a sitting position and let his hands curve to the sides of her neck and slide onto her shoulders. The blouse dropped away and joined his shirt. Then Judson was unfastening the clasp of her lacy bra.

Despite the urgent cravings of their flesh, the undressing of each other was a slow process, a thing to be savored. The same held true when they were once again lying together on the soft bed of grass. Their rediscovery of each other was thorough. It was an experience that refreshed an intimate physical knowledge, but there was more.

There was the added excitement and awesome pleasure that accompanies lovemaking when there is emotional commitment.

"I love you, Katy," Judson declared huskily, as he lowered his weight onto her.

"I love you, too." It was an aching admission, an ache that intensified into sweet torture in the minutes that followed. The union of their flesh came in a sweeping rush of sensation that carried them both to dizzying heights. It was a glorious, spiraling ascent of pleasure that swelled and finally burst in a golden rush of fire. It left them weak and exhausted and wholly satisfied.

Lying in the protective crook of his arm, with her head pillowed on his shoulder, Kathryn had the feeling she had come home after a long, long absence. She felt strangely boneless, and utterly content. Her hand trailed over the flatness of his stomach and up to his chest, where she threaded her fingers through the curling mat of hair.

Judson captured her hand, stilling its movement while he pressed it to his chest. Beneath her fingers, Kathryn felt the steady beat of his heart. She tipped her head back to look at him. He held her gaze, the ebony darkness of his eyes probing in its search for something.

"Are you happy?" he murmured.

"Yes." Her body still tingled with leftover pleasure, and she was enveloped by Judson's warm musky scent. She had no desire to leave this place—or this man. It had been the same the last time they'd come here.... Her dreamy expression began to sober. She lowered her head and closed her eyes, trying to shut out the memory of Judson leaving her the very next day.

A fine tension rippled through him at her change of mood. "What is it, Katy?"

"Nothing," she insisted, determined not to let old hurts and new fears spoil this moment.

She tried to snuggle closer, but Judson removed the pillow of his shoulder, raising up on one elbow to look at her. "Tell me."

"It's nothing, Judson." She sat up and started to reach across him for her clothes. "We should probably start back."

He snared her arm before she reached her objective. "It's something," he insisted with an edge of impatience. "And I want to know what it is."

There was a turbulent darkness in her eyes when she looked at him. She didn't want to discuss the past. She just wanted to forget so she could embrace these warm feelings inside her a little bit longer. She didn't want to remember how fleeting they could be.

"Are you regretting what happened between us?" His narrowed eyes and the tone of his voice made it sound like an accusation.

"No." How could she?

"Then what is it?" There was a roughness to the demand, an almost desperate need to know. It confused her.

"I told you—"

"You told me that you didn't know what you wanted," he reminded her tersely. "Now I guess

I'm wondering if you've managed to make a decision yet.''

Her eyes widened, shocked and a little hurt that he could think that she could still be deciding between him and Charles. She hadn't consciously made a choice, but her actions should have spoken volumes. The act of love had certainly cleared up her own confusion. At least to the point that she now knew she could never marry Charles, regardless of the outcome between herself and Judson. And what would the outcome be?

He misinterpreted her silence, taking it as hesitation. His features hardened as he let go of her arm. "So what was this, Katy?" His gaze raked her nakedness to let her know what he was referring to. "Just a one-night stand?"

She didn't understand his attitude at all. "I don't know," she said, because it was true. "You tell me."

A frown drew his brows together and took away his anger, leaving only confusion. "You were the one who was having doubts," he accused.

"Can you blame me?" she asked, wondering why he couldn't understand her state of mind after all she had been through.

"Yes, I can blame you," he snapped. "Your indecision is tearing me apart. You keep dragging strings in front of me, then snatching them back before I can get a good enough grip to hold on to you."

"Do you really want to hold on to me, Judson?" There was an ache in her voice to know the answer—and to be able to trust in it.

He laughed shortly in disbelief. "I've wanted to hold on to you and not let you go ever since the first time I saw you. You got to me like nobody ever had before—and no one has since. I've traveled a lot of miles during the years we've been apart. Seen some of the most beautiful country in the world and done some things most people will never get a chance to try. But it never seemed to matter where I was— Texas, Colorado, Montana—or what I was doing. My heart was never really along for the trip. It's been in Deepwater, Kansas, with you, for the last seven years. And I've been cursing myself for leaving ever since."

Kathryn didn't—couldn't—doubt the sincerity of his words. They tugged at her emotions while also supplying grounds for some hope for the future. Without her, his life had been lacking something. Kathryn knew that he needed excitement to feed his restless soul. But if his travels and experiences could no longer provide the excitement, and losing her was really the cause of the void, maybe she could be enough for him—enough to insure that their love would last.

It was such a heady thought, Kathryn was almost afraid to believe it was possible. If she could have Judson and feel a reasonable amount of certainty that she would always have him, life could offer nothing better.

Tentatively she reached to touch his arm, drawing the wary sharpness of his glance. Overcoming the past wouldn't be easy, but she now knew she wanted to try.

"Promise you'll never do it again?" she urged fervently. "Leave me, I mean."

There was a sudden darkening of his eyes as Judson realized what she was saying. There was no more indecision. She had finally made her choice.

"Oh, Katy." Her name was a groan that was dragged from his throat.

He pulled her into his arms and kissed her with a sweet, raw longing that expressed what spoken promises never could. Then he buried his face in the curve of her neck and held her. She clung to him, arms around him, hands splayed across the bronze of his back. In his presence there was reassurance, and the hurt that had gone before faded in significance.

The pressure of his body pushed her slowly backward. His mouth hovered above hers for an instant. "I'll never leave you, darlin'. I swear."

His hard masculine lips fastened onto her mouth. The kiss was gentle and deep, a low-burning flame that was slow to ignite passion. Their passion was a building fire that had no danger of burning itself out before its time, because there was a higher plane to be reached.

And in time, they reached it. They were joined in a sweeping rush of ecstasy that melted them together as if they could never be separated again.

IT WAS ALMOST DARK before either of them was inclined to leave the shelter of the willow tree behind. After pulling Kathryn to her feet, Judson parted the curtain of branches and they emerged hand in hand into the fading afternoon light. The familiar stillness of a summer evening was settling over the land, warm and slightly sticky, without a breath of breeze to stir the humid air.

It was a lazy time of day. The stillness all around them seemed to dictate slow speech and slow movement. Even the horses had fallen under a languorous spell, moving only their tails as they lazily swished at flies.

"Seems a shame to disturb them, doesn't it?" Judson murmured, inclining his head toward the sleepy-eyed animals.

"Mmm," Kathryn said in agreement.

Releasing her hand, Judson wrapped an arm around her shoulders. Kathryn let her head rest against his chest. The position was both natural and utterly satisfying. A contented sigh escaped through her slightly parted lips. She was reluctant to leave the place where she had found so much happiness in so few hours.

"I suppose we should be getting the horses back before it gets dark and Old Bill starts wondering if something went wrong." Judson looked as reluctant to leave as she, despite his words.

"Buck is probably wondering about us, too." Kathryn tipped her head back to look at him. "You know he's going to be thrilled about this."

"This?" An eyebrow lifted, asking her to identify the subject of discussion.

"Us," Kathryn murmured, lowering her gaze. While it felt completely natural to be with Judson, it still seemed a little strange to refer to them as a couple. For so long she had deliberately put the possibility from her mind. Speaking about "us" as a reality almost seemed like tempting fate, which had never been kind to her.

"Buck was really shaken when he found out about my mother...the way she interfered," Kathryn told him, sobering at the thought. "I think the fact that it was all a mistake will make him twice as glad to see us back together. It won't seem like such a waste."

"But that's exactly what it was. A waste." The pressure of his arm around her shoulders tightened, as if to hold her there even though she made no move to free herself.

"Yes," she murmured.

"Did you love him, Katy?" It was an outwardly calm question, threaded with emotional undercurrents Kathryn sensed rather than heard.

"Who?" Turning, she braced her hands against his chest and levered enough space between them to look into his eyes.

"Your husband." The word didn't come easily for him.

Kathryn hesitated, startled by the mention of the nonexistent man. She had to tell him. There was a painful tightening of her throat as she recalled the time Buck had tried to convince her that Judson had the right to know the truth, the same as she did.

"Judson, I..." She licked her lips nervously, wondering where to begin, afraid he would be angry with her for not telling him sooner.

"I know. You didn't think I was coming back," he said grimly. "Under the circumstances, I guess I can understand why you'd marry someone else— but that soon?" His features darkened, and his intense gaze pierced her.

Kathryn closed her eyes, hearing the pain in his voice, knowing what he must be feeling. "I was never married, Judson."

There was a second of stunned and doubting silence. His hands gripped her shoulders.

"What?" he demanded.

When Kathryn opened her eyes, his hard, wary gaze pinned her to the spot. She nodded her head, emphasizing her claim.

"It was a story my mother made up to save my reputation." There was irony in her faint smile, because her reputation had been saved while everything else had been lost. "I was pregnant... with our child."

Her announcement rippled through him, bringing a pallor to his face. "Is that true? You were pregnant when I left?"

Kathryn nodded again.

A slow rage began to boil, returning the color to his face. "And Mattie knew it," he stated with a biting contempt that surprised Kathryn with its force.

Releasing her, he swung away. His handsome, rugged profile was turned to her, his features rigid as he fought to keep his anger under control.

"We can't blame her, Judson." Kathryn automatically began to defend her mother, but a distant part of her registered the fact that she meant what she was saying. Not only had she come to understand and feel sympathy for Mattie, but Kathryn no longer felt any real blame or bitterness. It had been a tragic waste, but she could accept it without hate or ill feelings toward the one who had caused it. It was better that way, because her mother had been a classic example of how bitterness only serves to destroy the one who harbors it.

Taking a step toward Judson, she sought to diffuse the anger that was hardening him against her mother. "She had a lot of personal problems that we never knew about," she began, but got no further as Judson jerked his gaze to her. It wasn't the anger that stopped her; there was something else in the darkness of his eyes. She was confused by it.

"What happened to the baby?" His voice was hoarse.

"I lost it," she murmured. "In my eighth month."

A muscle clenched in his jaw. "No wonder you didn't want anything to do with me before you knew I had come back for you. You must have hated me all those years." A harsh, derisive laugh escaped him. "And who could blame you?"

The dark glitter in his eyes was guilt, Kathryn realized, even though he wasn't to blame for what happened. Her expression softened.

"I never hated you," she admitted. "Sometimes I wanted to, but I couldn't." Because she had loved him all this time. She had simply failed to recognize it until recently. "I didn't want anything to do with you—before or after I learned the truth...because I was afraid." She paused, staring at the ground. "Judson, almost everyone I've ever cared for, I've lost, one way or another. I never want to go through that cycle again."

A finger was crooked under her chin, lifting her face for his inspection. The gentle, loving light in his eyes seared her with its warmth. Then it was his mouth that was searing her with its kiss, and the excitement that was both old and new moved swiftly through her veins.

Lifting his head, Judson looked at her and sighed. "We've got a lot to overcome, Katy. More than I realized."

She nodded soberly, knowing how very right he was. Too much had happened for them to simply forget. There were too many years of hurt that couldn't be wiped away with the wave of any magic wand—even the magic of love.

"I know." She bit pensively at her lip.

Judson detected her worry. He caught hold of her shoulders, gripping them hard. "Life isn't perfect, Katy, and neither are we. We're going to have our share of troubles like everyone else. But if we can understand that, it'll carry us a long way toward overcoming them. What we had seven years ago was special, but we can't go back. We aren't the same two people anymore. Life has taught us some things, and a lot of them we'd have been better off not learning. Now it's time to forget, start fresh with what we've got and build on it. We love each other and that will have to be the foundation. We can't let the past start eating away at that—the way we feel about each other—or our chances together aren't good. We have to hold tight to what we've got, Katy,'' he asserted, his voice hard with conviction, ''and make it even stronger.''

She listened to his voice, hearing the determination that rang through it. Her gaze searched his features and noted the strength etched into the hard angles of his jaw and the planes of his face.

''Yes,'' she said softly.

At the simple, firm agreement from her, Judson smiled. Her heart began tripping over her ribs as joy spilled through her, flooding her system and finally bubbling up in the form of laughter.

''Yes.'' Her green eyes sparkled up into his.

He took her hand, linking his fingers through hers. ''Come on.'' He led the way to the patiently waiting horses. ''We'd better get back.''

The ride back to Old Bill's place seemed very short, even though they kept the horses at a walk most of the time, not in any real hurry to reach their destination. When they did, they took care of the horses and the tack, then stopped by the house to talk with Old Bill for a moment. Judson had seen the bent, grizzled man earlier in the afternoon, when he'd stopped to ask permission to borrow the horse. As everyone in Deepwater seemed to, the man remembered Judson from years ago.

After they'd chatted for a few minutes and thanked Bill, they walked hand in hand to the graveled driveway. The tan car was parked next to Kathryn's.

"Why don't we just take one car home," Kathryn suggested on impulse, not liking the thought of being away from him for even a few minutes. There was such a warm, wonderful glow around her, and she didn't want it to fade.

"Why?" Judson arched a questioning eyebrow. "We'd just have to come and get the other one tomorrow."

She smiled, recognizing the logic of his statement. "I'm being silly, aren't I?"

"No." He shook his head. "It's a nice change of pace to have you wanting to be with me instead of telling me to get lost. That's hard on a man's ego, you know."

"Somehow I don't think you have to worry about having a shortage in the ego department," she teased.

"I'll take that as a compliment," Judson drawled.

"Of course you will." She mocked him warmly, conscious of how at ease she felt in his presence. As long as he was by her side, it seemed that nothing could ever go wrong.

They stopped beside her car and Judson opened the door for her. She glanced inside, but made no move to get in, wanting to postpone the moment of parting.

"What are we going to do about dinner?" She took it for granted that they'd have it together.

"I hadn't thought about it." He shrugged. "Whatever you want to do is fine with me."

"We could go to that little Italian place like we used to," she suggested.

"Sounds good," he agreed, and slipped a hand under her elbow to help her into the car. Leaning down, he kissed her with drugging force. The afterglow made it a little easier to smile when he closed the door and backed away. "I'll meet you at the house." He winked at her, then moved off in the direction of the sedan. Her eyes followed him every step of the way, loving the sight of him.

She waited until he pulled out of the driveway, then put her car in gear and followed. It was a short drive to the house. By the time she parked and switched off the ignition, Judson was out of the car and waiting. She hurried to catch up with him.

"Long time no see." Warm amusement slashed grooves in his cheeks as he commented on her haste.

"I thought so, too," she agreed on a teasing note. But she meant it.

As they walked to the back door, his arm settled naturally onto her shoulders. It was an entirely possessive gesture and the feelings it evoked were entirely pleasing. His hand shifted to the back of her waist as they entered the house. Buck was sitting at the kitchen table. One look at their expressions told him all he needed to know.

"Well, well, well," he murmured, a slow grin spreading across his face. "It looks like you two have finally come to an understanding."

With a downward glance, Judson let his eyes caress her features. "Of sorts," he murmured, a smile quirking his mouth. "I've heard of hard-headed women before, but this one takes the cake. I was beginning to think I'd have to carry her off somewhere and torture her into giving in."

Kathryn had an instant image of Judson's brand of torture. It was a heady thought—one that pinkened her cheeks because it had been voiced in front of Buck.

"Mmm-hmm," the older man replied with a dry sound of agreement.

"I think I'll go up and change," Kathryn murmured, feeling self-conscious. "There's coffee in the pot if you'd like to have a cup while you're waiting."

"Hopefully you won't be gone that long," Judson said with a slow smile.

The warmth of his expression dazzled her and Kathryn was positive she floated up the stairs. She couldn't remember her feet touching the ground once. When she'd closed the bedroom door, she felt Judson's absence keenly, as if part of herself had been left with him. It was a sensation of belonging to someone that she'd never felt with Charles.

It didn't take long to wash and dress. In less than ten minutes Kathryn was leaving the room, wearing fresh white slacks and a deep-aqua blouse. Her white heels made attention-getting clicks on the kitchen floor. Judson's glance ran over her with eloquent approval.

"Ready?" he asked, pushing away from the table to stand.

"Yes." She walked over to join him.

"Care to come along, Buck?" It was a good thing Judson was in control enough to issue the polite invitation, because Kathryn wasn't. She seemed blind to everything but Judson.

"You gotta be kiddin'," Buck snorted. "Sittin' around watching two people stare at each other is a long way from bein' my idea of a good time." Beneath the feigned disgust there was unspoken approval.

Kathryn laughed and pretended ignorance. "Do we do that?"

"Do we do that?" Buck mimicked her voice, then waved a hand toward the door. "Go on. Git, before I decide to come along as chaperone."

The Italian restaurant was a small, "hole in the wall" kind of place, with shabby red vinyl booths, plenty of beer on tap, and pizza that was as delicious as she remembered. A seemingly constant string of cowboys sat at the bar. A jukebox wailed continually in a back corner.

"This place hasn't changed a bit," Judson mused. He pretended to study the men on the barstools. "I even think those boys at the bar are the same ones that were here the last time we came."

"I wouldn't doubt it." She absently traced the cigarette burns on the tabletop with a fingernail. "You have to admit the place has character."

"I noticed you didn't say atmosphere." It was a dry comment. "Do you come here often?"

"Never," she admitted. "I like the place, but it isn't exactly Charles's style." Kathryn sobered as she realized she hadn't given Charles much thought. "I'll have to see him," she stated, but she wasn't looking forward to it. She hadn't treated him fairly and the knowledge didn't please her. "I owe him some kind of explanation."

"I painted a pretty explicit picture for him." There was a click of a lighter as Judson lit a cigarette. "I seriously doubt that any more explanation is necessary."

"You what?" Her glance sharpened. "You had no right to do that. It wasn't your place." She nibbled the inside of her lip. "How did he take it?"

"I think he'll survive." His voice was dry. "He wasn't so shattered by the discovery that he wants to quit working for me."

Her head came up in disbelief. "Are you serious?"

"Yep." He gave her a crooked grin. "So I don't really see the need for you to try to comfort him. He found his ring on your dresser and took it with him."

"Just like that," she murmured, and realized just how right her decision not to marry Charles had been.

Mistakenly she had believed she could conquer her loneliness with someone like Charles, but Kathryn knew now that that had never been true. Without love, there was no purpose for marriage.

Even if that weren't true, she had been foolish to think it could work. A few rough and rocky patches could sorely test a marriage that was built on the solid foundation of love. It would only take a minor bump or jolt to break up a union that was already flimsy because it lacked emotional commitment.

"Are you sorry Charles wasn't more upset that the engagement's off?" His eyes were narrowed against the smoke curling up from the cigarette that dangled from the corner of his mouth while his hands were occupied—one holding a glass of beer, and the other absently turning over the check the waitress had just left facedown on the table.

"No, I'm not sorry," she answered truthfully. "I wouldn't wish a broken heart on anybody." But his total lack of loyalty wasn't something she could take pleasure in having to acknowledge.

"But you're still a little bit disappointed." The cigarette was removed from his mouth as Judson quit fiddling with the check.

"A little," Kathryn admitted. "But I guess I'm mostly disappointed in myself." She shook her head slowly, a soft sad laugh coming from her lips. "More and more I'm discovering what a rotten judge of character I am. My trust in people has always been rather misplaced."

She watched him take a drink of the beer, hold it in his mouth for a second and swallow. All the time, the darkness of his gaze was focused on her. The silent expectancy in his look prompted her to go on. "I trusted Charles to give me two things I need—emotional safety, and the security of knowing he'd always be there. But after what you've told me, I have the definite feeling that if I had stayed with him, he would have let me down sooner or later anyway.''

An I-told-you-so glint appeared in his eyes. "Surprised?" The tone of his voice said she shouldn't be.

"Not really," she admitted. "Although I would have been if it had happened before you came back." A small accepting smile curved her mouth, hinting of the sense of having lost something, of disillusionment. "Until then, I trusted Charles. And my mother—"

"And not me," he inserted.

"No." Her smile grew wider, more natural. "Not you."

The sweating beer mug was sitting on the table. Judson wrapped both hands around it and tipped it toward him while he studied the contents of the nearly empty glass.

"And now?" His glance drifted idly back to her, but there was nothing idle about the inspection behind that look.

"Now?" Kathryn repeated, and looked away as she tried to sort through her feelings for him, making an attempt to separate the recent ones, the relevant ones, from the deeply rooted fears and ideas of long ago.

She felt his eyes watching her, reading the source of her hesitation like a child's book. When she met his gaze, an awareness of her inner conflict lurked behind his bland expression.

To say she trusted him totally would be a lie,

and Judson would know it. In time she would grow more secure in his love. Each day that it lasted would build certainty, strengthen the bonds between them—bonds that were, right now, both fierce and fragile.

"I don't have any reason *not* to trust you, do I?" It wasn't a direct answer, and that seemed best, since a completely honest response could hurt him. But he already knew the truth.

"No." There was a flatness to the reply. "But it looks like that's something I'm going to have to prove to you." He slid to the edge of the booth and stood up. "One of these days you're going to have to face the truth," he stated, stretching a leg straight so he could get a hand into the pocket of his snug-fitting Levi's. "You're stuck with me, darlin', like it or not." He pulled some bills out of his pocket and left them on the table. "Get used to the idea."

"Yes, sir." Her smile was a little bit tremulous and teary. The compassion and understanding he was showing touched her deeply.

There was an easy silence between them during the drive home, both of them caught up in their own thoughts. So much had changed in a day, yet it seemed the most natural transition in the world.

The house was dark when they returned. As they walked into the kitchen, Judson lifted a speculating eyebrow. "Does Buck usually sack out this early?"

"No," she admitted with a soft chuckle.

"I didn't think so." He gave the door a push to

close it. Then he was pulling her into his arms. His mouth grazed warm trails over her cheek and neck. "I'll have to remember to thank my old friend for knowing when to make himself scarce."

"Yes." It was a breathless response as her lips parted in trembling anticipation of his kiss.

Slipping her arms around his middle, Kathryn tipped her head back to accommodate his descending mouth. His teeth pulled sensually on her lower lip while his hands roamed the curves of her body with intimate knowledge. Longing surfaced in a rush, leaving her dizzy and clinging.

Her hands moved up around his neck, applying the necessary pressure to deepen the kiss. Her senses were alive to him—the hard feel of his muscled body, the manly scent of him and the taste of him, uniquely his own and druggingly potent.

His tugging fingers pulled her blouse free from the waistband of her slacks. While he kissed her senseless, his warm hand made contact with the bare skin of her stomach. The muscles contracted involuntarily at his touch.

There was a heavy reluctance in the way he lifted his head. His breathing was ragged, like hers.

"I guess I'd better go," he muttered in a thick voice.

"No!" The word was startled from her. A clawing panic began to attack her at the thought of him leaving. Earlier she had experienced a vague uneasiness when they'd separated to make the drive home from Old Bill's place, but the feeling had been easily dismissed because the length of separation was only a matter of minutes. Now Judson was talking about hours apart. . . or more.

Kathryn tried to push the idea from her mind. This day had brought revelations about Judson that made such fears seem groundless. Yet she couldn't seem to shake them. She brought her hands around to spread them flatly on his chest and lever a little distance between them.

"Don't go," she insisted earnestly. Not yet. Not until she began to feel sure that he would come back. That day would come, and with it the freedom to love completely. But after so many years of guarding her heart against total commitment, opening it up to full capacity would be a gradual process.

His gaze made a deceptively lazy scan of her face, missing nothing—not her love, nor the sudden fear in her eyes. "The neighbors might talk," he murmured.

"I don't care." She shook her head emphatically, the feeling of alarm growing as he showed no signs of giving in.

"Since when?" He appeared to playfully mock her, but there was a seriousness beneath his smile.

"Since right this minute." Kathryn forced herself to sound calm.

"What about Buck?"

"He leads his life and I lead mine." She didn't care what anybody thought. Her relationship with Judson was too new. She wouldn't take any chance of losing him again.

He studied her for another minute. Then he was

scooping her into his arms and carrying her up the stairs.

STIRRING, KATHRYN ROLLED ONTO HER SIDE and felt her thigh brush the hair-roughened length of a man's leg. A dreamy contentment pulled her mouth into a smile as she opened her eyes. There was a crazy little leap of her pulse at the sight of Judson. Her eyes roamed lovingly over his relaxed features—the strong, smooth cut of his jaw, the ridge where his nose had been broken, and his mouth, so hard and male and sensual.

Propping herself on an elbow, she leaned over to brush his mouth with her lips. His hand flew up to curve itself to the back of her neck and pull her down for a hard kiss. When he let her up for air, she was breathless and laughing.

"I didn't think you were awake," she accused.

"Let that be a lesson, darlin'." His voice was thick and husky with sleep. "Don't offer a starving man an appetizer unless you're prepared to follow it up with the main course."

Tucking a section of her hair behind her ear, she gave him a provocative look. "I can't seem to decide whether that's a threat or a promise."

Judson put a hand behind his head and let his gaze sweep over her. Kathryn looked soft and tousled from sleep. The covers were down around her waist. His dark eyes grew even darker. Her breath caught in her throat.

"I guess it's a promise," she murmured with a husky laugh. It took all of her effort to pull away from him. She swung her legs over the edge of the bed and reached for her robe. A finger trailed down the length of her spine. She shuddered involuntarily. "I have to get up." She turned down his silent invitation to remain in bed. "I'm already running late. I'm going to have to rush to open the shop on time."

"You're the boss. Open it late." He absently ran his fingers over the curves of her waist and hip.

"I can't." It was difficult to reject his suggestion. Before she gave into him, she pushed her arms into the sleeves of her robe and stood up. She didn't trust herself to face him until she'd closed the front of her robe and securely tied the sash. By that time Judson had propped himself up against the headboard, the move causing the covers to ride low on his waist.

"That's too bad," he drawled, a crooked smile of regret tugging at his mouth. "What time is it, anyway?"

"A little after eight." Which gave her less than an hour. She started toward the bathroom.

"That late, huh?" With a sigh, he sat up in bed. "I've got to get going, too."

"Going?" Her mouth went dry as Kathryn abruptly stopped and pivoted around. "Where?"

"To the motel." His look was half smiling, half frowning, saying very clearly that he considered her question ridiculous.

"You can stay here." Kathryn realized she hadn't made herself plain enough the night before, so she hurried to correct the omission.

"No, I can't." He swung his legs over the side of the bed and reached for his pants.

His flat declaration started the old fears churning in her stomach. "Why not?"

"Because all my things are over there." He zipped his pants and turned to give her a questioning look. "Besides, I've got work to do, too. I'm expecting some important phone calls later this morning."

"Why don't you bring your things over here?" she suggested. "You can have your calls forwarded to this number."

"Are you asking me to move in with you?" he questioned with surprise.

"Yes," she said firmly.

His eyes narrowed. "Why?"

"Why?" She was a little startled by his question. "Isn't it obvious?"

"Maybe. Go ahead and tell me anyway." He cocked his head to one side.

"Oh, I see." A small knowing smile touched her lips as Kathryn wandered over to him. She slid her arms around his bare middle. "You want me to tell you how wonderful you are, how much I love you and that I want you to move in because I can't stand the thought of us being apart."

He studied her upturned face and appeared to turn her words over in his mind, as if testing them. Then his tension seemed to leave him. He linked his arms around her waist.

"If I'm going to move in here, we'd better be thinking about setting a date, so I can make an honest woman out of you.'' He smiled lazily at her stunned expression.

"A date?" she echoed. "As in wedding?"

She was suddenly thoroughly happy. But it was a fleeting emotion, almost instantly chased away by a storm of doubts.

"That's what I had in mind." A warm glitter was in his brown eyes. "Unless, of course, you have some objection?"

There suddenly seemed to be a hundred objections, although Kathryn couldn't really identify a single one. She loved him enough to ask him to move in with her, so why on earth was she holding back?

"No." She shook her head a bit vigorously in an attempt to shake away the nameless doubts that were intruding on her joy. "No objections."

"Good," he said with warm satisfaction. "Does the end of the week sound okay to you?"

It was a full second before the import of his words made their impact on her. The end of the week. Married. Kathryn was paralyzed by the prospect. She suddenly understood the reason for her hesitation. It was too soon to make that kind of total commitment. The first glow of reborn love had not yet had time to dim. . . if it was going to.

Right now the idea seemed totally impossible because they were so happy. But Kathryn thought it would be wisest to wait until the newness wore off. Even though it went against everything inside her that was crying to say yes, she began to shake her head.

"That's awfully soon," she protested. "Why don't we wait a little while and—"

"Why?" Like his voice, his gaze was sharply questioning, the warm glitter fading from his eyes.

The way he was looking at her made Kathryn uncomfortable. "I'd just like to give things a little time to settle down. The wedding announcement for Charles and me was in the paper only yesterday. As a businesswoman, I don't want to deliberately start a lot of gossip. . . ." She sensed he had already guessed her reasons, but she went ahead and gave him a different excuse. The truth, in this case, would solve nothing. Only time would tell.

And Kathryn desperately hoped that, in time, she could lose this nagging fear that everything could blow up in her face at any given moment. Living with it was like waiting for an explosion, knowing it was coming, but not knowing when.

Avoiding his gaze, she rested her cheek against his bare chest. Her arms tightened around him and there was a trace of desperation in the clinging embrace.

It simply seemed too good to last.

CHAPTER FIFTEEN

THE NEXT COUPLE OF WEEKS Kathryn and Judson seemed intent on making up for lost time. They spent every spare minute together—even Sundays. While a freedom day had seemed important with Charles, Kathryn couldn't tolerate the idea of being away from Judson for an entire day. It was totally unthinkable.

He'd set up a miniature office in a corner of the sitting room off her bedroom. He was only a phone call away from his office in Dallas, and only a flight of steps away from Kathryn. The arrangement worked out beautifully.

She managed to find twenty excuses a day to run upstairs during working hours. She told herself that this consuming desire to be with him was strictly a result of her love—it had nothing to do with a need to make sure he was still there. But in rare moments of honesty, she had to admit it was a little of both.

When the last customer left the shop, Kathryn escorted her to the door. She locked up, put the sign in the window, and abandoned the ever-increasing pile of paperwork in favor of going upstairs. Hurrying through the bedroom, she rapped lightly on the door to the sitting room and walked in without waiting for an answer.

Judson was standing in front of the desk, with his back to her as he put some papers into a briefcase. The usual clutter that covered the desk top was conspicuously absent.

"What's this?" she asked curiously. "Cleaning day?"

Partially turning, he looked preoccupied as he glanced in her general direction. "I didn't hear you come in," he said absently, and snapped the briefcase shut.

"What are you doing?" She rephrased her initial question as she moved farther into the room. Instead of completing his turn and meeting her with an embrace, Judson swiveled back to pick up the briefcase. Then he walked over to her and draped an arm across her shoulders, propelling her into the bedroom. An odd feeling inched up her spine.

"Judson...." Any questions she had intended to ask were choked off when she saw the suitcase sitting beside the bed. Her widened gaze flew to him, panic churning in her stomach until she thought she was going to be sick.

There was a frown of concentration on his face as he scanned the room for something he might have missed. "I just got a call from Dallas." Letting his arm fall away from her shoulders, he walked over to set the briefcase next to the suitcase. "An urgent situation has developed. I'm going to have to fly back right away."

The blood was pounding so loudly in her ears, Kathryn could hardly hear him. "You're leaving?" Her words were a hoarse whisper.

When he faced her, there was a long probing look from his dark eyes. "Yes. There's a matter that needs my immediate attention," he explained again.

"Can't you send someone else?" There was a desperate quality in her voice, almost pleading.

It was too soon for a separation. The two weeks they'd shared had been wonderful, but it wasn't long enough to give their relationship the strength that would insure nothing could come between them. And the possibility of losing him now terrified Kathryn. Stark fear entered her eyes.

"Why should I send someone else?" Judson asked. It almost sounded like a challenge.

"Why not?" she countered, striving for a calm that seemed totally unattainable. "If you don't absolutely have to be there...."

"There is one man I could send," he admitted, hesitantly.

Kathryn couldn't conceal her relief. "Good." She sighed, a smile spreading across her face. "Now that that's settled, what would you like to do this evening?" She was anxious to change the subject. The thought of his near-departure made her extremely nervous.

His gaze narrowed on her face in a way she'd seen many times since they'd gotten back together. It was a look that probed deeply, always searching for something, yet never appearing satisfied. Turning, he walked to the window and laid an arm high on the frame, bracing himself against it while he stared outside.

"Why don't you want me to go, Katy?" It was a flat question, as if he already knew the answer.

"Do you want to go?" Kathryn asked, alarm returning at his failure to drop the subject.

"It's my job," he stated. "My responsibility. It isn't right to push it onto somebody else's shoulders."

Kathryn heard the indecision in his voice and knew he was warring with himself. Some instinct told her to keep silent, that any pleas for him to stay would have the opposite effect. Her hands curled into fists while she waited tensely for his decision.

Finally he turned from the window. "Katy, I...."

There was something in his expression that made her breath catch painfully in her throat. "You want to go, don't you."

It wasn't a question. Kathryn knew it was true. She'd seen that look before—the restlessness, that hint of dissatisfaction with present surroundings. There was a cold, sinking sensation in the pit of her stomach.

Then Judson's simple yes nearly ripped her apart.

Kathryn could feel the color draining from her face. He didn't have to go. He wanted to. After a short two weeks together, he was choosing to be away from her. She should have known. Drifters couldn't change. Nothing ever satisfied them for long. Why had she believed differently? Then she realized that she hadn't believed it, not really. The little nagging fears had never gone away. If only she had listened to their warning.

"I'll only be gone a few days," Judson said with quiet calm, although he was observing her reactions closely. The obvious fact that she was upset didn't appear to affect him. "Or maybe a week," he amended. "It will depend on what kind of mess I find myself in when I get there."

"So it might take longer?" The question was a sharp, stinging challenge to his indefinite plans. "Should I just expect you whenever you get back in the neighborhood?"

Her questions bordered on accusations. Judson didn't appear surprised by them, but his expression hardened. "You should expect me when I tell you to," he replied in a controlled, level voice. "When I get there and find out what exactly is happening, I'll call to let you know when I'll be back."

"Or *if* you'll be back?" Kathryn hurled the words at him with an anger born of fear. Why had she let this happen? Why had she become involved with him again?

"*When* I'll be back." Judson emphasized the word, a tautness in his voice. "You're just going to have to trust me, Katy. I have a business to run and I'm going to run it."

"No matter what it does to us," she said, rubbing her arms to ward off the sudden chill.

"It won't do anything to us—unless you let it."
It was a grim statement.

Kathryn laughed harshly. "I only wish I had as much control as you're implying." As it was, she would always be living on the edge of a precipice, constantly wondering if he would come back to her time after time. "I can't handle the uncertainty, Judson."

"If you trusted me, there wouldn't be any," he said in a tone that challenged her.

"And if you loved me, you'd stay and give me the time I need to build that trust." She held his gaze, matching his challenge with one of her own.

"You've had time, Katy." He raked a hand through his hair, a suggestion of impatience in the action. "It isn't getting any better between us. It's getting worse."

"But these last two weeks have been wonderful," she protested, and felt the sting of tears in her eyes because, apparently, the joy had been all one-sided.

"They haven't been wonderful for me," he stated, confirming her suspicions. Reaching into his shirt pocket, he took out a cigarette and lit it, dragging the smoke deep into his lungs before letting it out on a long breath. "It's no good this way, with you being afraid to let me out of your sight for a second. You can't lock me up in a box, take me out when you want, then put me back for safekeeping. It—"

"I don't do that!" It was a shocked denial. "I

only wanted to be with you.'' The quaver in her voice revealed her hurt.

His eyes softened as he watched her, then hardened as he squared his shoulders in a way that suggested he was exercising self-control.

''Judson?'' The single word was an appeal for time—time together. If he loved her, he would do whatever was necessary to make things work.

''No, Katy.'' He shook his head decisively. ''No more. This private little world you're trying to create for us is suffocating. We can't go on this way. It'll end up killing anything we feel. I don't want that to happen.'' In sudden agitation he walked to the dresser and crushed his cigarette in the ashtray sitting on top. ''I don't know what it's going to take to prove that I love you, but until you believe it, we don't stand a chance.''

''Stay here,'' Kathryn urged. She twisted her fingers together and tried to hide the desperation that was welling up inside. ''That'll prove a great deal to me.''

''Only until the next time I have to go somewhere,'' Judson asserted, unswayed by her claim. ''Maybe my leaving and coming back will prove something—I don't know. But one thing I do know is that if we keep doing things your way, we're both going to lose.''

He held her glance for a pulse beat. Then he moved to pick up his suitcase and briefcase. Panic gripped Kathryn.

They had only had two weeks. Now he was restless. He claimed he still loved her, but it was too soon to trust the strength of ties formed in such a short time. *Out of sight, out of mind.* Old sayings always had their basis in truth. For a man like Judson—a drifter, a follower of impulse and whims—the adage was surely twice as appropriate. As of now, he intended to come back. But once he was away from her. . . .

"I'm not ready for this yet, Judson," she insisted. "Don't go."

He hesitated, indecision flickering briefly across his face. Then his jaw became set with grim determination. "I have a plane to catch." Turning, he started for the door.

"If you really love me, you'll miss that plane," Kathryn challenged, her voice low with all the violent emotion she was trying to suppress. "So if you walk out that door, it'll tell me all I need to know. You don't need to worry about coming back."

Her words made him tense visibly. He turned slowly to face her. "You don't mean that."

"I mean every word." Kathryn was trembling with the desperate need to hold on to him. "If my wants and needs mean so little to you that you can completely disregard them. . . ." She left the sentence unfinished, but her meaning wasn't lost on Judson. Her chin lifted to an angle of defiance. "When you walk out the door, be assured that you're also walking right out of my life. . . for good."

His expression hardened in reaction to the threat. "Are you sure that's the way you want it?"

"That's the way it is." Her hands were clenched into tight fists at her sides while she stood tall and unmoving before him.

For endless seconds they faced each other, each waiting for the other to back down. Hope flared in Kathryn when Judson bent to put down his suitcase. But it was only so his hand would be free to open the door, which he did. Kathryn felt an agony like she had never known as she watched him pick up the suitcase and turn away.

His footsteps were loud on the stairs, as if he was pounding into her mind what was taking place. He was leaving her, for good. Kathryn clamped her hands over her ears, but the echoes of his footsteps rang clearly in her memory. The sounds twisted together, and she felt as if a crushing band of pain threatened to break her. She couldn't stand to let him go. Not again.

Choking back sobs, she ran for the stairs. They were empty now, and the old familiar panic started to rise. Her feet flew over the steps. At the bottom she paused for a split second, then hurried to the kitchen. But he wasn't there. Her heart hammered. Reaching the porch door, Kathryn yanked it open and stepped outside. Her searching gaze caught the flash of a tan fender as the car rounded the corner, then disappeared. She was too late.

Numbly, Kathryn entered the house. A shaking began in her hands, then spread through her body, weakening her knees. She sank into a kitchen chair and pressed her fingers against her throbbing temples.

It was best that she hadn't caught him in time. In the long run it wouldn't have solved anything. Judson didn't really love her with the kind of depth that would sustain them. His emotions were intense, but they wouldn't endure. At the very most, she might have been able to postpone this moment when it had all come to an end. But sooner or later, the pain had to come.

And it was sheer agony.

THE OCTOBER WIND whipped and howled outside the house, whistling around the corners and filling the early-morning silence of the kitchen with its eerie, haunting sound. The last remnants of summer were being chased away for good by this strong, blustery gale. It was only the first sign of the long cold winter that lay ahead.

Shivering, Kathryn pulled the thin satin of her robe more tightly around her. The small amount of warmth it provided couldn't begin to take the chill from her bones. It was the coldness of loss, a sensation she'd felt too many times before to mistake it for anything else. The only cure for it was time, lots and lots of time. Which was something Kathryn had plenty of.

The days stretched before her, dark and bleak and empty. The path she had to walk led nowhere, promised nothing. Kathryn knew this, because she'd been on that lonely path before. Only this time it was going to be worse. After six weeks the pain was growing sharper rather than beginning to dull.

"Couldn't sleep again?" Buck entered the kitchen and flipped on the light.

"No."

Kathryn turned her head to the side, averting her face from the penetrating blue of Buck's eyes. She was leaning against the counter, her back to the sink. Buck's never-changing pattern from cupboard to coffeepot eventually brought him to stand next to her. She listened while he poured the hot black brew into a cup. Kathryn felt his glance on her but didn't turn to meet it.

She pushed away from the counter. "I'd better start getting ready for work." There was plenty of time, but she needed an excuse to leave the kitchen without sounding rude. She didn't want company or conversation.

"Kathryn?"

She stopped, hesitated for a second, then looked at him. Concern furrowed his brow. Kathryn knew he saw the traces of her recent tears. Her eyes were puffy and red, her face bearing telltale blotches.

"What?" She questioned his reason for stopping her.

"You been cryin' again?" His gaze was sharp under eyebrows pulled together by a disapproving frown. "That's all you been doin' for weeks."

"Believe me, Buck, it's not because I want to." Kathryn felt a need to defend her behavior. "What I want to do is forget, but it isn't that easy." She paused briefly. "Why do I let him do this to me?"

The line of Buck's mouth tightened at her question. A response wasn't expected, so none was offered. He raised the steaming coffee cup and drank from it.

"Heard some talk around town yesterday." Buck changed the subject to one that was less painful than Judson.

"Oh?" Kathryn tried, and failed, to sound interested in whatever gossip was being circulated.

"I was over to Tiny's for lunch, and the women at the next table were grumblin' about the shop, sayin' they never knew when it was going to be opened or closed, and the service they been gettin' was downright 'atrocious,' " he said, giving the last word the haughty inflection the woman had used.

"Oh," she murmured. "I hadn't realized it was that bad."

"Guess so." Setting his cup down, Buck braced one hand against the counter and let the other hand rest on his hip. "I'd say it's about time you started tendin' to business."

"Sounds like it," she agreed, then sighed. "You know what it is, Buck. It's the nights." She crossed her arms, hugging them against her stomach as the chill returned. "I never get any sleep anymore. I'm so tired during the day, I can't get any work done." She sighed again, her gaze dropping to the floor. "Before Judson came back, I had a life I was content with. Now it doesn't interest me. My shop's falling apart right before my eyes, and I don't even have the energy to do anything about it. Worse, I don't really care." A small wry smile touched her mouth. "Judson's not even here, and he's managing to ruin the only part of my life that was still intact when he left.''

Buck released a breath that was rife with impatience. ''That shop ain't got nothin' to do with Judd Taylor. It's up to you to get your work done, Kathryn—nobody else. So don't go blamin' all your problems on other people. It ain't right, and it don't solve nothin'.''

Kathryn was a little startled at Buck's declaration, which seemed to have come totally out of the blue. ''I know it's up to me to make the boutique a success,'' she told him with a frown. ''All I was saying was that the shop doesn't mean that much to me right now. Nothing does.''

''It better mean somethin' to ya,'' Buck said bluntly. ''It's all you got left.''

''I know that,'' Kathryn retorted, not liking to be reminded of the fact.

''Ain't much is it?'' he observed. ''Considerin' what you could have had with Judd.''

She flashed him a hurt and angry look, wondering why Buck wasn't being more sensitive about the subject. ''No,'' she admitted, because her life was so empty right now, sometimes she thought she'd die. Her chin began to quiver. ''Why did he have to come back, Buck? Now I have to get over him all over again.'' Her head ached with the thought. ''I'm not sure I can do it a second time.''

''I don't see as how you got much choice.'' Buck shrugged.

''No.'' His callous attitude stung. Buck had always been her comforter, the one unshakable force she could cling to in the face of any tragedy. If she'd ever needed someone to lean on, it was now.

"The way I see it, you can go one of two ways," Buck said. "You can keep on mopin' around, feelin' sorry for yourself. Or you can pick yourself up by your bootstraps and hope like hell that someday you might be able to crawl out of the hole you been diggin' yourself into for the last seven years."

"What are you talking about?" Kathryn was stunned. "The only thing that's wrong with me is that I was fool enough to set myself up for another broken heart. Which I got—as usual!"

"*That's* what I'm talkin' about." There was a hard glint in his eyes. "I got a broken heart 'as usual,'" he said, repeating her final words. Then he began to shake his head and click his tongue. "Poor, poor Kathryn. Always lovin' and always losin'. Ain't it a pity nothin' ever goes her way."

Kathryn blinked furiously, trying to fight back stinging tears. "It's true," she retorted. "And you know it."

"I don't know no such thing," he denied. "Not anymore anyways. It used to be true—or so we thought. You used to have a reason to run around feelin' like the victim. I think you got so used to playin' that role, you couldn't snap out of it when it stopped bein' a fact."

"That isn't true," she protested.

"Ain't it?" There was a skeptical lift of an eyebrow. "Can you look me straight in the face and tell me you honestly expected it to work out for you and Judd?''

"I hoped it would." She pressed her lips together tightly and sniffed, trying to hold back a flood of tears that were on the brink of spilling forth. "I wanted so much for it to work out."

"But you never really believed it would, did ya?" Buck said. "You always figured it wouldn't last, and in the end, you'd suffer for takin' a chance on him."

"Well?" Kathryn challenged, because that was exactly the way it had happened.

"Well what?" Buck frowned. "Whose fault was it that it ended?"

"It wasn't mine!" She drew back, putting a hand to her breastbone, stunned at his implication. "Judson didn't love me enough to try to work things out, Buck. That's all there was to it." It was an aching admission.

"Didn't love you enough, huh?" Buck straightened away from the counter, placing both hands on his hips in an attitude that was at once defensive and challenging. "I never seen a man make such a damn fool of himself over a woman. He was jumpin' through hoops for you for over two months! You kept slappin' him down, and he just kept comin' back for more, tryin' to make up for things he never even did, for cryin' out loud! Did you ever once stop to think about that?"

"I don't want to talk about it," Kathryn declared hoarsely, unable to take a lecture on top of everything else. "Judson is gone. That one glaring fact makes everything else irrelevant.'' And it made the memories very, very painful.

"Maybe it does and maybe it don't,'' Buck asserted. "Did you ever ask yourself why he left?''

"I know why he left!'' Kathryn cried. "And I don't want to talk about this anymore—'' Her voice broke. She covered her mouth with her hand, trying to contain the sobs that choked her and prevented speech.

"No. You don't want to talk about it because it hurts. For the last seven years that's been the story of your life. Don't do, think, say or try anything that hurts or *might* hurt some day twenty years from now. You got hurt real bad once, and all you been doin' ever since is concentratin' on makin' sure it didn't happen again. You've been so wrapped up in yourself—how *you* feel, what *you* want, what *you* need—you can't even think about how anybody else might feel.''

"You don't know what you're talking about, Buck!'' Kathryn flared, brutally wounded by the way Buck saw her. His attitude seemed the final betrayal. When he started in again, Kathryn spun away, intending to leave. But he caught her by the arm instead.

"I know exactly what I'm talkin' about, and if you'd listen it'd do ya a world of good. Just like if you'd looked outside yourself for even a few minutes, you'd have seen how much Judd loved you and that he suffered just as much as you did—maybe more! How do you think he felt when he learned you'd married some other guy? That hurts, Kathryn, I know. But it didn't stop Judson from tryin' with you again. He ate his pride over and over and over tryin' to win you back. He finally thought he'd got the prize, but instead he got a kick in the teeth, because after all he went through to get you, you didn't believe he cared. I'll tell ya' somethin', Kathryn. I'm glad Judd's gone. A man can only go so far and still call himself a man. If he'd come back, I'd have lost every ounce of respect for him I ever had.''

That was too much. Kathryn was trembling with brutal pain and wounded outrage. "If you're so glad he's gone, maybe you should leave, too!'' She hurled the words, wanting to transfer the hurt he'd inflicted on her, back to him. "I don't need either one of you! Neither of you gives a damn about me!''

"Kathryn—''

"Go! Just get out and leave me alone!'' Kathryn almost screamed, struggling to control the raw, aching sobs in her throat.

Buck recoiled as if he'd been slapped. Shock wiped the anger from his expression and the color from his face. There was only a split second's hesitation before her wrist was released. Kathryn shut her eyes tight as tears scalded them, and she heard the sound of Buck's shuffling footsteps. When they stopped she lifted her gaze.

Buck was standing by the door, looking at her with a raw pain that ripped her clear through. There was a wet sheen on his high cheekbones. He met her gaze with sorrow and pain-filled eyes.

"Lookin' at you is like seein' Mattie all over again." His voice was very quiet, sad. "You got her same beauty, Kathryn. And now you got the same bitterness burnin' in your eyes. It destroyed your mother. Now it's gonna destroy you. I hoped to God I could help you stop it, but—" His voice broke. A tear slipped over the craggy roughness of his cheek. Then, dipping his head in defeat, he turned and left.

The door banged shut behind him and the sound resonated through Kathryn, nearly shattering her. Her legs crumpled beneath her and she went down on her knees, weighted with pain and guilt. She covered her face with her hands, but the action didn't block out the image of Buck. She had wounded him deeply and the realization pained her deeply.

"I didn't mean it, Buck," she whispered to the empty house. "I didn't mean for you to leave." But he was gone. Like Judson. And she had driven them both away.

The sobs that had been silently shaking her shoulders were given voice. Only the tears were no longer for herself. She was crying for Buck. And she was crying for Judson—the two people she loved most in the entire world. The two people who loved her just as deeply—or had at one time.

The tears continued to fall until there were no more left.

HER HANDS WERE CURLED around a cup of coffee that had long been cold as Kathryn sat at the table, lost in thought. Despite the fact that it was nearly noon, she hadn't yet changed out of the blue satin robe and nightgown. The shop was still closed and she didn't care.

Yet the indifference she felt toward the boutique was not the result of the lethargy that had laid its claim on her the past six weeks. The morning's argument with Buck had given Kathryn plenty to think about, which, of course had been Buck's intent.

Why hadn't she seen that at the time? Angry and impatient with herself, Kathryn pushed the coffee cup away and leaned heavily against the back of the chair. She folded her arms across her stomach in self-disgust. Buck loved her. She knew that. He would never say or do anything to hurt her.

Granted, his observations had wounded, but only because they contained far too much truth for Kathryn to be able to turn the comments aside. His words had stayed with her long after Buck had left the house. And Kathryn had been forced into a period of thorough self-examination that was years overdue. The conclusions she'd drawn were hardly pleasant. She had no choice but to agree with Buck.

Preoccupied with her thoughts, Kathryn was only dimly aware of the sound of footsteps on the porch. By the time she recognized the noise and attached a meaning to it, the door was being opened—very slowly.

Her gaze centered on it, hopeful yet wary. It

had to be Buck. All morning she had been praying he would come back, and now he was here. Relief surged through her, but Kathryn was careful not to let the feeling blind her to the possible reasons behind Buck's return. She knew she had hurt him deeply, wanting to lash out when his only motive had been a desire to help. If he was here now for nothing more than to collect his belongings, Kathryn wouldn't blame him a bit.

The door finished its slow, creaking arc until it stood halfway open. Instead of walking in, Buck poked just his head inside the opening. Keen blue eyes swept the kitchen, stopping on Kathryn. He held her gaze for several silent seconds. His expression revealed nothing.

"Is it safe yet?" The gruff, wary question was accompanied by another quick glance around the room, giving the impression that he was checking out a battle zone before entering.

And Kathryn knew it was going to be all right. "Yes. It's safe." She tried to laugh, but the sound was choked off by a tiny sob of relief. She got to her feet. "Come in. *Please.*"

Opening the door wide enough to accommodate his long lanky frame, Buck stepped inside. A watchful glint was in his eyes.

"Sit down," Kathryn invited, anxious to restore their relationship to normal. "Can I get you something? Coffee? Maybe some lunch?" She hesitated, aware that Buck was making no move to take his usual place at the table. "Buck, I...I'm sorry. I didn't mean—"

"I know."

The simple statement of understanding filled Kathryn with the warm security of knowing she was loved, despite the fact that she wasn't always lovable. It also seemed to take the tension from the air. It suddenly became easier to talk. In a matter of minutes Buck had restaked his claim on the chair that had always been his; Kathryn had filled his favorite coffee cup and set it before him. She joined him at the table and they talked, openly, honestly, naturally.

"I know I came down a little hard on you," Buck told her. "But I've been sittin' back and watchin' you go downhill for a month and a half now. I had to try to do somethin' to wake you up before you destroyed yourself." Large-knuckled fingers toyed absently with the handle of the white cup. "That's the same thing I did with Mattie— the reason I fought with her all those years. It would have been a whole helluva lot easier to just give up on her, but when you love somebody, you have to love 'em enough to fight *for* 'em and with 'em if it'll help straighten things out."

"I never really thought about that," Kathryn murmured, remembering the strange relationship her mother and Buck had shared.

"It might be kinda hard for you to believe this, Kathryn. But love can't always be gentle and understanding. Sometimes it has to be tough, willin' to cause a little pain if it'll solve a big problem." His mouth slanted in a crooked smile. "It'll make a lot more sense to ya when ya have kids."

His glance fell to the tabletop. "Course, I'm a fine one to talk, since I never had none of my own, but—"

"But you had me," Kathryn inserted, knowing, it was what he was thinking, and knowing, too, it would be difficult for him to say.

"Yeah." His eyes returned to her. His grin was a bit sheepish. "Anyways, this tough love I was tellin' ya about. It's like when the parent has to spank the kid—hurt him a little to protect him from somethin' big. It ain't an easy thing to do, cause it hurts the parent, too."

"I'm sure." Kathryn was beginning to see how difficult it had been for Buck to be so hard on her—and how much he had to care, for it to be worth the effort.

"Now, the way I see it, Judd was at that point when he decided to leave, even though he knew how much you wanted him to stay."

"But. . . ." Kathryn stopped the automatic protest that came to her lips. So far, Buck was making a lot of sense.

If she'd listened to him a long time ago, she and Judson might have been together this very moment. She pressed her lips together, determined to pay attention.

"Don't you suppose that'd be a hard decision for him to make? Knowin' he'd be hurtin' you if he left? The whole idea of it had to hurt him, too," Buck insisted with a frown. "But he knew you had to learn to trust him. Somehow, he had to prove that he loved you. If he left, it gave him the chance to prove that he'd also come back. That trip was for your sake, Kathryn, not his. He'd already fought for ya. The time had come to get tough and fight with ya.''

"But he didn't come back," Kathryn pointed out immediately. Then she sighed, correcting the thought in her mind until it became truth. "He didn't come back because I told him not to," she mumbled. "It was my fault this time."

With the admission came sadness, and guilt for what she had done to Judson. But there was something else, too. There was a sense of strength in admitting her own mistakes, in taking responsibility for her actions and facing the consequences. After the first time with Judson, she had fought against love, considering her happiness to be too precious a thing to place in someone else's hands. She had wanted to be in control of her life, her future, her happiness.

But to have control of anything, one must also accept responsibility. No one had forced her to try again with Judson. It had been entirely her choice. She had retained control over her life, but only until the time came to accept responsibility for the decision she'd made. She'd chosen to seek happiness with Judson, then sat back and expected him to supply it. In reality it was up to her to see that her needs were filled—not by selfishly demanding and taking, but by supplying Judson with the things he needed from her.

In giving him freedom, she would have received the security of knowing that if he left, he'd return.

That pattern would have eventually created the trust on her part that Judson had sought. Which, in turn, would have insured that his love for her would have grown, rather than being smothered by her fears.

Kathryn leaned an elbow on the table and sighed. In retrospect it all seemed so clear.

"You were right, Buck," she admitted. "About everything. I never gave him a chance." Again she sighed. "And now it's too late. When he tried to fight with me to save what we had, I threw it away." Tears began to collect in her eyes as the impact of what she had done really hit her.

"Poor, poor Kathryn." Buck shook his head and clicked his tongue.

"Buck!" It was an instant protest against the need for another lecture.

But the minute she looked at him, Kathryn realized the grave expression he wore was only one of mock seriousness. His blue eyes twinkled and humor underlined every groove in his leathered face.

"You're hopeless," he declared, but there was warm amusement in his voice. "You don't even need a villain before you start playin' the victim. If nobody's done you wrong, you'll just turn all the blame on yourself and accept that things just weren't meant to go your way."

In her mind's eye, Kathryn had an instant image of a victim—a sufferer; a person who would desperately like things to be different, but has no control over his situation. Did she fit that image anymore...or not? One thing was certain. The role was not appealing.

"Buck." Kathryn hesitated, wary of false hope. "Don't you think it's too late for Judson and me?"

He sobered, growing thoughtful. "I ain't got the answer to that one, Kathryn. You're the only one who can find out. Talkin' to Judd is takin' a risk on gettin' hurt, but at least you'd be movin' in the right direction—goin' after what you want instead of takin' and acceptin' whatever comes your way." He shook his head slowly. "You can miss out on a lot of good things by not makin' the first move."

Her hesitation evaporated when she saw the loneliness in Buck's eyes. It offered undeniable proof of the truth in his words. "You're right, Buck."

With that, Kathryn came to a decision. She stood up and walked to the phone. A minute or two later, she had placed her call.

"Hello," she said calmly and with a new sureness of purpose. "I'd like to make a reservation, please. What time is your next flight to Dallas?"

The line clicked as she was put on hold. Kathryn glanced over her shoulder at Buck. There was warm approval in his grin. He winked.

"That's my girl."

THE TEXAS SUN warmed the morning air and bounced its rays off the mirrored windows of the high-rise office building.

"This is it, miss." The taxi driver pulled to a stop at the curb and glanced at Kathryn through the rearview mirror.

She frowned. "Are you sure this is the right place?"

"Yep."

"All right." It was a hesitant acceptance of the accuracy of his information. Kathryn wasn't sure what she'd expected the offices of Monument Oil to look like, but she was startled and a bit intimidated by the impressive structure before her. A frown continued to crease her forehead as she paid the driver and climbed out of the cab.

For the hundredth time Kathryn questioned the wisdom of her impulsive decision to come to Dallas in person when it would have been so much easier to call. She had arrived last night, after rushing to Topeka and catching the first plane headed in Judson's direction. From the airport she intended to go directly to see Judson, but his office was closed by the time she'd arrived in Dallas and there had been no way to locate him until this morning.

As she entered the building, her stomach churned nervously. A receptionist directed her to a suite of executive offices on the top floor. The spacious reception area was plushly luxuriant, from the thick beige carpet to the walnut-paneled walls and the furniture that was covered in the finest-grain leather.

Unconsciously Kathryn stopped, hovering near the exit while she tried to adjust to her surroundings. This was all Judson's—the empire he'd built in the past seven years. It didn't seem possible for anyone to achieve so much in so little time. Yet he had always been determined to make something of himself, she recalled. And when he was determined to do something. . . .

Her gaze traveled anxiously to the receptionist, but Kathryn was remembering the way Judson had been so determined to win her back. It was difficult to accept the knowledge that the man whose word was law in this place was the same man she had rejected time and time again. Kathryn kept seeing flashbacks of their summer, ending with the hard look he had worn when she'd told him not to come back—ever. The possibility that he would welcome her now with open arms seemed to grow more remote with each passing second.

"May I help you?" The dark-haired receptionist prompted Kathryn to state her purpose in being there.

She froze, struck by the impulse to turn and run, yet pulled by the desire to see him at least one more time. The latter won out.

"Yes." Her smile was stiff. "I'd like to see Jud—Mr. Taylor, please."

Surprise flashed briefly in the brunet's eyes. "I'm sorry, he's not in. Could someone else help you?"

"No." It was a very definite response. "Could you tell me when he will be back?"

"Sorry." She smiled the apology. "Mr. Taylor is in Dallas only very rarely. I'm afraid he's out of the state right now."

"Oh."

Her face mirrored her disappointment as Kathryn realized just how badly she had wanted to see him, regardless of all her qualms. Fear of his rejection hadn't managed to stop her from coming. Instead, she had conquered it.

In her opinion it was a huge step in the right direction. Going home to Deepwater without seeing Judson would be like going backward when she needed to go forward. It became imperative that she follow through until the matter was settled, one way or the other.

"It's very important that I see him," she informed the receptionist in a tone that clearly said the woman would have no peace until she provided the answers to Judson's whereabouts.

Twenty minutes later, Kathryn left the office building, triumphantly clutching a slip of paper with names, addresses and directions scribbled on it. She stopped by the hotel only long enough to collect her luggage. Then she headed for the airport.

BENEATH A CLEAR SKY that seemed to go on forever, a lone pickup truck bounced over the two rutted tracks that formed the private road. In all directions, vast rolling plains stretched to meet the sky. Not even the dust plumes kicked up by the truck's tires could provide a screen that in any way softened the stark beauty of the landscape.

"Ever been to Montana before?"

If the truck's driver hadn't already guessed the

answer, the way Kathryn kept craning her neck in every direction would have told him. She was amazed by the seemingly endless reaches of unbroken grassland. Once she had thought Kansas was a land of wide open spaces. But that was before Montana. Kathryn had never seen anything so wild and untamed in all her life. There was a primitive ruggedness about this place that both fascinated and excited her.

"No. This is my first time here." She glanced at the driver, a short rounded man with a full black beard and a shyness that was in complete contrast to his robust appearance.

When she'd arrived at the temporary branch office of Monument Oil this morning, this man had informed her that Judson had accompanied a team of men to look over a potential drilling site, or survey the land, or some such thing. The purpose of his absence hadn't mattered to Kathryn. All she'd really heard was that Judson would be gone for the entire day.

After flying such great distances to find him, Kathryn had been in no mood to wait. Tension and frustration had been building in her for the last two days. She was coiled tight with nervous energy. The knowledge that her search might end in rejection only made the waiting worse.

"I really appreciate your taking the time to drive me out here." She thanked the man for the third or fourth time. If he hadn't finally agreed to bring her, she was positive she would have exploded. "How much farther is it?"

The black beard was bent against a barrel chest as the driver looked down at the gauges. "Speedometer says we've come fifty miles, so we've only got about ten to go."

With a nod, Kathryn accepted the information and looked out the window. The minutes dragged. She curled her fingers over the curve of the armrest to keep from drumming her nails against it.

"There they are."

The driver jerked his head to the left to indicate where he'd spotted the crew. With a turn of the steering wheel, the pickup bounced off the road. Kathryn gripped the armrest more tightly to brace herself against the bone-jarring ride.

The small dark dots the driver had noticed from the road were rapidly becoming distinguishable as pickup trucks. Men were scattered around the area to the right of the trucks, clustered in groups of two or three. Kathryn felt her pulse begin to race as her eyes tried to single out Judson's form from the others.

The jackets everyone wore to protect themselves against the nipping north wind gave added bulk to their frames. Not yet close enough to see their faces, Kathryn couldn't tell one man from the next. Impatiently, she glanced at the driver and silently urged him to hurry.

When her eyes swung back to the collection of trucks, Kathryn realized she'd been looking in the wrong place. Apart from the others, Judson and another man were standing next to one of the pickups. Kathryn would have known that tall broad-shouldered form anywhere. There was a sudden tightness in her chest that made it difficult to breathe.

His dark head was bent, his arms spread wide as he held a large sheet of paper that could be a map, which he and the other man appeared to be discussing. As the truck rolled to a stop nearby, Judson glanced at it briefly, then returned his attention to business. He had an air of authority—and an ease in carrying it.

Her hand was on the door handle, but Kathryn paused, taking an extra few seconds to study the picture he made. His suede jacket was hanging loose, exposing the creamy whiteness of its sheepskin lining. The wind combed its fingers through the darkness of his hair and blew it back from his forehead. The angles of his face were proud and strong, stamped with a rugged earthiness that made him seem a natural part of his surroundings.

Watching him, Kathryn was struck by the thought that the only grounds she'd ever seen him on were hers—her town, her home, among her friends. Out here, surrounded by nothing but endless amounts of space, Judson was in his element. In this land that could so easily dwarf a man with its incredible vastness, Judson stood tall.

Perhaps because he was like the land, Kathryn mused. Wild and free and untamed. Yesterday she had visited his offices in Dallas, and she had been impressed. Yet *this* was the environment that suited Judson. Kathryn was glad for the opportunity to have seen him like this. It was a vision of

the essential man—proud, rugged, strong, free—
and it was something she knew she'd never forget.

"That's Judd Taylor, ma'am," the driver
said, pointing him out. "The one holding the
map."

"Yes, I know." The admission held an added
fervency, because Kathryn knew this was her first
real glimpse of the man he truly was. And she definitely liked what she saw. If she had the power to
change anything about him, it was a power that
would go unused.

With a deep, calming breath, she opened the
door and slid out of the truck. The noise drew Judson's attention. The preoccupied quality in his look
vanished when his gaze focused on her. There was
an instant of shock, then whatever he was feeling—
if anything—was kept inside, locked behind an unreadable expression.

Disappointment welled in her throat, but Kathryn tried to swallow it. A joyous welcome was hardly to be expected after the way she'd treated him.
Her legs were a bit unsteady beneath her as she
willed them to carry her across the distance that
separated them.

She could feel his eyes on her, watching her with
a new wariness every step of the way. The low pitch
of his voice reached her as he murmured something
to the man standing next to him. Judson's compa-
nion looked at Kathryn curiously, then moved off,
leaving them alone.

With a nonchalance that Kathryn envied, Judson
began rolling up the map. "What are you doing

here?'' he demanded. The tone of his voice bordered strongly on indifference.

It stung, but Kathryn reminded herself that he'd been hurt. "I...I came to apologize." She smiled a little self-consciously, knowing it had to be obvious that she hadn't traveled all these miles without some hope of reconciliation.

His expression remained closed. It neither encouraged nor discouraged. It was as if he no longer cared one way or the other. His reaction hurt, but Kathryn knew she had to try. She wouldn't leave this place without giving it her best effort.

"I know now that I was wrong," she admitted, finding this confession a lot more difficult than she'd envisioned it would be. If he'd only stop looking at her with that hard, flat stare. She took a breath and forced herself to go on. "I was wrong about a lot of things. Buck made me take a good look at myself, and I realize how selfish I've been...how unfair I was to you."

There was no flicker of interest at her admission of guilt. Kathryn couldn't tell whether he thought she was lying or whether he simply had no feeling left for her at all.

"I shouldn't have held you responsible for the past," she went on. "You went through just as much as I did—maybe more. I should have trusted you without expecting you to prove yourself. I was just so wrapped up in my own problems, I couldn't see what I was doing to you." Looking at him now, so cool and composed, Kathryn wondered if she was having any effect on him at the moment. Her hopes began to burst, like the fragile bubbles they had been. She felt very awkward and foolish. "Well...I just wanted you to know that I finally woke up to reality. If I hurt you in the process, I'm sorry."

"And that's supposed to make everything all right." Judson snapped, showing the first sign of temper—of emotion, period. "I'm sorry I hurt you, as if I fell down and skinned my knee! I went through hell with you, Kathryn. Words don't just take all that away."

"No." She lowered her gaze, blinking back tears for the way she had hurt him. "They don't. And you don't have to tell me how hard it is to forget the pain. I know, Judson. And I understand. I really do." A few painful seconds passed. Kathryn had to wait for the lump to leave her throat before she could speak. "Well...I guess that's all I have to say."

Before she made a complete fool of herself, Kathryn turned and walked quickly away. She should never have come. That much was clear. It was too much to expect Judson to forgive and forget simply because she'd had a change of heart. Forgiving was one of the hardest things in the world to do. But forgetting was even harder.

"Katy."

There was a low demand in the way he said her name. It stopped Kathryn in her tracks. Quickly she brushed away the few tears that had slipped down her cheeks. Then she turned around.

The time she had taken to collect herself had given Judson the time to close the distance between them. He was standing only a foot away. The light that glittered in his dark eyes made the breath catch in her throat.

Lifting a hand, Judson slid his thumb over her cheekbone to wipe away a tear she'd missed.

"My beautiful Katy," he murmured. "Maybe now we can forget together."

SEATED IN HIS USUAL CHAIR at the kitchen table, Buck glanced from Kathryn to Judd and grinned from ear to ear.

"I guess my gambler's instincts are still reliable," he declared. "I was bettin' that neither one of you would give up without a fight."

"Without a fight?" Judson mocked. "This pretty little gal darn near wore me out!" He slung an arm around Kathryn's shoulders and pulled her more tightly against his length. Chairs didn't offer the closeness they sought, so they were standing side by side, leaning against the counter.

"I had to admit, I wondered for a while if you mighta gave up," Buck said.

"Me, too," Kathryn agreed.

"No." Judson shook his head. "I was just resting up for the next round." His gaze glittered warmly over her. "You know what they say, Buck. If something is easy to get, it isn't worth having."

"There's some truth in that." Buck nodded.

The porch door rattled as someone knocked repeatedly in a quick, steady rhythm.

Kathryn raised her eyebrows. "I'll get it," she murmured. "And I think I'd better do it quickly. Someone sounds determined."

When she opened the door her mouth instantly relaxed into a smile at the sight of Ruby Weatherby.

"Ruby! Come in and have a cup of coffee. We're just having a little engagement celebration...." The words trailed off as Kathryn remembered Ruby's own engagement. She glanced at Buck, and saw his expression had sobered.

"I'll pass on the coffee, Kathryn, but thanks, anyway. I won't be here long enough to drink it."

The widow never even looked at Kathryn. Her gaze was fixed on Buck. She walked toward him, her posture unnaturally rigid, hands clenched at her sides. Tension suddenly filled the room.

"Hi, Ruby." Buck was frowning, trying to discern the woman's attitude. "Somethin' wrong?"

"I just wanted to know one thing, Buck." She hesitated for a second, then blurted out. "Are you ever going to marry me or not?"

Buck drew back, shocked and showing it. "Marry you?"

"Yes or no." It was obviously a strain for Ruby to maintain control. The pressure had finally popped the cork.

"But what about Hank?" Buck was reeling in confusion. "You told me you two was engaged."

"I told you Hank proposed," Ruby stated. "Never once did I say I accepted. That was supposed to be your cue. I thought if I told you about

Hank, you *might* get some ideas of your own. Did you or not?''

Recovering from their own shock, Kathryn and Judson began to smile at the situation. Judd leaned close to her ear. ''It doesn't sound like Buck's instincts are so great after all,'' he whispered.

Kathryn, filled with so much happiness that she couldn't contain it, laughed softly.

''Well?'' The inscrutable Ruby was close to tears. ''Are you going to answer me, Buck Weston?'' She blinked.

Her question finally penetrated Buck's daze. He pushed to his feet, a wide grin splitting his face.

''I thought you'd never ask,'' he declared, and kissed the startled widow soundly to let her know he meant it.

Kathryn shook her head and smiled up at Judson. ''I can't believe that just happened,'' she whispered.

''Neither can I,'' he murmured in agreement. ''But I do like a woman who goes after what she wants.'' His gaze narrowed. ''Speaking of which, did you mention that we were celebrating our engagement?''

''Aren't we?'' Then Kathryn realized there had been no formal proposal this time around. ''Well?'' she prompted.

''Well?'' he countered.

''Are you going to marry me or not, Judson Taylor?''

''I thought you'd never ask,'' he said, his dark eyes dancing.

**April's other absorbing
HARLEQUIN *SuperRomance* novel**

A LASTING GIFT by Lynn Turner

Jennifer had been happy, married to Michael Page.
He died after a tragic illness, and now all she
wanted was to be left alone.

Then Nathan Page, Michael's younger brother,
arrived, determined to take care of her. Tempers
flared, but temper turned to tenderness when they
admitted their mutual loss. Something special had
begun. . . .

Nathan was first to realize he was in love—with his
brother's widow. He knew he should leave. But
Jennifer had already lost one love, and she could
not let him go. . .

A contemporary love story for the woman of today

These two absorbing titles
will be published in May
by

HARLEQUIN
SuperRomance

THE AWAKENING TOUCH by Jessica Logan

Jan Jordan had spent all her life in the peaceful isolation of her mountain home in Maine. Even in her wildest dreams she could never have imagined a man as compelling as Jason Farrell.

Jan had helped rescue the wealthy businessman's son, but Jason felt more than gratitude. He wanted her to leave her home and go with him. He wanted her.

She knew his ex-wife's betrayal had left him bitter. Love no longer had a place in Jason's life—only passion. Yet still a powerful force drew Jan to him. If only things could be different. If only . . .

LITTLE BY LITTLE by Georgia Bockoven

The former weather girl no longer brought disaster to the job. She was an incisive reporter now—and an exciting woman.

When NASA spokesman Mike Webster tried to get close to Caroline Travers, she backed off. Her ex-husband had shown her the selfishness of love; she wouldn't risk humiliation again.

But Mike was one to give, not take. Forced to abandon his dream of space flight, all he craved was a home with Caroline. Mike was warm and sexy, honest and altogether lovable, and Caroline was sorely tempted to believe in him . . .

These books are
already available
from

HARLEQUIN
SuperRomance

If you experience any difficulty in obtaining any of
these titles, write to:

Harlequin SuperRomance, P.O. Box 236,
Croydon, Surrey CR9 3RU

Look out this month for

VERDICT OF LOVE   *Beverly Sommers*

Casey didn't fit the profile of a young lawyer. She sneak
cigarettes in the bathroom of her flat to escape the wrath of I
roommate, subsisted on peanut butter sandwiches, and dres
just as she had in college. In fact, when Sam Dreyfuss first I
eyes on Casey, he mistook her for a bag lady and gave her
spare change. But the second time they met, Sam demande
date.

Sam Dreyfuss was one of the best lawyers in Manhatt
Casey's courtroom opponent, and a sharp dresser to boot. Nat
ally, Casey was a bit mystified, and just a bit suspicious . . .

PUBLIC AFFAIR   *Sarah James*

Liza Manchester, outspoken member of Graham Universit
feminist community, couldn't stand Professor Scott Harburt
Scott, best-selling author of pop psychology books, was a nig
mare of positive thinking, so blithely self-assured that he refu
to leave Liza alone, despite her pleas, demands, and raj
Having recently completed a book on what women want, Sc
was confident that Liza would relent, proving his theories corr
as usual.

But something odd began to happen to Scott's experime
gleefully labelled "the affair of the professor and the feminist"
local papers. A new element crept in, one Liza never anticipa
one Scott couldn't identify . . .

IMAGES ON SILVER   *Rayanne Moore*

In the rugged terrain of Yosemite National Park, Christy Re
risked bruises, sprains, and broken bones for her hig
acclaimed wildlife photographs. Self-reliant, self-suffic
Christy didn't want or need any man's help. But Ranger Tra
Jeffords ignored Christy's protests and checked up on her, w
ried about her, cared about her. It was a little annoying at fi
but then it became wonderful and a little bit frightening.

Yet Travis kept asking Christy why she had worked alone
so many years. And though Trav was an extraordinary m
Christy knew her secret was something no man would und
stand . . .